"Part poetry, part penny dreadful, *World, Chase Me Down* grips you with an originality that will keep you rooted to your chair."

—Craig Johnson,
New York Times bestselling author
of the Walt Longmire mysteries

"The kidnapping that was called 'the crime of the century' in the early 1900s later became just a footnote in Omaha history, but Andrew Hilleman has again given it fascination and life."

—Ron Hansen, bestselling
author of *The Kid* and
The Assassination of Jesse James by the Coward Robert Ford

"Andrew Hilleman is a fine stylist with a great sense of fun and an impressive grasp of popular culture in the early twentieth century."

—Mary Doria Russell,
bestselling author of *Doc* and *Epitaph*

"A brilliant mix of pulp and balladry, narrated by an adventurous, philosophical, lovelorn outlaw, *World, Chase Me Down* reminds me of my favorite portraits of criminal lives—Jim Thompson's *The Killer Inside Me* and Ron Hansen's *The Assassination of Jesse James by the Coward Robert Ford*—and proves Andrew Hilleman to be as good a writer as any there is." —Timothy Schaffert,
author of *The Swan Gondola*

"A first-class page-turner, layered with ambition, greed, promises made and broken, and the powerful bond of friendship. The writing is pitch-perfect, the dialogue pops, the flashes of humor are just right, and the courtroom scenes are not to be missed. Best of all is the sophisticated portrait of the kidnapper, a complicated and unforgettable character. Bravo."

—Ann Weisgarber, author of *The Personal History
of Rachel DuPree* and *The Promise*

"Supremely compelling. Gleaming with dark beauty in every line and gritty truth in its portraits of both haves and have-nots, *World, Chase Me Down* is that rare thing: a novel paced like a blazing page-turner and crafted like a finely woven tapestry. Brilliant on all counts."   —Elizabeth Rosner, author of *Electric City, Blue Nude,* and *The Speed of Light*

"A thunderous debut: a raucous gallivant through the wild heartland of our American myth, an indictment of big beef money, and a portrait of the twentieth century's first great outlaw. This book will raise laughs from your belly and stab the wild meat of your heart. It sounds the barbaric yawp of a great new voice in American fiction."
—Taylor Brown, author of *Fallen Land*

"A riveting read that brings a turn-of-the-century crime into shivering reality. Pat Crowe, butcher turned kidnapper, is a fascinating combination of high hopes and dark desires."
—Jonis Agee, author of *The Bones of Paradise* and *The River Wife*

"The crime at the heart of this novel reverberates from dirty back streets to the halls of power. Once *World, Chase Me Down* grabs you, it won't let go."   —Brent Spencer, author of *Rattlesnake Daddy*

"Unforgettable: a raucous and engaging story told by a voice so convincing you'll think the author must be channeling his turn-of-the-twentieth-century antihero, with all his imagination, boldness, wry humor, and natural eloquence. Rich historical details bring the sights, sounds, and smells of rough-and-tumble meat-packing Omaha to life in this suspenseful and surprising novel."
—Mary Helen Stefaniak, author of *The Cailiffs of Baghdad, Georgia* and *The Turk and My Mother*

PENGUIN BOOKS

WORLD, CHASE ME DOWN

ANDREW HILLEMAN was born in Omaha, Nebraska, in 1982. He earned his BA and MA in English at Creighton University, in Omaha, and his MFA in fiction from Northern Michigan University. He has been published by *The Fiddlehead* and was a finalist for *Glimmer Train's* Very Short Fiction Award. He lives in Omaha with his wife and their daughter.

ANDREW HILLEMAN

WORLD, CHASE ME DOWN

A Nove1

PENGUIN BOOKS

PENGUIN BOOKS

An imprint of Penguin Random House LLC
375 Hudson Street
New York, New York 10014
penguin.com

ISBN 9780143111474

Printed in the United States of America
1   3   5   7   9   10   8   6   4   2

Set in Adobe Caslon
DESIGNED BY KATY RIEGEL

This is a work of fiction based on actual events.

For April

Nothing fixes a thing so intensely in the memory as the wish to forget it.

Michel de Montaigne

The righteous shall rejoice when he sees the vengeance: he shall wash his feet in the blood of the wicked.

Psalm 58:10

CONTENTS

WORLD, CHASE ME DOWN

All Things Long Past

IN THE HISTORY of all things, good stories one day become old stories and then cease to be told at all, and I suppose mine is no different. For the past twenty years I've been puzzling my way back to humanity, but all I'll be remembered for, if I'm remembered in the first place, is perhaps the foulest of all crimes: the kidnapping of a child. The apogee of a life nourished by lawlessness. When I was furthest from the aubade.

Oh, there's a litany of other transgressions.

For a short while, I was the most wanted man in America. This was around the turn of the century. Thirty years past and more now. After my final arrest, I drew a bigger crowd at a Nebraska train station than President Roosevelt when he made a campaign stop in the same town during his bid for reelection. A few scattered folks still talk about me like legend. I relished it all. Even the fake stories the newspapers trumped up about my escapades.

When I was young I believed that my tale would be threaded on parchment that never frayed and etched in tablets that would never erode and inked upon the presses from the wharves of New York to the goldfields of California. My role in it all would be auditioned for on stages the world over. I could hear the thunderclap of ovation like a madman certain of his own future and creation's reaction to it. I could see it all floating like glow bugs in a fortune-teller's globe. But, let me say this: the world is not a skirt to be lifted. There's no redemption for the devil. I have returned to the teaching of my childhood. I have suffered, have been hungry and homeless and cold and for want of anyone to share with me a kind word since those days now long since passed. It's been mighty rough trotting, but I will not repine.

I've robbed banks and stolen diamonds, nearly killed three police officers in a Cicero gunfight, escaped a burning building and a prairie fire, and even looted the entire town of Shinbone, New Mexico, after me and my old pal Billy Cavanaugh locked up the village marshal in his own jail.

Poor goddamn Billy. Had I never stepped in to break up that fight in the stockyards all those years ago, the stupid kid, fortuned by his own stupidity, probably would've made a life out of things much longer and brighter than what he came to finally afford.

I laugh at that memory still.

How gorgeous it is to be sad.

Yet he is here still, even if he is only here to me. Love and money and happiness—they are dead sea fruits. All have had their own short running meters in my life. But the idea of friendship operating on that same arrhythmia is too depressing a thought to contain. Let me say this: I have found no happiness in evil. I will not paint roses on the life of an outlaw. Here there is only truth without imagination.

What is over for me now was over long ago. It's the second-to-last day of October, nineteen and thirty-nine. Either my sixty-eighth birthday or my seventieth. I'm not certain which. My hair's gone white with the snow of age, my livery hands are spotted like trout skin, my clothes stink worse than old breechclout. Ragged light of new day. The world turns like she always has. A tonnage of stars around a half moon yet to vanish, and steam rising from sewer grates all along the flagstone of Farnam Street.

I lurch out of my squalid flophouse into the awful darkness of morning. My staggering walk is like that of a clubfoot gimp for I'm near ruin and emptied of all heart and I expect no pity for these things. It's a mammoth struggle to button my shirtfront. Lamplights flicker yet in the early gloss. The street is empty, sunken between lopsided buildings like the floor of a canyon. I tamp my pipe. Only a few leavings in my tobacco pouch. A loud noise startles me like gunshot. In an alley across the street a young boy chucks crab apples against a brick wall. Thud, thud, thud. Like a pitcher warming his arm in a bull pen. I curse the tramp child and struggle against my cane. A spume of low cloud like mist in evenfall. My big spurs jangle as loudly as if I were wearing chain mail. Silly to wear spurs at my age.

Silly to be anything now.

It's my morning ritual: a short walk to the lagoon at Hanscom

Park to feed the pigeons as the sky fills with color. I scatter seed and candy. Twenty birds gather at my feet. Spearhead cloud cover. Acorns fallen from their cups. Dogwoods limp in cracking sun. Cattails long in the orange mud. An omen of first snow in the dawn.

I halloo the pigeons. Give them hallowed names.

"Hullo there, Billy," I say to one.

"Hullo there, Hattie," I say to another.

"Hullo there, Matilda," I say to the smallest of the roost.

The birds give no response. They bob their heads and peck the seeds and take counsel with one another in their own cooing language around my worn boots. I speak to them like they are people. I mumble to myself. Lose spittle down my last clean shirtfront.

They're speechless to reply.

I can see them all yet.

There is Billy in our very own little butcher shop. Both of us not much past thirty. CROWE AND CAVANAUGH, BUTCHERS, the storefront sign read in cursive script. Our long end of a dream. Days spent skinning carcasses and rolling sausages out of a grinder. How often I find myself lost inside those memories. Even the banal acts of scrubbing tile walls and mopping up wastewater are a fantastic caprice when remembered from a great distance.

There, too, is Hattie. Her startling yellow hair piled up in waves under a leghorn hat. Her lipstick as messy as if applied in a fun house mirror after a long night of necking. She bore a rare beauty often seen in women painted on cigar boxes but hardly in everyday life. Her china blue eyes as big as hailstones. Break your heart quicker than a plate dropped on the floor, those eyes could. Her throaty laugh that shook the china in your hutch. The nightgowns she wore as thin as mist to bed every night. A complexion the color of moonstone.

I will never be shed of that woman.

There she is under a cluster of noisy apple trees, leaves rustling as loudly as wrapping paper, blotches of sunlight turning her yellow hair pink. A thunderbolt flash and she appears naked in our bedroom during an electrical storm. A skunk stripe of moonlight on her back as she turns and beckons me to bed while rain slashes the window.

How she still affects me now from such a great distance is a special kind of madness I cannot parcel. The moon is not tanned by the sun, after all. Still, there she is, a spectral visitor, clear in my mind but forever gone. Nothing left here but the empty.

It occurs to me now that I have created legendary days of her in my own memory. I've never seen her under any goddamn apple trees or made love to her during a thunderstorm with moonlight on her skin or any of the other cruel and haunting images conjured up in retrospect. My remembrance of her is invented out of the same cotton as perfectly shaped clouds in a child's artwork. Such things never existed nor ever will. The contemplation of her love for me and raising our daughter Matilda together in a pink house with a quiet but substantial life was as grossly paradisal as the notion of Eden.

It had been that way all along. All things of any beauty are lost before they are gained, and they stay lost forever after, and the gaining of them in the first place is just a temporary figment, and that's just the natural way of the world, and not a damn fool ignorant to all around him or a genius aware of too much for his own good can remedy their way out of that.

Here I am now. Here I sit among the birds. An old man galled of crotch from poor bathing and thin as fish line from poor diet who quivers yet against the capsizing of the world. My right leg jerks in spasm and the pigeons scatter in fright.

"No," I call to them. "Don't go. Come back, friends. Come on back now."

"It's just my leg quaking," I say.

Just my heart, going.

I am still here. There is a twinkle left yet.

I wipe my mouth with a cloth and stuff the cloth back in my pocket and scatter more seed for the birds. Most of them do not return. You've never known me, never had the capacity to know me, and I don't know any of you except by your markings, but I very much love you still, and my love is an obsession despite all that has made it absent. I cackle and spit again. My paper sack empty of feed. I sit on the bench by the park lagoon for a few more minutes and accidentally fall asleep. A policeman comes by and pokes me with the end of his baton.

"Hey there, old timer, no sleeping in the park."

I snap awake, dazed.

"Best get now," the officer adds.

"I'm Pat Crowe," I say.

"You're loitering is what you are," the officer tells me and continues his beat.

The day browns in color and falls in temperature. Sun streaked and freezing both. Autumn given way to new winter in two hours. Wind empties trees. Shadows lasso, and hearthstones glow in the growing dark like the eyes of rodents. Ten more degrees plummet, then twenty. Flurries settle on stoop pumpkins. Day passes into evening.

I stagger home. What I now call home.

I totter about my flophouse room. A miasma of dust and velvet. The curtains dark as liver and mossy with age. A bloodstain from a previous tenant the size of a throw rug on the wood floor, scrubbed to a faint pink square. I reheat leftover coffee and fry wholemeal with fatback in a spider pan. A medicine show crackles on my tube radio. I peel away my socks. What effort it takes. The cotton crunchy with ice. My toes nearly black from frost and neglect and poor circulation. I fill a deep pot with water boiled on the cookstove for my feet. My toes come alive again in the boiling pan.

Outside my window, the world.

Omaha, Nebraska.

A glittering sedan sputters in the season's first snow. A Chevy Master with four doors that hiccups and stalls and sputters like an invention still in the throes of imagination. I peer out into the slanted snow. An elderly Negro woman is shitting into an old tin can between a narrow crevasse of clapboards.

I laugh and say aloud to myself, "Good for you, old girl."

It's high time for a gill of brandy. My hands quake on the glass like it was a heirloom long lost and now returned. I stoke the pitiful fire in my cookstove with the few chips left in the scuttle and watch the snow accumulate on my window. Rising from my cane rocker is a considerable effort and I plod about the room as if I were shuffling my feet over ice.

A whole day come and gone. Nothing more I can manage than to survive it. My pocket watch clicks against a glass of water on the nightstand. I hang my mothy suit on a wickerwork chair and swallow two barbiturates the size of small toes as per my doctor's orders following my stroke this past Christmas. The pills are strong enough to put a dog to sleep and I must cut them into thirds. They have a pleasant effect in small doses. My hands shake as I climb into bed. In old age, it's harder and harder to fall asleep in a timely fashion. I often sit up for hours before I'm relaxed enough to close my eyes.

I don't want this world to vanish. There's nothing left for me in it, and still I cling. As I listen to the ticking of my windup alarm clock, my mind wanders from one thought to the next. On some occasions, I can still see that Cudahy boy squirming in his chair, bound by horse hobbles and his face covered in an old baby shirt, smoking cigarette after cigarette under his makeshift blindfold. Young Edward Junior. He was an alright skate if there ever was an alright skate on this grim planet. A truly brave soul. And yet he whimpered and cried at night, begged us to return him to his mother and father. I can hear those pleas still. Let me say this right off the bat: I am a guilty man. Make no mistake. I kidnapped that young man and held him for ransom and got away with it scot-free for five long years before my spirit completely broke and I returned to Omaha for my just desserts.

At this late hour of life, I am glad of one lasting sliver of redemption: Edward Junior's fate was not the same as the young Charley Ross that inspired my crime in the first and, in later years, the Lindbergh baby whose abduction was, in turn, modeled after my foul deed. I can imagine no greater horror. A delivery truck driver discovered the toddler's corpse on the side of the road: the tiny skull fractured by a massive blow, the body half-burnt and bearing the marks of animal bites. I pray the infant was chewed on after his passing and not before, and that is perhaps the most macabre prayer ever sent up through the grapevine. For so long my life was nothing but darkness, and I've been battling my way back to the light ever since.

And still.

Some evil cannot be sewn up.

What progress I've made I cannot discern. It is said in Genesis that God divided the light and the darkness and gave them different names. Yet, in these dwindling hours that still remain for me, in looking back on a life divided as severely as night is from the day, I wonder if there is any difference between them at all.

Snow clicks against my window pane. A guttered candle floats in a pool of wax atop my cold radiator. The panther paces inside my chest. My mind full of history. Despite the fact that I'm so close to the end, my thoughts are not of the darkness near to come but of the advent of darkness long ago.

BOOK ONE

THE CRIME
OF THE CENTURY

I

ON THE EIGHTEENTH day of December in that first year of the century, when the old earth was nearing her darkest calendar day, Billy Cavanaugh and I parked our horse and buggy at the corner house on Dewey Avenue. Billy held the reins to our ragged silver pony. I ignited a calabash pipe with two matches after the buggy jolted to a stop, thumbing the bowl to get the tobacco rolling. Billy fit on a pair of cloth gloves and stared up at the darkening slab of sky, a low rind of winter sun in the west. The last whiskers of daylight. There was no wind. A light snow fell as gently as dust swept off a rooftop.

Neither of us said a word to the other as we sat parked along the curbstone. The hour approached seven. I jumped down from the buggy and fed our pony an apple from my trouser pocket. I scanned the street: a brick neighborhood avenue—void of traffic—that was lined on both sides by opulent mansions, the types with cupolas and double chimneys and crawling ivy. A scarf of river fog blew over from the Missouri. A lamplighter made his rounds, igniting gas street lights with a long wand. Coming around to the other side of the buggy, I elongated a spyglass and focused its sight at the mansion on the corner. The estate, a twenty-two room Victorian surrounded by a gable fence, sat on a half acre of land and was home to Edward Cudahy and family. I glassed the young man inside the room, sixteen-year-old Eddie Junior. He was knocking around balls on a baize-covered snooker table.

After a moment of studying the youngster, I collapsed the spyglass and returned to my seat on the buggy, crossing my arms across my chest.

"What's he doing?" Billy asked.

"Playing billiards against himself."

"Against hisself?"

"Nine ball by the looks of it."

Our pony shivered in the cold. Twenty more minutes passed and the snow fell harder: fuzzy and diagonal. Night arrived in full. A new moon hung over the trees, low and fat. Billy socked a wad of leaf tobacco the size of a walnut in his lower lip and collected his spit in an old pineapple can. Spitting on the street came with a ten-dollar fine, which was twice the amount of money either one of us had in the wide world. I pulled the large storm collar of my overcoat around my neck.

Halfway past the hour, a police officer in a bell hat and wool tunic approached from the opposite side of the street, doing whirligigs with his nightstick as he walked his beat. Billy and I both offered a friendly nod as the officer passed.

"Good evening, gentlemen," the officer said.

I doffed my bowler. "Good and cold."

"You fellers have business on this street?"

"What else?" Billy said.

"Forgive him, officer," I said. "He's Florida born, and the winter makes him somewhat choleric."

Billy sneered and spit into his old can. "I'm merry in all weathers."

"Yes," I said. "Ordinarily as kindly as a Texas cyclone, this one."

"Don't go to upsetting me, now."

The officer asked, "What are you twos doing on this block?"

"Waiting on a fare," I answered.

The officer craned his neck to get a look at the handle of a revolver bulging from a shoulder holster inside my coat. "You got a permit for that roscoe?"

I eased myself off the buggy and stood in front of the patrolman. I pulled open the left side of my overcoat to reveal a fake badge pinned to my suit lapel. "I'm Detective Dobbs of Sarpy County. My less cordial partner here who gets grumpy past his suppertime is Detective Saunders. We're scouting a young man who escaped from reform school yesterday and robbed his poor auntie of five hundred dollars this morning. She's one Mildred Finnegan, resident of 3710 South Dewey," I said and pointed at the house next door to the Cudahy mansion. "Which is that one right there."

The officer considered the house. "You boys are good ways out from Sarpy County."

I flipped open my timepiece. "Three and one-quarter miles to be exact."

Billy began, "The longer this mule sticks around—"

"Quite right," I interrupted him. "If our young runaway would happen by and see us conversing with a uniformed lawman, it might just may scare him off."

"It common practice in Sarpy County to send out two detectives to retrieve a juvenile escaped from reformatory school?" the officer asked.

Billy and I exchanged a look.

"What precinct in Sarpy are you boys from?"

I furrowed my brow. "What's your name, officer? I'd like to have it in case I have to report to my captain that a third-shift beat boy of the okey-doke variety spoiled our opportunity to apprehend our suspect."

"My name is Donald Marsh. And you can report me to President McKinley if you want. I'm doing my duty, and I asked you a question."

"South Sixteenth Street Precinct," I responded harshly. "Now, I can appreciate you doing your duty, but I'm going to ask you this once to be on your way out of respect for our surveillance. Surely you have other routes on your beat that are in need of your attention. But if I have to ask again, you'll be stripped of your badge and folding sheets in a Chink laundry before the week's out."

The officer backed away. "You Sarpy boys are a real pair of sweethearts."

"And a merry Christmas to you and yours on the Douglas side," Billy said.

"Detective Dobbs, was it?" the officer asked me.

I tipped my hat in a parting gesture. "That's right."

"Detective Saunders," the officer said to Billy as a farewell. "Happy hunting, gentlemen."

We watched the officer leave. He walked briskly to the corner of Dewey and turned left, heading south. He'd been whistling a tune when he came down the street, but was silent during his exit. No longer was he twirling his baton.

Billy paid heed to the difference. "Man left with a purpose."

I climbed back onto our woeful buggy.

"Suppose he heads to the nearest call box and dials up central station to check on those names you gave him?"

"Suppose he does," I said and opened my spyglass again to examine the Cudahy mansion. Eddie Junior was no longer in the parlor. "He'll find out that Detective Dobbs and Saunders are real fellers. Came into our shop a couple times for chops."

Billy chuckled without amusement. "You and your split tongue. How many times have you lied to me and I've not known it?"

"If I ever lied to you, you'd know it good and well by the sixth syllable."

"If he doesn't come out soon, we best pull it in for the night," Billy said and nodded toward the Cudahy residence. "Come back tomorrow or the day after."

I collapsed the spyglass. "He's coming out now."

The front door of the mansion opened and exiting the house was Eddie Junior, carrying a bundle of books bound in a belt strap. Tall and pale and thin-shouldered, he wore a knitted cap and knickerbockers. Following him down the drive was the family pet, a spotted collie with a bobbed tail like that of a lion. He closed the front gate behind him, calling out for his dog to stay close as it was without a leash. Billy shrugged a cape of monkey fur around his shoulders and bent his head low, leaking more tobacco juice into his can. I jumped down to my feet again and watched the young man from behind the buggy.

Eddie Junior stopped three houses down: a three-story, Georgian Colonial affair with sash windows five across on the top floor and a wraparound porch. He rasped at the door and was greeted by a woman in a gingham apron who invited him inside immediately. His collie waited on the porch, pacing.

I ran a pocket comb through my beard. "Get the rig ready. When he comes back out, we'll scoop him up on his way home."

"Suppose he stays for a while?" Billy said, taking up the reins.

"Beware the fury of the patient man."

"You and your literature."

Four minutes passed. The entire block was dark save for the flicker of the gas streetlamps. Our pony whinnied and snorted the frosty air. Snow fell in fat wet patches. Billy dug the grassy chaw out of his bottom lip, flung it into his fruit can, and wiped off his mouth with the back of his hand. Finally Eddie Junior reemerged from the neighbor's house, offered an indistinct farewell to someone back inside the foyer, and closed the door behind him. The books he'd been carrying by a belt strap were gone. His collie yipped and took up behind him again, staying close to his heels.

Billy whipped the buggy around, making a full turn to come up the other side of the street. The pony clopped at a trot over the icy brick, and Billy steered the coach halfway up onto the sidewalk, tipping the carriage as the two left wheels bounced over the curb. Eddie Junior was heading straight toward him and paused at the sight of the man in the fur cape seated on the platform. Darkness between the streetlamps hid his face.

I crossed the avenue on foot, taking a long route to get behind the young heir to the Cudahy meatpacking fortune. I approached with my five-shot revolver drawn at my side and the big collar of my overcoat hiding my face. My hat scrunched down low past my eyebrows. My crunchy footsteps in the new snow made Eddie Junior turn around. He was blocked from escape in both directions.

"We've got you now, Eddie Jones," I said, keeping a distance of five feet.

The young Cudahy stammered. "My—my name's Cudahy. Not Jones."

I threw open my overcoat, revealing my fake badge just as I had done for the inquisitive police officer. "Sure it is. I'm undersheriff of Sarpy County, and you're under arrest."

Eddie Junior looked as if he might sprint away. Billy drew his Spencer rifle from a scabbard hidden alongside the buggy and held it sideways in his lap.

"I live in that house right over there," Eddie Junior said and pointed toward his home less than thirty yards away.

I stepped closer. "You escaped from reform school last night and stole five hundred dollars from your aunt. You're not fooling me, Eddie Jones."

"But I'm Eddie Cudahy, and I live right there!"

"That game won't work, son," I said, drawing the young man's attention away from his house. As I moved to take him, Billy bolted off his seat and threw his monkey fur over the boy's head. Young Cudahy tried to fight off the garment, but Billy was quick to wrap his arms around the boy and tackled him to the ground. The collie dog snarled and barked but didn't attack. Eddie fought and screamed, but his fists and voice were muffled under the heavy cape. I whacked his head through the fur with the checkered grip of my revolver, rendering him motionless. Billy stood up gasping from the effort. After wiping the snow from his pants, he found his hat on the ground and dusted off its crown.

Together, we lifted the boy's body and carried it to our buggy as casually as furniture movers hauling a sofa. After propping up the young man into a sitting position to give him the appearance of a cloaked passenger, I canvassed the street in both directions. There wasn't a person in sight. I glanced at every house on both sides of the block, making sure no one had come to a window or front porch.

The commotion set Eddie's collie into a frenzy. Billy kicked at the pooch, just missing its muzzle with the spurred heel of his boot. The dog ceased its hysterical yipping long enough for us to resume our seats on the buggy platform, the unconscious young Cudahy squeezed between us. Billy clucked his tongue twice and we were off at a trot. The buggy rocked back and forth with its newly added weight. The boy's collie kept pace with our carriage until the end of the block but gave up the chase as we rounded the corner and disappeared from view into a flurry of sideways snow like a ship lost to storm.

II

THERE'S NO DENYING it: a man outside the law's pale revels in an existence unmatched by anything else in creation. A clever man, a pretty famous desperado in his own right, once told me that being miserable ain't the same as being good. And he was right. But he also left the equation half short.

I was eleven years old when the Big Nose George Gang descended on my family's ranch in Colorado. Daylight silvered out, the sun under the mountains and well on its way to causing the other half of the world its share of trouble when four riders crested the brow of a stony hill. I was the first to see them. In the goat pen harassing a rattlesnake with a tree branch, if memory serves. Their shapes as oneiric as shadows in a dream. The lead rider bellowed a greeting from a distance. He rode a cinnamon mare and wore a stovepipe.

"Hey there, youngster," the man said and spit. He moved around a wedge of tobacco as big as a jawbreaker in his cheek. "Your pops somewhere abouts?"

I nodded and ran for home, past the chicken coop, to fetch my father. The leader introduced himself as George Parrott and politely asked if he and his men could be served a supper and take shelter for the night in the barn, as he calculated a rainstorm advancing in the red clouds over the Rockies. He said they'd rode nearly a hundred miles in the last twenty-four hours without rest and badly needed a spot to recuperate for the evening.

"Sure enough," my dad had said and shook hands with all four men. "You can stable your horses yonder and see to your washing at the well."

The man who'd introduced himself as George thanked him mightily for the hospitality, and his gang watered their horses at the goat trough. I brought the strangers' horses two buckets of forage and sweet feed apiece and showed the men where they could wash before supper. George patted me on the head, told me I was an alright tyke. He gave me a silver dollar and a stick of horehound candy for my effort. A second man brought a bag of lemons inside and asked my mother if she could make lemon pies with whipping cream. She accommodated him with a mite of exasperation.

I was sent out to the springhouse to fetch fresh milk and butter. My two sisters gathered potatoes and canned tomatoes from the root cellar. A five-pound jackrabbit cooked in the fireplace, the logs snapping and the hare spitting juice as it rotated on a spit. My mother dressed the table with her best linen and set out our queensware dishes usually reserved for holidays. The four men came into the house in a bawdy temperament. They arranged their boots by the door and hung their mackinaw coats on the hall tree and all around otherwise regarded their presence as if they'd graced our family an audience with the queen.

The leader of the gang had a nose as big as a bird's beak and his last name, Parrott, was a humorously fitting circumstance when regarding his large snout. He was not guarded about his physical abnormality. He even drew attention to it by tapping on his left nostril three times and saying: "After I was born, my folks changed our family name from Gerardo to Parrott on account of my schnozzle. Too bad. If I'd been born with a big something else, they might've changed our last name to Wienerschnitzel and named me Colossus."

I had seen his likeness before. His mug was pasted on circulars in town. Impossible to forget a nose that size. Every telegraph pole in Leadville bore a poster of his profile.

WANTED. GEORGE PARROTT. ALSO KNOWN AS BIG NOSE GEORGE. DEAD OR ALIVE.

He carried a bird's head Colt on his hip, wore a melon-colored shirt with butternut trousers, and kept his sundown orange hair cropped above his ears. He took his time poking about the kitchen cupboards as if he owned the place until he discovered an earthen jar of muddy whiskey. He poured out five lashings: four for his men and one for my father. They sat and drank, and George asked if he and his weary travelers might indulge a second slug before supper. My daddy did not refuse them.

That night we dined on roast jackrabbit, boiled potatoes, biscuits with blackberries, and three lemon pies for dessert. The men were profane but in good humor. They masticated the rabbit and slurped berries straight from the spoon and poured the whiskey as freely as if it came from a spigot over the concrete kitchen sink. Soon their voices fell easy out of their mouths, their tongues as loose as if culling remembered song, when just twenty minutes prior they hardly had the stamina to answer a simple yes-or-no question.

By the time the pie and coffee were served, the gang recalled their latest forays into crime as casually as if they were conversing about the weather. There was no want of conversation once they got enough whiskey in their bellies. They talked on numerous subjects with engorged vocabularies. My mother cringed and offered more coffee. She sent my sisters to bed, but I begged to stay up, and she didn't have the energy to argue. The kerosene stove warmed the house and the men bundled themselves by the fire with their cups.

I studied George as if trying to memorize his every characteristic. I was enamored. The life of those men galloping off to every new horizon and slapping around their pistols and bringing in bags of lemons for strangers to make them pies seemed as marvelous as the fables I read from my sisters' fairytale books. After dessert, the rainstorm George had forecasted came in over the mountains sideways. Rain hard enough to bend lampposts and drown night toads. The whole house complained in the wind, ached as if it were weak as pasteboard.

"I canny thank you enough, Mr. Crowe, for your family putting us up and for that fine meal," George had said after his second slice of pie as he swept crust crumbs off his vest. "We come all the way down from Montana."

"What was your business there?" my dad asked.

George considered the question and how truthful an answer he might divulge with another swallow of whiskey. He turned the cup in his hands. Truth won out. "Well, it ain't no secret we're not merchants. We robbed us a military convoy south of Powder River. Army payroll. It's all corrupt, you know? The troops never see but a dime on the dollar of what they're owed and the big Washington fat cats skim from that payroll like it was milk boiling. So we helped ourselves to a little before they could. We was soldiers, used to be. All four of us."

The man who'd brought in the lemons said, "God, we've been

running eight days on now without much for sleep or pleasure. It sure is fine to be sitting here in front of this grand fire with a good meal in the belly and a dry roof over our heads."

He turned to me. "Be grateful always for the small delights, young'n."

Come morning I was the first to wake. I played with the silver dollar Big Nose had given me the night before, had even slept clutching the coin in my little hand, and went out onto the porch to watch the sunrise. Our goats were still drenched from last night's downpour. The rain had stopped only an hour earlier. They shivered and bleated and bemoaned their station. Fog hung low in our valley. A damp kind of dawn.

After a short while, George came out from the barn wearing only his union suit with his mackinaw coat hugging his shoulders like a cape. He stopped at the water pump and sloshed some cold on his face and wandered over to the porch with his mustache dripping.

He said, "That sunrise looks like a painting of a sunrise."

I sat silently.

"Look at all them perfect pinks and oranges," he continued. "I never seen one quite like it. If that sky was done in oils and hung in a frame on a wall, I'd say that such beauty never existed anywhere on God's green earth. It's a damn wondrous thing, kid. Man's notion of nature is almost always grander than the actual thing. And now here we are staring at it."

I turned the silver dollar in my hands. "I've seen your picture before."

George chuckled, spat. "On circulars in town, I bet?"

"My dad says you're an outlaw."

"Well, your daddy's by-God right about that."

I bent my head low.

"Your mama got any coffee boiling in there yet?"

"She's still asleep."

"A lollygagger then, is she?" George said and chuckled again.

"Why do you do it?" I asked.

"Do what? Call people names? I was only funning about your mama."

"I mean rob people."

"Because I'm good at it," George said. "The simple, honest life? That game ain't worth the candle, son."

I nodded to feign understanding the same way I did sitting at a desk in the back of my schoolhouse, fiddling with the coin still.

George tongued his wet mustache. "That the first dollar you ever been paid?"

"Yes, sir."

"You obey your moms and pops all the time?"

"Yes, sir. I try to."

"Well, you get used to too much of that and it'll be mother-me-do and yes-sir-papa your whole rotten life. I'll tell you one something I wish had been told me when I was a sprout. Being miserable ain't the same as being good," he said as he studied the new day, as attuned to the sunrise as would be a mapmaker upon seeing a new tract of land to cartograph. Not long after, his pals came out of the barn in their goat-hair chaps and galoshes and snap-button shirts, ready to ride out. George dressed himself in a hurry. They saddled their horses and rode up to the porch where I sat playing with his silver dollar.

George considered me one last time.

"Tell your ma and pa we're sorry we couldn't stay for breakfast," he said, nickered at his horse, and the four riders bolted off. I kept the silver dollar safe until I was old enough to spend a little on myself. Later in life, I couldn't remember what I purchased with the coin and, from time to time, wished I'd kept it still.

III

FOR THE THREE months leading up to the kidnapping, Billy and I had rented a frame cottage on a lane north of Grover Street that belonged to an old German seamstress. The house, vacant for more than a year before our arrival, had fallen into disrepair. The roof was patched up like a quilt with squares of heavy napped cloth that swelled during rainstorms and leaked runoff into pots and buckets. The floorboards were warped. Plaster crumbled off the walls. Wallpaper peeled down in long curls. Once painted white, the house had been stripped of nearly all its color, and the exposed wood had rotted from the elements. There was a good barn at the back of the property that was nearly as big as the cottage itself.

The home sat on a pronounced slope of upland above the southwest corner of the city, just beyond the South Omaha limits. The hillside leading up to the sandy drive was covered in dead wildflower so parched from the winter that it broke apart underfoot like dust. From the main window at the back of the house, we had a view of the Union Stockyards and the Cudahy packinghouses pitched in the valley below. I stared out the window for more than an hour before finally settling on the rent. The cottage was perfect.

"We'll need to fix it up some," Billy said.

I disagreed. "Yeah, what this outfit needs is some nice Irish lace on the windows."

"If I'm to live in a place, it's got to be livable."

"Well, it ain't the penthouse of the Belvedere. I'll give you that."

Billy paced the main room and then wandered into the kitchen. I followed him, watched him examine every crack and crevice.

"I guess it'll do," Billy finally said.

"I'm guessing it will," I replied.

For a whole month we set about preparing the house. We pasted oatmeal paper on all the windows to cut out the sunshine.

There was a gun rack on the wall to the left of the front door where we could stash our rifles. I brought a few pieces of discount furniture into the hideaway: a wicker rocker, a pair of ladder-back chairs with rope bottom seats, a kitchen table full of knots, a pair of collapsible iron cots.

Billy cleaned out the woodstove, which had been inhabited by a pair of rattlesnakes honeymooning for the autumn. He nearly got bit twice trying to shoo the rattlers with a willow broom and finally unloaded six shots from his revolver into the stove. He missed both snakes entirely at point blank range but made them uncomfortable enough to slither out of their iron nest so he could finally sweep them past the front door. He fired five more rounds as they bellied away into the weeds, and missed again altogether.

I watched with a smile from the front porch, my hands dug into my trousers, my pipe crooked in my mouth. "That's some fine shooting."

Billy spun around. He didn't know he was being watched. He nodded at the snakes slithering away. "You go to hell. They're skinny."

"I seen kids with slingshots got more accuracy than you."

"I've been domesticated some."

"Suppose you have. Suppose I'll just keep you on the scattergun."

Billy cursed and went back into the cottage to put some wood into the stove to heat up the drafty front room. I set about to the chores of stocking the pantry and barn. Oats and carrots and sugar cubes for our pony we had yet to purchase. Brandy and ham and banana taffy for me and Billy. I made several trips into town to shop for a good horse and used buggy before finally settling figures on a white mare with a silver star on its forehead and an old Stanhope with a collapsible carriage top.

The horse was an agreeable creature with a pearl mane and enough life left in her to pull a good draft. I fell to liking her immediately. Billy was as indifferent about the animal as he was the cottage and everything else.

It seemed he'd lost all sense of wonderment in life. All month long he mooned about in a droll. The man couldn't even manage the enormity of the moment we were about to create. Nothing I said or imagined could stir Billy's emotions. There was only the salving of pain with brandy and whiskey and plenty of it until the first thin light creased over the hills and the pain returned harder and more pronounced than it had been the day before.

After the expense of our preparations, including the three months of rent paid for in advance, we were down to our last ten dollars between us. To pass the empty evenings, we cut cards at the small kitchen table and shared slugs from a gallon woodjacket can of drug-store whiskey. Come morning we were both usually ale sick and took turns dunking our heads in the freezing horse trough by the barn before pulverizing some coffee we drank as strong as coffin varnish in tin cups.

For five weeks we studied the comings and goings of the Cudahy home. Billy sat in the carriage with the top raised for cover while I stood in company with our white horse, puffing my clay pipe. We spoke little and, when we did converse, we talked in hushed tones.

In the afternoons young Eddie Junior came home from school around three o'clock. He played shinny with his friends in the street before suppertime and practiced his piano in the front room. The evening hours were spent holed up in his room with his schoolbooks, and the hour before his bedtime was largely employed at his father's billiards table. We followed him in the evenings on his occasional errands. We lurked in shadows between the flicker of lampposts. I made notes about his routine on a lined pad, noting what times he left the house each day and for how long he was gone.

It was a sullen month of winter that December.

The weather didn't clear out but for an hour or two at a time. Icy rain fell in nailpoints. Clouds ribbed like needlecord, allowing only for the faintest bit of threaded sunlight. The Missouri froze overnight only to thaw again the next day. Come the middle of the month, on a rare day clear of weather save for a few ragged clouds ghosting in a white sky, Billy and I readied ourselves for what would prove to be our final day of observation.

I fell out of sleep in a mad dash and got into my woolens to start the kitchen fire. I parched coffee beans in an iron pot and chunked out some water from the cistern pump to brew the beans. Billy was coughing himself awake by the time the coffee was ready. I stepped outside into the quivering morning in my long johns and sheepskin boots to peel a mealy apple and have a morning toke from my pipe.

On the downslope toward the river, a huddle of cows stood in a field of dead and snowy clover. A buckboard pitched high with manure passed by on the road below our house, a shovel handle jutting out of the stinking mound. Billy joined me outside, wearing only his skivvies under his long coat and a rabbit pelt for a hat, hacking up the nighttime from his lungs. I sat on the front steps and looked south toward the stockyards.

I peeled my apple bald as a stone. Balanced it on the porch railing and undid the flap of my woolens and pissed off the front porch.

Billy said, "We take the kid tonight."

I auditioned the idea in my head. "Supposed to snow this evening."

"I'm not waiting any longer. I wait another day and I might change my mind about the whole damn thing."

"Getting nervy on me?" I asked.

"Just losing patience is all," Billy said and spit phlegm. He crammed a plug in his lowers and leaked tobacco from his mouth and stirred molasses into his coffee mug. "We ought to have us a pail of suds. Steady our grit."

"No grog," I said. "We need to be clearheaded."

"You got that letter finished?"

I nodded. We went over the plan step by step for the remainder of the day. After supper we readied ourselves for the crime. I lathered foam on my cheeks with a pig bristle brush and shaved using a broken piece of glass for a mirror. Billy darkened his pitiful mustache with lampblack from the bottom of one of our oil burners. He found a little courage from a few swallows of baldface leftover in an old apothecary jug. We both dressed in laundered shirts and fresh pressed trousers and stitched boots.

New weather filled out over the city: a high batting of snow clouds waiting for sunset, a scarred sky veined with the last light of day. We set out on our buggy down a winding farm road of packed sand. The temperature dropped ten degrees in less than an hour by the time we ambled our coach into the city.

The winter sun pulsed like muscle over the naked trees. Wintery brume traced the streets. Everywhere inescapable angry cold. I pinched a clot of tobacco from my carrying tin and sent pipe smoke up to the heavens in long drafts. Billy wrapped himself in his monkey fur and sat chattering his teeth. Twenty minutes passed and young Eddie returned home from academy on his regular clockwork, his schoolbooks slung over his shoulder by a belt strap as he kicked a stone down the sidewalk.

I watched him and scribbled another calculation on my nickel pad. I tamped down my pipe bowl and said, "The kid keeps schedule better than the railroad."

"I could've told you that three weeks ago. I did tell you that three weeks ago. Then two weeks ago. Then last week I told you the same thing."

"We canny rush it. There's only the one chance we'll ever have."

Billy reached down and took his rifle out of its scabbard. He laid it across his lap to admire its weight and polish before wagging the gunstock at the Cudahy house. "Let's get it over with then. Let's take him tonight."

"Not yet," I said. "There's one thing left to do."

"There's nothing left for us in the whole world but this," Billy replied and slid the Spencer back into its housing.

"I need to go see him one last time."

"The kid?"

"The old man."

"The old man? Edward Cudahy?"

"Yes. Edward Cudahy."

"You cannot be serious."

"I cannot be anything else," I said and situated myself again on the buckboard. I took the reins from Billy and clucked my tongue to get our pony marching.

Dusk dimmed the earth in a giant fold. Around the corner of Dewey Avenue, wagon traffic clogged to a standstill. A dog had run into the lane only to be trampled under hoof by a string of stagecoach ponies. Three dirty Polish children in black rags were weeping over the stomped bones of their beloved shaggy pet, the mother trying to shoo them back inside away from the horror.

While we sat waiting for the bottleneck to clear, Billy spit tobacco in giant globules. I lit the iron lantern dangling from a rod over my wagon seat. A man, presumably the father of the family who'd just lost their pet, had wrapped the dog in a blanket and was carrying it back toward their house with his sobbing children following him. We finally crossed the avenue where the poor mutt had been trampled, loped over a sopping wet mushroom field in the new snow as the sky pinked.

Seeing the dead dog reminded me of another time long ago when my first horse had drowned in a flash flood. I was thirteen years old and living for a summer on my uncle's ranch in Shinbone, New Mexico. The desert rains came heavy that night and washed the sky clean of all atmosphere as if it were picture glass. I thought hard on that moment as Billy and I pulled into the lane leading up to our Grover Street cottage.

We'd barely escaped the flood that night—me, my uncle, and two cousins. A rain of such weight it flattened crops into tillage and bent cornstalks at the knees, the floodwaters often places deep enough to drown a horse with a current like a river. And drown my nag it did, an old twenty-dollar California horse as reliable as sunrise. The poor beast carried away on its back with its legs flailing in the air.

How easy it was to be carted off this life. All night I could think of naught else. Be it beast or man, rich or poor, strong or weak, it was all too easy for any of us to be swooped up by darkness in a single whoosh, screaming and screaming.

IV

I FIRST MET Billy almost two years earlier. It was the last summer of the old century, eighteen and double nine. The streets bright with rain from the previous night's thunderstorm. All of Omaha sequined by sunlight on raindrops still clinging to windows and store signs. Yellow trolleys and dinging streetcars zipped along their routes, carrying full loads of people to work.

Shop doors had opened for business: photography suppliers, confectioneries, a ten-story department store where a person could buy anything from a portable sewing machine to a tub of jelly. A clothier balanced a tower of hats for sale on his head. A woman in a cocktail dress entered a syphilis clinic, last night's thunderbolts apparently not the only thing that shook the bedposts.

A mangy mutt missing whole chunks of fur lapped up gutter water streaming down from a roof pitch. Youngsters in wash suits and soap-lock haircuts played stickball with broom handles in the street, using manhole covers as bases, between the bouts of passing traffic before the sun was full out and the whole city purple with heat. Another advertisement for Mennen's Toilet Powder—this one pasted on the side of a bulletin wagon—came to a halt at a sidewalk flag stop. Drying linens garlanded fire escapes. Wash lines were hung between tenement windows. Neighborhood laundry the flags of the alleys.

My days were spent hauling hogs on my back, with a meat hook over my shoulder, from the slaughterhouse to the railcars. They were cut in half lengthwise with the heads still attached, weighed upwards of eighty pounds. My spine felt as weak as shoestring most days by noontime. Dry manure dust clouded the air, perpetual as a London morning fog. Some days I'd had a shovel in my hand for so long that when I finally got to setting it down at quitting time it felt like I'd lost a third limb. During my long workdays I hardly spoke a word to anyone. Many took me for a mute or an invalid. My facial expression always suggested that of a man looking for paradise over the next bend.

One afternoon in the stockyards, after lunching on ham and white bread from a tin cookie box, a scuffle broke out in the gravel yard in front of the loading docks. I was sitting on the ground against a pigpen wall and starting my pipe when I first heard the commotion. Four big Bohemians circled around a feller about my age. He was bleeding from his block-shaped head and dancing around with his fists raised, poised like a rattler for the next attack. If it weren't for the foolish attempt at a beard growing on his cheeks, I might've thought him to be twelve or thirteen years old.

The four men around him kicked up dust in the air, hooting and hollering. At first I didn't move. Nor did any of the other men seated alongside me in a row against the pigpen wall as they finished their lunches. One of the Bohemians wielded a jackknife. Another held a chunk of broken pavement as big as a brick and launched it at the back of the young man's head, knocking him flat on his stomach.

The four crushers threw up their hands in excitement and hopped around shouting as if celebrating a last-second sporting victory in a gymnasium. The young boy groaned on the ground, still conscious but barely so. His hair full of blood. He tried to stand up but couldn't lift his own body. The thirty odd men who'd been watching the fight were as indifferent about witnessing the beating as if they were reading about it in newsprint the day after.

I had seen enough.

I stood slowly, as if getting out of a rocker, and wiped the dust off my pant legs. My pipe clenched between my teeth, smoke rolling. A roll of wall clouds pushed through the sky. A distant rainband moving in from the north. I approached the four Bohemians with all the urgency of a man without a thought or care in the world, my hands dug deep in my pant pockets. Their whooping stopped as I stood before them, working my pipe. A whistle sounded that the lunch break was over, but not a single man seated against the pigpen wall moved except to get a better view of the action.

I said, "Alright, that's enough now, you hear? You boys have had your fun."

The four men stared at me blankly. I might as well have been speaking in tongues for all the comprehension their faces held. I wondered for a moment if they knew any English at all.

Many who worked the yards didn't.

The biggest of the four stepped forward but said nothing.

I tried again. "Looks like you boys got yourselves a snoot full of itch somewheres. Can't we all just have us a quiet lunch without stirring up the nonsense?"

"What's it to you?" the big one asked. His mouth hung open so wide he lost a bit of drool down his shirtfront.

I groaned as if pondering an unanswerable question. "What's it to me? I'm trying to enjoy my pipe before I got to go back to lugging around dead hogs for another six hours and you boys are spoiling my smoke."

"Jesus, Aleksander. Look at this big sommabitch come to play," one of them said to the first man standing in front of their circle. He walked straight up to me and flashed a knife toward my chest. He had a mangled left eye as yellow as a cat's and a week's worth of buckbrush on his cheeks. "This ain't none of your business, stranger."

I considered the blade. It was no more threatening than a letter opener. A fishhook might have been a more foreboding weapon. I removed my worn felt hat and held it over my heart as if bidding a friend farewell. "If you aim to frighten me, you'll need something a lot bigger than that toadsticker."

The man with the knife looked at his blade as if he'd never seen it before. He gestured at the beaten chap who still hadn't the power to get off his stomach. "That boy there done hurt my little sister."

"Hurt her how?" I asked and took out my pipe to spit on the ground.

"Broke the poor girl's heart."

"Broke her heart?"

"That's right."

"So it takes four of you to beat the pulp outta him? Now if you'd said he raped her or roughed her up some, I might just as soon walk on outta here and let you fellers go about whatever you saw fit to do next. But a broken heart happens to us all at some point or another. That, well, that there's just a part of life."

"He left her for another woman," the man with the little knife said. His three friends shifted behind him.

"She good-looking?" I asked and spat again. "Your sister?"

"Like a sunset over the mountains."

"Well, every man thinks his own geese to be swans."

Laughter burst from the crowd against the sty wall. The Bohemian with the knife walked right up to me with his blade at the ready. He was close enough that he could cut a hole into me with one jab.

I kept my hands in my pockets and said, "If you all ain't outta here in under a minute you'll see one of the hottest times you've ever had in a cattle yard."

There was no more discussion after that. The Bohemian slashed his blade crosswise, aiming to spill whatever was inside my stomach in one long gash. I sidestepped the swipe as easily as dodging bad weather and grabbed the man by his forearm without removing my other hand from his trouser pocket. I pulled back and snapped the man's arm as if it were as hollow as a bird bone. The knife dropped from his hand. His radius fractured completely, sticking out of his shirt as he collapsed to the ground grasping his elbow.

The biggest of the group charged me but didn't make it two full steps before I socked him in the temple. He staggered back dizzily. I spat out my pipe and coldcocked him once more, square in the nose. I'm not much for boasting, but I will say this: my punch was as blunt as a worn bolt. His face would've incurred less damage if he'd been whacked with a stove lid.

He fell on his back and whined in a babyish way. Clotted blood gushed out of his nose and mouth. If his friends hadn't picked him up and drug him off, he might have just as soon choked to death on his own teeth and the world wouldn't have missed much from his absence. A wet piece of his nose was lying on the ground and the rest of it had collapsed into his face. I stepped away and wiped off my knuckles with a ratty handkerchief as casually as if I were washing up before supper.

The two remaining Bohemians dropped their courage awful quick as they helped their other two friends to their feet. The man

I punched in the face couldn't stand under his own power or open his eyes. The other's arm was in such torture that his legs seemed to fail right along with it as the entire foursome wobbled away. The rest of the curious and murmuring crowd packed up their lunch tins to get back to work, leaving only me and the beaten young man in front of the slaughterhouse.

I touched the tip of my boot to the kid's stomach. He moved, but only barely.

"You alright?" I asked.

A series of moans implied he was still alive.

I went over to the work pump where everyone drank from the same greasy cup during water breaks. The pump needed a good priming before it coughed up any water. I worked the lever five or six times until it spewed a blast of brown silt into the communal cup. I dumped the water over the kid's head. He moaned louder this time and turned over onto his back. The chunk of pavement stone that hit him in the back of his skull had split into two and lay on the ground a few feet away.

"You oughta get up if you can manage it," I told him.

The boy mumbled something indecipherable.

"This ain't no kind of place to be lying around," I said and crouched down to help the poor sap to his feet. He staggered as if completely drunk. I hoisted him up and put my arm over his shoulder to help him walk. Together we carted ourselves to an alley between a pair of brick slaughterhouses. I let the kid down with a thud and went to retrieve my pipe I'd spat out on the ground. I washed it off under the water pump, shook off the excess, and stuck it back in my shirt pocket upside down.

Sitting down again, I pulled my knees up to my chest. "You think you ought to get yourself to a hospital?"

The boy smacked his lips and gingerly touched the back of his bloodied head. "I ain't never been no good in fight."

"Well," I said stoically. "That's a keen observation."

"Where did you learn to throw a punch like that?"

"Colorado."

"That's a rough and tumble place I hear."

"I suppose so. If you walk past the wrong gatepost."

The kid tried to stand, but his legs buckled. He fell back against the wall and gave up any aspirations to walk out of the stockyard under his own power. Silvery rain fell from an empty sky. We both looked up. There wasn't a cloud to be seen between the tops of the buildings.

"God alive," the kid said. "I feel like I got hit with a whole half of planet earth."

"That or a piece of cobblestone. They both pack a pretty good wallop."

The kid spat into his hands and rubbed his saliva between them as if it were soap.

"What's your name?" I asked.

"William Cavanaugh. Everybody calls me Billy."

I stuck out a hand and Billy wiped off his and we shook. "Pat Crowe here. Next time you get in a bind you ought to just run the hell away," I said and stood to get back to work, readjusting the hold of my belt and the fit of my shirt.

"Listen, listen," Billy said, holding up a palm to halt my leaving. "Those boys might come back. They were pretty dead set on sending me to mine. I, well, I can't do much about it. But maybe if you were around, you know, like a pal or something?"

I rubbed my mouth. "Like friends you want to be?"

"Yeah, yes. Friends."

"Isn't that a little sentimental?"

"What's senty-mental?"

I thought on that some, dug wax out of my ear with my pinkie finger. "It's kind of like being happy and sad at the same time."

"I'm always more one than the other, myself," Billy said and patted at a line of blood above his eyebrow.

I stared down the empty alley. My voice caught in my throat. "Friends, huh?"

"I ain't got many."

A long pause followed. A man at the other end of the backstreet was eating a banana with such intent that he appeared spellbound by the fruit.

"Hell, I ain't got any," I finally replied and helped Billy to his feet with a good pull, and we both set off down the alley as the new rain quickened into a downpour.

V

IN THE ALCOVE of a bedroom on the second floor of our hideaway cottage, we bound young Eddie's feet to the legs of a ladder-back chair with a pair of horse hobbles and cuffed his hands to the chair's arms with iron manacles. We blindfolded him with a baby shirt and set a demijohn of water between his legs, nestled at his crotch.

If Eddie bent over enough, given the foot of slack in his manacles, he could lift the jug to his lips for a drink. He glugged down four or five heavy pulls, spilling more down his shirt than he got in his mouth. There was no furniture in the room save for the chair to which Eddie was tied and a large rattan rocker. The floorboards echoed every footfall. A lone window on the eastern wall, double-sashed, was blacked out with a giant cut of old carpet nailed into the paneling.

I collapsed in the rocker. It wasn't situated close enough to the window. I pushed the chair over, angling so it was within arm's reach of both the window and the woodstove in the corner of the room. A peg of sapwood broke apart in the stove's belly. A coffee kettle hissed steam. The room was sweltering. I opened the fuel door and tossed three ladles of water on the fire, hoping to find some balance of temperature. Since bolting him down to the chair, the young man hadn't made a sound. He didn't whimper or struggle, but allowed us to position him as we pleased. His steadiness took me by surprise. I watched Eddie for five long minutes. The only movement he made was to lift the carboy to his lips again, slugging down the water and sloshing it all over his shirtfront. Billy sat in the far corner of the room, his legs pulled into his chest, sipping whiskey from a dented cup.

I looked at him and sighed. The inebriate couldn't keep a bottle away from his lips even at the apex of his life. There was nothing to be said. No conversation worth being had. I sighed again, and all three of us sat in silence for a full hour. I lifted the carpet guarding the window and peeked outside. A grin of moon. Snow ticked against the warm glass.

Two miles away, in a deep gash cut through the bottom hills of South Omaha, I spied the distant workings of the Cudahy plant. Midget smokestacks funneled exhaust no longer than cigarette plumes from my vantage. The entire industry ran day and night, the locomotives hustling without cease, the factory lights glowing like a glut of stars alone amid endless blackness, a constellation stranded by millions of seemingly uninhabited miles.

Finally the stove went cold and thereafter the whole room. I relit the kindling with a cotton oil wick and nudged the wood with the toe of my boot to allow some oxygen into the gasping flame. I creaked back and forth in the rocker and broke the unnerving silence by asking young Eddie if he was comfortable.

"You want some of my dad's money," the young man said.

"It's not his money," I said. "Your father is a thief."

"And what are you?"

I laughed. "They call me Little Lord Fauntleroy."

Eddie scoffed. "Dad thinks a great deal of me."

"That's exactly what I'm counting on," I said and sparked my last cigarette.

"Could I have one of those?" the young man asked after a moment. I looked to Billy. He'd fallen asleep against the wall.

"An accommodatable request," I said and rolled the makings of a smoke from a purse of coarse tobacco and a leaf of papers. I handed the square to the young man and sparked the end for him with a paper match. Eddie leaned over and drew on the cigarette madly until it was extinguished and asked for another. I acquiesced. The young man had made no fuss, and if the most he asked for was a smoke, I would roll him cigarettes until daybreak.

I rose from the rocker and paced the room with a hand dug inside my vest. I walked to the peeling wallpaper scrolled with a wild rose pattern that had been falling away in strips from years of neglect. Inside one of the tears, I removed the ransom letter I'd written in print with a pencil. The letter, immaculate in spelling and punctuation, had gone through numerous drafts. A little more than a page long, it was as finely manicured writing as I could muster. Every pain I'd ever suffered throbbed inside those words. I unfolded the letter, as neatly creased as ironed trousers, and studied the scrawl in the light of the stove door.

When I was satisfied that every syllable was as flawless as I planned it, I took up the rocker again and said to Eddie, "I have here a bit of correspondence your father will be receiving bright and early tomorrow morning."

"My ransom letter?"

"Yes. Would you like to hear it?"

"I'd like another cigarette," the young tobacco fiend asked.

I glanced at the baggie and papers. There was no sense in rolling them when the young Cudahy was smoking them faster than they could be constructed. With a grunt, I was on my feet and searching Billy's pockets for a pack of machine rolls. I found a box of cross cuts in his overcoat and handed over the whole bandage to Eddie along with a book of matches.

"You can help yourself to as many of those as you want," I said. "But when they're gone, there's no more."

"If you'd take off this blindfold, I could help you with your grammar," Eddie said.

I chuckled halfheartedly through the side of my mouth. "You've a world of nerve, son. That I won't argue."

"You're not the first man that's wanted easy money from my father."

"Oh? You've been abducted before? A regular thing, is it?"

Eddie sparked a match after some fumbling. "Men have tried swindling dad before."

"This is no swindle, son. It's solatium."

"How's that?"

I snickered. "Like fringe benefits, you might call it."

"You're a little cracked, aren't you?"

"Broken in all places but my gut."

"My dad's a tough man. He won't repine to your threats," Eddie said. His voice trailed out aimlessly with a wasp of cigarette smoke curling up under his blindfold to the ceiling. He swiveled his head about in his blindness. Didn't know whom he was talking to or where in the room anyone might be.

I snapped open the letter. "Maybe you ought to give this a listen before you rush to judgment, my young friend."

"I'm comfortable," Eddie said and eased back in his chair, his newest cigarette burning away in between the fingers of his cuffed right hand.

I cleared my throat and adjusted my reading spectacles to the tip of my nose. The room was too dark to read the letter from my spot in the chair, so I turned up the globe of the iron lantern at my feet.

I began: "'Mr. Cudahy, we have kidnapped your son. You must pay six hundred thousand dollars in gold coin for his safe return. Mr. Cudahy, you are up against it and there is only one way out. If you don't the next man will, for he will see the condition of your son and realize that we mean business. If you fail to follow any of these instructions, he will be returned to you permanently harmed beyond repair or even perhaps not at all. If you stray from the following direction, you may forever walk endless fields hoping to find his bones disintegrating amongst the corn, his tiny skull buried in dirt only to be discovered centuries later like so many other fossils of once vibrant animals now lost forever to time and unspeakable sadness.

"'Men of the future might wonder at how they came upon such an artifact and the story behind its place buried in the earth. Yet none of them, no matter the exactness of their instruments and gadgets of which we now have no conception, will ever be able to figure the heartbreak behind their discovery. Your story of suffering will not be written in literature. It will be absent in the annals of history. Your child will have died alone and in pain of immeasurable magnitude that, in the grand scheme of what is precious in life and what is not, will only have cost you a dime on the dollar when held up to the light of your incalculable fortune.

"'Thus we give these instructions, which are to be adhered to with the finest detail. The entire six-hundred-thousand-dollar sum must be paid in twenty-dollar gold pieces, in canvas bags containing ten thousand dollars each. Each bag must be placed in a bank messenger's regulation valise. Put a red lantern on the front of your carriage. Leave your house at ten o'clock sharp, tonight, December Nineteenth. Drive out along Center Street, which runs from Omaha for forty miles. Some place along that road you will come to our lantern with a black and white ribbon tied to the bail.

"'Leave the money there. Turn around and drive back to your home. If there is any attempt to capture us we will not try to get the money, but return your son to you after we have put acid in his eyes and blinded him. We will castrate him surgically with a pair of elastrator pliers so that he may never bear children. Being your only son, he will not be able to pass on your family name. The Cudahy line will end with him.

"'Then you may lead him around blind and fruitless the rest of your days and tell the world the story of how you loved gold better than you loved your own flesh and blood. Don't be misled by the police as Old Man Ross was, who never recovered his kidnapped son, Charley Ross, and died of a broken heart. Follow the instructions in this letter and no harm will befall you or yours. Sincerely, Bandits.'"

I removed my eyeglasses, folded the letter along its creases, and tucked both into my shirt pocket. I studied Eddie's mouth, the only part of his face visible under his blindfold. It did not quiver or tighten. His jaw was loose as he continually sucked a cigarette. Already a pile of squashed butts were at his feet. If the letter had any effect on him at all, the young man did not show it. I wondered how I might solicit some emotion out of him. I broke off a piece of chicory stick for the coffee kettle and scooped ash from the legless stove with an old sardine can and looked out at the winter rain streaking tin down the window.

"Well, what do you think of that?" I asked.

Eddie cocked his head. His cigarette crackled with another inhalation. "I'd make it twenty-five thousand. Dad might pay that."

"Is that your worth to him?"

"Would you stand for that cut?" Eddie asked. "Dad's wealthy, but he doesn't just have six hundred thousand dollars' worth of gold lying around."

"He's a multimillionaire."

"On paper and in his investments. His wealth is measured on his factory."

"You're a smart skate."

"He's a resistant man."

"What about your mother? Is she the resistant sort?"

Eddie sat silently at that remark.

"You look a little pale, kid," I said and patted my pockets. Inside my trousers I found a vial of stamina tablets. I shook the pill case like a maraca. "How about a little medicine? I have here some of Dr. Williams' Brand Pink Pills," I said, reading the label. "They might restore some color to your complexion."

"I'm naturally light of pigment," Eddie said.

"Perhaps something else, then? A spot of whiskey maybe? The stuff we got ain't no goddamn good, but it'll warm you up all the same."

Eddie fussed with his handcuffs and squirmed in his chair to get comfortable. The heat from the stove was making him sweat. He'd already soaked a salty line into his baby shirt blindfold. "You're a bad man," he said.

I rocked in my chair. "I still have the material in me to do the right thing."

"Having it and using it are two different things."

"And you'd do well to remember it, seeing as how your fate is still on the balances."

"There are probably five hundred men scouring the city for me right now."

I looked out the window again, peeling back the carpet curtain. The Cudahy factory was still humming at a full tilt though it was nearing midnight. "Not yet there ain't. I doubt some whether your parents have noticed. Strange, the sixteen-year-old son of an empire gone for a whole night and nobody's keen to your absence."

"When they do get keen they'll rain hellfire down on your head."

I thought on that some. I'd weighed the repercussions in my head so many times in the last two weeks I could no longer fathom all the possible consequences of the crime. There was no more logic to be calculated, only the panther pacing back and forth inside my chest. Still, Eddie's suggestion to lower the ransom made practical sense.

Twenty-five thousand dollars' worth of gold would weigh nearly a hundred pounds once placed in bags. Six hundred thousand would tilt the scales upwards of two and a half thousand pounds. Transporting that much weight in gold was hardly worth the effort even if we could manage the feat.

The math was economical, especially given the need for fleetness of foot in the face of what surely would be one hell of a tracking party at our heels. I groaned and removed the letter from my pocket again to make one last revision. I erased the figure demanding six hundred thousand and substituted twenty-five thousand. I might've asked Billy if he was willing to take such an alteration. But when the man had knocked himself out on granddaddy syrup at this pivotal hour, he lost his vote.

The matter was settled in my mind.

"Better get some shut-eye if you can manage it," I told our captive. "Tomorrow's going to be a long day for you."

Eddie licked his lips. "Maybe a little whiskey would help me sleep."

I agreed. "Trying to sleep sitting up is rough business," I said and poured a tall glass of whiskey from the bottle Billy had been drinking. I placed the glass in Eddie's hands forcefully, spilling a little. "It's rotgut. Best to drink it down quick."

"Have you a mixing agent?"

"This isn't a taproom."

"I've not a trained tongue for hooch."

I laughed and adopted an aristocratic tone. "Oh, many pardons, monsieur, perhaps a peck of twenty-year-old scotch, instead?"

Eddie let out his first unexpected whimper of the night.

I softened at his cry. "I think there's some milk in the icebox downstairs," I said and lumbered down the steps to retrieve a bottle of yak from the highboy. I brought the milk upstairs and filled Eddie's tumbler to the brim. "There you be, kid. Slug it down."

Eddie gulped the elixir in three labored pulls and smoked two more cigarettes before he relaxed enough to quit squirming in his chair. I leaned back in my rocker and closed my eyes for a few interrupted hours, waking every few minutes, dreaming for short bursts of things long past that would never pass me again.

VI

WHEN I FIRST came to Omaha, I had nothing to my name but my daddy's old wool suit, a wooly peach, two cheese sandwiches smeared with white mustard, a dollar plus sixteen cents, and one half-smoked green cigar I'd been saving since my train crossed the Colorado border. I'd never seen a building taller than two stories. When it came to towns, the biggest I'd ever known was a hovel called Soda Springs: one mud street with a canvas saloon, a sheet iron hotel, and a combination bank and general store. Omaha might as well have been New York City to my young impression.

My elder sister had been living in the city for some time and operated a brothel in the downtown sporting district. The Sallie Purple. She named it after herself even though her name wasn't Sallie and there wasn't a speck of purple in the whole place. Her given name was Mary Elizabeth, but that seemed too virtuous a combination for a woman running her own whorehouse. I, for one, would've appreciated that kind of raillery. Maybe even named the place Saint Mary's Parish. For kicks. Just to rile the Catholics and confuse a few Lutherans. Still. It's not good business to upset your most loyal demographic.

The Sallie Purple was unpretentious in every sense: a two-story, white clapboard affair with a flat rubber roof and a tangle of telephone wires snaking out to their connecting street poles. Old whiskey barrels filled with water were spread out on the wooden sidewalk to combat future fires. For all its aesthetic modesty, the spot was one of the most raucous harems in the city. Besides whores, it proffered gambling of all stripes: billiards, roulette, poker, faro, dice, and a lottery wheel. The sign above the front entrance—in sharp green lettering—declared: IF YOU HAVE A FAMILY THAT NEEDS YOUR MONEY, DON'T DALLY HERE.

Why the sign was done in green lettering instead of purple still remains one of the great mysteries of my life. Forget the existence of God, what happened to the dinosaurs, and all the hooey about the pyramids. What I really want to understand is why my sister, of sound mind and body, started calling herself Sallie the Purple, named her whorehouse as such, and then painted her sign green.

This world. There's nothing in it but the daffy.

And no one was daffier than Tom Dennison.

Sallie had warned me about the man. All I was hoping for was a job. Maybe working behind the bar on some nights.

"That's easy," my sister told me the day I had arrived in town. "But you got to understand something. You won't be working for me. You'll be working for Mr. Dennison."

I'd never heard of the name Dennison before but could assume what kind of man he was. Every city had one of them to some degree or another. "I'm not sure I'm one to get mixed up in the politics of it all."

"You'll have to whether you want to or not."

"All's I want is a job, sis," I said.

"Look, if you want a job in this city, you got to pay for it. Most people pay with a vote. Some pay with their particular skills, if they have any. But everybody pays. I pay. Mr. Dennison is my partner. If he wasn't, I wouldn't have a place to call my own."

"So he owns you and you own that whorehouse? That's how it works?"

"He owns the city. And let me tell you straight out, there's no bucking it. These are dangerous men. They don't carry their guns just for the company. You toe the line like I toe the line and you'll find that you can make some serious money here."

I laughed. "What a gag."

"It's no gag. It's good business. The only business, actually. Everyone needs the assistance of a go-between these days. That's how the world spins, and that's how money gets made for both sides, I hate to tell you."

"Right, this Dennison feller is the finger, and you're the one wrapped around it."

"No, he's Mr. Dennison and I'm Madam Purple."

"Madam Purple, huh? You know, I've been meaning to talk to you about that."

Sallie grabbed my arm. She had the strength of a man. A two-

hundred-pound former Irish beauty queen with a streak of hippopotamus mean in her blood. "Smarten up, would you?" she said.
"You want to make your own way in this city? Then you have to play
by its rules. You want a job? You can have it. You want to start up
your own business someday like me? You can do it. But what you
can't have is the naiveté to call me a pawn. I'm a middle-of-the-road
proxy, nothing more."

"Oh yes. I'm sure I've sorely misjudged you. I'm sure the reason
you're sitting in that basement going through those gambling tick-
ets is to put the winnings in your pocket."

"Believe it or not, there are things more valuable than a dollar.
Especially when you already got barrels full of them."

"Like what?"

Sallie stepped forward and straightened my jacket lapels. "Like
friendship. Like allies. And, like I said, I'm a fence. You think I get
along all by own gumption?"

"You're getting fleeced is what you're getting."

"Well, everybody needs friends."

"You sure got a funny way of making them."

"And yet I still have them."

I exhaled.

"What's got you all bollixed up anyways? You just blew into
town an hour ago, and already you want to upset the apple cart?"

"You're getting shook down is what's got me bollixed up."

Sallie took my hand by the wrist and pulled me so close I could
smell what she had for breakfast. Eggs and pineapple. She said, "Let
me tell you a little something. You can think what you want of me
but that mouth of yours could get us both into a lot of trouble if the
wrong person heard you talking like that. Mr. Dennison comes by
for a weekly visit, and I don't want him stopping by any more than
he already does. My house used to be run by a woman name of Beth-
any Bashman. She was the second or third biggest player in this city.
Bigger than you or I will ever be. Woman used to swan around town
like she'd just stepped out of a bandbox, and now she's got to buy her
groceries on credit down at Blubaugh Brothers. I wouldn't want that
happening to me. Or to you."

A few days later, Mr. Dennison came calling when I was closing down my sister's whorehouse for the night. He walked in from the street like a man ready to split lightning. The main billiards room was empty, all the chairs stacked upside down on the tabletops and the stiff organdy curtains pulled shut across the picture windows when Dennison came up to the counter, dressed neat as a new coin. He wore a brown herringbone suit and a brown felt crusher with the brim nearly touching his eyebrows. His ocean gray eyes cased behind a pair of owlish spectacles. A diamond stickpin centered in his white tie. I was busy restocking the shelves behind the bar and didn't hear him come in at first, didn't even know what the man looked like, when Dennison tapped his large onyx ring on the oiled counter three times to get my attention.

I spun around and wiped off my apron. "Sorry, pal. Closed up for the night."

Dennison smiled. Two big goons stood just inside the doorway, wearing suits that looked like they'd been bought off the rack and bulged under the arms from the pieces in the shoulder holsters. "I know you're closed. I left my coat in here a few hours ago. A single-breasted fox-hair coat."

I knew the jacket. It'd been left on the coat tree in the private smoking room reserved for the bigwigs and big gamblers. All checkered flooring and felt walls, dim as an opium den. I had checked the pockets during my closing duties and found thirteen hundred dollars in one of the side pockets. No one in the city carried that much cash, and very few would ever see such an amount all at once in their entire lives. I retrieved the coat from a broom closet behind the bar and handed it to Dennison who folded it over his forearm like a waiter's towel and searched its pockets, finding the cash still intact.

He counted out the cash in front of me: two five-hundred-dollar bills, a one-hundred-dollar bill, and ten twenties. Sucking furiously on a toothpick, Dennison took his time in considering my disposition and appearance.

At last I asked, "Is something the matter?"

"What's not the matter? I got over fifty whores out of commission this month with the only French thing in this city that's not on a dinner menu," Dennison said, referring to the recent syphilis outbreak throughout the city, "a police commissioner who thinks he needs to raid a bunch of my stuss houses next week to pacify the new reform mayor, and a wife who spent more money redecorating our guest bedroom than Ida McKinley did renovating every room of the White House."

"I meant with the coat," I said.

Dennison peeled off a hundred-dollar banknote from his stack, reached out, and forced the bill into my palm. "You go on and keep this for yourself. What's your name, son?"

Startled by the gesture, it took me a moment to reply. "Pat."

"Pat what?"

"Pat Crowe."

Dennison raised an eyebrow and looked back at his two gunmen, who hadn't moved from their spot by the front door. "Sallie's brother?"

"That's right."

"The brother the bartender, huh? You enjoy this kind of work?"

"I enjoy anything that pays me, sir."

"Forget money. What gives you pleasure?"

I pursed my lips, unsure of how to respond.

"Do you know who I am?"

"You're Tom Dennison," I said, then added, "the political boss."

Dennison chuckled and held out his jacket with an outstretched arm. One of his gunmen stepped forward and took it off his hands. "That's the name for it, I suppose, silly sounding as it is. But it's a job just like any other."

I held out the bill Dennison had given me. "Not saying I don't appreciate the offer, but I can't keep this."

"Why can't you?"

"You don't even know me."

"I know you're just about the most honest person I've met in a long time, which is a lot more than I know about most people. Never heard of a man returning that kind of money to a person. Never in my life. Probably never will again. You seem like a smart kid. Good size, too. I could use a man like you. You ever need to make a little extra money, you come see me at my place on Farnam Street. You know where I am on Farnam Street?"

I nodded affirmatively. Everybody in the city knew where

Dennison's place was on Farnam Street. He shook his head several times as if finally getting a joke. He slapped the bar counter twice and left the whorehouse, one of his gun goons holding the door open. As he disappeared into the street, the words "Don't forget now, come and see me soon" trailed behind him like a scarf tail in a stiff wind.

I saw the man soon enough when he returned to The Sallie Purple a week later, this time early in the evening with a pack of people in tow, including mayor Frank Moores. The mayor had a voice as shrill as a teapot on the scald whether he was giving a speech or ordering drinks. He took malt whiskey barefoot and had to explain to me that barefoot meant neat. I brought five more whiskeys and two bottles of wine to their table in the private smoking room, where Dennison had left his coat the week before. Smoke leaked from gigantic cigars, filling the room to the ceiling.

The other two men seated on the serpentine booth around the table were Tom's right-hand man Billy Nesselhous and Ace Diamond, a civic reformer whose party alliance was as fake as his name, a man who flip-flopped his politics as frequently as if his loyalty were something hot on a spatula, depending on which party member's ear he was bending. Four women were also with the group, all of them dolled up in glittery boas and crepe dresses. Two of the four were squeezed in on both sides of the mayor, his arms draped around them as if posing for a portrait. The poor dames appeared as bored as a group of schoolgirls listening to a lecture on household economics, and maybe just as young.

I uncorked the first bottle of wine and poured a dash into each stemmed glass. Dennison waved his hand over his, refusing the alcohol.

The mayor crossed his leg at the knee, a nearly feminine posture that didn't match the bulk of his beefy thighs. He tapped a cigarette on a pewter case. "Ain't you thirsty, Mister D?"

"I like to keep my wits about me," Dennison said graciously. He was the only man without a moll tucked in next to him.

"No whores or booze, huh? Howsa fella supposed to sell products he don't use himself?"

"Would you be asking me that if I worked behind the counter of a lingerie shop?"

The mayor let out a belly laugh. "Boy, you sure are nutty. That's a good ol' poke in the ribs, eh Ace?" he said and nudged the man with his elbow. "Imagine that, ol' Mister D here walking around in a pair of frilly step-ins to show them off for the customers. What about you there, Ace? You wear woman's undies?"

Ace Diamond—elephantine in a beige suit—patted his ample stomach. "I got on a corset right now. Reason how I got such a tiny waistline."

"What a crack-up. You two are a couple a doozies." The mayor laughed again and looked at me hard. Like a dunce, I was still standing at the head of the table holding the wine. I couldn't take my eyes off the woman tucked under the mayor's left arm. The first time I ever saw hair that yellow. There's nothing in the world for words when you finally see real beauty. Her lipstick was smudged—she'd been necking with the mayor when I entered.

The mayor tossed a double eagle on the table. "That'll be all, waiter."

Dennison tucked the curls of his eyeglasses behind his ears. "Mr. Mayor, this is the boy I told you about. The one who found my coat last week."

"Oh yes, quite right. Good to know that even in the lower ranks of society there's still those with some amount of moral fortitude."

I titled my head and groaned softly as I looked the mayor over. "You have a soft spot for the poor and grafters alike, do you?"

The room went silent. Dennison sighed disappointedly.

The mayor sat forward and crossed his hands on the table. "What exactly are you implying there, young man?"

I shrugged as if the answer was obvious. "You're a friend to all walks of life."

The mayor rubbed his mustache and smiled. Dennison lit a cigar and pulled at a chipped pottery ashtray.

I picked up the double eagle and was about the leave when Dennison asked, "Hey Pat, you're probably the most honest person in the room. Tell us, what do you think of our new mayor here? Doesn't he always speak the truth?"

"I don't know," I said, holding the drink tray at my side. I looked ridiculous in that silly apron and sillier bow tie. "I've never asked him for a loan."

The four men in the room laughed together. I was still staring at the girl on the mayor's left and exited through the privacy curtain as the laughter subsided.

Slightly past the dinner hour, the main barroom was a saturnalia of pipe tobacco, cackling laughter, pine paneling, and ragtime pounded out on an upright piano. My sister, the most disinterested madam in the history of whoredom, was bent over the counter next to the beer taps, reading the *Omaha Evening Bee* while undressing an orange with her thumbnail. Billy sat at the far end of the counter, nursing a glass of brewed choc.

It'd been two weeks since I'd broke up the fight in the stockyards and every evening since he'd come into the whorehouse by himself. Sometimes he played checkers all night long until closing time and even then was skittish about heading home alone. It wasn't exactly a friendship, though I slowly developed a fondness for him in the way a big brother does for a runt of a younger sibling. And those Bohemians were sure to come back some time or another. It wasn't in a Bohemian's blood to let well enough alone. Billy's head hadn't stopped hurting since getting pelted with the chunk of pavement, but he didn't have money to see a doctor.

When I came behind the bar, he asked me for some headache powder. I slid the bottle down the bar top. He stirred two tablespoons into his choc and slammed it down in one draught. I poured him another mug from the tap and examined my appearance in the mirror behind the liquor bottles, straightening my hair with my fingers.

My sister looked up from her reading. "You're so darned pretty."

"Who's that looker come in with the mayor?" I asked.

Sallie looked back toward the curtained entrance of the smoking room. She knew the names and faces of nearly everyone who ever set foot in her place. "Which one?"

"The one with the yeller hair."

"That'd be Hattie McCoy. Or Hattie McCoven," Sallie said. She flipped over to the next page of the evening paper and threw a scrap of orange peel onto the floor, her attention focused on the fruit as acutely as if she was crocheting a sweater.

"Who brings whores into a whorehouse, anyway?" Billy asked.

Sallie ruffled her paper. "Whoever can afford to."

"Well, which is it?" I asked. "McCoy or McCoven?"

"Why don't you go ask her yourself?" Billy added with a nasally wheeze that made his words sound as if they came out of his nose instead of his mouth.

Sallie sighed and finally quit fiddling with her orange. "Don't get cutesy now, you hear? You go nosing around one of the mayor's pin-ups and it's bon voyage, little brother."

I wasn't hearing any of it. "That's the most beautiful woman I ever seen. Woman like that, you could stare at her till you grew cornstalks on your eyes."

"Yeah, she's exotic as an apple," Sallie said and chuckled absently.

"You don't see it?"

Sallie folded her paper. "You ain't supposed to be drinking on the job."

"Maybe you ought to make her your wife," Billy said.

"Maybe I ought to yet."

"Or maybe you ought to go upstairs and get a foot rub and a frog dinner and a real piece of Nebraska cooze that won't cost you your life," Sallie said.

I brayed. "I ain't one to pay for it."

"Not with coin, anyway," Sallie said.

"Money well spent," Billy added and raised his glass. He'd emptied his pockets on such slick over the past two weeks. If he wasn't at my side, he was upstairs getting bounced around by a meaty Ukrainian whore twice his size. Poor Billy Cavanaugh—a tiny man with tiny hands and a rumored tiny something else—loved himself all things large and had a rash or worse to show for it, constantly tugging and itching at his crotch.

The night drew on toward closing time. Dennison and his gang of political bags stayed past the final hour. I served them exclusively until everyone but Tom was beaming drunk. When they'd had their fill of whiskey and wine, it was out with the Swedish coffee and snifters of apricot brandy. Twice the mayor fell asleep for a spell. Dennison, Ace, and Billy Nesselhous spoke in hushed tones so as not to wake him. I couldn't keep my eyes off the young woman my sister told me was named Hattie. She'd returned my look on several occasions, albeit very briefly and with as much impudence as if I were weather expected.

By two in the morning, the place was empty save for Dennison's party. Billy always stayed planted at the counter until I walked out and locked the door behind him. Sallie had retired upstairs in her boudoir for the night, leaving the closing duties to me. I was drying off glasses with a rag when I looked out to the street and saw them: two of the blond Bohemians I'd roughed up at the stockyards. They stood on the far sidewalk against a streetlamp, smoking, waiting. Billy's back was to the window. He was playing rummy against himself, flipping over cards as worn as old soap slivers.

I set down the rag and walked to the far end of the bar and got the thirty-thirty out from under the till. I kept the rifle at my side so Billy wouldn't see it and told him I was headed out back to take out the trash. As soon as I left the bar, the Bohemians dropped their cigarettes and walked across the street, looking in both directions.

They came through the front door as quiet as quick thieves and scanned the front room. Billy was the only man in sight. The bigger man who'd gotten his nose busted wore a piece of plaster between his eyes. The second man had his arm in a sling and his other hand was filled with a truncheon the size of a baseball bat. I came around the back of the bar and stood just outside the front door, waiting for them to make any kind of move that would justify emptying my rifle into their backs.

"Hiya there, Billy boy," the big one said as the pair stepped behind Billy's stool.

Billy turned from his cards and his eyes went dead.

"Your protector ain't here," the second one said and slammed his club on Billy's hand against the counter, breaking bones in more than one spot. Billy held his hand against his chest. It throbbed and bled. He couldn't bend his fingers.

"I ain't never meant your sister no harm. We just wasn't compatible is all," Billy whined through the pain.

"Wasn't compatible?" the first one said. He leaned over and took Billy's mug and drank from it and set it back down and wiped his mouth. "You were set to be wed, and now our poor sister hasn't come out of her room in a month."

"I just ain't got the marriage gene in me."

The two Bohemians looked at each other. The big one yanked out Billy's stool from under him. His head hit the edge of the bar with such force that he bloodied his mouth and loosened three of his front teeth. The second man kicked the stool out of the way and jumped over the bar and helped himself and his brother to a couple pours of whiskey while Billy flopped around on the floor. They both laughed at his misery as he cupped his broken hand over his throbbing mouth.

I bolted through the front door five seconds too late, my rifle raised, the buttstock pressed against my shoulder. "That'll be a dollar and a half for the drinks and fifteen dollars for my friend to get his hand fixed," I said.

The Bohemians set down their glasses simultaneously.

"Fifteen dollars?" the big one repeated.

"Plus ten more for a dentist to put his teeth back right," I said and cocked the rifle.

"You gotta be fooling us."

"I wasn't fooling you the last time, and last time I didn't have the business end of a smoothbore pointed at your heads. So you can imagine I ain't anything but fooling now."

The Bohemians, unarmed except for the club and a pair of brass knuckles, had no choice but to acquiesce. I led them out of the saloon around to the back alley with their hands raised over their heads. The alley sloped down a hill toward a little spit of creek so narrow a man could step over it without widening his stride. A rail fence separated the alley from the water. Billy limped after us, spitting out clots of blood and holding his broken knuckles against his shirt. I knelt the Bohemians down in the mud and searched their pockets with one hand while I gripped the thirty-thirty with the other. All total I fished out eight dollars between them and handed the sum over to Billy.

"This will cover either your hand or your teeth, whichever's more pressing," I said as Billy took the money and shoved it down his pants. "Don't go spending it on a whore or this sister of theirs."

"You calling our sister a whore?" the big one asked without turning around.

I put my left boot up on a crate, steadying the thirty-thirty against my thigh. "No sir, I'd never say that about anybody's sister, even if she was that very thing. But that hot-headiness right there is what's got you in this mess and the one before it. Not everything's an insult. It'd do you well to learn it."

I handed the rifle to Billy and asked him if he had the ability to keep it trained on his friends long enough for me to go back inside and dial the police. The only telephone in the bar was powered by a large glass jar of batteries on a shelf in the storeroom and sometimes it took more than a minute to get a connection, even within the city limits. Billy held the gun as if it were heavy as an elephant tusk and said he could manage, broken hand or not. I nodded and headed back inside. A thin rain pinged against the whorehouse roof as if it were made out of pie tins. Huddled next to a bin fire at the top of the alley were three panhandlers wearing oilcloths for snow coats.

The first shot rang out when I wasn't halfway up the slope. I didn't turn fast enough to see the second. All within eyeshot was the glint of the creek and the gun smoke rising fast above Billy's head. He'd shot both Bohemians in the back of the head without a word spoken. I raced back down to the fence line. The bodies had fallen face first into the mud as if tripped. Their sprayed heads were missing entire sections of skull and jaw. The exposed parts of their brains were a dullish gray color. Billy lowered the gun and picked up a discarded cartridge at his feet. The other he couldn't find in the dark.

I yanked the gun away from him. "What in the hell have you done?"

"I killed them," Billy said as plainly as if he'd mended a pair of socks.

"I can see that."

"Police or no, they'd keep coming back. I haven't slept more than an hour at a time in two weeks. This was the only way."

"In the back of my sister's goddamn cathouse?"

"When the opportunity arises," Billy said and stopped short as if leaving the other half of his thought unspoken.

I held the rifle in my hands lazily. "I told you not to do anything."

"Don't get spooky on me. Let's just throw them in the river," Billy suggested.

"I ought to throw you in with them."

Billy hung his head. "I'm sorry. I'm just sick of being scared all the time."

"This is some goddamn mess," I said.

Billy's eyes darted back and forth like he was working out long division in his head.

I felt nothing for the boys dead at my feet even though I tried hard to conjure up some emotion. Just wasn't no feeling for those that had it coming no matter which side you might be upon. I'd never seen a dead body before and was thankful I wasn't around when the passing occurred. It struck me seriously enough just hearing the shots and seeing the after of it all.

"There just weren't no other way," Billy said.

I spat and turned back to the whorehouse. "There's always another way."

"Where you going?"

"Just stay put, and this time I fucking mean it," I said and hustled back inside. I threw open the curtain to the smoking room. Tom Dennison and his cohorts were still deep in conversation, their table littered with empty bottles and dirtied glasses and muddy ashtrays piled up like anthills. The mayor was asleep again with his head against the booth, his mouth open. Spittle on his tie. His shirt stained with drool. The women had left, Hattie included, swept off aboard some late-night carriage to wherever women like that were kept.

Dennison squashed his nickel cigar into the bottom of the mayor's whiskey glass, which still held an inch of amber. It sizzled out in a sigh. "You ready to lock up?"

"Not entirely," I said, unsure of how to broach the subject. "Mr. Dennison, sir, we have a bit of a problem outside, and I'm not quite sure how to handle it."

"What kind of problem?"

"Maybe it's best if you came and saw for yourself."

Ace Diamond and Billy Nesselhous rose to come outside as well, but I asked, politely as I could, for them to stay behind.

"A tricky situation," I told them.

When Dennison came around to the back and saw the pair of bodies and Billy holding the Winchester, he didn't need any further explanation. The man was as pragmatic as a sewing machine. He waved his hat over the corpses as if they were already giving off a stink.

He said, "Hell, Pat, remember when I asked you if you knew who I was and you said I was a political boss?"

"I said I guessed you to be Tom Dennison."

"Well, that too. At first I got the feeling you thought me some kind of Boss Tweed whose only aspiration in life was to stuff ballot boxes and get my picture on the cover of some tobacco label in my favorite top hat. A kind of disdain you might say. Well, I'm glad I was wrong because you figured out awful quick what I'm good for and what I'm not. This mess here? I got a couple associates that'll make these two poor sonsabitches disappear before daylight. And what your sister don't know stays what she don't know."

Billy stood staring out beyond the creek as if on third watch, cradling the rifle. I had only one thought on my mind, and it wasn't the dead Bohemians.

"Who was that blonde with the mayor?" I asked.

Dennison smiled at me as if I were the stupidest person he'd ever seen. "Just some skirt tail blown in from Little Poland. I saw how you fancied her. Mayor Moores did too. Either that or he's just as absentminded about his women as he is his politics."

"It'll be daylight soon," Billy said.

Dennison flipped open his timepiece. "Four hours on yet. But you're right. No time to waste. I'll get on the horn, take care of everything. You boys just go on back inside and get that blood by the door mopped up, whosoever it was."

Billy spit another clot. "That's mine. The bastards."

"How much does something like this cost?" I asked.

"Cost?" Dennison repeated the word curiously. He put a hand on my shoulder. "I told you that sometime or another you'd need me."

"Actually, you said you could use a man like me."

"Same thing. Now, you come see me Monday morning. And I mean this coming Monday morning. Not Tuesday or Thursday or the Monday after."

I nodded and thanked him twice, and we shook. Billy had wandered down to the creek edge and was urinating in the water, holding the thirty-thirty across his shoulders lengthwise. I called out to him. He buttoned up and followed me toward the alley.

We weren't twenty feet away when Dennison hollered, "Say, Pat? I'm not sure if you're crazy or stupid or both, but that gal with the mayor you were fawning over all night? There's a dance this weekend at the Hotel Boutique. She'll be there most likely, done up as pretty as a ribbon on a candy box. I'm not advising you in either direction and, well, pursuing this one is probably about as silly and dangerous as anything else, but I'll be goddamned if I don't allow for a man to make his own mistakes."

I turned. "What's her last name? McCoy or McCoven?"

"I'm sure I don't know," Dennison said as he crouched down to examine the corpses.

"Well, how do you know she'll be at that dance?"

Dennison stood and wiped his hands together. "Because it's my hotel."

VII

AN HOUR BEFORE dawn I rose and left young Eddie chained to his chair in the room next to the panting radiator, securing the door from the outside with a padlock. I gave the young man my last three cigarettes to tide him over for the rest of the morning. Billy was still passed out on stump whiskey and would remain in some faraway fantastical sleep for the rest of the day and probably longer if I left him unmolested. He was one hell of a glorious drunk. Every night for the past month he'd drank his eyeballs to float. Sometimes he shat himself up his backside after he passed out for the night, blamed it on the quality of the grog. He'd have gulped pig urine if it would muddy his mind.

A man like that, there was little to be done for him.

I went to the wood frame barn at the back of the cottage and greeted our stabled pony with the distinctive silver star on its forehead. She whinnied me a good morning. I hadn't thought to name her. Not right to own a nameless horse. I weighed it in my mind. Silversmith, I finally said to her. I'll call you Silversmith. I led her outside into the cold and fed her a breakfast of sugar and corn in the snow. I stroked her neck and hummed calmingly into her ear.

"Yes, that's right, you're a fine old nag, ain't you?" I cooed, cinched on her saddle, and tied her reins to the trunk of a vase oak just beyond the shed door.

Inside the lean-to, I kicked around some old tools and found an axe handle I'd carved to a point on one end. I wound a length of string around the stick five times until it was taut and put a pin through the ransom letter. I carried the stick out with me to our horse and ambled back into the Omaha city limits, toward the Cudahy mansion.

When I reached the front lawn where just hours ago we'd nabbed young Eddie Junior, I stood in the stirrups and launched the stick like a javelin at the front door. It landed upright in the cold ground, pitched straight as a fence post.

There was no commotion on the street or in the home. All the lights were off, the windows dark. I circled my horse three times, its hooves squeaking on the ice. The Cudahy yard had not been walked all night. Suncups were still visible in the snow. I snorted and fled the neighborhood at a trot. Gigged my pony's flanks gently and traversed back toward our cottage on winding abandoned roads and slick hillsides.

Less than a mile away, I halted on a shallow bluff to study the world below. Alpenglow streaked the horizon. In that blue hour before sunrise, I marveled at creation. I couldn't recall ever feeling such a sensation. The entire city so small I could pinch it between my fingers. The moon bright in a belt of predawn shadow. The skyscape burst with the first columns of winter daylight through low cloudbreak.

I clucked at Silversmith. The silence and lack of activity at the Cudahy home unnerved me. I chewed over the possibilities. The papers should've been pasting the story all about town in an hour when the morning edition hit the pavement. The police wagons should've been crowding Dewey Avenue in every direction. I never imagined it all to be so easy. I spat again and doubled back down into the city, stopping at a Czech bakery on William Street. I tied our pony to a large wooden Indian on the walk in front of the store. She dropped five huge clumps of green dung while swishing her tail. I laughed at that and went inside to use the telephone.

At the counter, I purchased a five-cent cup of coffee as weak as rainwater and a sweet roll, and tried to envision the coming conversation in my head. An oak phone booth took up the back of the store. I kept staring at it over my shoulder.

The bakery's proprietor watched me suspiciously. He was covered in flour dust and wore a paper wedge cap. "It's a phone booth, not a ghost," said he, rudely.

"My horse took a shit on your walk out there, right by the front door," I replied and got up to seclude myself in the booth. I lifted the earpiece off its cradle, wiped the bell rim with my handkerchief, wound the crank, and asked the operator for a local connection.

"Central? I need a line through to Spruce 7132," I said.

Two minutes passed while the operator punched in the route of the call. The baker watched me the whole time. He hollered out from his post behind the counter, "Rarely get through in anything but dry weather. Snow's been taking down wires all over the city."

I ignored him and waited a minute longer. Checked my nickeled timepiece. Five minutes to eight. Finally a connection came clear on the wire.

"Is Edward Cudahy there?" I asked in a low tone, altering my voice so as not to be recognized. I sounded like I was gurgling water.

A woman replied, "He is. Who's calling?"

It was their colored maid who'd answered. I graveled my voice deeper, "Never you mind who I am. Just get the man on the horn."

A moment passed. A heavy cough sounded on the line. "Hello? Hello?"

"I want to speak to Mr. Cudahy."

"Speaking," Cudahy said.

I put my coat collar around my mouth to distort my voice further, speaking through the fabric. "Do you know where your son is, Edward?"

Another long pause. "Who is this?"

"Darkness is falling all around you."

"My son is asleep in his bed."

"After you find his bed empty you might want to go out to your front yard. There you'll see a post with an attached letter. Follow the instructions."

"Say," Cudahy stammered, "you hold on there. I want to talk with you longer."

"Follow the instructions," I said again and rang off.

VIII

THE DANCE AT Tom Dennison's hotel turned out to be a necktie sociable. The Hotel Boutique was a lopsided four-story brick structure with a tiny ballroom. I outfitted myself in a silly jacket and ascot tie that made me appear comically aristocratic when the look I had hoped for was that of a cosmopolitan businessman. On my walk over to the hotel, the once cloudless autumn sky filled up from one minute to the next, and a downpour fell about as hard as it could for half an hour without knocking out the bottom of the universe. I sprinted through the cloudburst and entered the hotel soaked down to my nightclothes. I stood dripping on the lobby carpets like I'd fallen out of a fishing boat.

The lobby was a tall atrium of overstuffed sofas, spills of oriental rugs, amber marble, cathedral glass. The hands of a gilt edge clock marked the time as a quarter to seven next to a painting of a timber wolf howling at a thumbprint of acrylic moon. Canvasses under the hotel roof bagged with rain. Everyone else arrived aboard covered coaches and under umbrellas and were all as dry as September hay.

For the necktie sociable, each eligible lady brought two distinct bow ties with her. One she wore and the other was thrown into a large basket with all the others. The bachelors then paid for the dinner by purchasing one of the bow ties, and the woman who wore his match was his date for the evening.

I searched the lobby for Hattie. The hotel was full with a whole payload of maiden ladies, each wearing a unique bow tie around her neck. I thought I might never find her until I glimpsed her startling yellow hair—she was standing at the edge of the room by a rough pine table set with stacks of dinner dishes. The string band started playing. Men and women searched each other out. The bow tie I drew from the basket was deep red, not the match of Hattie's periwinkle blue knot. I wanted to crush it in my hands and go home, for I was dripping and silly looking and without any chance to court the woman I came to see. The bow tie matching game was something I'd never expected or heard of in my life.

On my way out the door, I spotted a little man with a stringy comb-over holding a periwinkle bow tie. He was scanning the crowd on his tiptoes like a lost child looking for his mother in a department store. I went right up to him and offered to trade him ties.

"Hardly," the little man said. "If you want to trade you've seen your match and went running. I will not be duped."

I dug a gold piece out of my pocket, the same coin the mayor had given me for a tip two days before. "I'll give you twenty dollars."

"Thirty."

"Twenty's all I got."

The little man sniffled. "Fine. Trade. I'm no prize, and maybe a fat ugly woman is the only chance I got without having to pay for it."

"I haven't seen my match," I admitted. "I'm only in love with yours."

"Love? Don't you even know her?"

"I intend on pursuing that end."

"You intend on it? My boy, my dear silly boy. I'm an alchemist of sorts, and I've got just the remedy for your ailment. The name's Doc Ruggso, and I have—" the little man said in his best salesman's tone, but I had already bolted off for the bar.

I yanked off my asinine ascot and fastened the new bow tie to my collar. After two short bourbons chased with a chalice of beer, I mustered enough dizzy in my bones to circle up to that celestial system, holding my hat with both hands on the brim. Hattie was seated alone on a camelback divan next to a stone fireplace gone cold for the night and a stand-alone ashtray full of twisted cigarette butts.

I said to her, "Hello, miss. I believe I'm your date for the evening."

Hattie McCoy. Or Hattie McCoven. Her flaxen hair was held back with a taffeta ribbon. A chiffon velvet dress adorned her slim freckled shoulders. The architecture of her corset held up her bosom as tautly as catapult ammunition.

She smiled at me and fit another cigarette into her opera-length holder. "I was wondering when you'd come over. Do you think me an Apache?"

I swallowed like it was my first time swallowing. "An Apache?"

"You're scared to death of me."

"You, well, you wreak havoc in the heart of every bachelor in this hotel," I stammered with a twisted tongue and gestured around the lobby with a sweep of my hat.

Hattie sat back against the divan and crossed her legs as if waiting for a camera bulb to flash. "At least you don't stutter."

"I'm sweating more than is pleasant," I said and wiped at the glaze on my forehead with the back of my hand.

"Honest, too. You're quite the catch. Aren't you going to sit down?"

I sat down.

She laughed. "It's a small wonder you haven't soiled yourself yet."

"My jitters? That's just compliment in costume is all," I said and pawed at my face again.

"How's that now?"

I tugged at my heavy shirt. "Beautiful women cause all men some measure of dewiness. That's something I'm certain with which you have considerable experience. Why, the more beautiful the woman, the more copious the perspiration."

Hattie curled her lips. "That's an impressive vocabulary for a barkeep."

I regressed. "My mother made my sisters and me read from the family dictionary every night. That and the Saint James Bible. Only two books we kept in the house. By the time I was thirteen when she passed, I had gotten all the way through the Rs."

"My," Hattie said mockingly. "You're a horse of a different color, Mister—"

"Pat Crowe," I said. "I've come to find out if your last name is McCoy or McCoven."

"Is that all you came for?"

"For starters."

"Don't you want to know my first name?"

"I already know it to be Hattie."

"Call me Hat. I hate Hattie."

"Okay, Hat. Hat McCoy or Hat McCoven?"

"Neither," Hattie said through her cigarette smoke. "My last name is Munro."

I thought on the sound of the name and all its variations. Hattie Munro. Hat Munro. Hattie Crowe, given enough time and luck. Hat Crowe. Hat and Pat Crowe.

"I saw you pay the man with the curtain hair a gold piece for my ribbon," she said.

"I can afford it," I lied.

"You're a barman at The Sallie Purple. I've seen you there."

I bowed my head.

"Don't tell me you're in love with me."

"No, ma'am. By the end of the night you'll be telling me."

Hattie laughed. "Boy, I can't get a read on you."

"They wrote all about me in the book of Amos."

"I never went in much for the prophets."

"Yeah," I defected. "Know-it-alls."

After the dinner and dancing—deviled ham sandwiches cut into tiny triangles, pheasant, pear salad, partners for a quadrille, an opera reel, all the happy footfalls and violin music and creaky banjos—we went outside and sat at a small bistro table on the sidewalk in front of the hotel. Hattie sipped from a cup of tea, and I from a glass filled with whiskey and a whisker of water. The sky had cleared. The stars looked as close as I'd ever seen them. The entire galaxy strewn about the bottom of a cup. Decorative paper lanterns hung in the trees lining the sidewalk.

I told her about all my ambitions in life, my lonely stag condition, and my pet tabby cat, and finally asked: "You don't think to be married to a gorgeous young critter like yourself would be far ahead of loneliness?"

"Who am I to say? I've never been a bachelor with a tabby cat."

I swirled my whiskey as if it were a glass of green and yellow paint I was trying to mix into an even blue. "You don't parade yourself around in show goods."

"You're quite the artist with the compliment."

I sat the whiskey down and took off my hat and examined its stained felt lining as if the proper response was stitched into the fabric. "You have lips upon which the honeybee might like to linger."

Hattie smiled. Lipstick on her teeth. "That's more like it."

"Maybe you like it enough to sprint up to the altar with me."

"You haven't even tried my cooking."

"I don't think of women as washers and darners."

"Don't speak nonsense to me."

"Am I pressing too hard?" I asked.

Hattie popped a new match, lit another cigarette, and extinguished the match in the last tepid inch of her tea. "You're distressingly attentive. I'll give you that."

I hung my head again. Hattie smirked.

"You're a serious boy," she said.

"You go in for the goofballs, then, do you?"

"You've seen who I go in for."

I shrugged. "The mayor's already got himself a wife."

Hattie laughed. "Yes, isn't it just the holiest of sacraments?"

"How's that?"

"Marriage," she said, flicking ash. "It's all one big gaffe."

"There's some measure of silliness in everything, I suppose."

"You're a smart boy. But I might not always agree with you as well as your tabby does."

I sighed and stood, offering my hand to help Hattie out of her chair. "I'll get rid of the goddamn cat."

Early the next morning, I lay in bed with Hattie in my boardinghouse room. She was still asleep, her wealth of yellow hair spilled out over her pillow. I put on my pants and went down to the parlor shirtless except for my suspender straps and filled two chipped mugs with coffee from a communal kettle sitting atop a potbelly stove. I brought the coffees back upstairs and set one down for Hattie on the toadstool table next to the bed and pulled a chair up to the window. The disintegrating curtain was as greasy as a cook's apron. Peeling it back, I peered down onto the street.

Outside the morning bore oily fogs and a wrinkled sky. Daylight arrived cold and pink with clouds as low as the building tops. The coffee was burnt and had the hard taste of a batch that'd been reheated three or four times and sitting in the same pot for even longer than that. I took one more sip and tossed the rest out the window.

Hattie woke a few minutes later, blinking as slowly as an owl. "Don't drink the coffee," I said. "It's gone bad."

She sat up and sniffed the air. The carpet reeked of odors trapped deep in the fibers from previous tenants: tobacco spit, toe jam, blood. I had hung a simple cross on the wall above the bed, but other than that, the walls were bare. "You really need to find a new place to live if you want me to keep coming over," she told me.

I pinched some tobacco from a canning jar and filled the bowl of my pipe and stared down into my empty cup. "Like what kind of place?"

"A nice apartment. One with clean floors and its own kitchen. Or a house even. I always dreamed of living in a pink two-story house."

"A pink house?"

"Mmhmm. Ever since I was a girl."

"I don't have the money for that."

"You ever plan on getting more money?"

"Everybody in the world has that plan," I said and was about to say more. Instead I pressed my lips down on my pipe stem and sat blowing smoke out the window. The thousand-dollar band of money my sister had given me on loan to set myself up in the city was hidden away in my tobacco can along with my other savings. I still couldn't believe it. A thousand dollars. I wanted to tell Hattie everything. How if things went right, I might be able to buy the exact same kind of home she dreamed of, one with vivid purple carpet and a covered porch and a pair of plum trees in the backyard. One with a new cookstove where she could bake butter cookies and a dry cellar where we could jar and store spicy pickles. But there was no use in talking about any of it before it could happen.

I went over to my icebox and filled my cat's dish from a quart of buttermilk. The silver coins used to keep the milk fresh rattled inside the bottle. I petted the tabby and returned to my chair by the window.

"You're a window watcher," Hattie said. "Just like that cat."

I looked down on Cherry Street. Alleyways as wide as the avenues. A child in a black straw hat carried a large package out of a fabric shop. A group of khaki-clad Negroes were huddled around a telegraph pole, showing each other their teeth. I blotted my mouth with my handkerchief and said, "I like to see the world wake up. The streets filling with people starting out their day."

"You'd rather look at them than at me?"

I turned my gaze to Hattie and then was back at the window just as soon. "The other morning I saw a hatcheck girl hurrying home after a late shift. She stopped at the corner store down there and bought a pound of cigarettes. So I went down and asked the clerk for the exact same item the woman who just left had purchased. He sold me a pound of Turkish cross cuts that came in a silk-lined box."

I gestured at the very box now sitting atop a pile of books in the corner. I'd opened the package but had smoked only one of the cigarettes. "I like to make up little stories in my head about all the people I see. Who they are, what they do, what their lives are like. Then I got to thinking. What if I could know one thing about that hatcheck girl? How much closer would my imagination of her be to what her reality actually was?"

Hattie stood up, wrapping her body in the bed sheet. "Why are you telling me this? Is there something going on with you and this hatcheck girl?"

"I only saw her the one time," I said, putting my finger inside the curtain again to look down on the street. "I'm telling you this because you might as well be any one of those people down there right now."

"What're you saying?"

"I'm saying I don't know anything about you."

Hattie sat back down on the bed. She was as stunned as a bird that'd flown into a show window. She wiped her nose and looked away. "You're very much a serious boy."

"I'm not very much of any one thing in particular."

"You're very content to live in a room that doesn't even have a working sink."

I sighed through my nose. "Tell me something about yourself."

"Well, last week I was making it with the mayor and eating

stuffed quail for every meal, and now I'm here with you in this god-awful little room with stained carpet, and I can't even get a decent cup of coffee in the morning. So, that should tell you something."

I thought on that. I sat thinking on it until my pipe bowl went cold. Hattie threw off the bedsheet and began to dress. The clothes she'd worn the night before were hanging on a nail protruding from the wall. She was right. Knowing that much was enough for now. The night I first saw her come into my sister's place, nobody seemed to know anything about her, and even if they did, they weren't saying. I wondered how much she even knew about herself.

Yes, this was enough.

She could've been one of many gals with the mayor. Instead she was my only gal.

I was a packinghouse stinker with one good pair of checkered pants paid for in full and a beet red farmer's neck. She was a hired girl at the opera club who dreamed of one day living in a pink two-story house.

Yes, that was enough for now.

When we lay together two days later, I booked a parlor suite at the Hotel Windsor, a palatial mammoth with turrets like a castle. A birdcage elevator was manned by a one-armed bellhop in a pill-box hat. He kept the sleeve of his missing arm folded and pinned to his shoulder. Our room on the top floor was decorated in gold leaf, had a stone bathtub filled by hand. The private balcony was garishly decorated with trellises of climbing grapevine, a baroque balustrade, and marble statues of Apollo and Daphne. The expense of one night cost me two weeks' salary at the stockyards.

We ate our dinner alfresco on our balcony under a cloudless autumn sky. A liveried waiter brought us a bottle of port with smoked sausage and chilled blueberry soup and a loaf of macaroni bread.

Afterward, lying in the giant canopy bed, the posts draped with tasseled cloth, I tried as I might to equate my feelings for Hattie to something I'd experienced before. The closest thing I could conjure was when I was bit on the wrist by a copperhead as a young boy of eleven while playing in a field of tall grass next to my daddy's farm.

I sprinted home holding my dripping wrist. My mother dropped a plate on the kitchen floor when she saw me. She used a warm piece of chicken flesh to soak the venom out of the wound. My whole left arm was spotted, but within an hour the swelling diminished. When my wrist finally stopped bleeding, she washed the bite mark with tobacco water and covered it with a poultice of skunk root. Most of what I remembered was my lonely and delirious sprint home, my head dizzy as I contemplated my own destruction. Even the next five minutes of life seemed as distant as a glimpse of some far sky. If it was love I was feeling now, the only sensation that had ever come close to it in all my born days was a neuralgic affection.

I went to the liquor table. The decanter of port was wrapped in a towel to keep it warm, and I poured a wisp into a snifter. I said, "I don't think I'll ever get a beat on you."

Hattie played with the ends of her hair. "I'm not so complex."

I stared at her curiously. I could write a lot of awful school-house poetry about her if only I knew enough different words to describe her yellow hair, my drooping heart.

"You're giving me the goo-goo eyes again," she said.

"Can you blame a fella?"

"Patrick Joseph Crowe," she said and slapped me playfully on the wrist. "I do declare. I believe you're in love with me."

"And what if I told you I wasn't?"

"I'd tell you that you're a damn liar."

I was in love. Or at least that's what I figured the syndrome to be, as all its symptoms were foreign to me. It could've just as well been heat illness or a stomach bug, and I still would've misinterpreted it as love, called it by that name.

In the morning, a doorman delivered coffee to our room. I stirred milk into my cup and sat outside on the balcony to watch the young sun skim rooftops. Down on Douglas Street, under the awning of a drugstore, a shirtless man balled up his fists and screamed at a clot of pigeons that had descended from a sagging telegraph wire.

"Beat it, you scavengers!" the man said, rolling his fists in the air like a prizefighter circling an opponent. "Fuck outta here!"

The birds continued to bob their heads absently, hoping to find a bit of bread. Their feathers blue in the morning light. While the man continued to threaten them, a native woman sat on the ground with three blankets wrapped around her. She bellowed, "What is

you trying to prove, Harold? C'mon there, Harold. What is you trying to prove?"

After a few minutes of watching the scene, I learned the man
trying to fight the pigeons wasn't named Harold. The woman was
really just screaming at a leaf that had fallen at her feet.

IX

SEVEN MILES WEST of Omaha, along Big Papio Creek in a paddock grove on the south side of the road, Billy and I sat waiting on our haunches. From our hiding spot in the dead brush that overlooked the only passable thoroughfare to Fremont, we could see for half a mile in every direction before the sun set. I left a lantern with black and white ribbons knotted to the handle on the side of the road, waiting to ignite the wick until we saw Cudahy's carriage.

The hour approached nine. A thirty degree night, moonless and cloudless both.

I continually opened and collapsed my spyglass, scanning the eastern traffic on the road of which there had been little in the last hour and none whatsoever in the past twenty minutes. Billy had his lips around a choice cigar, seated against a rock that blocked our position from any travelers below. He blew smoke rings and kept his free hand down the front of his trousers. Our white horse was hitched in a hollow on the other side of the hill for quick access.

"How are you feeling?" I asked after I collapsed the looking glass again.

Billy clamped his mouth shut, his speech halted by pain. He had one hell of a katzenjammer from all his whiskey the night before and probably wouldn't be right of mind until the next day. Even at dinner earlier that evening, he hadn't said more than a few words, commenting only on the good quality of his steak. What a fine meal it had been. Before setting out to retrieve our ransom, we dined at The Little Owl, one of the finest restaurants in the city. The inside was all silver brocade and purple velvet and Bavarian china. For our meal, an exquisite offering of smoked herring topped with banana puree, steak tartar with shirred eggs, oyster scallops, turtle soup, and asparagus soufflé.

All total, it was a seventy-dollar supper.

Enjoy it while we can, I had said. After this, it's all paper towns and sleeping by creek water for us. For many months, maybe. After this, come tomorrow and every day after, we will never again be anything else but fugitives.

We left little Eddie tied to his chair in the cottage. Leaving him alone for such a long time worried me, but we had the good sense to gag him and chain his chair to the woodstove. The kid had been a real sport about the whole thing, even when we crammed the cloth in his mouth and taped it shut. It was hard for me to wish him anything but the best after the rotten affair was over.

I glassed the road again. Nothing.

From my vantage, the Big Papio, frozen over since November, was a crooked strip of silver through the darkened snow. There was a small wind. The barren trees ached like settling floorboards. For the fifth or sixth time, I checked the ammunition in my short caliber rifle. My polished revolver was fully loaded. I lazily spun the cylinder like a pinwheel to pass the long minutes.

I said to Billy, "All my life has been the wrong time in the wrong place. I doubt very seriously if that pattern will change tonight."

Billy had his hat tipped down past his eyebrows. His hands were folded in a steeple across his stomach, and he was practically lounging against the rock as if he were reclining on a divan without a care in the world. He spoke with the cigar in his mouth, "Relax, will you? You're going to give me a condition, fussing around like that."

I looked at him sideways. "There's not a condition in this world you don't already have that I can give you."

Billy chewed his cigar stump like a teething toy.

"How can you be so calm?"

Billy sat up, perturbed. "Our letter said for Cudahy to depart at nine sharp. I guarantee you the man left at the exact stroke of the hour. It ain't much past that now, and we're seven miles out from the city. Eight and a half from his house. Even if he was saddled up on leopard back, he wouldn't be here yet."

"You have no mind for extenuating circumstance," I said. "What if he sent police out early to scout the road ahead? What if he hired detectives to currycomb from the west?"

"You underestimate the power of fatherly love. The man will

not risk the safe return of his son. He might unleash the law dogs after the kid's home, but not before then."

"That's another thing. Once this is over that's exactly what he'll do. He won't stop with just the Omaha police. That won't satisfy a man like him. He'll put a reward out for our capture across the national wire. It won't just be lawmen on our trail. Every set of eyes in the country will be peeled for us."

Billy singed out his cigar and tossed it into the snow. "Did you honestly think it would ever go any other way than that?"

"I keep lying to myself about it if you want the truth."

"Honesty is the best policy."

"And the best people can have all of it. They want it. They even wanted the little bit I thought I wanted. They're welcome to it. I'll never play the honest game again. The cards are all marked, and the dice are all loaded."

"Yeah," Billy said too loudly for my liking. "Now that you finally got that figured, you'll see it ain't such a tough old world after all."

"Hush up," I said and elongated the spyglass again. The road was still empty. I wiped dust and snow off my coat sleeves. The countryside all over my clothing. I'd convinced myself the entire forty-mile stretch of road between Omaha and Fremont was teeming with scouts covering every rod.

I said, "He'll hire Pinkertons for certain."

Billy waved off the idea. "So what? Let that bastard waste more of his money. Those Pinkerton thugs give up easy."

"They do like hell. I heard it once that Frank Geyer tracked down H. H. Holmes for five months over three states. They hanged him fast after he was caught. Son of a bitch strangled for twenty minutes after the trap dropped because his neck didn't snap."

"Yeah, in Philly that happened. My sister tell you about that, too?"

I stared through the spyglass again. "Gruesome thing to die from lack of wind. Rather I'd be chopped up by an axe."

"I'm hoping for a quick heart attack in a whore's bed at the age of ninety."

"Quiet," I said, aiming the glass. "I see something."

Billy turned onto his stomach and peered over the rock. "Where?"

"Yonder." I pointed. "Yonder."

In the distance, half a mile off, a faint red glow appeared between the trees. There was just enough gray in the sky to make out the distinctive shapes between the actual roadway and the hills that surrounded its sunken course like the bottom of a valley. The only real light was trapped inside the silver creek, the ice cutting through the black ground. I stared at the red blip through my scope. It grew in size, slowly, until I could see it flicker.

"Hot goddamn," I said to Billy. "That's Cudahy's lantern."

"How do you know?"

"It's on the dashboard of his buggy."

"I mean, how do you know it's his buggy and not the chief of police?"

I collapsed the spyglass and covered the looking window with the eye piece and shoved it into an umbrella bag tied off to one of my belt loops. I stood and wiped off my trouser legs, making sure I had the matches in my pocket.

"We won't know unless I light our beacon," I replied and scrambled down the hillside to fetch the lantern I'd left on the shoulder of the road.

I opened the glass door and sparked the wick just as the approaching buggy rattled over the plank bridge a quarter mile away. I watched it near. If two vehicles crossed the bridge instead of one, I would've doused the glim and let them drive past. But there was no second carriage. Cudahy's buggy was quite alone. Maybe Billy was right. Maybe Cudahy hadn't involved the police yet. If he had contacted the authorities, they were not within a mile in either direction. I set the lantern in the middle of the road with a heavy clank and sprinted back up the hill where there was hardly any snow left on the ground so as not to make tracks. The law might've been able to snuff us out at a designated spot, but not every tract in a forty-mile stretch could be scoped no matter how many men Cudahy hired. Every foreseeable circumstance had been covered. Our plan was without flaw.

X

A LOW BANK of snow clouds spread out over the city as I entered The Sallie Purple a month after Hattie and I started going steady. The first flurries of the season. Winter drizzle fell and sang in the gutters. The sky was as dark as dusk despite being the height of the day. In the distance, a church bell marked the midday hour. A group of children rode trash can lids like sleds down the enamel of a frozen hillside. Netted bundles of winter radishes and cabbages hung from yokes outside the greengrocer next door, its store windows sweating like the glass of a hothouse. Mr. Bram, owner of the greengrocer, was salting the walk in front of his shop.

I tipped my hat hello to the man and entered my sister's whorehouse. I went behind the bar and poured myself a quart of beer and a short glass of brandy. I cracked an egg into the beer, slugged it down in one huge swallow, and carried the liquor with me toward the parlor in the rear of the building.

"Hey there, Pat," the morning bartender said. "What're you doing here?"

"It's my day off. Thought I'd come and moisten it up some," I replied, raised my brandy in a salute, and entered the gaming den which doubled as my sister's office. Two oval-shaped faro tables were covered in green baize. A snooker table was littered with bright billiards balls next to a bank of glowing slot machines. A policy wheel game with rubber tubes and a large chalkboard slate scored the previous day's winning numbers.

My sister was seated at a card table with Tom Dennison and Billy Nesselhous, going over the previous month's numbers. It was collection day. A whole heap of loose cash and banded coins were strewn over the table. Sallie sorted the bills into stacks, but there seemed to be little organization to her piles. Dennison leaned back in his chair with his arms behind his head. He wore a giant hat and a red plaid suit with a boiled shirt, the kind with a detachable collar unbuttoned in front. Nesselhous hunched over a tablet of lined paper, working a short pencil with the concentration of a man composing meter. For a moment they didn't notice me enter. I stood in the doorway swirling my brandy.

Dennison was the first to look up. "Say, if it isn't Pat."

Sallie glanced at me as if squinting against the sun. Nesselhous waved a hello without taking his eyes off his accounting.

I cleared my throat. "Broke open the piggy bank again, did you?"

"Come on over here and join us," Dennison said with an inviting sweep of his arm. He lifted a bottle of white satin gin from the center of the table, picked up a glass, wiped out the inside with his finger as if checking it for dust, and poured a healthy swig. "Come on over here and have a little eyewater with me."

I sat down at the table. Dennison and I drank together. He licked his lips and poured himself another. The man was an enigma. He hadn't taken an ounce of liquor with the mayor when they came in on a Friday night and now was drinking gin straight at lunchtime. A couple of half-eaten cold lamb sandwiches lay on the table in wax paper wrappers next to the gin glasses and disorganized money.

"What's the scuttlebutt?" Dennison asked.

I said, "I thought I might bend your ear, if you have a few minutes."

Dennison tilted his head.

"In private, perhaps?"

"This is as private as any of my conversations ever get."

"I'm thinking of starting up my own business."

The room stopped. Sallie was in the middle of licking her thumb to get a better grip on the bills and was so stunned she kept her tongue on her thumb for a full five seconds before snapping out of it. Nesselhous shook his head and giggled. Dennison leaned forward.

I said, "I've been working in the stockyards since I got into town. And I've been working with meat long before that, back home on my family farm. I know more than most when it comes to the butcher trade. It wears on a man to put his skills to use for somebody else when he could be using them to better his own life."

Dennison furrowed his brow. "You want to open a butcher shop all by your lonesome?"

"Not alone. Me and my pal Billy. He's just as good with a blade as I am. Maybe better."

Sallie winced. "Every tailender in this city and their goddamn aspirations. It's an illness, you know? Never being satisfied with what you have."

"Nobody wants to stay a stockyarder forever," I said.

"Don't get soggy on me," Sallie said.

"Weren't you the one who told me that one day I could have a place of my own if I played my cards right?"

"Yes. But by one day I didn't mean six months after you breezed into town."

"Your pal, this Billy what's-his-name, is he a straight card?" Nesselhous asked.

"Billy Cavanaugh," I said.

"Straight enough to blow your head off for you," Sallie said knowingly. She looked at me with a condemning stare. It seemed we hadn't actually gotten away with murder. At least not from my sister's compass. I wondered how much Dennison had told her. How much he had not. The real danger was in the difference between the two.

"Little Billy the tugboat," Dennison said with a chuckle and gave Nesselhous a playful whack between his shoulder blades. "He's the backslapping sort."

I clamped my hands in front of my groin.

"C'mon, Pat," Dennison said. "If you're going to vouch for the man, then vouch for him. Tell Nessy here that your pal is all right."

"In what way?" I asked.

"In being reliable."

I shook my head. Thought of Billy's penchant for the bottle and the bimbo both in equal intensity. "I'd be responsible whether the place succeeded or not. Wouldn't vouch for any man besides myself. You never know what another might do."

"Especially not that gump," Sallie said distractedly as she continued to count through a stack of bills, most of them in low denominations.

Dennison put in a plug of tobacco and leaned over to aim a line of brown spit into the spittoon on the floor. He pressed his tie against his shirt with a flattened hand to keep from staining it. "What's the matter with that kid anyhow?"

"He's affected in the head," Sallie said.

I grimaced. "He hasn't gone mad."

"Gone?" Sallie said. "Sure. He hasn't gone mad. It isn't a recent development, I assure you. Kid sits up at the bar five nights a week talking to himself while he plays checkers."

"He's not of unsound mind, I mean."

"No, no. Not all," Sallie said. "Kid's all wool and a yard wide."

I stared my sister down. "He's just sick of getting the shit kicked out of him."

"Aren't we all?" Dennison laughed.

I said, "I'll be honest with you, Mr. Dennison. I want to run my own butcher shop like my sister here runs this place. I'd be asking you for a loan, make you a partner in it all. But I also want a fair price."

Sallie stood up so quickly she nearly knocked her chair over. "Excuse me for a minute, gentlemen. I need to have a quick word with the entrepreneur here," she said and led me by the bicep into a smaller counting room without windows and a safe as big as an ice-cream freezer. She pushed me up against the wall. There was that hippopotamus mean flaring up again.

"Let me draw it mild for you," she whispered. "You go into league with Tom Dennison and you're in his pocketbook for life."

"I'm not getting into a row with you over this."

She put a finger in my face. "Let me tell you how this works since you seem so keen about making company with wolves. Say your start-up capital to get the place running is four thousand dollars—"

"It'd be more like five, I'm thinking."

"Stop talking and listen. Five, six, ten, it doesn't matter. Whatever the number, Tom will take fifty percent of every dime you make every month until his investment is paid off. If half is too low, he'll up the gratuity until you're paying him off in chuck steak. Then say you manage well enough to pay him back. Most don't get that far. They have to sneak out of town overnight. But let's say you do. After that, he takes twenty percent of your monthly income for life. His finger will be in your pie forever. Do you know what twenty percent amounts to for most businesses? That's your profit. All of it. You'll be working twelve hours a day, seven days a week, and making zilch. You'll be sleeping in the back of the place because you can't afford a room. Not even one in that shithole you're staying in now. You'll go crazy and try to cook your books so you can put five dollars in your hip pocket every once in a while. You'll end up babbling to yourself in an alley next to a bin fire wearing a rubber fishing hat."

"You sure know how to paint on the roses."

"Goddamnit, Pat. You're barely thirty years old and making the mistake of your life."

"You've gone and done well enough to wear your fancy gowns." I lifted Sallie's hand in the air. Three of the five fingers were adorned with colored stone rings. "You got two mortgages on your left hand alone."

Sallie yanked back her arm. "What I've got is two hoodlums out there going through my couch change, and I'm going to have to sell these damn rings in a dolly shop to make up the difference. Don't you think it's strange them caring so much about two hundred dollars? That's chicken feed to a man like Tom. But he'll still spend three hours having his friend with the winged hair pore over my ledger and count out every dime I got on hand to make sure he's not missing a red cent. What do you think will happen to you when you owe him half a grand? A thousand? More?"

I giggled. "He'll make me sell my fancy rings, I suspect."

"Keep laughing. Go on. Laugh yourself all the way into the poorhouse. Or the cemetery."

"Or into an alley? In my rubber fishing hat?"

Sallie threw up her hands. "You want to beard me? Be my guest. But don't say I didn't warn you when the man guts you down from soda to hock."

"Glad to know I got your vote of confidence," I said.

"How long have you been working in them stockyards? Six months?"

"Damn sight longer than I ever wanted to."

"And you and this Billy character, you've got your whole business figured, do you?"

I said, "We've dressed hogs, geese. Pheasants. We both of us can butcher a cow better than most Injuns could ever skin a buffalo."

Sally raised an eyebrow. "What about the numbers?"

"Damn the numbers," I said. "I'm sick of lugging around carcasses and cutting up sows for half a dollar an hour while the rest of the world gets rich doing a lot less."

"You have no idea what it takes to survive in this world," Sallie said.

I blew a raspberry.

"You better get serious."

"What about you? You're daffy is what you are. How hard could it be? A mother comes in to order her Sunday roast, and we give her kid a slice of bologna over the counter for being a good tyke. We talk about the weather while we cut their chops to order. Or trade a few jokes while we wrap up their London broil."

"No one ever got rich owning a butcher shop."

"Tell that to Edward Cudahy or James Boyd."

Sallie said, "Those men are tycoons. They own whole stockyards. Factories. Shipping."

"Well, maybe not rich. But it'd be mine."

"Yeah, it'd be the nuts. Just imagine all that glitz and glamour."

"You know what? You might think the idea is above my bend, but there ain't no need to give me any snoot about it," I said, walked back into the game room, stood behind my chair, and said, "Mr. Dennison, I want you to know I plan on selling outside of the city. In South Omaha. There's this little place for sale on Hickory Street. Used to be an old harness shop. I know you already got a stake in a couple butcheries in this district. I'm not here to step on anyone's toes, especially yours."

"That's a good idea," Dennison said as he slammed back another cap of eyewater. He was as drunk as a sainted pig. "But if you're going into business for yourself in that part of town, you better be careful of Ed Cudahy."

"Man's an ogre when it comes to territory," Nesselhous added.

"I work for him," I said.

"Yes, a hardworking employee of the Cudahy Meatpacking

Company," Dennison replied. He picked up one of the cold lamb sandwiches and examined it but then thought better of taking a bite and set it back down on the wrapper. "But do you know anything about him? Have you ever even laid eyes on the man?"

"I'm not afraid of competition."

"Yeah?" Dennison said. "Well, you ought to be."

"I wasn't born in the woods to be scared by an owl."

"Well, fair warning, you open up your own shop in his part of town, even a little rinky-dink deli with no prospects of expansion, and he'll be hot to bust you. Which makes me wonder. Why in the world does a fella with your kinda size want to waste his time out in fucking palookaville selling a bunch of cut-rate cow? That's going to be a tough racket. I tell you what, I got some idiots around town I've been meaning to beat the living hell out of if that's something you might be interested in."

Sallie let out a snorting, despairing laugh.

"Shut your trap," I told her.

She continued to snort.

I said to Dennison, "You do the work of a thug, you make a bandit's wage."

"As you please. I guess it's nothing but the floral wallpaper for you, huh?"

I touched the brim of my hat in gratitude. "I appreciate your time."

"Sure," Dennison said and shook my hand. "Come back and see me anytime. I trust you and Mr. Nesselhous here can work out the details on your own."

I thanked him and left the whorehouse. The streets were messy with wastewater. I climbed aboard a hired wagon, and the driver got his balky old horse marching. He was the cheeriest driver I ever met. Tipped his hat and clucked a surly hello to every woman our wagon passed. "So many pretty skirts in this burg," he said. "So many."

I paid him no heed. I was thinking about the larger aims of life. Of a life Hattie had only mentioned once before, but one that I'd expanded upon in my own mind. It'd become part of my daily thoughts. A little pink two-story house on a quiet avenue. A parlor room full of maple furniture with a great big picture window so we could see who was coming to call. Coffee brewing on the back stove in the mornings, reading the newspaper in a deep armchair next to a fireplace full of pearwood clicking down into fruit smoke in the evenings. A pair or two of troublemaking kids who minded their manners when it counted. The whole world a constant reminder that most beautiful things were often as simple as the arithmetic it took to gain them.

XI

"Our plan's got a flaw," Billy said when I returned to our spot behind the rock, heaving deep breaths. I collapsed against the rock and opened my mouth to the sky. The carriage on the road below approached. The red lantern on Cudahy's wagon grew brighter, bigger. I spat up some phlegm and sparked my pipe for a short toke.

Billy continued, "What if he leaves us a phony package? Like what happened to those fellers who kidnapped the Ross boy?"

I turned and sat against the stone. "He's too smart for that. He wouldn't dare."

"You never know for certain. What if he leaves us a hundred pounds of kitchen starch?"

I sucked air, squinted my left eye. "Then we blind his son and snip off his manhood with the cow pliers, just like we warned."

"You're not serious. Who's going to do it? You?"

"I was hoping you'd be crazy enough."

"You're a fine friend."

"What?" I gulped three more frosty breaths. "Syphilitic insanity and all, right? It gets worse with time, don't it? Ain't you still nutsy?"

"I got papers say I ain't."

"Papers? What kind of papers?"

"Official papers. From one of those evaluation wards. They say I'm of sound mind."

I chuckled once, quick as a hiccup. "No fooling? How about that?"

"The kid, Eddie, he's not a bad skate," Billy said. "You said as much yourself. You really want to put acid in his eyes and castrate him?"

"Of course not. But if his pops doesn't follow the instructions—"

Billy interrupted. "Wouldn't you like to be sure? Say he leaves us soft soap. Wouldn't you like to be down there to catch him in the act? We got guns, we got masks."

I inhaled twice more and, with some quick consideration, nodded agreement. We both rose and donned old gunnysacks we'd cut eyelets and mouth holes into just in case of unwanted police presence. After fitting the homemade masks over our heads, we smashed our hats back on and hightailed it down the slope, falling to the ground on our bellies a good ten yards away from the road in a clump of dead weeds.

I removed the thirty-thirty from the strap around my back and Billy drew his pair of repeaters. Our labored breathing was as loud as barroom shouting, or so it seemed as we both tried to hush our lungs in equal measure. The Cudahy coach stopped with a jolt. The two handsome black horses bridled to the cart snorted and hoofed at the gravel. Driving the rig was a bald man who wore a clawhammer coat with big tails. He swished the reins lightly.

"There be the lantern," he said.

Cudahy's bulky figure wiggled on the passenger side of the wagon seat. His face was obscured by darkness, but his shape unmistakable. "See if it's the right one."

The coachman stepped off the wagon.

I whispered to Billy, "If you see anyone else get out of the back of that carriage, we unload all we got into them without so much as a how-do."

Billy nodded. Each breath a quake.

"Yes, sir," the coachman said after examining the lantern. "This is the one."

"Has it got black and white ribbons tied to the bail?"

"Yes, sir. Black and white."

Cudahy lifted a heavy valise from the carriage floorboard and set it on his lap. His breath as visible as smoke in the frigid air. "Put the money next to it."

The coachman did as instructed, heaving the bank messenger's case with some effort, and set it on the ground with a thud. He went back to the carriage and gathered up a second bag and placed it next to the first in a neat arrangement. He looked at his work, then the lantern, then spied all around him, swiveling his head in every direction. He snorted and gave a passing rub to one of the horses before mounting the wagon again. Cudahy said something that was inaudible to us from our hidden position in the weeds. The coachman clucked twice and steered the horses around, turning the carriage to head back the way they came.

Still no moon in the sky. Wouldn't be for another night more.

I leapt to my feet in a rush, rifle butt deep in my shoulder. I shouted, "Hold them ponies right there or I'll put a little short caliber in your heads."

The carriage stopped instantly. It had turned sideways in the road. Billy, his courage ten seconds short, joined me after a brief delay. Both of his hands were filled with aimed revolver.

"Both of you, get down on the ground," I demanded.

Nobody moved. Even the horses were motionless.

"Are you deaf?" I asked. I cocked my rifle hammer. Even a sound as small as that had an echo in the middle of nowhere. "Get off that rig. Now."

Another moment passed. Cudahy was the first to move. His weight shook the carriage as he stood and stepped down, his back facing the other direction. His driver replied in kind and I directed both of them to the other side of the road with their hands aloft. They marched into the snow side by side, arms raised. When I instructed them onto their knees, Cudahy asked, "Where is my son?"

I came up behind him, each footstep a wet crunch, and jammed the end of my rifle into the back of his head. "Skin for skin if that's the way you want it," I said, quoting the Satan of the Old Testament. "All that a man hath will he give for his life. All I'm asking you for yours is to keep quiet."

"Are you not a man of your word?" Cudahy said, ignoring the threat. He was on his knees now, an effort that was as laborious to him as a turtle trying to flip over after being capsized on its shell. "I followed your instructions to the letter, and now you're robbing me?"

"Not robbing. Double-checking," I said and kept my rifle trained at the back of his head.

Billy searched both valises.

Inside each was a pair of canvas bags filled to the brim with gold coins in ten- and twenty-dollar increments. He lit a match and pawed through the coins, making sure there wasn't a counterfeit amount of nails or buttons filling out the bottoms. Nearly ninety-five pounds' worth of gold. He could barely contain his excitement.

His voice was a wheeze, "It's all here."

I turned and nodded to our original camping spot at the top of the hill where Silversmith was hitched just on the other side of the draw. "Get it loaded up."

Billy holstered his guns and picked up the two bags, one in each hand at fifty pounds apiece. It took him quite the effort to manage the hill with the weight, like carrying a pair of kettle bells. He slipped twice, cursing the heft of the gold. I watched him but kept my rifle sighted on Cudahy and his driver.

The dark thought came to me: it would be easy to execute both men and maybe, just maybe, forever satisfy the panther prowling in my chest.

"I know who you are," Cudahy said.

I thought: put one in his brainpan. Instead I said, "Do you, now?"

"You won't get away with this, Pat Crowe."

I stepped back, relaxed my rifle over my shoulder. "Stand up!"

Cudahy stood.

"Turn around."

Cudahy turned. He looked right at me. "That mask doesn't fool me, son."

I breathed through my gunnysack. After a heavy moment, I bashed Cudahy in the mouth with the barrel of my rifle. The huge man collapsed to his knees and fell over onto his side. His front teeth were completely smashed. Blood poured out of his mouth and gushed over his cupped hands as he pressed them to his face. He moaned like a kicked dog and spit out a mess of broken lip, blood, teeth. I watched him writhe in pain. I chuckled through my cloth mask and knelt down beside him.

With a great deal of calm, leaning against my upright rifle, I said, "Now you listen to me. You're in a good heap of pain. Come time, you might need a set of false teeth. I do hope you have a good dentist. Man as rich as you must have. It might be hard to hear anything but the ringing between your ears right now, but you better pay attention anyway. I'm not releasing your son for three days. In seventy-two hours he'll be set loose. But that's on one condition.

"Are you listening? You don't tell anybody he's gone. Not the police, not your sister in Burlington, no one. I really mean it. If I pick up a paper in the next three days and see that this story's made ink, I will kill your boy. And it won't be quick, either. I'll torture him. I will burn his feet. I'll chop of all his fingers. I'll use his stomach to put out my cigarettes. If a minute goes by where he stops screaming, I'll shoot him in his kneecaps. If he passes out from the pain, I'll put his head underwater until he drowns or wakes up. When he's coherent, I'll tell him all of this happened because his father couldn't keep quiet.

"You better hope your wife hasn't made any bad choices. I really hope for your son's sake she hasn't phoned anybody while you were out on this errand. And your driver here? Well, let's just say you better trust the man with your child's life. We have two scouts keeping an eye on your house around the clock. If one suspicious carriage parks in your drive or anywhere near it, I'll break your son's arm in three places. If anyone enters your house that even looks like police, I'll brand him with a hot iron from your stockyard. He'll bear your company mark like he was one of your cattle.

"That brand will be the only way to identify his body, if you ever get lucky enough to find it, because his face will be unrecognizable. I'll scalp him like an Injun. Then I'll cut off his nose and ears and pour acid in his eyes. That much pain will surely render him unconscious. But I'll stick a plunger of morphine in his arm to shoot him awake again to make sure he enjoys every agonizing moment. Are you hearing all of this? Nod if you understand."

Cudahy nodded and spit more blood.

"Good. That's good. Just remember, after I get bored of torturing your son, I'll slit his throat. Not with a good knife, no. That would be too clean. I'll rip him open with an old nail. His throat will rupture jagged. Then I'll dump his body in some nobody lake or piece of pasture way the hell out in the middle of nowhere.

"Birds will pick at his remains. Fish will nibble on his skin. A wolf or a coyote might tear him apart. And that will be the end of this tale. You'll forever have an empty chair at your dinner table where he once sat. His sisters will have forgotten what he looked like by the time they've grown. Your wife will never come out of the house. She'll probably lose her mind to unspeakable grief. And when you die or retire, somebody with a last name that isn't yours will own your company. They'll change the name. Your family line will fall to ashes, never spoken again on the tongues of men."

I stood and slung the rifle over my back, adjusting the strap. Cudahy squirmed on the ground. A pool of blood stained the snow in front of his head as if he'd sneezed it out. I considered the driver. He hadn't moved since he had gotten down on his knees. Probably he was one of their house servants. Or one of Cudahy's cattle salesmen. There was no telling what he might do, but there was no justice in doing him harm.

I didn't even know his name.

"Driver?" I said. "You of a mind to help Mr. Cudahy remember what I just told him?"

"Yes, sir," the driver replied weakly.

"What's your name?"

"Ernest Cartwright."

"Well, Ernest Cartwright, answer me truthfully. Who knows about the boy's abduction?"

The driver stuttered. "Just, uh, just the family, sir."

"You're not family."

"No sir. I'm not."

"Who knows? Think. Give me names. And if I get the idea you're lying to me, I will shoot you in the head. Do you believe that?"

"I believe it, sir," the driver said. His voice was powder soft. "There's me."

"Speak up now, so I can hear you."

"I said there's me. I know."

"Goddamnit, of course you know. Who else? Who are you?"

"I'm a stableman, sir. I keep up the grounds and animals on the family ranch."

"A stableman?"

"Horse trainer and caretaker, sir, by trade."

"Leave him alone," Cudahy gurgled as he kicked his legs in pain.

I whacked him in the side of his head with the stock of my rifle. "One more word out of you and I'll blow your head off."

Cudahy rolled over onto his back, spitting clots.

"So you know about it, stableman," I said to the driver. "Who else?"

"There's—there's the mister and the missus. The two younger sisters. The housemaid."

"Anita, right?" I asked.

"Yes, sir. Anita."

"Who else. The police? Neighbors? Extended family?"

The driver fumbled his words.

I pressed my rifle to the driver's head. "Tell me."

"No sir. No police. No one else. When Mr. Cudahy got your letter, he was very concerned that it be followed exactly as written."

I slung my rifle over my shoulder again. I'd spent way more time in discussion than I wanted. For all I knew, Billy had already bolted off with our horse.

"You know something, Ernest? I believe you," I said and hustled over to the pair of draft ponies stationed to their carriage and unhooked them from their bindings. I took off their headstalls and bits, unclasped their harnesses and breast collars and whacked them both on their hindquarters.

"Giddyup, c'mon, hiyah!" I said with a loud cluck of my tongue. Both horses trotted forward four paces only to stop again. They were well trained. I fired my rifle into the air, sending the horses into a fit. They galloped away down the road, and I watched them until they disappeared from view.

"You remember what I told you," I hollered back to Cudahy and his driver. "Three full days. Anything short of that and little Eddie Junior will suffer a death indescribable."

XII

AT FIRST SIGHT, our butcher shop looked more like a novelty store. We adorned the front with a pair of bull heads carved out of mango wood on each side of the entrance and painted the windows in gold lettering advertising the meats: VEAL LOAF, BRAUNSCHWEIGER, LIVERWURST, OXTAIL SOUP, GOOSE LIVER SAUSAGE. The overhanging eaves were draped in holly and trim for the grand opening, which fell on the Monday before Christmas Day.

Occupying the corner of Second and Hickory, the store literally sat in the shadows of the Cudahy Meatpacking plant when the afternoon sun was in the sky. Most of the neighborhood was a seven-block district of warehouses nestled between the looming Union Stockyards. The building itself was three stories tall and skirted with canopies above its entire second floor. Nearly every structure in the district was of equal height and constructed of redbrick above brick streets cut through with railroad spur lines.

I made the storefront sign myself from a piece of sheet iron and a bit of pink paint, which read in fancy cursive script: CROWE AND CAVANAUGH, BUTCHERS.

Inside, the butchery was much more functional and drab. A huge ice table and sawbuck carving block as large as a church altar occupied the back wall where customers could order their meat to any specification. Kerosene lamps hung from the low ceiling. By ten o'clock in the forenoon, the tile floor was slick with water and blood and slush brought inside on customers' shoes. I mopped the slurry down the floor drain every hour to keep it dry and clean. To coincide with holiday shopping, whole geese and pheasants lined the walls, dressed with berries. Billy and I each wore a uniform of all white, our aprons slashed with blood.

Billy was an ace with a blade. He could undress a whole steer as neatly as peeling the jacket off a banana. He used an air pump to spray animal blood on the hanging carcasses on display to heighten their color. I dealt with the shoppers directly and left Billy in charge of most of the butchering to save him from any unpleasant exchanges. When it came to customer service, he was either foul in manner or spitting tobacco or stammering his words or all three at once. The kid was death on a scattergun, powerful in chewing snuff, offensive with his halitosis, a surgeon with a cleaver, deft at making nervous people more nervous, and nearly as unwelcoming in his demeanor as he was loony.

Most of our patrons were poor Polish and Irish laborers who came into the shop wearing patchwork coats without collars. They had unkempt hair and rotting teeth and hardly a lick of learned English between the entire lot of them. I tried my best to make friends when I could, offering up compliments and complimentary samples of chipped beef. I wrote down their names next to their physical descriptions in a nickel pocketbook.

When I showed Hattie our shop on the second day of being open for business, a heavy snow cooled the earth. The sky woolen with cloud cover. She arrived aboard a taxi carriage as if attending an opera, dressed in a long coat with a cape and kid gloves. I was waiting for her on the plank sidewalk in front of the store with my hat in my hands. I gripped it so tightly I crumpled the brim on both sides. I smoked a strong pipe and pushed my long bangs behind my ears while I paced back and forth, nervous as a boy on his first day of school.

Hattie stepped off the carriage and looked at the storefront as if it were condemned. She fixed her sneer and said, "This place is some pumpkins. You've done good for yourself, Pat."

I blushed and waved my hat with a panoramic sweep. I'd never been so proud in my whole life. "She's a great gal, this place. Come on inside and let me show you the works."

"I don't want to get blood on my new boots."

"We keep the floors as clean as a baby's conscience," I said and took Hattie by the hand and led her to the front door. Before we entered, I pointed at the sign above the windows. "See that there? Crowe and Cavanaugh. This is my own place. Now whaddaya think of that? By the time we get her running full steam, it's no more rental rooms and shared wash buckets for us. Nothing but the cream from here on out."

Hattie sniffed the putrid air. Even the clean smell of heavy snow couldn't disguise the odor of dead animals. She broke free from my grip and said, "I thought you and I might take breakfast somewhere nice."

I stammered. "You don't want to see inside?"

"I've been in a butcher shop before."

"I spent four weeks getting this place up to snuff."

"And I'm sure it's lovely."

"Is something the matter?"

Hattie bit her lower lip and covered her mouth with her hand as if catching a hiccup. Her face cringed as she held back tears.

I sighed and smashed my hat on the back of my head. The dangling store sign flapped in the cold wind. We'd had only five customers in our first two days, and only three of them made a purchase. All three had been given credit. I exhaled through my nose. No other business in South Omaha extended credit to the Polacks and Micks and Negroes. Even the Cudahy shops, unsinkable empire that they belonged to, took cash only. A man couldn't get a new button sewn on his threadbare coat at a haberdashery in that part of town without payment up front.

I looked back at Hattie. She'd started in with the boohooing.

I took my hat off again and gestured with it while I spoke. "You think I won't make it? You and everyone else, huh? Well, let me tell you something. I ain't one to strain my future through a piece of cloth. Not by a jugful. I'm going to make something good out of this life, and I'm going to make it honest even if it's hard trotting along the way. And let me tell you something else. I ain't doing it for me. I could've gone on hauling hogs and sleeping on hay till I croaked and never thought twice about it until I met you. I'm doing it for us. This store here? It's for you. All of this."

Hattie dabbed at her eyes.

I shrugged. "I'd go to hell across lots for you."

After a moment she said, "You're getting bamboozled."

"Bamboozled? That's a funny word. What's that mean? Like tying on a long one or something? Because I tell you what I haven't had, a drink in a month."

"You know what it means," Hattie said coldly.

"I don't at that. I ain't familiar with woodland sayings."

"I know the men you've thrown in with."

"The men I've throwed in with, huh?"

"Quit repeating everything I say like you don't know what I'm talking about. You'll make a poor go of this business and they'll close it down in three months and you'll be on the outs for the rest of your life."

"That's a helluva thing to say to me after I just got done carrying on about hogs and hay and all. Christ, I ain't even had my morning banana yet, and already you got me feeling almighty blue," I said.

"That's just what they want. You've trusted too many to your own sorrow."

"Just who is this 'they' you think you know so well?"

"You know exactly who. They give out loans on short meter and then take it all back and more like they were planning on failure all along. It's how those gangsters make their money."

"You've had some interesting pillow talks, I guess," I said.

Hattie's face dropped. For a moment she looked poised to slap me across the face and walk off down the avenue all the way to forever and never come back. But she didn't. We just stood there in the snow not saying a word to each other.

I rubbed my mouth and blinked against the purpling sky. There was still plenty of moon left in that early morning. For all I didn't know or only knew a part of, I also knew that Hattie knew more than most men ever would about the workings of fellers like Tom Dennison and those in his circle. She'd lain with the mayor on who-knew-how-many nights before I came along and probably with many others of his same paint. There was no blame for it. None that I held, anyway. But there was also no getting around it even by the long route. It was the kind of dark knowledge that spilled out faster than bad gossip in every gold-papered bedroom in every harem in the city after a night of whiskey and romping.

I had seen it myself from the girls who worked at The Sallie Purple. All the men who called city hall their office, all the deputized officers who walked a beat, every businessman who owned a topcoat, and every thug who ever fired a pump gun or cheated at cards—the working girls of the city knew all their secrets. Most could dish them up in alphabetical order or spread them around faster than a newspaper switchboard, depending on how you wanted your meat cooked.

And still I asked, "What do you know about it?"

Hattie wavered and looked across the street. A huddle of women in homespun rags stood in front of a tenement house. They'd come out to part with a few pennies for the man driving the neighborhood milk cart. She said, "I know you won't see twelve cents back from all those widows and destitutes you plan on giving credit to."

I took out a length of butcher string from my pant pocket and began wrapping it around my hand for want of something to do besides just standing there like a dunce getting the pretty business.

In a reminiscing tone, I said, "You know, when I was boy back home on my daddy's farm in Colorado, there was this family living in a soddy about a mile down the road from us. The Woodrow family. They had something like six or seven kids all younger than me. Well, papa Woodrow, he was a candle maker and a drunk. Stored away lard in these big old stone jars and rendered it into tallow for making the candles."

I paused and unwound the string from my hand only to ravel it around my knuckles again. I did this over and over, fiddling with the string like I was bandaging a wound and looking at the ground the whole time.

I continued, "They was poorer than a parlor maid on account of candles don't sell for but a short bit a dozen. That and the fact that Mr. Woodrow kept his weight in whiskey. Anyhow, they couldn't afford the gut fat from an old shoat let alone a good Christmas bird come the holidays. But there was this French butcher in town who let them take home a twelve-pound goose on loan every Christmas Eve. I remember that butcher shop better than my own bedroom. That Frenchy kept his mustache glossy and turned up at the ends like he was really something. And you know what? He never should've given a Hoosier like Woodrow credit for a single gizzard knowing he owed tabs yards long at every grog shop within wagon distance. But Frenchy did. And every year come February or March, ol' Woodrow paid off that bird because he knew if he didn't, that next year his family would be eating crackers for Christmas. And I always thought, what if that old Frenchy didn't give out no credit? Those kids would've had nothing better on their plates than johnny-cakes is what."

Hattie shuddered in the cold. Her facial expression suggested she'd been forever lost to all human feeling. "That's the most you've ever told me about your family."

"My family? Didn't you just hear me tell you it was about the Woodrows?"

Hattie looked away and wiped her cheeks with a gloved hand.

I waved at the store sign again and finally pocketed the butcher string. "If you don't want a look-see at the place today, that's alright. Ain't nothing but hung meat and a five-cent crazy man in there, anyhow. Come on, I got something else to show you that you might like a touch better."

I took her by the hand and hailed a hansom cab driven by a pair of claybank ponies. The top-hatted driver drove us to Orchard Avenue. We rode through Vinegar Flats and Squatter's Row as morning spread its mantle over the city. When the cab stopped, I threw open the back curtain. There in front of us was a pink catslide house with a picket sign in the yard that read: SOLD. The house wasn't much for looking at, but it had good bones and a working stove and, most importantly, two stories and pink paint. It cost me eleven hundred dollars. My tobacco can didn't have much left in it save for some old coins and few wrinkled bills after the purchase, but I owned the place outright.

The windows on the top floor were as crooked as poorly hung paintings. Maybe probably the porch needed a fresh coat and mended steps. I pictured us sitting on a matching pair of cane rockers every evening to watch away the end of the day. I'd run water pipes through the walls so we could have a bathtub upstairs and, boy, would that be something most folks couldn't calculate even in fantasy.

It was all so easy to imagine. Maybe put a garden in the backyard. Can the vegetables in the root cellar for winter so we'd have peaches and zucchini come February. There wouldn't be a stick of carved furniture or a piece of English silver in the whole place, but what we did have, we'd have plenty of. We'd keep our eggs fresh in a pail of lime water, and I'd bring chops home for dinner in deerskin wrappers.

I couldn't stop smiling. I felt like the biggest toad in the puddle.

"You bought a house," Hattie said plainly, as if it didn't impress her a breath's worth.

"A two-story pink house. Just like you said you always wanted."

"I said that?"

"I remember it pretty clear."

"You're the sweetest boy I've ever met."

"You ought to marry me then."

Hattie looked at me like I was a museum piece.

I scratched my scalp. "My mother always said 'sweet' is the marrying kind."

"Now what kind of proposal is that?"

"Best one I got, I fear."

Hattie considered the house again with a bunged-up expression as if all she could imagine were flies crawling on the window glass come summertime and drafts that would set her to shivering in her long nightshirt when the winter wind got to howling.

"If you were my wife, you'd never have to tie on apron strings."

"That's good because I can't make chicken fixings or slapjacks."

I said, "I could think of all the pretty girls I've ever seen in my whole life, and they wouldn't amount to a parcel compared to you. You? You take the dust off everything in creation."

"Do your compliments always come all on the same rod?"

"Jesus. I don't know."

Hattie poked me in the stomach. "I'm only funning you."

"You'd like to make me feel like I should be put in the corner wearing a tall pointy hat is what you're doing. When I say I don't know what you mean, I don't know what you mean. You think I do, but I ain't as smart as you think. I keep trying to think of ways of telling you I love you, and you keep acting like I need to keep on thinking."

"You scare too easy, Pat Crowe."

"Yeah, when it comes to you. You can put that on my headstone."

Hattie giggled. "Such a serious boy."

I shook my head. The sun was new up, and the last of the snow clouds were fleeting easy across the sky faster than a drink spilled across a tabletop. "That too. Etch it in. But I'll be goddamned if you ain't the silliest girl I've ever known. Show me another like you anywhere minus all the silliness, and I'll be there straightaway."

"You're awful strange, but I love you," Hattie said and put her arms around my neck. She reared up on her toes and kissed me on the mouth. "If you stop acting like a jackass, I'll marry you. So long as you don't mosey off in a heat every time I give you a little jab in the ribs."

As soon as she said it, a feeling of dread spread over me when it should've been the happiest moment in my entire life. One day all this would be gone. Not just me and Hattie. We were the least of it. But the house, the street, the whole history of our lives together in this place would be forgotten. Even the memory of it all would be gone. I didn't know why I was thinking it then, but it'd crept into my head and there was no getting rid of it and the thought was this: all moments both good and bad alike soon enough belong to the lovely land of long ago.

XIII

FOUR DAYS BEFORE we set off to kidnap Edward Cudahy's son, I went to visit the old man myself. After moonset it was dark as pitch, and I walked the streets far into the midnight hours until my face was swollen. A strangling rain mixed with sleet blasted store windows opaque with frost. The globes of streetlamps seemingly floated in the air, hazy and untethered balls of light, their iron posts disappeared into the blackness. The streets were checkerboards of mirrored ice. Old snow had to be shoveled into the back of flatbed wagons and driven down to the banks of the Missouri where it was dumped into the river like trash.

I turned up my coat collar and waited out the worst of the wintery rain under a bridge archway in Hanscom Park. An hour before dawn, I walked up the pea gravel drive of the Cudahy's castellated house, as big and gothic as a cathedral. Wetness soaked through my boots. Icy water ran off my hat brim in an unbroken stream. I approached the front door coughing in fits and rang the bell. My mouth was in my coat collar. A moment passed and I pounded the door with my fist. At once, two windows filled with light. A dog barked somewhere deep inside the house. There was a shuffling of footsteps. A colored maid with heavy breasts opened the door, asking me what my business was at that early hour.

I told her in a weak voice I was there to see Edward Cudahy.

Yes, yes, it wasn't even seven o'clock yet.

"I'll wait in the rain if I have to," I told her.

The maid frowned and admitted me into the lobby. Inside was all buttered warmth and amber light. The smell of rich stained wood and stove smoke. My draggled boots stained the giant carpet, a dizzy smear of paisley and intertwined fish patterns. I shook myself off like a wet dog. The maid handled my sopping threadbare coat with disdain, as if it were some dead animal the family cat had brought inside, and hung it on the coat tree where it dripped a mess onto the floor.

I gawked at all the gapeseed. A spiral staircase wound up like a corkscrew, the like of which I'd only ever seen before in pictures of ballrooms in luxury ocean liners. A plate-sized pendulum knocked back and forth behind the glass door of a granddaddy clock. A candle chandelier with eight ivory wood arms was hung from the ceiling like a frozen octopus. I couldn't help but whistle in amazement.

"This is some kind of joint," I said.

The maid frowned. She did not like whistling at that early hour or compliments about the estate or anything else as far as I could tell. She disappeared behind a swing door and returned a minute later, telling me to make myself comfortable in the parlor.

I took up a mohair couch next to a giant stone fireplace. A library ladder was hooked to shelving carved with acanthus leaf, able to glide along the floor-to-ceiling bookcase to reach the highest leather-bound volumes, books on every manner of subject: Civil War battles, countless law and economic texts, matching violet-colored editions of the complete Charles Dickens library, history of the Byzantine Roman Empire, haberdashery. A Christmas tree was covered in tissue paper, oranges, and stick candy. A toy train set ran in a circle around its base. Outside, a barren tree branch scratched at a window. The walls were hung with mahogany paneling, dark as chocolate.

I allowed myself a smoke while I waited without asking if it was admitted inside of doors. I coughed and spat through the whole thing. Finally the tobacco was too much for my ailing lungs, and I knocked out the pipe's contents into an ashtray shaped like a seashell. My face still swollen with cold. My cheeks and nose hurt to the touch. It was no matter. I'd see the thing through even if I lost a lung.

After nearly half an hour of waiting, the master of the home entered the parlor. Edward Cudahy, in all his excess heft, carried his mountainous weight with a certain sense of pride as if in mimicry of all those caricature cattle barons in Chicago and Kansas City who ate quail eggs for snacks between meals and drank cream even on the hottest of summer days and dabbed at their neck sweat with embroidered hankies while fussing over their stock numbers. He stomped into the room fully dressed for the day in a worsted suit, the woven fabric as thick as carpet. A chain connected his pocket watch to his vest buttonhole. He stood a few feet away from the sofa, patting his belly, studying me.

"Do you recognize me?" I asked and stood.

Cudahy's eyes leapt back and forth behind his spectacles. He came up behind a deep armchair with big buttons. "Glad to see you again, Patrick."

"I bet you are. I bet you're just tickled to see me come in from the storm."

A loaded pause filled the room. The magnate unfolded his eyeglasses and stuffed them into his suit coat pocket. "A touch early to come calling, but I'm glad you called nonetheless."

I said nothing. I just stood there staring.

"I was sorry to hear of your marital woes. I gave Hattie a job some couple years ago when she came calling for one. Made her quality overseer in our new north lot, no questions asked. She's an admirable woman."

"I might've supposed that's where she met your brother, but we both know that happened long before that," I said and returned to the sofa. I was quite at ease save for my whooping lungs. "Anything else your family would like to take of mine?"

Cudahy grimaced as if the notion of such thievery was the most asinine thing he'd ever heard. "You're soaked, poor boy. Have you gotten yourself a cold?"

"I'm warm enough."

Cudahy scoffed again. He was unnerved to the bone but pretended otherwise. He didn't respond for a moment, his eyes blinking wildly, and swallowed a globule of spit.

"You're looking a tad peak-ed yourself," I said.

"Anita," Cudahy hollered for his maid from his position behind his armchair. "Anita, dear, bring Mr. Pat here some asafetida and hot water. Poor fellow's got an awful cold."

The maid peeked her head into the room after a moment. "Asafetida, sir?"

"Yes. And boiling hot water. And I'll take my breakfast in here this morning."

"Right away, sir," the maid said.

She was about to disappear when Cudahy opened his hand to

me. "I was just about to have breakfast. Perhaps Anita could prepare you something?"

"Not for me. I never have a stomach at this hour," I said. "But a spot of asafetida would be much appreciated. Doc tells me I got, what? An abscess of the antrum?"

"That sounds ungodly."

"Gives my lungs the fits, I'll admit," I said and coughed twice more.

Cudahy nodded to his maid, and she vanished to retrieve the requested medicine. When she was gone he finally rested himself into the armchair he'd been standing behind and crossed his legs, revealing his sock supporters. A tea table separated us. After an awkward few moments of silence, the housemaid brought in a serving tray and set it on the table. A single hard-boiled egg sat in a stemmed holder, a stick of butter rested next to four slices of toasted pumpernickel. Two upside-down coffee cups with gold-edged brims were stacked on a folded cloth napkin next to a spouted kettle. I reached forward first, helped myself to a pour of hot water and medicine, stirring it together with a tiny spoon.

Cudahy smiled beneath his thin mustache, which didn't match his bulging face. His fingers were too big to fit through the handle of his mug, and he held it like a stone. "This is quite uncommon, showing up unannounced at someone's home at such an hour."

"You mean it's rude," I said. "You can say what you really want to me."

"You always were quite the talent with the blade. Yes, sir, one dandy of a meat man, you were. Experience in our business is of rare value," Cudahy said as he picked up the egg from its holder and peeled off the shell in delicate fashion, removing the tiny cracked pieces like flecks of lint. "I remember the good work you did for us."

"You might remember more than that."

Another pause filled the room.

I rested my medicine cup on my knee. I was either serene or homicidal. It was impossible to tell the difference. Maybe I felt both ways. I really didn't know.

"Well, you can always come work for us again," Cudahy said nervously and nodded at the wet mess that had formed under my feet. My clothes were soaked through as I shivered and coughed. "You're dripping like a leak, son. Where's your coat about?"

"Making a mess of your foyer, I believe," I said and gestured back toward the entryway where my shabby overcoat was hanging on the coat tree.

Cudahy peered over my shoulder, caught sight of the garment making a puddle on his dizzy carpet. "That old rag? It couldn't warm a post."

The giant man then rose after popping the whole egg into his mouth and walked to a closet just outside the parlor. He returned with a double-breasted coat of his own collection. He petted its cream fur, examined its gold buttons, and handed it to me in a giant fold while he continued to chew a yellow mess of egg. "This might do you better. Bought it on holiday in Naples two years ago and have only worn it twice. Good Italian wool. Give it a try."

I slipped on the mammoth garment. It sleeves hung down to my knuckles and its girth could've fit another man my size inside its material. "It's a handsome piece of drapery, Ed."

"Well then, it's yours. Consider it a Christmas gift."

"Are we trading now?"

"Trading?"

I sat down and snorted as loudly as a man alone in a field. I let loose a brown clot of sickness through my mouth into a fancy cuspidor. "It's a nice coat. But it's not as nice as a wife and a child. Not to mention a whole business."

Cudahy shrugged his shoulders. "That sounds threatening."

"I'm not threatening you with anything. Whaddaya think? That I might come in here before sunup and flash a revolver around the room?"

"That's just about enough of that. I empathize with your situation, I truly do. But your wife left you. I didn't steal her off some store shelf. Nor did my brother. And as for your little shop failing, that error lies squarely on your shoulders. You think you have reason for hatred, but you best reserve that feeling for your own shortcomings. So let me save you the trouble and say I'm not influenced by your unwarranted accusations of thievery, and I'm certainly not shaky at the knees because you own a few guns."

"I don't own any guns, friend," I said and pulled at the collar of Cudahy's gifted overcoat. "I didn't even own a decent coat until a minute ago."

"Friend, you say? We're friends now?"

"Yeah. Good old pals. Everything's jake between us."

Cudahy shook his head and scratched butter onto a piece of toast. "We need a foreman for our new knackery out in San Francisco, by the by," he said after a heavy moment, anxious to switch gears as he continued to butter his toast. "You'd be a good candidate, if it's a job you're needing. I'll give you a traveling advance, put it on receipt. Two hundred dollars would get you to the coast in fine form with a little extra for sport on the side. Then you can report to our supervisor out there. Mr. Jim Davis. I'll give you a contract."

"You'll get me out of Omaha, you mean."

"It's a job offer," Cudahy said. "An honest one with good pay."

I coughed again in five loud successions. My hanky full of blotted sickness. "A good kick in the stomach would be just about as pleasant a concern."

"You ought to go to a hospital. You're in miserable shape."

I looked about the room while I dabbed my mouth with my pocket cloth. On a tray along a far counter, crystal decanters with big knob tops were filled with enticing amber liquid. Probably some of the best liquor in the Midwest. "I'd be better off with a lashing of whiskey if you can spare it."

"At this hour? How long have you been on the bum?"

"Oh, give me a swish," I said. "It'll clear up my lungs."

Cudahy hesitated but poured a swig of campfire despite his reservations. I accepted the heavy glass with two hands, cradling it like a cup of coffee warming the palms, and knocked it back in one slug. Before the whiskey hit the bottom of my stomach, Cudahy's son, sixteen-year-old Eddie Junior, came into the parlor. He was dressed for school in a tunic with knitted knee socks and flannel trousers with a coordinating academy jacket. A large gold crest was sewn into the jacket like a police badge over his heart pocket, a bundle of books slung over his shoulder.

"I'm off for academy, father," he said, standing just inside the room. His hair was slicked down with brilliantine and he kept pawing at a particularly troublesome tuft of cowlicks on the back of his head.

Cudahy looked back. "Have you got your lunch pail?"

"Yes, father."

I stood and approached Eddie Junior with an open hand, offering a shake. "Little Eddie Junior, I presume. How do you do? I'm Pat Crowe."

We shook hands.

"Yes, son," Cudahy said. "Mr. Crowe here used to work for us."

I was still shaking Eddie's hand. "Your Aunt Hattie used to be my wife, and your little cousin Matilda is my daughter."

Cudahy lunged off his armchair. "Off you go now, son. The academy won't stand tardiness."

Eddie Junior smiled faintly and bid us farewell as he left the room. Once he was gone, I went to the mirrored liquor table and helped myself to another pour from the crystal decanter. I swallowed half of it and watched Eddie Junior, heir to the Cudahy packinghouse fortune, slink his way down the street from the parlor window.

"He hasn't got any earmuffs or a scarf, even," I said, gesturing with my glass. "He'll catch cold like I did walking around like that."

"You didn't have to tell him all that about Hattie and Matilda. He's got nothing to do with it," Cudahy said.

I finished my second helping of whiskey and set the glass down on top of an oak music cabinet with a hard clank. "The truth is nasty business."

"Suppose I'll be having an interesting dinner conversation tonight. I thank you for that."

I laughed. "And what will you tell him?"

"The truth. Every nasty part of it, as you say. Including yours."

"You're a good man, Mr. Cudahy," I said disdainfully. "Thanks for the coat. I suppose I'll cork off."

"Why did you come here?"

"To find out who you really were."

"And what did you find?"

"That you're a good man, just like I said." I sniffled and thumbed my nose. I spun around slowly, admiring the Cudahy family portraits on the walls, each set in a gaudy frame. In one painting there was

Edward with his son Eddie Junior and five of their wirehaired terriers at a dog show, all smiles and leashes and wagging tails. In another, Edward, his wife Sue Anne, and their children—Eddie Junior and his two sisters—posed against a washed background. A third showed Edward and his family again; this one while on vacation for a weekend of river fishing. Edward Junior held up a dangling line of glimmering trout.

"A good man," I repeated. "You and your family. A portrait of wholehearted American goodness."

"And what're you?"

I was halfway to the door. "I don't know what I am."

Cudahy sat back down, exhausted. The man was so fat that his trousers bunched up around his crotch as if they'd been inflated. He was confused and still had bits of egg in his teeth. "That's enough of the cryptic stuff. What do you want, Pat? You came here for something, and I'd like to know what it is you think you're owed, exactly."

"A good secondhand coat and a nibble of whiskey is all," I said and examined the cream overcoat. It was the finest garment ever to dawn my shoulders.

"Tell me straight. I don't like being goaded."

I was in the doorway with my back to Cudahy. I leaned an arm against the frame and shook out a few more wet coughs. Finally I turned around so Cudahy could get a good look at me in all my inexpungible misery. My jaw muscles worked in and out as I chewed my anger, my bottom lip trembling. "I just wanted you to see."

Cudahy waited for me to say more.

I gave him nothing.

"See what?" he asked.

"What hell has made of me," I said without a shred of emotion. I put on my hat as clumsily as if it were a giant pot and left the mansion. The front door, heavy as a drawbridge, slammed shut behind me with an ominous thud.

A new nickeled morning brandished new hopes. Yes, I thought as I buttoned Cudahy's oversized overcoat to the collar, I will have my story written forever across this mighty continent. I will secure my place in the annals of this monster land.

There was nothing in my pockets but an old apple, which I'd

been eating the night before. I headed east. Tails of ice fog weaved between the magnificent houses. Snow fell in pellets and the sun appeared to be only a foot high over a city dizzy with winter. The first bits of quailing daylight in shards. My muscles corded up in the cold. In the giant coat, I must have appeared like a hobo who'd hastily stolen the garment off a rack in a department store without caring to measure its size.

I turned left on Dewey Avenue. How the winter winds had wrecked the city. Fallen branches and roof shingles were cloven about front yards. A telegraph cable, thick as a corn snake, lay on an opposite sidewalk like a forgotten garden hose left out overnight. So assured was I in my rightness that I deciphered my own crystallomancy in the hiccupping morning stars. A smattering of blackbirds lifted off a naked tree branch, cawing across the page of the sky like spilled blots from an ink pot.

This was not about redemption.

Redemption was a fanciful notion for salvation. For repair. There was no repairing anything. Only bringing obscurity into brightness, only cracking open the machinery so that the world might have a good long look at the hidden anatomy. Look upon these innards and judge for yourself what I have done, the only thing I could do.

It would take an equal or perhaps even greater measure of villainy to expose what I hated most about the villainous world. The children in rags who came pawing at the gigantic carriages parked along the decorated boulevards, and the men inside who tossed out a few coins on the street only to shoo the children away. The stockyarders who worked for half a dollar a day only to have to pay twice that for the same meat they labored over to fill their families' tables.

Whole neighborhoods of shacks constructed with scraps from the city dump. An impoverished wife who loses her husband to cholera and her son to influenza in the same month. A clapboard tenement full of the elderly and the widowed and barefoot children, jammed into a single room, unable to both refill their coal bins and eat ever day of the week. It was one or the other. Warmth or supper, take your pick. The holiday handouts of frozen turkeys and children's toys for the poor that were bought and paid for by their own political patronage. The generosity of the wealthy nothing but a long-running gag.

I walked the city all morning just as I had all night before, fueled by a hate so compound that the word itself—*hate*—was as insufficient a vessel for encompassing the emotion as a cup assigned to contain the sky. But there was no other word for it. No other. Hate, I am not a phoenix rising. Hate, there is only this pile of ashes. Hate, I used to be something else, but I have not transformed. Do not look upon me anew. You have seen me before. I am that hated thing, and I wear no mask. I am not standing up to the wicked. I am the wicked. And I have never been anything else but this all along.

XIV

THE FIRST SEVEN months of my marriage to Hattie passed in a spall that felt more like feverish hallucination than actuality. Soon enough the grandeur of it all would smear in my memory, and the details would fade completely as a dream once so vivid is forgotten not long after waking. Hattie and I moved into our little pink house on Orchard Avenue. Spring arrived in a giant noise. Thunderheads dropped hailstones on our catslide roof seemingly every other day; the Missouri River was high up with floodwater, and even once a skinny cyclone came rushing down Hickory Street not more than four blocks from our house, bursting store windows and tossing mules over rooftops, a wake of glass dusting the avenue as completely as snowfall.

One day in April I returned home early from work on a balmy afternoon. Hattie was lounging on a divan with her legs spread open in front of an elderly white-bearded man seated on a stool. Her skirt was bunched up around her knees as the man lowered his head between her thighs.

My first instinct was to get the cattle knife off my hip and slit the man's throat open as wide as daylight. I was glad to have restrained myself from such action long enough for Hattie to explain that the man was her physician, Dr. Greg Arnold.

I offered him a glass of cold yak, and he politely declined.

The reason for his visit was the tardiness of my wife's menstruation. His words, not mine. That doctor was one odd skate. "One of my many specialties is urology," he said. "You can tell a great bundle just by the color of one's urine. Why, there are over twenty different hues." He produced a wheeled chart that detailed all the possible variations. Each meant something different. "There's chartreuse yellow, saffron, pear, chiffon, sun gold, mustard, and even a greenish tint if one were to eat too much asparagus." He went on and on about all the lovely uses for harvesting urine: neutralizing jelly fish stings, manufacturing gun powder, textile dyes, fertilizer.

Like I said, that old sawbones was an odd skate.

After his visit, Hattie stood up and led me in front of our cinnamon wood mirror by the fireplace. I put my arms around her waist and nestled my chin in the soft nook of her neck. When we both looked up at our shared reflection in the mirror. Hattie lifted her blouse, took my left hand, and placed it gently on her belly.

She said, "You're going to be a father."

Our daughter Matilda Rose was born on the last day of June. The three of us curled together in a bed draped with cheesecloth to keep the mosquitoes away. The first time I kissed my daughter's chubby pink cheek, the first time her little hand wrapped around my pinkie finger, I thought: this world could not be more grand.

Full days of glad in our butcher shop: hogs and steer split in halves and hanging in the cooling room, kept down to temperature with an ammonia machine; selling finely wrapped packages of bird and cutlet over a clean pine table. The smell of my wife's hair in my nostrils and the vision of my daughter's laughing eyes in my head kept a smile on my face until quitting time. Then, walking home as the sun dropped out of the sky, saying goodbye to Billy for the night with a few dollars more in our pockets than when the day began. A wife and baby girl in good health. A home in fine repair.

All of this could have repeated on and on until forever.

None of it ever would.

They are but dreams of things long ruined, long gone. After a certain point, the past is as vertiginous as looking down after a tall climb.

All that's left is dizziness. All that's left is the empty.

Perhaps it was how it had to be with those fleeting instances of inexplicable love: always brief and, maybe partly because of that brevity, always lasting.

Let me say this: my greatest fear when I became a father was that one day my daughter would discover just how wicked the world could be. Not more than seven months later, I would be committing one of the most wicked crimes in the world by stealing another father's child not more than fifty yards from his front door.

Come the height of that summer, at early candlelight on a particularly boiling Friday in July, a Victoria shaped like a giant slipper pulled up to the curbstone in front of our butcher shop. The coachman hollered out their arrival and spit masticated plug over the leeward side. Dark green hail clouds were making in the western sky. The two men who exited the carriage each bore a significant heft, and the Victoria rose a good six inches off its axle when free of their weight. They entered our butchery ten minutes before closing time. One of them pointed at the advertisement painted on the picture window: EVERY CUT! NECKS, RUMP ROASTS, AND OXTAIL SOUPS! CREDIT GIVEN. ALL WELCOME.

I was counting down the till in my batwing bow tie and Billy was in back dressing a cow for market when the husky pair approached the counter.

"What do you say, gentlemen?" I offered in my best salesman voice.

"Powerful hot day," the first man said as he pawed his handkerchief about his face. A mustache of beaded sweat coated his upper lip. He was bald, with a chin that sagged like a turkey wattle, and wore a seersucker suit so thin it was nearly transparent. "Hot enough to peel the scales off a lizard, yes sir."

"What can I do you for? We're running a special on veal chops by the half dozen and—"

"My name is Edward Cudahy," the man said and tapped his cane on the counter. He had a voice that could shake a house an inch off its foundation, even in whisper. He pointed the tip of his cane toward the window. "I have a large packinghouse myself hard by."

I slammed the till shut and studied Cudahy over something good. I'd spent my first six months in town working for the man and had yet to see his likeness in so much as a three-cent portrait, until now.

"Billy," I hollered into the back of the store. "Hey, Billy boy, come on out here and meet none other than Mr. Ed Cudahy."

The second man who came in with Cudahy went around poking each hanging carcass as if to make sure they weren't plastic. He had hands the size of a fielder's mitt and drake tails at his neck. Billy emerged from the refrigerated cutting room with so much blood on his apron he might have been field dressing a walrus. Every time he got to skinning a cow after hoisting it up in the air with a block and tackle, he messed himself worse than a back alley surgeon. He went right up to Cudahy and forcibly shook his hand and slapped him twice on the shoulder and patted his chest hard, saying, "Hell, Mr. Cudahy. Color me tickled. The king of pork town hisself. How do you do?"

He got cow blood all over Cudahy's hand, suit, and laundered shirt.

Cudahy broke away and set to dancing around in place as if a waitress had dropped a bowl of hot soup in his lap. "Good God, son. Haven't you got the sense God gave a goose?"

Billy ran back behind the butcher block and dunked his hands in a suds bucket.

I thought that was pretty funny. "He gets excited some whenever a big deal comes through our doors."

"He liked to ruin my suit," Cudahy said as he blotted at the red handprint on his chest with his pocket linen. "Ain't you got any seltzer on hand?"

"There's a soda shop down the road a piece," I said.

Cudahy quit fiddling with his clothes. They were ruined beyond wash. Seersucker stained easier than paper. He thumped the side of the till with his cane. "Enough of this shilly-shallying around. You have three thousand dollars in unpaid customer accounts. Not to mention you still owe at least that much to your investor."

"How's that any of your business?"

"Everything in South Omaha is my business, and I just so happen to own this tract of land. The man with the curls there is my banker. He tells me that if you can't pay off your balance in thirty days' time you default on your loan."

"I didn't take out a loan with a bank."

"Tell that to Tom Dennison," Cudahy said and took out a flat bill book from his suit pocket. "I spoke to the man just this morning. He and I play a little pinochle at the Jackson Street club on Fridays come lunchtime. I'm willing to offer you full title on this cocklebur outfit. Now you won't find that kind of deal anywhere else. That's six thousand dollars free and clear to shut your doors by Monday."

"A real bona fide offer, huh?"

"Either you walk away clean of debt this weekend or in a serious hole at the end of the month and I strip this place down to the tin and you can deal with Mr. Dennison directly about the balance owed. But, let me tell you, he's a tad prickly when it comes to finances."

"Just hang up the fiddle, you're asking?"

"It's a fair offer," the banker with the curls of hair said as he continued to poke around the steers hanging from the ceiling. "I advised against it. I told Ed here to let you boys flail around some more. Have a bit of patience, I said, and you'll be richer for it. But he's got a big old sappy heart."

I gestured at Billy. "Him and me? We used to work for you in your south lot. Near broke our backs working ten hours a day for sixty cents an hour."

Cudahy said, "And you can come back to work for me if it's a job you're needing."

"I know your type. You're nothing but a bully with a flower in his lapel. You'd clean a man of his shirt while his kids picked dinner out of a trash barrel in their bare feet."

"I hear you have a baby girl, yourself," Cudahy said and cracked his neck.

"I ain't selling. I've worked too hard to get this place running to quit before I even give it a chance to succeed."

Billy came back over from the suds bucket, shaking off his hands as he tugged at his crotch. "Something tells me this one is more than pinochle buddies with that Dennison bum."

Cudahy took out a bible of smoking papers and a rubber tobacco pouch to get the makings together for a cigarette. "Smart buzzard. But many more of stronger mind and deeper pocketbooks than you have faded like candlelight in this business. Either of you know of Sir Thomas Lipton? No? I drink his tea every morning. Well, he came here to Omaha some couple years ago hoping to export trade of bacon hogs back home to Mother England. Long story short, no farmer within a hundred miles of here was willing to sell their hogs. Man owned a fleet of yachts, a rice planation in South Carolina, half of Malta, the good half anyway, and still his venture to buy a few hogs in this city was an abject failure. Maybe someone in this room had something to do with that. And maybe that same somebody disposed of his plant and sent him back home across the Atlantic with a red hiney after spanking him good under his swallowtails."

"I heard that fable, too," I said. "Except for I heard you did more with his hiney than just spank it."

Billy shook his head and had himself a small chuckle. "Sodomite."

The word sent me into a fit of laughter. When it came to subtlety and innuendo, Billy was an artless creature.

Cudahy fumed. He was so perturbed that he left the paper and tobacco he'd been trying to roll into a cigarette on the counter like it was a failed experiment. "You run it over in your heads tonight boys, if you have any brains left in them. My offer stands until noon tomorrow."

For the rest of the summer, shadows seemed to follow me wherever I went. Imagined or not, I saw them grow long even when the sun was high and remain long after it had set. I was sure I'd been followed home on more than one occasion.

On one evening in early August, after I put my newborn daughter to bed, I came downstairs and looked out my kitchen window. Standing there under our plum tree were two silhouetted figures. Soft moonlight illuminated their shapes: dome crown fedoras, wide shoulders, knee-length overcoats. I grabbed my five-shot pistol and threw open the front door, but by then the shapes of what I thought were men had disappeared.

Two days later I was walking home from work after closing up shop. I said goodbye to my last customer of the day, Mrs. Francis Carver, a woman so delicate and reserved she called a chicken breast a chicken bosom when ordering her meat, for fear of using foul language. The last of the evening sun lighted the sky an apocalyptic crimson. Corncob smoke rose over rooftops in the distance. Fumes poured out from the packinghouse smokestacks. A pair of black leghorn chickens wandered about in the empty street.

I took a shortcut down an alley between two clapboard tene-ments. A cup of sugar was being transferred on a wash line from one apartment to another. When I got halfway down the alley, two figures appeared at the opening of Izzard Avenue, looking much like the shadowy figures I'd seen standing in my front yard. A trash can lid rattled to the ground. Laundry smoke poured out of a building pipe. I stared at the figures. I couldn't see anything except the shapes of their bodies.

The two men didn't move. One of them said something to the other, and they each lifted a heavy object from inside their coats. I balked for a moment and then sprinted back down the alley. With a giant heave of my shoulder, I busted through a locked door in the build-ing to my left that led into a chop suey restaurant closed up for the night. I sprinted through the kitchen and past the sitting area and came out onto the north side of the building. I needed to get off the streets.

A block away I saw light still glowing in the window of the Abbott Grocer, where I shopped once a week. I hustled inside and approached the register where the owner, Sal Abbott, eighty years old and wrinkled as wastebasket paper, stood with a weak smile. I smiled back and looked around the store, trying to remain calm.

"Hey there, Pat. Everything all right?" the old clerk asked. He was smoking a briar pipe with a nicotine cup that covered the bowl like a lid on a kitchen pot. The nicotine cup was clicked open, and smoke was coming out of every hole in the old man's head. A little bit even seemed to leak from his ears.

"Sure, sure," I said and slowed my breathing. "How's business these days, Sal?"

"Slow," the old man said, then corrected himself. "Slow but steady enough."

"That's alright, Sal. You don't need to be afraid of telling me the truth."

"Is something wrong, Patrick?"

I looked out the window. "I think a couple hooligans were trying to rob me on the street. Been a lot of muggings going around lately. I dunno. Maybe I'm just jumpy."

"I've had it with this city," the old man said. "Used to be

everybody cared for everybody else. Cared about their welfare, how they were holding up. And they meant it, their caring. Nowadays you can't shake a man's hand without keeping your other on your pocketbook."

I nodded in agreement and rubbed my hair after taking off my worn cap.

"Tell you what, old timer, I need to pick up some trimmings to take home to the wife," I said and loaded up a cloth sack as I went around the aisles, hoping to buy some time in a public place. I collected four cans of evaporated milk, enamel cleaner, peas, lemon snaps, a loaf of wholemeal, a box of puffed wheat. I returned to the front of the store and set the bag down on the counter.

"My credit still good here, Sal?" I asked.

The old man stared at the bulging bag. The total sum of the groceries couldn't have been more than four dollars. His voice quivered. "I can't. Not anymore. One of Mr. Dennison's men come by and told me no more credit's to be given to anybody until they pay what they—"

I raised my hand. "What about a trade? I got some good meat I could bring in tomorrow, first thing."

"No," Sal said. His voice was so soft it was barely audible. He rubbed his craggy hands over the counter as if smoothing it out. "That just won't do. I'm sorry, Pat."

I nodded. I understood.

I turned to exit, leaving the bag on the counter. "No hard feelings, old man. I guess I'll be seeing you around the bend sometime."

The old man stammered and told me to hold on one minute. He reached for a can behind the register where a sundry of toiletries took up their own separate section. He added a box of soap and tooth powder to my bag. Then he took out a handful of small change from the heavy can and counted it out in his palm. Even with his thick bifocals and plenty of light, it took him more than a minute to parcel out four dollars' worth of coin. He threw the coins into his till and pushed the bag toward me.

"For the family," Sal said.

"I couldn't possibly—" I stuttered.

"Quit it now. You're a good boy. Miss Sally told me so."

"Miss Sally?" I asked. "Old Miss Sally Jenkins? She comes in every Thursday for her kiszka and tongue loaf."

"She says you're the only man around here who has faith enough in folks to treat them like they're decent even if they ain't. She tells me you're just about aces. Loves your little shop. Plus, I know you got a baby girl at home."

I touched the bag. "But you said there's no more credit."

"Store can't give credit. But I can give credit," Sal said and pointed at his chest with his thumb. "You can owe me."

As I was stumbling to find the words to express my gratitude, the two men who'd followed me into the alley entered the grocer. They wore rubberized jackets and carried full-choke shotguns inside their overcoats, the muzzles visible through the bottoms of their knee-length flaps. They stood in the doorway like spirits, saying nothing.

"Sal," I said and waved my hand. "Go on and get out of here."

The old man didn't budge.

"Whatever you've come looking for, you've found too much of it," I told both men and stepped forward two paces with my fists clenched.

"Says the chump who's been running away from us for four blocks," the first man croaked, his voice as deep as a bullfrog's. An old knife scar ran up the side of his neck.

"What do you want?"

"We come at behest of the boss," the second one said. "Wants us to bring you in for a little chat."

I nodded and was about to go along when I heard a loud metal click. Old Sal had gotten out his ten-gauge from under the counter. He snapped open the back action and checked both barrels and then sighted the gun between the two men standing just inside the front door of his shop.

"It's loaded," Sal said. His frail arms trembled from the shotgun's weight.

"It's alright, Sal. Put it down. No need mixing up in this," I said.

The first bruiser lifted his own shotgun out of his coat, swinging it up into his arms by the strap on his shoulder. He was as quick at drawing the pump-action as most men—even veteran gunslingers—were with pistols, maybe faster. The second man took his weapon out much slower and aimed it as carefully as a hunter taking sight at a whitetail. "Best listen to him, old man. You got a shotgun, I got a shotgun, my friend's got a shotgun. This could all get awful messy in an awful hurry."

Old Sal cocked back both hammers. "I'm eighty-one years old and come down with the consumption and my wife's been passed on for a decade now. So, no, I don't reckon I'll be putting down nothing."

"You can barely hold that thing," the second man said. "How do you think you'll fare when it comes to hitting anything more than air?"

"Fair enough to put a little buckshot in your bellies."

I stepped in between the old man and the bruisers with my hands raised. "There ain't no need for this, fellers. I'll come along like you say. Just everyone put down their metal."

"The old man goes first."

I looked back to Sal and saw he wasn't of any mind to lower his weapon. His arms shook like the shotgun weighed fifty pounds.

A long moment passed. I kept my hands raised and was walking toward the men, but it did no good as the thug on the left let loose of both barrels and hit Sal square in his chest. The slugs thundered through his heart and sent him flying back against the wall. He shattered the beveled mirror behind him. His shotgun fell to the floor and harmlessly sprayed buckshot into the ceiling.

I cried out and charged the man who still had his barrels loaded. Before he could pull the trigger, I bolted him in the side of the head so hard he stumbled into a tall pyramid stack of canned goods. The tower of cans hadn't fully collapsed before I picked him off the ground by his shirt collar and walloped him four more times until his eyes rolled into the back of his head. I could feel the man's brain knocked loose in his skull, swimming. I lifted him up higher and threw two more punches square in his neck, hoping to collapse his windpipe and let him suffocate from a broken throat.

The man gurgled and his whole body went limp before I threw him off and turned to get a beat on the other man, who hadn't any shells left in his gun. But as soon as I got off the floor I was back on it, popped in the teeth with the barrel of the second man's shotgun. My vision blurred, and my eyes went crooked. I lifted myself up to my knees when the thug whacked me in the mouth a second time. I fell motionless to the ground among the rolling cans of dessert prunes and stewed tomatoes, my sight as bright as lamplight and my ears ringing for a brief moment before another blow to my head passed everything into darkness.

XV

AFTER I SET Cudahy's pair of wagon ponies free, I crested the top of the hill and stumbled down the other side where Billy and I had hitched our own horse to the trunk of a spruce. It was so dark I could barely see five feet in front of me. The terrain steep with old snow that had melted and refrozen as slick as pond ice. Each footfall sounded like snapping twigs. My boots, a cheap pair of two-dollar monarchs, had soaked through the leather. I raced as fast as I could manage down the slope.

Twice I lost my footing and fell on my backside so hard I bruised my tailbone. I tripped and rolled like a barrel before stopping my momentum by clawing at the ground. I could barely breathe through the burlap of the gunnysack mask and ripped it off my head and stuffed it down the front of my trousers. When I came upon the hollow where we'd left our nag, the entire spot was empty.

I panted and lit a match to aid my vision.

I should've mounted one of Cudahy's horses for myself.

"Goddamn you, Billy, where are you?" I called out, waited, heard nothing.

Billy had abandoned me.

"Goddamn," I said out loud to myself. "Goddamnit! Where's the goddamn moon when you need it?"

I collected my breath. The cold air burned my lungs. I sat down in the snow and heaved so hard my stomach nearly burst. There was no place in the world as quiet as a forest at night in the dead of winter. Tree limbs creaked in the wind.

I shouted again, "Goddamn you, Billy! Goddamn you!"

"Hey!" Billy hollered. His voice was part yell, part whisper. "Hey, you idiot. Quit your bellyaching. I'm over here."

I looked in every direction. Couldn't see a thing.

"Over here. To the west."

I lit another match, held it out like a beacon. Billy had moved our horse. He was down by a split of stream that branched off from the main creek, hidden among a making of dead trees. I climbed down in a dash. When I got to the bottom of the embankment I accidentally put a boot through thin creek ice. Water as cold as water gets. I was so furious I shoved Billy to the ground.

"You're a moron," I scolded. "Why in the hell did you move that nag? Goddamn. I couldn't see a thing."

Billy got back on his feet and procured a bent cigarette from his vest pocket. Before lighting the tobacco, he petted Silversmith on her nose and blew a calming warm whisper into her left ear until it twitched from the sensation. "She was getting spooky."

"Spooky? She's a goddamn horse tied to a tree in the middle of nowhere and can't see a thing. Of course she was going to get spooky. That's why you tie up a horse in the first goddamn place, so they don't run off when they get spooky. Goddamn you, I thought you took off on me. How the hell was I supposed to find you?"

"Just like you did."

I spat twice and made business searching through the bank valises that Billy had tied onto each side of our horse like saddlebags. I lit another match as I clawed through all the coin. There was enough color in the bags to fatten us both for five or six years, maybe longer if we budgeted the gold.

Neither of us would have to do another scrap of work until we were nearly forty.

"What the hell took you so long?" Billy asked.

"He knows," I said. "Cudahy. He knows it's me."

Billy shrugged. "So much for the masks."

I snapped the valises shut. "He doesn't know who you are. Far as I could tell."

"I'm sure he'll figure it out. Or the police."

"I bought us some time before they call the police. That's what took me so long."

Billy popped a match, inhaled deeply, and mounted our horse. "How'd you manage that? Christ. You killed the bastard, didn't you?"

I hoisted myself up, sitting bareback behind Billy. "He's going to need a new set of teeth, that's for certain. Come on, let's get out of here."

Billy put his heels into Silversmith's rump, and we bolted off at a canter through the glinting trees. We rode for ten miles, crossing around the outside of town just to be safe. At one juncture we had to clip off a section of wire fence to pass through a dead soybean field. I sniffled and spat phlegm the whole way. The huge sacks of coins, an extra hundred pounds of cargo, tired our horse in a good hurry. Soon all she could do was trot despite Billy's encouragement for speed. I told him to go easy on the old girl. I'd set loose Cudahy's wagon mares before I left the scene, I said, and it would be some time, probably daylight, before Edward and his driver would come across another traveler able to help them back into the city.

There were still five hours left in the night.

"Imagine that," I said. "Imagine that bastard rolling around in the snow looking for his teeth until sunup."

Billy considered the image. "This ends badly, you know. Maybe not for a while, but eventually this all goes against us."

"I'm glad he knows it was me. I was almost hoping he'd figure it."

"Well, wish granted."

"Two hours ago you were telling me to calm down."

"I'm calm."

"You ain't either," I said.

"Quit talking, would you? I'm tired."

I groaned. I searched my tattered coat for a pocket bottle I'd been saving for the glorious and wealthy ride back to our hideaway. I patted my biggest pocket. The bottle had shattered. A great wet stain all the way through to my long johns. A pint of quality brandy gone to waste. Most probably it ruptured somewhere during my scramble down the hill looking for Billy. My first notion was anger, but it quickly receded. There'd be plenty of time for celebratory brandy in the near future. Nothing but time. In ten days I might be drinking ten-year-old purple for ten dollars a pour at ten in the forenoon in a city so far north the temperature wouldn't spike past ten degrees until April or later. I put my lips together. We ambled over a frosted plate of land so desolate that if we didn't have our bearings it would be an easy guess to say we were a hundred miles between any kind of city in any direction.

When we finally arrived back at the cottage, I fed our horse a double helping of oats and gave her a bucket of water. I draped a giant monkey fur cape around her body—the same one Billy had thrown over Eddie Junior's head when we abducted him—and rubbed her down to warm her skin.

"You've got grit," I said to her while she fed on the oats. "Yes, ma'am, I'll say you got grit in spades. What a fine horse."

Come sunrise, with little more than two hours of sleep, we hitched our buggy to the pony and marched Eddie down the stairs. He was still blindfolded in the old baby shirt, his hands cuffed. Billy fried us some bologna in a skillet, flipping it like flapjacks, and boiled a pot of rye coffee. All three of us ate in silence. Young Eddie was grateful for the food. He masticated the bologna in a frenzy without a utensil. Unable to move all night, he'd pissed his trousers. The smell was unmistakable.

After the quick breakfast, we set him up in the wagon between us and removed the shirt from his eyes just long enough to toss a coat over his head. Bristles of daylight spread over the plain. Poor Silversmith was as worn down as an overworked mule and seemed to mope with every movement. Within the hour, we'd driven to the far north side of the city along a lonesome stretch of the Missouri River.

I stepped off the rig and looked out at the sluggish water, frozen in some spots and running free in others. Could smell the river in the gelid air. Billy and I both tied on bandanas to hide our faces. Billy took the coat off Eddie's head, unlocked his manacles, and told him to step down. The kid hesitated.

"It's all right," I told him. "Your papa came through. We're turning you loose."

Eddie blinked his eyes as if he'd never seen creation. A blind man healed. He was wobbly on his feet as he got off the wagon seat. I thought he might run away. Instead he walked right up next to me and stood rubbing his head.

I stared at the water. "Do you know where you are, kid?"

Eddie looked around. He looked at me, my face covered with the bandana.

"You got your bearings about you?" I asked again.

Eddie pointed. "That's the Missouri right there."

"Across the way is Iowa. If you head back south, you'll get to the city in about two hours on foot. Think you can manage that?"

"I think so. Give me another cigarette, would you?"

I gave him three. "For the long walk."

Eddie lit one and started off toward home. "So long, fellows," he said.

I looked behind me. I wanted to shake the young man's hand. He had the nerve of a man twice his age. Seeing him go was nearly a sad affair. No need to get gushy.

"So long, kid," I said.

XVI

THE BASEMENT FLOOR of Sal Abbott's grocery was packed dirt, and the walls were painted cinder blocks. Tom Dennison came to the bottom of the stairs in his Palm Beach suit and wool topcoat, with smoke wheeling off his cigar. He took a pair of dress gloves from his pocket and fit them over his hands.

The two whiskered gangsters who killed old man Abbott and knocked me senseless were digging a hole in the dirt floor in the back of the cellar. They'd drug Sal's body down the steps and left him lying face down by their growing pile of dirt. Both of their jackets were off and their shirtsleeves rolled to the elbow. They took turns making the hole with a grain shovel they'd taken off one of the walls upstairs. While one labored with his feet in what was to become Sal's grave, the man I'd thumped in the head and throat stood smoking and spitting. He couldn't quit rubbing his neck and had a rough time breathing. He wheezed like an asthmatic and was wobbly on his feet.

The cellar was barely tall enough to walk through without stooping. A pair of barn lanterns lit up the room as dimly as a cathedral during a vigil.

Billy and I sat in chairs in the center of the cellar with our hands bound behind our backs and potato sacks over our heads.

I had been unconscious for some time, and when I woke I couldn't see anything through the sack material. My mouth was full of blood. I tongued the cavity in my gums where two of my bottom teeth were missing. Billy was in his striped pajamas, having been hustled out of one of the beds at The Berryman Club, where he'd just finished making it with a whore named Lulu or Tulip or Lily—the namesake of some kind of flower or another. He'd been sucking down a warm beer and commenting on the calming effect of the Japanese comet fish in the tiny glass globe on her nightstand when a pair of masked strong-arms with oily revolvers broke into the room. They grabbed him up, threw a potato sack over his head, and tossed him in the back of their wagon for a ride over to the south-side grocery where he now sat beside me with a urine stain on his crotch.

For a long moment Dennison considered the setup and gnawed on his cigar before he finally drew up a third chair and sat down.

"Take those bags off their heads," he said to one of his henchmen, who went over and yanked off our potato sacks.

My eyes blinked wildly as they adjusted to the light and the surroundings of the cellar: Billy tied up next to me, Dennison sitting before us in a split-bottom chair, the goons digging the hole in the back of the basement by Sal's corpse. The old man had been tossed on the ground as if he was nothing more than a piece of luggage. I nearly started to cry but held back my tears as I looked up at Dennison and said nothing.

"Mr. Dennison?" Billy said. "Thank God. Hey, Tom, you know me. Tell your boys that you know me. We're old pals. If this is about the whores, I'll stop. I swear to God, I'll stop."

"I'll be with you in a minute, Bill, but first I want to have a word with Pat here," Dennison said and unfolded a sheet of paper from his breast pocket. He held it up in the air for me to see. It was the contract I signed with Mr. Nesselhous about the payments on our butcher shop. I sat stoic, spit a clot of blood.

"Evening, Pat, how's your week been?"

"You've come to kill me," I said calmly.

"Balderdash. Like Billy here said, we're all of us old pals. You, me, your sister Sallie. I just wanted to have a little heart-to-heart."

"The murderer's a comedian," I said.

Dennison smiled. "A murderer, you say? And a comedian, too? Hell, the only thing that's funny is the way you young fellows repay favors these days. It's not enough that you're living in a new house and running your very own business paid for by my dime, but you got to have your morals to go along with it and now the name-calling, too?"

"You killed old man Abbott," I said and looked again at Sal's body. The two goons had dug the hole about three feet deep. They must've thought that was a sufficient depth for a makeshift grave as they pulled the corpse into the hole by the legs and began to fill it back up with dirt. The first man used the shovel while the other brought over one of the barn lanterns and set it down on the ground next to Dennison's chair.

"That was unfortunate," Dennison said with some measure of agreement. "And believe you me, I'll be having a long talk with my boys about it after I'm done with our little chat."

The goon who'd carried over the lantern dropped a cigarette on the ground and squashed it out with his shoe. Dennison looked him up and down. His left eye was puffy and nearly closed shut from my first swing, which had sent him falling backwards into the stack of fruit cans. The lump on the side of his head would need to be lanced before it went away.

"Looks like you gave this one quite the polt," Dennison said to me.

The goon with the busted head patted at the knot in his temple that'd swollen up as juicy as a hunk of fruit. He opened his mouth to speak, which looked about as painful as anything he'd attempted in his whole life. His muffled voice made it sound like he was talking through a muzzle. He couldn't pronounce but a syllable at a time. "Kid's a bull. Hits harder than all creation."

Dennison said, "He could have your job if he'd learn to make better use of his talents."

"You're a bastard," I said. "And your thugs are cowards."

Dennison turned back to look at his man shoveling the dirt. "Cowards? I'm told that old Sal was armed."

I shook my head.

"Oh, he wasn't? My men said he had a shotgun and was threatening to use it."

I said, "He was eighty years old and near blind in both eyes, and you know it. Man could barely see well enough to make change from his till. Armed or not, he couldn't have hit a bull's ass if he tied off the end of that shotgun to its tail with a piece of string."

Dennison laughed, but not out of humor. "God, love you, Patrick. Tied up to a chair with your teeth smashed in and still as chatty as a dinner guest."

I spit more blood. "And you're still making fun before the man's even in the ground."

Dennison clucked his tongue. "Well, you're the one who ran into his store when you knew trouble was a-following. I'd say that makes you just as responsible as me."

"If you wanted to talk with me, why did you need to run me off the streets anyhow? You know where I live and you know where I work and I'm not running away."

"Because I want you to listen. And you haven't been listening for a good long while now," Dennison said and leaned back in his chair. He handed his cigar to his goon and hollered up the basement steps as if calling out for an absent waiter. "Hey, Ed? Ed, come on down here and say your piece to these boys."

Heavy footfalls sounded from the floor above. The wooden ceiling creaked under the weight of the man moving about in the grocery. Then the footsteps came down the aching steps. Edward Cudahy, with his chins shaking above his collar, made his way into the cellar with no lack of effort. He carried a peg lamp in a candle socket, holding it by its drip pan.

He surveyed the scene. "Sakes alive, what has this come to?"

"What was needed," Dennison said.

"This is too far."

"Things got a little out of hand, I'll admit."

Cudahy looked at the man filling the grave. An arm and a foot were sticking out of the dirt. "Who's that got killed?"

"Some nobody grocer," Dennison said without a shred of pity.

Cudahy couldn't stop shaking his head. "All of this over a piddly little butcher shop?"

"No, Ed. Over principle."

"Principle?" I said. I could barely hold my head up. "Some men never have any."

Cudahy said, "I want you to explain something to me, Pat."

I stared down at my shoe tops. "I'm not saying another word. You already went and made your mind up about things, so I won't give you the satisfaction."

"You want this resolved, don't you?" Dennison asked me.

"You only gave me a few months before you started trying to shut me down. It takes time to get a business off and running. You ought to know that better than anyone."

"A few months?" Cudahy said. "That's how far behind you are on your payments."

"It's over, Pat," Dennison added. "Time to face facts. Either way you leave this cellar, dead or alive, that shop is no longer yours."

Billy squirmed in his chair, working his shoulders as if trying to free his hands. One of Dennison's goons stepped forward and pistol-whipped him across the face. Billy let out a whimper. A quick line of blood dribbled down from his eyebrow.

"Sit still," the goon said and spit a long string of tobacco juice on his face.

"Alright, that's quite enough. Man's not going anywhere. Can't you see he already pissed himself?" Dennison snapped. He stood, untied Billy's hands, and handed him the folded square of a hand-kerchief from his pocket.

Billy wiped the blood and spit from his face. "What's this all about?"

"I already told you once to hush up, or do you want another smack?" Dennison said and sat back down. He nodded to one of his men who, in turn, shuffled over behind Billy's chair. Redirecting his attention to me, Dennison continued, "This is the last thing I wanted. But you broke faith with me. We had an agreement. But what good are agreements if you cast the terms to the four winds and turn down a perfectly good offer to break even when you know you'll never do anything but keep on losing money? My money."

"I thought you were a businessman," I said. "I never agreed to work for a gangster."

Dennison craned his head around the room to look at his men with a smile, amused by the word. "There you go again with the name-calling. Gangster? You mean like a hoodlum?"

"You know exactly what I mean."

"No, I beg your pardon, but I surely don't. A gangster is some-body who brings society down. A gangster is somebody who uses violence because they don't know no other way."

"What would you call this?" I asked.

"A powwow," Cudahy said.

Dennison hunched forward in his chair until I lifted my head. He said, "A gangster is somebody who goes looking for commotion. For trouble. That ain't me. No, sir. I'm for peace and order. A gangster? All he wants is to disturb the peace. But a man, even the most peaceable man, he knows there can't be peace so long as he's getting kicked by his pals. And no man who calls himself a man can stand there and take a kicking and not do anything about it. You, Pat, you're more a gangster than anybody in this room. And you surely ain't no man."

"Tom, whatever's been done, we can repair it," Billy said.

Dennison snagged his handkerchief out of Billy's hand. "I thought I told you twice now to shut your trap. Boy, I got one of you who don't listen and the other who crosses the fella who pulled him out of his no-avenue stockyard job and put him all the way up in his own shop, no questions asked. Now, what kind of sense does that make?"

Billy sat there silently, afraid to speak again.

"Crossed you?" I said. "I haven't crossed you in any way."

"You haven't been able to pay me in three months. You might as well have pickpocketed me on the corner," Dennison said.

"I'm only trying to do what's right," I said and looked again at Dennison. "What's good. You say I'm not a man. But what is a man if he doesn't stand by his principles?"

Dennison bolted out of his chair and slapped it across the room. "Principles, you say? What, you got principles now of all sudden? That's news to me. I'd say your principles changed mightily once you got what you wanted. And what did you want? You wanted what every man wants. A good job with good pay, a home for his wife and kids, a high place in society. And I gave it to you. Gave it to you better and faster than you could ever get it on your own. And you took it. Yessiree. You took it, and you stood there and shook my hand knowing it was that hand that gave it to you. And now that you've gone and got yourself tied up to a chair and facing your losses, you want to talk principles? Well, let me tell you something, Paddy. Principles are all well and good if they are unwavering principles. But that ain't what you got. What you got is an elastic conscience,"

Dennison said as he paced the cellar, his hands flying about in the air until he calmed himself.

He took in a deep breath, crammed his hands back into his pant pockets and continued with more reserve, "And you say you're a man. You ain't no man, and there are all kinds of men. A man might be any other breed of filth so long as he's not a double-crosser. But that's exactly what you are. And then you have the nerve to sit there and call me a gangster?"

Dennison went to the other side of the cellar and picked up the chair he'd launched across the room. He set it back down and was about to take a seat again when, instead, he drew his gold-plated pistol from his shoulder holster. He cocked it with a gloved hand and pressed it hard against my forehead. I winced and closed my eyes. One of Dennison's goons grabbed Billy by the shoulders and held him down in his chair. He tilted Billy's head back as the second man came up and forced his pistol barrel into Billy's neck.

"Mr. Dennison, please," Billy begged, "please, this ain't the way. I didn't have nothing to do with this. I'm just an employee. Whatever Pat did, he did of his own accord. I ain't got no say over the books or nothing."

"Of his own accord?" Dennison repeated the words. "Wasn't you the one who told me you wanted to go into business with him right down the middle? A fifty-fifty split, you wanted? But now that you got the steel on your skin, all of this has nothing to do with you?"

"I'm not afraid of death," I said, my eyes still closed.

"I'm sure you ain't. If you were, you'd be apologizing like Peter after the third cock crowed," Dennison said and momentarily took his gun off my forehead. "But at least you're finally sticking to something, late though it is. But what about your doting wife and your pretty little baby girl?"

"I got a wife and kids, too," Billy pleaded.

"Lord have mercy, Billy, you ain't got neither," I said. "You'd say just about anything to miss the bullet, wouldn't you?"

Dennison sighed. "You know kid, with all your yattering I'm more inclined to put you on the slab."

Billy cried as a stream of urine ran out of the bottom of his left pajama leg, soaked his sock, and began to puddle on the floor. "God, please. Honest out, I didn't know Pat wasn't paying you. If I did, I would've acted against it."

"Goddamn, he's wetting himself again," the second goon said and lifted his Bostonians one at a time to examine their soles as if he'd just stepped in a horse apple. "These are Martin's Scotch grain."

Dennison chuckled briefly. "Quit your assing around and act like a man who can afford a second pair for chrissakes."

The goon shook his head and reapplied his pistol to Billy's neck.

"So how about it, Pat?" Dennison asked. "You still ready to find out what's on the other side of this life or have you changed your mind again?"

I opened my eyes slowly. "Alright, goddamnit. I'll sell the place. I'll go back to work for you doing whatever you want. For my daughter and wife, I swear it."

Dennison tilted his head and cocked the hammer of his pistol. At the sound of the tiny click, I closed my eyes and braced for the bullet, but none came. Dennison lowered his pistol, stuffed it back in his holster and snapped the button shut. In turn, the goons released their grip on Billy and holstered their guns.

"Well then, it's settled. That wasn't so hard was it?" Dennison said, sniffled twice, and readjusted his felt hat straight on his head. "Everybody deserves a second chance, but nobody deserves a third. You just remember that, Pat. You remember that Tom the gangster gave you a second chance and spared your life on this night."

I panted and heaved but could not raise my head.

"Pat, tell me you're hearing me."

"I'm hearing you," I said.

Dennison turned to his men. "Alright then. It's getting on past my bedtime."

He pulled his overcoat back on his shoulders and bounded up the cellar steps two at a time to the main floor of the grocery with Edward Cudahy lagging behind.

XVII

I DID NOT arrive at the idea to kidnap Cudahy's son through fevered dream or criminal inspiration of any stripe. Rather, I came upon the notion by accident and from the most unlikely of sources—Billy's younger sister, Mabel.

For a time after we lost our butcher shop and I lost my family, Billy and I took to the rails. We hopped a train as it was leaving the Burlington Station, carrying only a carpetbag of clothes and a jar of inky brandy. My shirt pocket was stuffed with six cigars, my money purse tucked into my waistband along with a piddly five-shot revolver. We stowed away in the caboose with ten yellow cows headed for auction and slept against a sack of potatoes the whole night long.

I didn't wake until the train was somewhere east of Des Moines. For breakfast I skinned two of the potatoes, and we ate them raw off the blade of my hawksbill knife like apple slices. The cows' refuse filled the car with a humid green stink so pungent it was near poisonous. Billy and I stuck our faces out of the cabin slats to keep from turning our stomachs inside out.

The train chugged on and on across aprons of swaying corn and low oat fields and hard swaths of what seemed eternal nothingness, the forever machine of tomorrow and tomorrow again. At a junction stop in Chicago we switched trains. We had enough coin between us to share a cab in a Pullman sleeper on the Northeastern Railway. In the dining car, we ordered à la carte service of beef tongue and insipid soup and sunshine cake with orange icing and discussed our prospects. An elderly Negro with a starched porter uniform served us with great dexterity, bringing forth the tasteless broth without spilling a drop. Billy lapped the pale soup. It rippled in the bowl as the train clunked over the rails.

I cut my meat furiously. It was tough as firewood.

"We had some high times, you and me," Billy said out of nowhere.

"It wasn't always so. We had more bad than good between us."

"We'll have us high times again. You'll see."

I stared out the window. Telegraph wires as taut as catgut zoomed along. "Running that butcher shop with you was the happiest I ever was."

Billy set down his utensils and asked the porter for two brandies. The porter disappeared behind a curtain and returned a moment later with two stemmed glasses that held a scant amount of liquor.

I dumped the brandy into my mug of beer.

Billy acted in kind and we toasted our mugs. The train roared onward.

"Just you wait till we get to Philadelphia," he said. "My sister will put us up for a couple nights until we get our bearings. A change of scenery will do us both a heap of good."

I rolled the idea around. "How's she for looks, your sister?"

"Don't get started on that. Haven't seen her since I was twelve and she was in pigtails. It might be maybe that she's humpbacked or hog-bellied or hog-tied in a bad marriage or all three at once. All I'm saying is that she's family and we need a place to stay."

"That's what hotels and brothels are for."

"We haven't the money for that."

I nodded. "We haven't anything, friend."

We arrived in Philadelphia two days later. A vivid sash of dying light over the dusking hills. Lightning bugs as fat as bumblebees emerged from the cracks in the sidewalk, from their daytime slumber under the grasses. Billy wore a porkpie with a blue band. Me, a sweat-stained plug hat and a sports shirt with the sleeves rolled to the elbow.

A torrid sunset pushed the mercury past ninety even though daylight was already on the thin. We hired a hackney cab to take us to Billy's sister's place, a woman's home on the north side of town. Pink smoke rose from the evening chimney so lopsided it appeared ready to topple. The hitch rail before the porch was commandeered by a row of drooping and dying sweetbriar hanging in handled pots.

"Where in the hell do they put their horses?" I asked Billy as I considered the sign in front of the house: GERMANTOWN WORKING

GIRLS' HOME. FOUNDED 1891 BY THE YOUNG WOMEN'S CHRISTIAN ASSOCIATION.

I looked to Billy. "A working girl's home? Like a whorehouse?"

"It's the opposite of a whorehouse."

"A kind of nunnery then, is it?"

Billy shook his head. "No. It's like a boardinghouse for dames."

We climbed the steps and rasped the door with the brass pineapple knocker. The house matron, Miss Leslie, greeted us glumly. Her prematurely gray hair was wispy as spider silk, and her bosom sagged despite the stiff support of her ribbed blouse. Billy crushed his hat in his hands and told her he was kinfolk of Miss Mabel Cavanaugh, his kid sister.

"We normally don't allow men on the premises," matron Leslie said. "Your sister has just returned from work. I'll call on her if you both would be so kind as to wait on the porch."

I chimed in. "We're not stray dogs, ma'am."

"I beg your pardon."

"We've come a long way, miss. All the way from Nebraska we've traveled to pay family a visit. Four long days by train and none the less weary for it. I for one would much appreciate being able to sit in your parlor out of the heat and rest my feet if you'd be inclined to a little hospitality."

The matron frowned more pronouncedly but opened the door all the same. "Please remove your shoes before entering. I don't want mud drug in on our carpets."

Billy and I followed the matron inside the parlor after shrugging off our caked boots and set about to sitting on a chaise lounge in our stinking humid socks. One of the female residents who earned her keep as the housemaid brought us each a glass of sun tea. I thanked her as genuinely as I could.

I drained two glasses of that tea by the time Billy's sister came down the spiral staircase. We both stood to greet her. First I saw her feet, then the rustle of her floor-length dress, then her bosom, and finally her face. I didn't know what to expect. Maybe a stout plump girl with the disposition of bad weather if genetics had anything to do with it.

Instead I was quite taken. Mabel resembled Billy about as much as Aphrodite resembles a bulldog. She wore a dress covered with a white pinafore and her hair was done in ringlets like a schoolgirl, with a curled lock over her left earlobe.

Billy kissed his sister on both cheeks and hugged her into a spin around the room. She squealed with delight and begged her brother to put her down before she got woozy. I watched with my hat held behind my back. Billy made the formal introductions.

Mabel extended her hand.

I shook it daintily. "You shore are pretty, Miss Mabel."

Billy groaned.

Mabel waved a hand toward the dining room. "You should stay for dinner. Both of you."

I massaged my hat brim. "Your superintendent doesn't seem too keen about that. She hardly let us inside the house in the first place."

"Miss Leslie? Oh, she's a soft spot once you get to know her."

"Well," I said, "if you can arrange it, we'd both be mighty grateful."

Billy sniffed the air. "Yeah. We're famished. What's cooking?"

"Pepper pot," Miss Leslie said from the entryway. She'd appeared without warning, her hands folded piously across her coatdress.

"Couldn't be any worse than the soup we had on the train," I said graciously.

The matron seemed to soften, but not by much. "Our evening meal begins at six o'clock sharp. If you two gentlemen can find time enough to wash up before then and illustrate good table manners, you'd be welcome to join us. If you cannot abide by decent protocol, I will have you expelled from our table posthaste."

To pass the evening after supper, Mabel insisted I take a coach ride with her through the north side of the city. Billy had rushed out of the house as soon as the meal was finished. He said he was off to find a grog shop for the night and if I wanted to find him I'd have to come looking. I laughed at that and escorted Mabel out of the house. We hired an idling carriage parked across the lane. Together, as the sun westered toward setting, Mabel and I toured Germantown in a runabout shaped like a piano box with an open roof.

The seats were fashioned of fine goat leather. Even bouncing over chuckholes in the street was no strain on our pleasure. The reinsman wore a stovepipe with a stick of tallow balanced on its crown, stuck to the hat's felt with melted wax like a birthday candle atop a cake. I wondered if the wick was ever lit until, at the snap of a match, the driver reached up and ignited a flame without taking off his hat. It served as a kind of comic lantern when there was, as of yet, no need for light.

Mabel pointed out a few sights along the way. We rumbled along through the outskirts of town, riding over a covered mill bridge that spanned a catfish creek. I nodded at every sight, saying little as I continually thumbed my pipe. Color fell out of the sky. A middle moon rose over the darkening plain, faint as a thumbprint on glass. I draped my cow coat over Mabel's shoulders, and she thanked me. The coach turned left on Washington Lane. The avenue was freshly paved. A bucket of wildflowers dangled from every streetlamp.

Mabel asked, "How is it you came to know my brother?"

"We ran a butchery together for a few sweet months."

"That I know. I mean originally. How did you meet?"

I cogitated, my memory thin. "Billy got into a scuffle with a couple of stockyarders this one time. I stepped in to break it up, but he still took one hell of a lump."

"He always was one to attract trouble."

I stoked my pipe. A promenade of ash trees blocked out the sky.

"He dotes on you," Mabel said.

I studied Billy's sister as if taking inventory of a store shelf. She was unlike Hattie in every manner. She kept her figure concealed in deep clothing: a high collar, a pigeon breast blouse, skirt tails long enough to sweep the floor. Her hair, dark as deep soil, was piled atop her head over a horsehair pad, and her apple-shaped face was scrubbed clean, free of paint. I knew her to be a learned woman, one who could play the piano from sheet music, farm a garden three seasons out of four, balance arithmetic in her head without a pencil. Billy had told me that a couple times a week she recited epic poetry to the other women of her house for their after-supper entertainment, a crackling fire in the communal parlor.

She scared me to death.

I wanted to tell her so. But airing that emotion in the back of the carriage would've been like fire riding a breeze. Plus, there was no brandy in my blood. I looked at Mabel again. I would have smashed a whole planet for a kiss. Instead I sank in my seat, feebly smoked my pipe, wished the horses would drive us off a steep embankment.

Mabel caught me staring at her bosom. "You're a wolf," she said playfully.

"I'm worse than that."

"There's nothing hostile in you. You've a gentle soul."

I thought: look harder. I said nothing.

"You don't say much, do you?"

"I never was any good at cutting up touches."

"We ought to talk about something. It's such a lovely night."

"I'm sorry," I said. "I'm a damn awful date on wheels."

Mabel giggled. "A date, Pat Crowe?"

I shied at her laughter. "Your brother wouldn't be too fond of me calling it that."

"What do you think of him?"

"He's as silly as a hen wearing a bonnet."

"Be serious. I've not seen him much since we've grown, and his behavior, his whole life really, is a mystery to me. I'd like to know about him."

"I am serious when I say he's silly."

"Silly how?"

I moved my pipe around in my mouth. "I don't know. Goofy, you might say. None else like him. He'd go raking a pond at night to get the moon out of it."

"There's not much space in him for comedy. Not even as a child there wasn't."

"I don't mean it like that."

"How do you mean it?"

"Him and me? We're not good men, Mabel. Neither of us cottoned much to the better ways of the world. Me especially. Most everything I've ventured has become a terror."

Mabel put a gloved hand over mine. I frightened at her touch but had never been more thankful for such a simple gesture.

"You're trying to paint yourself a way that's just not in you."

I considered that. "I've never been one for doodling it up otherwise."

"What do you think of yourself? Really?"

I stoppered my pipe. "I'm divided of opinion."

"There's strength to be found in pain."

"There's only pain to be found in pain. That's why they call it that," I said and looked toward the heavens. The carriage rolled on under a strangely green night sky. The pair of big Clevelands driving the wagon snorted chilled air. The candle burning away atop the coachman's stovepipe was melted to the nub. Wax ran down the sides of his hat like dove shit streaks a building front. We were less than a mile away from returning to Mabel's women's home.

"We've all committed sin. We were born into original sin," Mabel said consolingly. "All we have to do is ask God for forgiveness and we shall be saved. We can thank his son Jesus for giving his life for ours."

I brayed. If I never again heard talk of a divine inscription upon my life and all the hokum of salvation that came along with it, it would be a reprieve truly worth thankfulness to a deity. I said, "God doesn't give a good goddamn what we do. Anyone who thinks otherwise is operating under ego I cannot fathom."

Mabel took away her hand. "You talk like a nonbeliever."

"I talk like I got brain working behind my tongue."

A full minute of silence passed. Wheel spokes rumbled over cobblestone.

"Maybe I had you figured wrong," Mabel said.

"Best not to figure me at all," I replied.

Mabel sniffled. She looked truly hurt.

"Bless your heart," I said and, this time, was the one to take her hand. "You're a good woman. A pure person. You don't deserve the doldrums of riding around a beautiful lot getting your spirit squashed by the likes of me."

Mabel straightened her posture. Her face was stoic. She was no hothouse flower. She stared at me hard. My disposition made no effect on her. "Billy told me you had a wife."

"And a child. Little Matilda."

"Were they not dear to you?"

"They were as dear to me as good weather," I said. "And as rare."

"Rare? How do you mean?"

"You don't get much of neither in Nebraska. Love or clear skies."

Mabel frowned. "You're a depressing sort."

I picked at my right thumbnail. My hands were shaking. "I suppose that might be one of the reasons why she left me then. Nobody likes being married to a rain cloud."

Mabel didn't know how to respond to that kind of sadness. There was no conversing with me. Everything I uttered came on a knife's edge and clipped all possibility of retort.

"I've had my fill of your gloominess!" she shouted and covered her face.

I sat solemnly. I hadn't wanted to turn her away. Sometimes subrogating my sour mood meant others had to get in the way of it. She was a good woman. A beautiful creature. I pulled in my lips like a mule showing its teeth. "I like having you around."

The carriage came to a traffic stop. Mabel blew her nose in a hanky and drew my attention to the second house from the railroad station. It was a double estate built of imported sandstone with a piazza on three of its sides. The yard was guarded by a brick wall overrun with crawling ivy, the yard populated with so many evergreens that all the second-story windows were blocked from the street view.

"What a sad sight," Mabel said, staring at the home.

"I'm sorry if I've depressed your mood," I said.

"Not you. That house. Did you ever hear the story of Charley Ross? The four-year-old boy who was kidnapped?"

"Not that I can recall."

Mabel pointed to the house. "They kidnapped him right there. In his own front yard while he was out playing with his brother."

I spat over the side of the carriage as it rolled forward again. "Four years old?"

"They never found him, either, the poor dear. Just heartbreaking. His father might've got him back, but a big inspector from New York came down and told Mr. Ross to ignore the demand for money. He promised Mr. Ross they'd get his son back and punish the fellas who took him, without having to fork over a dime."

"But that inspector never made good on that, huh?"

"The kidnappers were keen to his plan. He planted a trick ransom sack, but they didn't rise to the trap. Lord in heaven, what a sad story. The whole city was in a tizzy. Men didn't go into work, just to join the search party. Every police officer in Philadelphia worked double shifts trying to find the stolen child."

I sparked my pipe again. "Their plan was doomed from step one."

"How do you mean?"

"When it comes to awful doings, it's best to do them awful fast," I said and shook out the match just as it burned my fingertips. "They ought to have made sure the boy's father would deliver the coin from the outset and not blab to the bluecoats."

"You're a cull, aren't you?" Mabel said as our wagon pulled up to the front of her women's home. "Their fault wasn't the plan. It was in them. What kind of person abducts a child? I've never heard of such evil except for that one time."

I agreed halfheartedly, bid her goodnight as she leapt off the wagon. I flattened out some money for the driver and then decided to follow Mabel to her doorstep. She kissed me on my cheek and thanked me for the ride. I removed my hat and wiped out the inside with a bandana, my hair matted and slick. I'd sweat a line clear through my riband. Replacing it on my head, I asked if I might come in for a spell, have a cup of tea before parting.

Mabel smiled weakly. "Courtship isn't allowed inside of doors. We're not even supposed to be conversing with boys on the porch."

I swallowed. I'd ruined her impression of me in just under an hour, that much was clear. No matter. I bade her goodnight again and left the porch with little hesitation. I nearly caught myself skipping down the block. Billy's sister was one hell of a beauty, but there was beauty to be found elsewhere, and it wasn't in the folds of a dress or on the softness of scented skin. I was smitten, but not with Billy's little sister.

Inside me now was a strange kind of love, the love of a grand idea.

XVIII

DENNISON'S MEN RELEASED Billy and me from the grocery basement, and we staggered out of the cellar into a soggy dawn. A stippling rain fell faintly as a patter. We hobbled across town to our butcher shop. The sky streaked hard and glossy over the tin roofs of Sheelytown when a pair of men driving a team of ponies came to padlock the doors on our butchery. Gas streetlamps were still lit, giving off a brown glow. Smokestacks poured out plumes of coal exhaust. Telegraph wires and streetcar cables sagged over brick streets.

From an Albanian café across the street, we watched the men lower our sign. When we first entered the café, a row of cranky old men seated along the counter kept staring at us as if we'd killed one of their cousins. They all had scratchy whisk-broom beards and drank their fig wine as hot as coffee in handleless mugs. I ordered our drinks and stared back at them with the ferocity of a bobcat. When they saw I wasn't one that'd be easy to go around the stony yard with, they returned to their foreign babbling about Balkan politics and lemon soup recipes and Kosovo women, or so I imagined.

I'd gotten to know many of those Albanian types: the poor Aleksanders and haggard Blerinas who'd started to sprout in the neighborhood and came into our shop asking about any leftover animal intestines I was planning to throw out. They used lamb innards to make fried dishes with butter and cheese and corn flour. I caught them rummaging through our trash in the mornings and waiting in the alley behind our store in the evenings with hopes of snagging a good length of sheep gut to take home and dolly up into gutter soup. I hated them all with a purple passion. They wanted what I couldn't sell and nothing else. They could never pay for anything. Sometimes when the men got drunk enough on a hot day, they loitered around in front of our shop with their shirts off, and

Billy had to scare them away with a broom like they were nothing more than a huddle of pigeons.

I splashed a bit of specie on the counter for the drinks without caring to ask how much I owed. One of the old men sitting along the counter hollered at me in words I couldn't understand. I sat the glasses back down on the bar and kicked the man's stool out from under him. The man fell backwards and likely cracked his spine as hard as the cold floor was. I stared at his row of pals, waiting for any of them to make a move or say another word, whether I could understand it or not.

A moment passed and the entire café was silent. I felt awful as sin for acting the bully but didn't break my stare. These people had to beg for most of everything they got, and here I was lashing out at them when the poor bastards couldn't fill their coal boxes without trailing a delivery cart to pick up the loose briquettes on the street. I cleared my throat and helped up the old codger I'd kicked to the floor back onto his stool. I threw another handful of coinage on the counter and went over to the far end of the café with our drinks in hand.

Billy sat at a battered table by a grimy window. The tabletop peeled like old wainscoting and was sticky with spilt ale that probably hadn't been wiped up in weeks. I came over with the whiskey and beer and continually dipped the end of my kerchief in a glass of celery tonic. I rubbed it against the growing bulb on my mouth where one of Dennison's goons had staved in my lower teeth. Billy was so tired he could've slept standing up like a horse. He was still in his pajamas covered by a long overcoat. His eyelids sagged, and I had to nudge him every few minutes to keep him awake. We had a smile of bourbon apiece and sipped tentatively from our cardboard containers of lukewarm beer.

I traced my finger around the rim of my beer and stared across the street at the building front that just yesterday was still our butcher shop. "Well, that's that, I suppose."

"I'd like to get on before the sadness sets in," Billy said.

I was just as exhausted. I dabbed my mouth again. "Stick around for a bit. I ain't got nothing left and I'd like someone to share the feeling with."

"That ain't true."

"It is true."

"You got you a wife and a kid. And a nice little house fixed up right."

I thought on it all a moment. I thought about it ten times a day, sometimes more. A year ago I was fresh off the train from my daddy's ranch in Colorado and living among a bunch of Chinese and Polish bachelors in a cold-water flat covered in silver radiator paint. There were still things to be thankful for, and I was ever mindful of them.

Billy looked at my mouth. "God, they really knocked your slats in, didn't they?"

I rubbed my wound with my kerchief. I wanted to respond and thought I had said something intelligible, but was just muttering to myself, brokenhearted.

"Old King Lear," Billy said and sipped from his beer. The men across the street had finally finagled our huge butcher shop sign into the back of the wagon and were covering it up with a piece of tattered tarp.

"You know Shakespeare?" I asked.

"It's just something my dad used to say whenever I was acting blue and crazed and crying the buckets. He'd say, 'Quit your bellyaching, King Lear, and get on.'"

I snorted angrily and spat on the bar floor.

After a moment, Billy asked, "You believe in God, Pat?"

"I guess I don't."

"Yeah, the more I see of this world the more I don't either, I reckon."

"I believe in porterhouse steak and good brandy and having a woman around to tell you she loves you even if she don't."

Billy raised his smudged glass of whiskey. "I'm thinking of marrying, myself."

"Marrying yourself, huh? I guess you're crazy enough."

"There you go making fun again when the mood ain't right," Billy said. "I'm telling you I got the itches for this Ukrainian gal I've been seeing over at the Oak Street House."

I nodded at Billy's crotch. From the way he'd been clawing at himself for the past months, either he had a cactus flower in his pants or had come down with syphilis from one of his many romps in the lesser houses across town. I said, "You ain't got the itches for her. You got the itches from her."

If Billy had been a foot taller and three sizes wider and had any other friend in the whole world, he'd have slugged me in the face for mouthing off. Instead all he could do was sit there disgusted and clammed up like a spurned sibling. I felt just plain awful.

"I'm sorry," I said after a moment. "You know I don't mean no harm."

"You sure are cruel when you want to be."

"It ain't my intent."

Billy took down the last of his whiskey.

I looked up at the counter. The old man I'd kicked off his stool was fumbling around with his fork like a toddler as he scooped up a bit of pale egg from his plate. If there was any better way of measuring sadness in the world, I couldn't fathom it.

"What's she like?" I finally asked when our drinks were gone.

"Who? Fannie?"

"Yes, her. The one you fancy marrying."

Billy shrugged. "She's got black hair."

I waited for more, but it never came. As if black hair was all I needed to know and all Billy was willing to tell. "Well, you're the poet between us. I'll give you that."

"Whaddaya want me to say? She was never one of those whores I used to see, like you might think. She's a class gal. Our first date was a picnic under a pecan tree. I don't know what else to tell, I suppose, other than she's picked my heart clean. So it's either we get married or I go around putting the blocks to every new big 'un they bring into the Russian part of town for the rest of my days, and I'm telling you I can't handle me the mastodon babes no more. I had a fit for them for a while, but that's all drained out of me."

I nodded solemnly.

"I really mean it. I really love her."

"I don't doubt it an inch," I said. "Maybe they'll write an old-timey tune about you two someday. 'Picnicking Under the Pecan Tree with You,' they'll call it. A duet."

"You're never serious about nothing."

"I'm serious about every lousy thing in this world."

"You sure got a way of hiding it."

"The day you get hitched, I'll be the first one to chapel. You're my only pal."

Billy waved me off. "You're giving me that eighth-avenue funny business."

"I ain't either. But just some couple hours ago you were ready to sell me out for death to save your own hide, or don't you remember?"

Billy sat unresponsive. He had on a pair of green-tinted spectacles a doctor prescribed to him for his syphilis.

He'd caught the French pox from a Ukrainian whore in an oriental bedroom, or so he had been fond of saying. As if the blight he'd contracted made him worldly. All he'd really done was fork over a few grungy coins a few too many times in the aptly named Burnt District, for he'd been burnt but good and would be on a regimen of mercury chloride and wearing green eyeglasses and slowly losing what was left of his already pocked mind for the rest of his days until the whole world was just a lesson learned far too late.

I giggled at the silliness of it all. Little pug-shaped Billy. The man would never again be able to sit in a chair for five straight minutes without clawing at his crotch. Now he was bent on getting hitched to the dame that gave him all the trouble to begin with. As if just in case the syphilis didn't stick with him long enough, that damn crazy bastard had it in his head to go off and wed the source. The penance the lonely suffer for their sins is far greater than that of the wicked.

My snickering soon turned to sadness.

I looked out the window and blotted my mouth again and set to sobbing.

Dawn had arrived in full.

Billy broke wind. The noise sounded like fabric tearing. We ordered two more beers and shared a kretek, which cracked like snapping wood with each inhalation, and said our quiet separate goodbyes to our butchery.

One of the men lowering our sign into the rubberneck wagon

across the street wore a thick beard on a string he'd most likely purchased out of a catalogue. It was a foot long and as fake-looking as a costume prop. They'd gutted the inside of everything but the wallpaper and tied it all down in the back of the wagon. Even the picture windows had been scrubbed clean of the painted lettering advertising our meats. The place looked as if it hadn't been occupied in years.

After the deed was done and the doors were chained shut, I bid Billy farewell and wondered for a moment if I'd ever see him again. Most of my goodbyes were a permanent circumstance. I hoped this wasn't one of them. I went down to the Missouri River by myself and sat on the bank for the rest of the morning. I sat thinking for a good long while under a full ailanthus tree with its roots coming out of the ground crooked as witch fingers and listened to the foghorn of a riverboat pulling off the dock and drank from a pocket bottle of brandy until I fell asleep in the mud.

I came home late that afternoon to find my brother-in-law Ernest sitting in a rocker on my front porch. Ernest was Hattie's elder brother by three years and made it his special commission to oversee her well-being, just as he had when they were children growing up together. His beard was cut like that of the apostles in church paintings, and his hair clipped short above the ear. A high-water cut, it was called. He wore a new orange felt hat that still possessed the fresh blocking of a recent purchase from a high-end department store. His gold watch fob looped across his waistcoat.

The no-good braggart put his every penny on his shoulders and always made fun of my working clothes: my old overshoes, my butcher's apron, the sleeve holders on my cheap long shirts that put me in company with bartenders and blackjack dealers, the sad bow tie that made me appear more Sunday-strip comical than small-business owner.

Ernest held out his initialed cigarette case as I approached the vine-covered porch. I gave no response to his gesture, and Ernest lit one for himself. I looked away and spit into the dust. The scratch of a match, the popping of a flame, and Ernest smiled.

"Heard you sold some good shoats last week," he said, rocking. He kicked up his boot heels on the porch rail.

I stood at the bottom of the steps with my fists clenched at my sides.

"Fetched a pretty decent price, I hear," Ernest continued, his cigarette sagging in the corner of his mouth and bouncing up and down with each word he spoke.

I stepped onto the porch. "Six hundred dollars in one chunk."

Ernest whistled as if getting ready to laugh.

"That's twice what the others is getting," I said.

"Yeah. Some good money. A helluva lotta money for a butcher to make. Maybe you ought to sell everything you have now, shop and all, while it's still yours to sell. That's right. Yup. I heard about that offer you had to give it all up. The Cudahy company. Now there's a business for you."

"I did sell it. Just this morning I watched them take my sign down."

"How much did you get for it?"

"Nothing," I said.

Ernest had himself a big chuckle. "Nothing? How far in debt were you?"

"I'm not in any debt."

"For now."

"Not ever again."

Ernest couldn't quit chuckling. "You're a smart boy. A damn smart boy. Smart with hogs and cows and smart with women, too," he said, suggesting his sister's unhappiness. He reared back in the rocker and tapped on the glass of the bay window of our pink house, where little Matilda could be heard crying and Hattie trying to coo her.

"A smart man with women," I said as if musing over a philosophical thought. "I guess maybe so, especially after nobody else wants them."

That comment brought Ernest to his feet in a rush. He tossed his cigarette into the yard and came up a foot away from my face. I didn't flinch or blink, motionless as a horse who'd been struck over the head too many times. A baptismal silence between us.

"Thought that would keep you quiet," I said flatly.

Ernest brushed by me down the porch steps, cocking his hat.

"Tell you what, you'd better enjoy the rest of the day. It's the last one you'll ever have with your women, smart man."

"You ain't going to smoke me, so mosey off."

Ernest shook his head. "You just don't get it. Hat's coming home to live with our mama. Her and Matilda. She can't as well stick around here with a husband who stays out all night and loses his job and has no means to provide for her."

"Provide for her? She's got a roof over her head and food in the pantry. She's got more jewelry up there in her dresser than I got socks."

"She's coming home, and there's nothing you can do about it," Ernest said and stepped off the porch. Parked on the curb at the edge of our front yard was an uncovered wagon filled with a random assortment of things from inside our house: framed paintings, dresses, pots and pans, stacks of books, a reading lamp with the silly physique of a gooseneck, a rocking chair. I had come home in a stupor. Hadn't noticed the wagon at all until then. It was driven by a pair of old mules. A grease bucket hung from the rear axle.

I stared at the buckboard stoically and said out loud, as if to no one at all, "That's the second wagon I've seen taking away my stuff today."

Ernest sat down on the footboard. "You come around my sister or my niece ever again and I'll fix you good, you goddamn pig raiser."

I stormed into the house. Hattie was seated at the kitchen table, cradling our daughter as she fed from a liniment bottle. As soon as I entered, Hattie was on her feet and taking Matilda upstairs to our bedroom. Half of the house had been packed up, mostly smaller items that could fit into the wagon. Much of the furniture was still left, being too large to draw across town by a pair of decrepit mules.

I fumed and unwrapped a two-pound porterhouse from a parcel of butcher paper. The steak was as thick as an indexed atlas. The last cut of meat I'd taken from my shop before Cudahy's men padlocked the doors. I fried it up in a pie pan over the hob of our stove. There were no plates or cutlery left in the cabinets, and I ate the steak straight out of the hot pan with some yellow beans and drank a nibble of whiskey and had a smoke from one of the clay pipes I kept in a rack next to a crock of tobacco.

When I went upstairs to our bedroom, Matilda was asleep in her bassinet and Hattie was seated in front of her princess dresser, filling a large oat sack. She hadn't seen me enter. For a moment I leaned silently against the door frame. I swallowed some more of my amber and set the glass down on the dresser.

Hattie startled at the noise of the glass hitting the wood. "You scared me."

"Uh-huh," I said absently and continued to undress, lowering my suspenders in one fluid motion.

"You didn't come home at all last night, and I was worried sick. I had my brother come over to look after us."

I inserted myself into a flower-patterned chair and began to remove my socks. "It seems your brother is under the impression that you're moving back in with your mother and raising our child on your own."

"I am moving back in with her. For our daughter's sake."

"And then what? Back to gallivanting off with the mayor and whoever else?" I asked as I stripped down to my undershirt and began to root around in the drawers of Hattie's dresser, looking under the folded stacks of clothes.

"We got into this thing too young."

I continued to search the dresser. "Folks younger than us have got into it and stayed in it until the end of their days. That's what marriage is."

"What on earth are you looking for?"

I finally stopped my search upon finding a red bottle of laudanum. I held it up in an accusatory manner, pulled the cork, and dumped a long pour into the rest of my whiskey. I gulped it all down before it had a chance to mix. "That ought to numb me out so I can get a few winks, at least."

"Dr. Arnold prescribes that to me for my nausea and postpregnancy pains."

"Oh I know," I said and pulled off my undershirt. "He also prescribes Guckenheimer rye for breakfast and cherry rum for boredom."

Hattie slapped me hard across the face. "Don't you dare talk to me like that. You come home smelling like brandy or worse most nights."

I rubbed my cheek and peeled back the bedspread. "Well, if the truth is going to be had in the house with the serrated edge out, I thought I just might return a little of it your way."

"And what truth is that? That you're gone every day and I hardly get to see you except when you're belly-up at the dinner table or holed away in your den with your nose in a bottle?"

"It's called working. Working to make a living for you and me and our daughter."

"Sometimes I don't see you for so long I forget I'm married."

I lay down and pulled the blanket up to my chest. "Is that so? Well, you go on and live with your mama for a while. See how that life suits you. You'll be mending rags for clothes and cooking pottage in your bare feet."

Hattie tied her silk robe shut and put her hand over her mouth. "She's afraid. I'm afraid. You're in big trouble with the worst kind of men. I'm afraid that one day I'm going to be telephoned to the hospital, and when I get there you're going to be," she paused, unable to even speak the word. "I have nightmares. I wake up in cold sweats and—"

I flung off the blankets, went over to my wife, and held her at the shoulders. "I ain't in any trouble no more. I sold the place and all's square. I'll go back to work rounding up hogs and bartending for my sister or whatever else I can find, and there'll be food on the table, and you won't have to worry."

Hattie looked at me blankly.

"All of this, the, the—" I struggled to find the words. "The rococo furniture, the gold wallpaper, your little silk articles," I said and yanked a small drawer out of her dresser. I spilled its contents onto the bed: a sapphire ring, gold broaches, a pearl necklace, ribbon bows. "What's all the stuffing worth to you? Because it makes me sick. I got folks who come to me every day, widows with three sick kids, men with no jobs, nigras who can't spell their own names, all of them hungry and tired and broke and some of them homeless, and they come to me begging for a scrap of meat that's gone bad or anything else that I might throw out. And you know what? That'll never be us."

Hattie swiped the jewelry off the bed in a flurry, scattering it across the room. "You think that's what I'm talking about? Frills? You think that's why I'm leaving you? A week ago two men tried to break into our house looking for you. Then last night you go missing and you come home bloodied up and covered in mud, and you're telling me we're safe? I won't have our daughter living in danger. I won't live in it."

I lay back down in bed and folded my hands across my stomach. Matilda had woken from all the screaming and was now wailing herself. Hattie picked her up out of the bassinet and carried her around the room, cooing her and patting her bottom to calm her down.

"What do you want me to do?" I asked.

"Do? What have you been doing for months?"

"You're staying here. I'm your husband, and that's my little girl. I won't have everybody, especially your own brother, making fun, laughing at me."

"Oh you won't, will you? What do you expect people to think when a jane like me what's got everything marries a wet smack like you?"

I shot up from the bed and stood stammering. "A wet smack like me? So that's how it is, huh? Well, this wet smack put you in the nice pink house of your dreams and filled it up with whatever your heart desired. Now you want to flee out when I get in a little trouble? Well, I won't be the one to stop you."

Hattie hustled out of the room with Matilda in her arms, leaving the oat sack filled with her jewelry and all else behind. She bounded down the steps and out the front door, crying the whole way with me chasing behind. I stopped on the porch again and watched her sprint across the yard toward the wagon where her brother stood and helped her onto the bench seat.

They were just about to depart when I finally called out, "I failed."

Hattie and Ernest stared at me from their seat on the wagon.

I came closer. "I failed everything. I don't know what else to do."

Hattie was stunned.

"But, please, don't leave me. Not now. Not ever. I won't always fail. And I promise so long as you're with me, you'll never be scared or hungry or want for anything. I'll—" I tried to speak as I came up to the side of the wagon, but my voice trembled. My hands shook so fiercely I thought my whole body might tumble apart like some old machine once the last bolt came loose. My words came out in a gurgle.

I continued, "I'll be here at home more often. The only reason I haven't been lately is because I wanted to make a good life for you. But I didn't. God knows I failed about as bad as any man ever could. And you warned me. You knew better because you're smarter than me. My sister warned me. Hell, even the man who took it all away from me warned me. And I cocked it up. I cocked it all up. Everything. But not you and not Matilda. Those things I got right. You, you're the only good choice I've made since I got the harebrained idea to come out here in the first place. Hell, in my whole life."

I paused and tried not to cry. I tried to not even blink so I wouldn't push the tears out of my eyes. The emotion even shocked myself. I drew up my words slowly, as if I needed a windlass to get them to the surface.

"You know," I said, "the first time I saw you come into my sister's saloon, I thought I'd be the goddamn luckiest fella in the world if I even got the chance to talk to you. And I was right. And every morning when I wake up and when I come home from work, even when I'm tired and grouchy, when I just get to look at you for a moment from across the room, I still feel the exact same way. And I should've told you that every chance I got. But I didn't. I didn't, and I'm a fool to have waited this long to tell you how I've felt about you every day. But please, I'm begging you. Don't go now. Please, Hat, stay with me."

Hattie repositioned Matilda in her arms. She'd swaddled the child in a blanket and held her to her chest like a package. Ernest pulled back on the mule reins, anxious to depart.

"Why should I?" Hattie asked.

"Because I love you. I love you, and I love our little baby girl and—"

Hattie looked down the street as blankly as if there wasn't a thing left in the world. "I don't love you. Not anymore."

I didn't know how to respond to that.

All I could think of to say was, "How can you say that? Love just doesn't go away like it was never there."

"Well, if it's there at all anymore, it's only there for you," Hattie said coldly and told her brother to get those mules walking. Ernest sashayed the reins and the wagon rocked forward into a sullen march. I hollered and fell to my knees. I hollered at her to come back until the wagon disappeared around a corner at the end of our street.

Nightfall arrived before I was finally able to lift myself up from the grass and hobble back inside. I stood in the dark kitchen for a long time. Moonlight came through the windows. I memorized the items in the room as if I might never see them in that exact arrangement ever again: a half-open bag of flour on the counter, a dishrag neatly folded over the sink faucet, the pudding mold I used to put upside down on little Matilda's head like a giant hat to make Hattie laugh nearly every night at dinner.

How many times had she reached a wet hand into the wire sponge basket on the wall? How many times had she accidentally spilt coffee grounds around the range kettle and cleaned them up in the crumb pan now hanging from a nail by the back door? If she never came back, I'd never move an inch of it. I'd let it all sit untouched even if mushrooms started growing out of the walls. None of it would change until God himself came down to wipe it all away.

It took me an hour to climb the stairs.

I sat down to rest on the fourth step for nearly half that time.

Daybreak arrived by the time I made it to our bedroom.

The bags she'd been trying to pack during our argument were strewn across the bedspread and the floor. She'd been in such a rush. Such a rush. I lost my breath at the thought of her scrambling around just to leave me. She wanted to get away from me so fast she didn't even have enough time to pack all that she wanted to take. The thought of her running about madly just to get a few things together in a couple oat sacks broke my heart worse than any other image I'd ever suffered in my whole life.

Matted squares were still visible in the carpet where the pedal sewing machine I gave her last Christmas had stood just hours before. Even the potted plants she grew out of old oatmeal drums were gone. The wedding ring I took out on loan was left in a dish on the nightstand along with her house key.

Some of her long yellow hairs were shed on the bathroom floor. She had a ton of hair, and it was almost like living with a heavy cat. One morning not long ago, I found a loose strand in a clean stack of soup bowls and had a mind to toss the whole stack into the trash out of petty frustration.

What used to drive me mad suddenly put me on the floor.

Instead of sweeping the hairs up, I sealed them in an envelope to save. I knew it was ridiculous. But it also might prove to be the last piece of her I'd ever have. The things we leave behind end up staying with us longer than the things we keep.

I went into the bathroom and collapsed on the ground by the washtub I'd put in that past summer, just like I'd promised. I lay there for two whole days without sleeping or getting up to use the toilet. I remembered more from the past year with Hattie than I once thought I could retain about my entire life. And while all of it now seemed so abrupt, tender things had occurred between us, and they would always be tender in replay. I remembered the first time I came to see her after the night we met at the hotel dance, when I'd paid a man twenty dollars just to get her matching bow tie.

A week after that dance, I finally worked up the gumption to get dressed in my best pair of pants and boiled shirt and walk over without invitation to ask her out to dinner.

She had opened her door with a disturbed look but then said playfully, "Ah, if it isn't the lonely boy with the tabby cat. I thought you might come snooping around my door sooner or later. Well, what's it this time? Come to ask my hand in marriage again, have you?"

"No, Miss Hattie, I want to take you out to a restaurant."

"Now, I told you I hate being called Hattie."

I gripped my bowler as tightly as a boat wheel. "Right. Hat. I forgot."

Hattie leaned up against the door frame in her sleeveless pajama suit. "I sincerely doubt you've forgotten one thing about me."

I was staring at her bare armpit. "Well, I, maybe—"

"It's cute when you stutter, but you should stop while you're ahead."

I regained my bearings. "I'd like to invite you out to dinner, but I'd also prefer to not be terrorized about it."

"A real date, huh? Like music and flowers and the whole ball of wax?"

"Unless you're any good at frying pancakes. In that case we might just as well stay in."

Hattie looked at me cockeyed, the door still only halfway open. "I thought you said you didn't think of women as kitchen maids and laundresses?"

"You remembered," I said and couldn't quit smiling.

"Of course I remembered. That was pretty bold talk for a man who lives alone with a stray cat he named Marmalade."

"It seems you didn't forget much about me, either."

"Hard to forget a picture as sad as a man with no one to keep him company but a kitty."

"Yeah, I shot that cat."

Hattie laughed and opened the door fully. "Well, just don't stand there with your hat in your hand. Come in. I can't go out in my nightwear, and I need a few minutes to change."

There were only a few pieces of sad furniture in her flat. A wicker sofa with mismatched cushions and a torn armchair. Unpainted walls, no windows. A pair of oil lamps lit up the front room. A canvas sheet hung across the doorjambs of the adjacent bedroom.

"Where are we going?" she asked as she disappeared behind the sheet on the door.

I stood in the middle of the main room, afraid to sit down or look at the walls or do anything but breathe. "I thought maybe the Antler Inn. It's not far. We could walk from here."

Her muffled voice came through the walls while she was changing. "Pretty fancy spot for a bartender. Who knows, Pat Crowe. You just might surprise me, yet."

That day I'd thought: yes, there are still beautiful things left in this world.

How distant that all felt as I panted on the bathroom floor.

Like watching it from the surface of Neptune or farther.

Tomorrow I'd have the strength to track her down. I'd go straight over to her mother's house and ask her all the questions I never got a chance to ask. But morning came and the next one after that, and I still couldn't summon the energy to move. On the third day, I was able enough to slump down the stairs into the kitchen and sleep on an old straw tick on the floor. The house wailed and creaked against a hard wind. When I really thought about it, there were no more questions to ask, not of any kind. What I knew then, what I knew the moment I saw her leave on that wagon, was all there was to know.

XIX

By the time Eddie Junior wandered back home, Billy and I had ridden well outside the city limits. We headed southwest, stopping only to urinate and water our new ponies, a pair of rangy sorrels we bought from a Tennessean making his way to Canada. We said goodbye to Silversmith, gave her to the Tennessee man for free, and told him that she was worn out but one hell of a good horse if given a week of rest to recover.

We made camp for the night in Fillmore County along the bed of Tuttle Creek. Some eighty or more miles put between us and the Omaha police. A new moon in the winter sky, bright enough to cast nighttime shadows across the old snow. We hitched our ponies under a barren eucalyptus tree that even at full foliage in the summer wouldn't have provided enough shade for a vole. Billy counted out the gold from the ransom sack three times. He could not believe it. Nor could I.

Twenty-five thousand dollars.

I sat in amazement at our feat, staring out at the wide-open tableland in front of us as if it hadn't begun to exist until I saw it then, at that very moment. As if it were created for the first time by the simple fact it was I who was gazing upon it. I stood with my back against the eucalyptus, looked in the other direction. I knew no one was coming but couldn't help but to imagine that at any moment a horde of police detectives would appear over the sunken snowy hills behind us, thrashing their horses with all the vexed deviltry of the riders from hell at the coming of the rapture. I filled my huge pipe with fragrant orinoco from a pouch dangling around my neck and stood puffing away without a thought in my head save for Hattie and my daughter Matilda and what they might think of me now.

There was no smoke bloom of magic or poetry with all the combined alphabets of the world that could bring them back. Of this I was certain. I'd crossed the dark river and there was only darkness more on the other side. After a while I emptied my pipe by banging it against the tree and wished I could only do the same with all the stuffing in my mind.

If I had one last mercy yet to be granted in this life it would be to hit my head hard enough and empty it forever.

An hour before we made camp, we'd crossed the headwaters of the Big Blue River on an old scow toward sunset. A filthy Norwegian man with hair as blond as barn dust ran the ridgepole ferry with a pulley wheel at the cost of ten cents per passenger. Maybe I could find some semblance of peace with such a profession, if I got far enough removed from my home, too tired to share pleasantries with my fares, only the exchange of money for service as I tugged stranger after stranger over a slothful bend of wide and deep water from one bank to the next, helping them to their destinations and never knowing where they came from or where they were headed.

Together Billy and I ate a sad dinner of brown beans in tomato sauce from the grub box with ironclad biscuits we cooked over a small fire of pitch pine. We sat with our boot soles against the flames until they were sulfur hot, looking over the low piece of snowy prairie that was as gray and expansive in the moonlight as the sea under storm clouds. The smell of new snow had been in the air all day. When it finally arrived, it fell all through the night like a featherbed ruptured. I sipped from my usual vessel of nourishment: a two-gallon jug of whiskey strong enough to polish a stove.

After supper we melted snow for drinking water in the same frying pan we'd used to brown the biscuits, and let our ponies drink to their hearts' content before filling our canteens for the long ride ahead of us tomorrow. I spread some hay on the ground once my head was misty with whiskey and rolled up in a horse blanket and closed my eyes.

Come daybreak the blanket was crusted in frost, and my eyelids were starchy with ice. We rose at five, breakfasted on more beans and scorched wheat coffee, cleaned and harnessed our horses, and were riding at full tilt by first light.

"Ought to pass into Kansas by sundown," Billy said as we started out our gallop.

I nodded. Every rod we passed was only another stretch of state

I'd never see again this side of the bourn. For lunch I shot a couple prairie chickens wandering around by the rim of a gulch. I fired both barrels of my shotgun at once and scattered buckshot all over a half acre of ground knowing that if I missed once I wouldn't get a second try. Billy set a pot of water to boil while I plucked the dead birds and put them in the pot with their legs dangling out of the lid and looked over the cow yard of a nearby farm. A half mile out, an old homesteader was using dynamite to blow up tree stumps.

I remembered the story of a young boy I once knew back in Colorado when I was just a boy myself. Bluebonnet was his family name. The boy's given one I couldn't recall. What I never forgot was how one day that boy was playing in his father's barn and pocketed one of the percussion caps from a dynamite bundle kept hidden high up in the haymow. Later that day, after he got into some trouble with his mother, she bent the boy over her knee and set to spanking him when she hit the percussion cap in his back pocket and blew them both up in the front lawn. All that was left of the clothes on the boy's dead body were the wrist cuffs of his flannel shirt.

The isolated details we remember and the grand entities we don't.

I felt for a moment as if I might cry, but was too bitter for tears.

No sir. I would not show the blue feather ever again.

I shook off the image with a pull from my whiskey jug and a good smoke from my pipe, drawing on it heavily as I canvassed the land ahead. Antelope were nosing around a stunted cornfield covered with winnows of snow, hoping to find a frozen ear of broom corn left behind from last autumn's harvest. Socks of old husks littered the cornfield like scraps of trash. The antelope were thin and looked as starved as alley pups, eating nothing but bark and dead grass in those lean months. The scheme of life, even for the foredoomed of earth who know nothing of God, is to create the idea of God in their own trampling. Northern winds were whooping and snow eddied off the ground like little white dust devils.

We rode on into the warming afternoon, passing towns that were nothing more than a flagpole and a few shanties. What both of us would've given for a night in a nice hotel with oak floors and floral wallpaper with a roaring fireplace in the lobby, listening to a clumsy piece of sunshine being banged out on an upright piano while we split a bottle of brandy with our belt buckles unclasped and our stomachs hanging out, fat as butter. Rich as we'd ever been in either our lives and we still wanted for more. More than we could ever have.

On our third day we stopped at a ramshackle drugstore, the last business within eyeshot before crossing the Nebraska border. It was the only building for miles and miles. The place was a sod house with holes for windows. The only way we knew it to be a business was the hand-painted sign nailed to the roof ledge that read in a gross misspelling: FARMACYST AND WET GROWCER. A huge bluetick hound snoozed on the lopsided porch. We hitched our ponies to a post and ate a snug breakfast of soft-cooked eggs and oat cereal with cream while sitting up at the counter on a pair of nail kegs that served as stools.

I asked the counter woman, "I've heard of a dry grocer, but what's a wet grocer?"

"One that sells alky."

"I don't believe that's the true meaning," Billy said.

The woman crossed her arms. A faint trace of mustache growth above her lip.

"I don't care what you call it," I told her and pushed aside my empty plate. "So long as you got some whiskey, that's good enough for me."

Billy and I stood and perused the aisles for whatever assorted supplies were in stock. We decided upon three pounds of cornmeal, salt pork, a slab of bacon, a new iron kettle that wouldn't litter tiny flakes of metal into our morning coffee like the peeling one we currently used, brown eggs, condensed milk, some hard candy, and six cigars. While the grumpy woman rung us up at the till, Billy spotted an odd apparatus in a painted box next to the colanders of candy. He picked it up and read the label curiously.

"'Marvel Brand Whirling Spray,'" he quoted. "'Vaginal Syringe. Cleans Instantly.'"

I looked over his shoulder at the box that bore an image of the contraption and the technique for its proper usage. The device was a combination of what appeared to be a perfume atomizer and a fire stoker.

"Well I'll be," I said and whistled. "Would you take a gander at that?"

The woman sneered at our childishness. "It's for feminine hygiene."

"Yes, ma'am," Billy said. "I deduced that for myself when I read here that it's a vaginal syringe."

"Suppose if you can clean a sink, you can clean a cooze," I said playfully.

The woman yanked the box away from us. "Will there be anything else?"

"And what if I wanted to purchase that for my old lady?" Billy asked.

I interrupted politely so as to save the woman from having to dignify Billy with a response. "Tell you what, miss. I'm feeling a little headachy. Whaddaya got for that?"

She huffed. "Syrup of figs always does alright by me whenever I get a spell."

I laid one of the Cudahy gold pieces on the counter. "Well, toss it on in then."

"Anything else?"

"Whiskey," I said.

"What kind?"

"The best you have."

The woman bent over and produced a mysterious looking bottle without a label from under the counter. She uncorked it and poured me a healthy sample. I took it down without effort and stood with my palms on the counter.

"How do you like that?" she asked and cracked her first narrow smile of the entire morning. "Isn't that just about made to order?"

"Yeah. Top drawer. I could go streaming banners of joy around your hearth," I said sarcastically, and soon as I finished speaking, my stomach seized up on me. My throat tightened, and my knees buckled. Billy stepped away from me like I'd broken wind. I hadn't felt that instantly ill since the time I drank a bottle of black wine I purchased from an Indian behind the monkey cages at a traveling circus when I was just a teenager.

"What do you call it?" I asked feebly.

The woman gave a deep-bellied laugh. "Ain't anyone who ever drank it has lived long enough to call it anything."

What she'd given me wasn't whiskey at all but a toxic mixture of homemade tipple colored to resemble whiskey: coal oil, turpentine, and navy plug flavored with soft soap and rat poison. I cupped my mouth to keep from vomiting all over the shop and sprinted outside. I was on my hands and knees in the snow, spewing so violently I thought I might pass out from the effort. My eyes swelled up, and my vision blurred to a haze.

I heard a loud commotion inside but had lost control of every motor function except for the unrelenting heaving. My eggs came up in the snow undigested, and my nose was bleeding as if I had been punched between the eyes. When I finally stopped puking long enough to roll onto my back and inhale air like a man coming up from the bottom of a lake, a pair of gunshots sounded from inside the shop. The twin reports echoed, and the hound on the porch leapt to its feet and ran inside howling. Its ferocious barking lasted only a few seconds before another gunshot cracked, and all was silent.

I didn't know how long I'd lain out on the snow next to my steaming pile of throw up, but I knew it wasn't longer than a few minutes. Finally I summoned the strength to stand up, though it was a wobbly effort. I nearly fell against the porch banister and opened the door to a scene as graphic as any I'd ever witnessed in my born days.

Standing in the middle of the shop was Billy, his shirtfront soaked in blood as he wiped himself off. His pistol was still smoking when he shoved it back in his holster. He held a cattle knife in his hands and started to clean the blade after drying the blowback off his face. He replaced the knife in his belt sheath. A fan of blood as large as a framed painting covered the wall behind the register like paint popped from a balloon. More blood pooled on the floor next to two dead bodies, one being the woman proprietor and the other belonging to a man about her same age whom I had never seen before. The mutt was lying on the ground by the door with a hole in its ribs and its hind legs trembling as if chasing a cat in a dream.

Billy smiled widely and said, "Set thine house in order for thou shalt die."

He was quoting Isaiah, albeit he most likely didn't even know that Isaiah was a book from the Bible. He'd probably heard it said somewhere before without understanding its origin or impact. I was pretty certain of that. The passage would've rung true if he had said it before he set to murdering two people and one gangly dog rather than after.

I was so dizzy I could barely comprehend what had happened from the evidence at hand. Billy ransacked the rest of the store, filling empty gunnysacks with extra supplies and raiding the till for the few crumpled dollars and dingy coinage in its drawer. He packed the goods onto his horse and helped me up onto my pony and gave me a canteen of water, instructing me to drink until my stomach could hold no more.

We bolted from the scene in a flurry. It was all I could do to lie across my horse's back and hold onto the reins. Twice more I vomited and got some of the mess in my pony's mane, the water helping me discharge the remnants of poisonous whiskey still left in my stomach. I couldn't tell how fast we were racing or which direction we were headed.

Two hours later we finally stopped at a clearing where an abandoned schoolhouse with a partially collapsed roof stood between a clump of spidery elms. Billy assisted me off my horse and walked me into the rotting structure where rural children used to learn their arithmetic and geography before some kind of tragedy shooed them all away for good. The western wall was caved in from floodwaters or prairie fire. It was impossible to tell which as the black decay could've come from either type of destruction. Sitting up against an old cracked chalkboard, I quickly fell asleep. My last conscious thought was that I might not wake up from this slumber, and I wouldn't have argued much with my maker if that was indeed the case.

Later that evening I did wake up, soaked in sweat despite the zero weather outside. Billy had covered me in two scratchy horse blankets and was burning a cook fire right in the middle of the schoolhouse floor with wood from the tiny desks. A huge hunk of salt pork was spitting in a pot, and eggs were frying in a pan, their whites popping like hot tar.

"God," I said with a groan. "Not more eggs."

Billy laughed, but the laughter sounded more like relief than anything else. He'd changed clothes while I was asleep and appeared ready for a night of gamboling in a frilly yellow shirt and straight pants with his hair combed. He laughed again and without prompting began telling the story of what transpired in the store.

He said, "When I figured that wench had given you some awful stuff, I just lost my mind. I grabbed her around the neck and thrashed my blade across her throat four or five times. Five times. I was in such a fury that I had no accuracy. I gashed her high up under her chin and lower by her collarbone. I cut her so deep I severed her windpipe. God, her whole head nearly came off at the neck. Well, then she dropped to the floor with a little bit of flair, and the next thing I know, some lam in the backroom was scrambling out of his bed after hearing the commotion. Rushed into the store wearing nothing but his night clothes. Maybe he was her husband. I do not know. But there he was, and just as quick he was no longer. Shot him in the gut, I did. The hole in his belly was so wide I could see clear through it to the other side of the wall. His pancreas was lying on the floor six feet in front of his body. Or maybe it wasn't his pancreas. Maybe it was his liver. It smelled god awful so I'm thinking most likely it was his liver. Some kind of organ or another. Then that damn dog came in, and I dispatched of him as well."

I pulled the blankets up to my chin. "Are you drunk?"

"Of course I am. Here I am thinking you're on your way out and me not being able to do doodley-squat about it. I needed something to help trim my emotions."

The morning came, and I felt strong enough to drink some canned milk for breakfast and keep on riding. We never spoke of the violence in the store. Not for the rest of our days. We would ride on through the tops of Kansas, crossing into the bottoms of Colorado and on past the alkali lakes of Utah, shoestringing the path of the sun until the weather turned spicy and the canyons of Arizona were a picture no longer dreamt.

We would find a place easy enough to break in what would become the remainder of the world for us both. Maybe a little cottage on the sea. I imagined long swipes of citrus groves and celery fields. Strolling barefoot along the beach, boots in hand. Jackrabbits and coyotes appearing in the wild grasses that grew in the sand all the way to the waterline. Flocks of fruit bats with the wing spans of sea birds sailing under the red clouds of dusk, leaving their canyon nests for the fronds of queen palms.

Earth's shadow forming a dark band over the ruffled sea.

The high tide combing the beach flat.

But for now it was the utter flatness of tableland in every direction and snow eight or ten inches deep in some places. Once in a while we'd spot a windmill or granary or a collection of wigwams as white as new sailcloth and shaped like huge sugarloafs with smoke holes leaking dense supper fumes. As glad as I was to leave it all behind and fortunate enough to be making the getaway clean, I knew that even in the middle of winter with a flour sack of scant provisions and a scratchy blanket for a bed and the whole made world set to chase us down now and forever after, one thing was still true and always would be: heaven was the only place that could substitute for Nebraska. One I was certain I would never see. The other I was certain I would never see again.

Knowledge of
All Dark Things

SOME NEWSPAPERMAN IN Baltimore called the kidnapping of the Lindbergh baby the biggest story since the resurrection. Most folks simply referred to it as "The Crime of the Century." I don't know if it was all that. There's still more than half of this century left to be had, and a lot of ghastly things can happen in sixty years if history is our truest oracle of all things yet to come.

A feller by the name of Adolph Hitler is causing quite the sensation in Poland. It might be maybe he could prove a lot of trouble for the world if his shenanigans keep going the way they're headed. His circumstance is all the hubbub in the daily papers.

At least from what I can tell.

Reading the dispatch of the day is no short work.

My eyes are not what they used to be. My astigmatism makes even the boldest headlines seem like an optical illusion. I have to use a pair of opera lenses over my bifocals for triple magnification just to fetch up a few back page baseball statistics. Still. I try to keep up to snuff on the spring fashions and all the Gotham society hooey, and not a day goes by that this Hitler fellow isn't stirring the pot.

This world. I do not know her anymore.

The atrocities are beyond my fathoming.

The Crime of the Century, as it is, may yet to be had.

For a while the dubious honor belonged to that dago who stole the *Mona Lisa*. Vincenzo something or other. I cannot recall. No matter. He worked in the Louvre and hid the most famous painting in the world under his frock one night after closing time and hightailed it right on out of a museum more heavily guarded than a royal bank as easily as if he were lifting a pair of shoes from the Salvation Army. Made it all the way back to Florence he did. Didn't catch the bloke for near on two years.

I understand the sentiment. An Italian masterpiece deserves to be kept in Italy. Not Napoléon's bedroom or Louis XIV's goddamn hunting lodge. And yet. Stealing a painting holds no candle to stealing a child.

If the world is bent on making a hierarchy of the century's greatest crimes, one cannot forget the trick Al Capone and his thugs pulled on Saint Valentine's Day a few years back. I enjoy a glass of spirits as much as the next bird, and prohibition was one hell of an idiotic time for an entire country in the middle of a depression and dust storms to try and collectively give up the drink. But mowing down six men with submachine guns in a goddamn warehouse over a bunch of cut-rate hooch? I've got the dipsomania something fierce, and the furthest I'd go for a cap of eyewater might be ransacking a gin mill.

Speaking of. It's past ten on the Lord's day, and it seems my tortured stomach will not be sending my morning pottage back up the pipe. So I make business pouring myself a whisker of purple. Quinine water on the side. I'm an old man with no docket and very little voltage left in my loins, and if I can't have a breakfast brandy, then what else is there in life?

I have a washbasin for shaving and a slop jar for pissing and a window that will not open, painted shut around the trim.

The bedding is filled with ticking. The pillow, flat as straw.

The flophouse is run by a widowed Japanese woman who, with a little eyeshade, isn't bad for looks. After I get some good morning grog in my belly, I knock on her door and ask if she might like a basting between the bedposts. She laughs in my face, standing with her kimono slightly open at the chest. It's decorated in an overlay of plum blossoms.

I offer ten dollars to go along with it, and she slams the door shut.

"Well," I say through the door. "Pardon me all to hell for asking."

I put my ear to the wood. No footsteps. My landlady, the widow Baba, is still near.

I try again, softly. "I'm torn all to bits by loneliness," I tell her. "I'm sure it doesn't suit you any better than me to sleep in a cold bed every night."

The door opens a crack. "You think I'm small-minded?"

"I think you're too big-breasted to be small-minded."

The door closes again. "Filthy lodger," she says.

"I'm not a lodger. I'm a badger. A gunman. A desperado."

"You're drunk at eleven in the morning," she says and locks the door in two places.

A deadbolt and a chain. And so it goes.

Yesterday's snows have ceased but the mercury is nearly in the negatives. A grip of zero weather brought Omaha to a complete stop. The trolleys and streetcars have abandoned their routes. A winter so cold that the dipper I use for drinking froze in my water pail overnight. I have to put it over the fire of my fuel box to loosen it. Earlier this morning I discovered a mouse had made a straw nest in the door of my fuel box only to freeze to death. The poor little fellow. The smallest things break your heart the most. Its body was so stiff I lifted it out of the straw by its straightened tail.

Hoarfrost veins my window. Snow echoes sough music in the scratchy trees. When there isn't peat for my fuel box, I heat my pottage over a can of jellied alcohol.

The remaining birds that haven't flown south—and there are a good many of those little bastards—are yelling at each other atop the telegraph wire hung not more than five feet from my flophouse window. Across the hall some hussy is screaming banshee in the throes of what's most probably some newfangled coital nonsense I will never have the pleasure of partaking. A child shrieks for milk at such a shrill pitch even the goddamn wallpaper is trying to hurry itself out of the building, and I think: God, in all your infinite mercy, please, take me now. Don't toy with me. I've seen the things. Done more than most have fantasized about.

I fought with the rebels in the Second Boer War in South Africa.

I once ate a frog dinner with John Dillinger in Daytona Beach.

I've cut as many capers as the Jesse James and Cole Younger gangs combined and carried enough luck in my socks not to have had some lawman from Topeka or Red Oak gun me down in a cornfield. Enough is enough.

Yet I can't help but wonder how I'll be remembered. It's only natural to ponder the contents of one's own obituary, and mine is soon in the coming. Despite all my other escapades, despite five years of lawlessness enough to fill a whole series of blood and thunder novels, there remains only this: the kidnapping of Edward Cudahy Junior.

For a while they called that "The Crime of the Century."

Of course that was ludicrously premature. The century was only a year into its stay on the night Billy Cavanaugh and I grabbed that young man off the sidewalk two houses down from his own. Then, four years ago, came the abduction of Little Lindy, the infant son of the famous aviator Charles Lindbergh. Not yet two years old and stolen from his crib out of his second-story bedroom window, carried down a makeshift ladder, and whisked away into the night never to be seen again on this side of the born. And to think that all the while his father was downstairs smoking his evening pipe and the housemaid was down the hall taking her bath and neither of them heard a sound. If only the child had hollered like the child in the room next to mine is hollering right now. If only that ladder had made a racket when hoisted up against the side of the house.

Anything at all.

Like I said. The smallest things break your heart the most.

In all truth, I'm glad to be shed of that sobriquet.

The Crime of the Century. The name bears such weight. Perhaps, in the end, my deed will merely retain status as The Crime of the Decade. Yes, we can call it that.

They say the man who perpetrated the Lindbergh abduction was inspired by my own evil three decades earlier. His name was Bruno Hauptmann, a thirty-two-year-old German immigrant and carpenter by trade. This was March of thirty-two. Seven years ago now. The first day of the month if memory serves. At the time, I was living in the Bronx and working as a night watchman at The Hut in Union Square. My life of crime long behind me.

Boy, what a racket that story made. When I discovered that my successful kidnapping and ransom of the Cudahy boy was a chief influence for Mr. Bruno's daring piece of theatre, I booked train passage south to Hopewell, New Jersey, home of the Lindbergh family.

I thought: I must help somehow.

Surely I can be of some assistance to bring the child home safely. After all, there are thousands of police in New Jersey but only one man in the entire country who'd actually kidnapped a child before and gotten away with it.

So. Hopewell, New Jersey.

The child had been missing for a week by the time I arrived. A good warm rain fell in fat drops. Overworked drainpipes played wet music. A gutter bucket overflowed, gurgled like a slow boil. I made inquiries at the police headquarters and the newspapers, and visited two private detectives hoping to fill their coffers from the case—all before somebody involved with solving the kidnapping gave me the time of day. And it just so happened that somebody was Thomas Sisk, FBI agent. Very hoity-toity. He wore a knit necktie with a square end and kept his hair slicked back with scalp mayonnaise. Man looked like he combed himself with a fork.

"How the hell do you get your hair slicked back like that?" I asked him when finally admitted to his office. It wasn't much of a place. A pair of wobbly chairs in front of a cluttered desk. A half-eaten apple cooked under a banker's lamp. An electric fan blew streamers. Mr. Sisk ignored my comment about his hair and offered me coffee.

"Yes, coffee would be nice."

"Well, Mr. Crowe, I only have a few minutes. But I suppose anything might be of service at this point. Now, what did you come all the way down to Hopewell to tell me?"

"I have a few ideas pertaining to the ransom exchange."

"And those are?"

"Have you made contact with the perpetrator yet?"

"The perp—? Mr. Crowley, please. I appreciate your wanting to help, but unless you have something of substance I can use—"

I leaned back in my chair. "Listen here, you little twit. You sewing machine detectives are all the same. You can't think like a criminal because you've never even stolen a candy bar before. You're just like all those fancy, whadyacallem, penologists? All them prison experts with their special degrees who think they know something about prison life but have never spent a day in jail in their born days. All you fancy badges, you're all the same. You know nothing of criminals and their way of thinking, and yet it's your charge to nab them."

"I thank you for that," Sisk said rudely. He gestured toward his door.

I asked, "Do you want to get Little Lindy back safe and sound?" Sisk sighed. Stared at the wall behind me.

"First, if you want to catch this man, you must consider how you will deliver the ransom. When I got that Cudahy ransom it was delivered in bank valises. Every bank in America uses them. They cost twelve dollars a pair. A million of those bags all over, identical. It must be something unique."

"And you suggest?"

"A custom-made wood box. Some sort of rare wood. Green-heart would do nicely. Comes all the way from South America. That way the box can be identified later."

Mr. Sisk was no actor. He was bored as hell and could not hide the fact. He fumbled around with the papers on his desk like he had other pressing business. "Is that all?"

"No, sir. Next consider the money. Gold certificate bills are being phased out by the government. Withdrawn from circulation. So, use those. Much easier to track."

"Uh-huh, all very enlightening. Now, if you please—"

"I'm not finished. Next, don't mark the bills. The kidnapper spots that and you'll never spot him again."

Sisk laughed in my face. "Mark the bills? We're not Scotland Yard."

"Record the serial numbers, though. That's how you track them."

Sisk rose from his chair. "You don't say? I thank you for your help, Mr. Crowley."

"The name's Crowe. Pat Crowe. Haven't you been paying attention at all? Before this Bruno came along, I was the only other man in the history of this country to have kidnapped a child with any measure of success."

"Yes. A reformed criminal. Glad to see a man come around and atone for his past. But I've got many other things and people that need attention. You can show yourself out."

I fumed. The man was not listening. Or so I thought. I stormed around Hopewell for two more days, hoping to be of some service. I tried ringing the Lindbergh family. Of course they had no time for the likes of me. I returned to New York with the doldrums all about me, and a month later they found the body of poor Little Lindy on the side of the road: burnt, chewed, and skull smashed.

But. This world is never without surprise.

Not even for a lonely old codger like me.

Come September two years later they finally nabbed their man. Bruno Hauptmann. And to my great surprise he was picked up by the feds after trying to cash a rare gold certificate bill when paying for gas. Drove a blue Chevy sedan. The clerk, made suspicious by the rare note, jotted down his license plate number. When they arrested Bruno, they searched his home top to bottom and found in his garage a custom-made wood box containing fourteen thousand dollars of the ransom money.

A greenheart wood box. Hand carved.

Well, well. I guess Mr. Crowley wasn't as worthless as he was assumed to be by that fancy FBI agent Mr. Sisk. No doubt he took credit for these things. He can have it.

All I want for these days is a good jug of brandy, one last bounce around every corner of a four-post bed in a two-story whorehouse, and to be buried in a suit that isn't crumpled.

The last request, I will have little say over.

But the first two, I can do something about.

It may be as cold as the weather in outer space and my widowed landlady may have slammed her door in my face. But. There's a yellow brick Victorian whorehouse with blue shutters just down the block, and I've got a little coin in my pocket for a tryst.

I garb myself in a heavy coat and brave the cold. The whorehouse is nearly empty. Only a few other heavy drinkers occupy the counter at that early hour. They glare at me suspiciously. I ease myself on a stool and place my hat on the counter like a dinner plate. My shirt collar dark with sweat despite the temperature.

A bartender approaches.

"You have any good brandy?" I ask.

"Sixty cents per inhalation."

"Well, suppose I could have me a peg."

The bartender sloppily pours a short glass, spilling some. I wipe the counter and lick the spilt brandy off my fingers. I down the glass before the barkeep can pick up the coinage.

"Will there be anything else?"

"You have any La Flor de Vergunas?"

"Speak English."

"Good cigars?"

"Nothing as fancy as you."

"Well, set the boys up here a box of your best," I say, gesturing at the other patrons and touch my empty glass. "And I believe I'll have me another."

One hour and four rounds later, I pay the tab and present myself to a cluster of whores loitering around the staircase that leads up to the bedrooms.

All but one frowns at me. Even hired gals want nothing to do with an old man.

Still, there is one willing to do her duty. She's no beauty queen, but neither am I.

Together we ascend the stairs and enter the last boudoir at the end of a frescoed hallway. A gigantic oval bed with a brass frame takes up the center of the room. I remove my boots and socks and unbuckle my belt. The whore sits up against the slats of the headboard and lifts her poplin skirt over her knees. I finish undressing all the way down to my union suit, tossing my trousers and shirt onto a rocking chair by the window.

After the transaction is complete, I put my pants back on and cinch my suspenders over my shoulders. I fish out a wad of money from my trouser band and flatten out three greenbacks and hand them over to the whore.

"The going rate is five dollars, cowboy," the whore says.

I walk shirtless into the adjoining bathroom. Unbutton my trouser fly and scrub myself below with a new cake of soap. I toss a block of ice into the sink and stab at it with a pick until it's in chunks and run the tap after plugging the drain with a rubber stopper. I submerge my head three times. The ice water renews my senses. I return to the bedroom drying out the inside of my ears with a towel and pay the whore the additional two dollars she requested.

Lying in bed again, I spark my pipe and consider the fish swimming in the globe on the whore's hope chest. It's red and white with a long flowing tail.

"What kind of fish is that?" I ask.

"How should I know?"

"Fish don't usually get into a place like that on their own accord."

"You can buy it if you want. Lord knows you bought everything else in this place. Which makes me wonder, where do you get all your money?"

"From the bank."

"I mean, what's your line of your work, cowboy?"

"I'm not a cowboy."

"I could call you sweetheart."

"Or you could just lie there quietly," I say, pinching the bridge of my nose to subdue an instant headache.

A silent moment passes. It isn't to last.

The whore says, "It's not every day you see an old man dressed up like a cowboy and pulling out pocketsful of coin."

"Are you damaged? I said I ain't no cowpoke."

The whore fusses, kicking off the bed sheets. "Where do you get your money?"

I think about gagging her but don't have the energy. "I invented a machine for buttering bread," I say.

The whore takes the bait. She sits up eagerly. "Oh yeah? What's it called?"

"A knife."

"You're some kind of asshole."

"Closer to that than a cowboy."

"You wear spurs and a hat."

"Fellers who sell Cottolene door-to-door wear spurs and hats."

"Who are you? Really?"

I stand and size myself up in a tall mirror. Not at all pleased with my reflection. My stomach sags, and wild gray hairs poke about everywhere. I run my thumbs down the length of my suspenders, still shirtless.

"Name's Pat Crowe," I say. "I rob banks. Banks and trains."

"An old man like you?"

She cannot picture me any other way.

"Well, I used to, anyhow," I say. "For a while I was the most wanted man in America."

The whore giggles. "Now you're really fooling me," she says.

I shrug. She can believe what she wants.

So can the rest of the world.

BOOK TWO

THE THRILL
OF THE NATION

I

FIVE YEARS AFTER the kidnapping of the Cudahy child, I was flopping at a dime mission in Butte, Montana. The chimney of the mission was broken off at the roof. Most of the windows were smashed, covered with sheeting and flaps of loose iron. The silver valley housed the entire city in a cratered pocket as if it were dropped from a universe above. I panhandled with a dented cup and dressed in rags so worn they would tear apart like paper if I got them wet.

I babbled to myself on the streets. I stopped shaving, and my matted beard, nearly a foot long and grown over my lips completely, was almost always full of crumbs and dried spit. My brittle fingernails were as long as a woman's. This is not a flattering light in which to paint oneself, but I was a man without. There's no other way to illustrate my condition than to color it with its own bleak but true cast. When I didn't have a dime to pay for a night at the Mission of Mercy, I slept in dead nettle weeds and prickly lettuce. On a few occasions, I wandered drunk into a pigsty and slept with hogs to keep warm.

On my last morning in the city, I woke up spooning a big red shoat like we were old lovers long accustomed to one another's nighttime habits. I entered the Figaro Saloon as the sun began to boil away the morning chill. My stink followed me inside. I plopped down at the bar as if I was combed and shaved and bathed and not covered with hog filth. The place was empty. One lonely man who served as both waiter and cook was standing up on a chair filling a chandelier with lamp oil from a spigot with a long spout. His back was to me. He didn't even bother to look at who had come inside as he said, "We don't open for an hour."

I rasped my long fingernails on the counter. "I'd like use of your telephone."

The man swayed on the wobbly chair, keeping his balance as he turned. His face lightened. "Uncle Rags. Goll-dern. I've told you, you ain't welcome in here."

"I have money."

"You stink, boy. Now go on, get out of here before I phone the sheriff."

I picked a dime from my pocket. "I'd be much obliged if you did. I'm turning myself in to the law."

The proprietor got off his chair and came behind the counter. He flung a damp towel over his shoulder and pointed to a chalkboard behind him. "See that sign?"

I read the script in descending order: NO WOMEN, NO COLOREDS, NO INJUNS, NO CHINKS, NO CHILDREN, NO VARMINTS.

"You're the last one on the list."

"I'll give you a dime for a beer while you phone the sheriff."

The barman pointed at the door. "Out or I'll force you out."

"Get the sheriff over here and he'll do it for you."

The barman shrugged and grabbed a candlestick telephone from under the counter and slammed it on the wood. He spun the dial, asked the operator for the sheriff, and handed the receiver to me. I flicked him my dime, and he caught it in midair. He huffed his disapproval but poured me a beer with a high foam collar. I put the telephone mouthpiece to my lips.

"County Sheriff's Office," a voice answered on the other line.

"To whom I am speaking?"

"This is Deputy Mills."

"Deputy Mills, this is Pat Crowe. I want to give myself up. I'm sitting in the Figaro Saloon and will wait here for one of your men to come arrest me."

Laughter sounded over the wire, and the deputy rang off. I pressed the receiver lever down and asked the operator for a new connection. I waited and sipped my beer. When another connection was established, I said, "Listen to me now. My name's Pat Crowe. I'm one of the most wanted men in the country, and if you don't come down here to the Figaro, I will just have to come to you. I'd rather not keep harassing you like this."

A new voice came on the line. The speaker's mouth was full of food. I could hear him chewing his breakfast over his words. "Stop calling here. We've no time for games."

"Who's this?"

"This is Marshal Goodman."

"Well, Marshal, you're speaking to Pat Crowe. I want to turn myself in."

The marshal laughed just as the deputy had. He called out into the room. I could still hear his voice as he said, "Boys? Boys? Hey, McCrery? Go on down to the Figaro and bag that bum that's trying to fun me to death."

The line went dead again, and I sat waiting for nearly half an hour before an officer showed up. He looked about the empty saloon, a sneeze of snow following him inside like trail dust flowing off a rancher's coat. His spurs jangled as he crossed the plank floor and took up a stool two seats down from me. "Uncle Rags. I thought it might be you I'd find here. Tell you what, I ain't going to arrest a bum."

"Why not?" I asked, disheartened.

"Don't have any cause."

"What about vagrancy?"

"Vagrancy? You're plumb mad. I don't have time for small stuffs. Hell, last night some cowboy killed two Chinks for spitting on his boots."

The barman said, "I want his hide out of here. He's driving away my business."

The officer looked behind him at all the empty tables. "What business?"

"He's a goddamn bum," the barman said.

The officer stood, making ready to leave. "Shoo him out yourself, then."

I opened my tattered coat, full of holes and patches, and dug around one of the pockets stitched inside. Both the barkeep and the officer watched me with mild interest. My coat was not lined with blanketing or duck stuffing, but with old newspapers. I finally found a folded, yellowing sheet and put the flier on the counter, flattening it out delicately. It was a wanted poster with an artist's rendition of my image from nineteen-aught-one.

I said, "There's a reward of ten grand on my head. Or used to be anyway. I'm sure Edward Cudahy of Omaha, Nebraska, would gladly pay double that. He once had a fifty-thousand-dollar bounty out for my capture. I believe it's still in force. You are encouraged to wire him. Or Chief of Police Bill Donahue. You tell him Pat Crowe wants to surrender."

The officer studied the poster. "The hell you say."

"I do say," I said, gripped my beer, and began to recite in soliloquy, "Stout Nebraskan once I was, to give all quizzical eye pause, the thrill of the nation they once heralded my cause. Forgotten but not unsung, many trembling snows since passed when last my tale was young, until worn became their tongues and exhaustion emptied their lungs. To make all things new is to make the old undone."

"You see there?" the barman said to the officer. "He's been going around talking like that to the got-damn trees. I seen him spitting poetry to a lamppost yesterday."

"Some things in this town never change," the officer replied.

The barman continued his protest. "There are lunatics locked up in Utica Hospital that got it more together than him. Tell you what, Rags, if you ain't out of here in under a minute, I'm just gonna smash you one over the head and be done with it."

The officer chuckled absently and cozied up at the counter. "Say, Bob, you got a fresh coffee?"

"Brandy'll warm you up faster."

"Coffee, Bob."

The barman poured him a spot into a cup. The officer sipped at it tentatively. He took another sip and spit out the sludge. "Goddamn, Bob, gimme a brandy after all."

"Hell of a salesman, ain't I?" the barman said as he uncorked some purple from a bottle and lapped an inch into a dirty glass.

The officer held up his unwashed jar to examine its spots. "Yeah, hell of a salesman. You ought to go peddle sewing notions door-to-door."

I stared at the bottle. "Gimme a nibble, too, would you?"

The barman corked the brandy and shelved it.

"Aww, let me have a little breakfast brandy," I begged.

"You can have mine, Rags," the officer said and slid the glass over. "I ain't one to drink from a soiled cup. And you deserve a swallow, you crazy bastard, asking to be arrested. Never in my life have I heard of such a thing."

I wolfed it down and belched. "This stuff's been cut."

"It's medicinal," the barman said.

"Come on, Bob. I'm going to jail for a long time in a few minutes. This stuff couldn't float an egg. Gimme something stronger than the baby medicine you keep in your cookie jar."

"Do you even know how crazy you are?" the barman asked me.

"I wouldn't be crazy if I knew that."

The officer picked up the arrest notice and stood from his stool. He put his hand around my arm. "Alright, Rags, let's go. We'll sort this foolishness out at the jailhouse. If what you say is true, you're the goddamn dumbest idiot I've ever known."

I drained my beer, wiped my suds mustache with my shirtsleeve, and went along without fuss. "Well now, lawman, you know what they say? It takes a brilliant man to be stupid at the right moment."

II

Sunflash of dawn, red and cold, and Omaha appeared on the horizon. Our chuffing train slowing over the Tenth Street Viaduct as it pulled into the Burlington Depot. Despite the zero weather, the platform filled with triple rows of excited people awaiting my arrival.

I peered out my window as the train jolted to a stop.

A handprint from long ago smeared on the glass.

Brake steam hissed. The locomotive a giant kettle on wheels.

People everywhere in their sullen raiment: men in tattered farm coats patched with sacking, women in muted ducking and smoke-stained furs and silly hats full of feathers. Here and there a child on his father's shoulders to get a better view. Tobacco smoke and frozen breath rolled in little clouds over the heads. Pockets of the crowd murmured in scraps of English pieced together from their quilted vocabulary: *Pat Crowe is on that train!*

A man in a brimless hat exclaimed that their hero was coming home. I didn't know what to make of that. I surely did not. The crowd hooted and hollered. Farther down, a woman with a dirty face and a jacket patched in poverty—and nearly all alone in the world because of it—prayed with a rag. Or so it appeared from my vantage. She twisted her hanky in her hands as if it were a rosary. Among the crowd were nearly forty uniformed police officers and a hive of newspaper reporters in fedoras with press cards in the hatbands, their paper tablets and short pencils at the ready. Some of the onlookers arrived still in their heavy wool sleeping clothes. Even a couple in bathrobes and slippers. Every rank of life anxious to glimpse what the morning headlines of the newspapers the country over had been declaring for the past four days: PAT CROWE CAPTURED!

My train had been delayed nearly a full day due to blizzards in the western part of the state. Railroad lines were impassable until rotary snowplows with two locomotives coupled behind them wormed through the heaps of powder. In some parts of the track, snow drifts were cut through ten feet deep, nearly as tall as the locomotive itself.

Finally the steam engine rolled to a stop. Newspaper cameras raised up by cogwheels and balanced upon tripods were draped with cloth over their maplewood boxes. Shutters snapped and flash pans burst magnesium powder into the air like gun smoke, hoping to capture the moment I exited the train. Under heavily armed guard, I stepped forward in a lockstep shuffle, chains connecting my manacles to my ankle bracelets.

The crowd pushed forward to the edge of the platform and erupted in cheers as if welcoming home boys from the war.

Hooray! they cried. Hooray for Pat Crowe!

I did not look up to greet them.

With my shoulders slumped and my long hair flopped over my face, I was guided through the masses by a pair of officers. Men strained to pat me on the back. Women reached out with gloved hands, hoping to get a glimpse of my face. Parting the throng was like carving a path through seawater. A pair of young boys on the platform balcony tossed a few pails of torn paper into the air and it fluttered over the masses like confetti. Some of it stuck in my hair and beard like faint snowfall.

In the depot lobby, a new mob swelled around me as I was led outside, bulbs flashing. I never looked up once. I concentrated on my feet as I lumbered down the marble steps. A police wagon waited on the curb, double-parked against a long row of buckboards. Men and women lined the sidewalks, the traffic carnival thick. In later days, I learned more people were present at the train station to witness my arrival back home than were there to greet President Roosevelt when he visited the year before on tour for his bid of reelection.

After I was seated in the back of the paddy, Chief of Police Bill Donahue stepped up to the van's rear doors and climbed in after me to ensure my delivery to the federal courthouse. A giant, hammy man with twitching black mustaches and a head as big as a schoolhouse globe, his weight rocked the wagon. Two of his men slammed the doors shut.

Donahue told the driver to get the rig moving.

With a jolt the police van kicked backwards, reversed out of the parking lot, and began to nose its way through the crowd.

"Well I'll be. If it isn't Pat Crowe in the flesh," Donahue said with a heavy Irish brogue. His accent was so thick and ancient with the old country he might as well have been reading the ingredients to a recipe for soda bread in a Gaelic bakery. His left cheek bulged with a huge cigar nearly a foot long and as thick as a broken thumb.

I said nothing, my head hung between my knees. My hair hid my eyes.

"You might have heard tell of me, boy," Donahue said.

"Take that cigar out of your mouth when you talk to me."

Donahue puffed smoke. "You want one? I get 'em for a penny a grab."

"You're stinking up the whole wagon," I said.

Donahue twisted the cigar in his lips. The wagon stopped and started as the crowd swallowed up around it on all sides. Newspaper boys hollered out questions as they pressed up against the bumpers. Camera bulbs flashed all around. The wagon rocked back and forth.

"This is some spectacle," Donahue said. "Half of Omaha is out there."

I lifted my head with great effort. "I got a lot of admirers, it seems."

"Most folks think you're some kind of hero."

"What about you, chief? What do you think?"

"I think that most folks are as stupid as the sky is tall and that you're about as lousy a criminal as ever there was."

I smiled. I was truly amused by the thought. The wagon jolted to a stop again and then kicked back up to speed. We hadn't been able to manage half a block yet. I stroked my beard like a pet cat. "Maybe they think I'm somebody else. The beard throws a lot of people off the trail. I've heard it told that I look like Oyster Burns."

"Oyster Burns didn't have a beard, Patrick."

"Did you know he stabbed his own teammate when he caught him sleeping in center field between games of a doubleheader? With a penknife he did that," I said, pantomiming a blade jab to my chest. "Boy, what a world we live in."

"And where in the world have you been these last five years?"

"Wouldn't you like to be the one to know?"

Donahue rotated his cigar with his teeth. "Oh, it doesn't matter much now, Paddy. I told the city that you'd turn yourself in, and here you are. I know you. You're a man inclined to companionship. You couldn't last out there all by your lonesome. I told this city that one day you'd walk on back here."

I laughed. "Is that how you conduct your police work? By waiting for the criminals of the city to get so lonely they turn themselves in?"

"It sure worked for you."

"You said that five years ago."

"I'm a patient man."

"A patient man," I repeated. "Yeah, patience. Haha. Patience. My man. I'd say you got patience in spades."

The paddy wagon rumbled through a turn, using all of its eight-horsepower engine. It was the first time I had ridden in an automobile, and I was enjoying myself thoroughly. I stared at Donahue with a crazy smile and asked him for one of his stogies after all. The chief patted his pockets and handed over a cigar as delicately as if it were a newborn.

"Got any tinder?"

Donahue tossed me a matchbox and brushed ash off his waistcoat. I sparked a match between my front teeth, ignited the cigar, and drew an aromatic pull as I wet the stump, chewing it to life. Donahue noticed my long fingernails.

"Good Lord, Pat. You need to trim them sonsuvabitches."

"As soon as I get hold of a pair of scissors I'll have 'em down to the quick for you."

Donahue sighed. "I just don't understand it. You were a good boy. A decent family man. Sure you had your struggles, but don't we all?"

"You don't know me that well, chief."

"I know enough. I know your story. Hell, you were a good fella by all accounts."

"You can toss the birdseed somewhere else," I said.

Donahue stared at me blankly.

"You got it out for me. I made a fool of your entire department and now you've gone and blown a gasket."

"There's nothing personal in it. I'm to do my job. I'm to enforce the law, Patrick."

I leaked smoke from my nose. "Well, you can't make people good by enforcing laws or we Americans would all have been saints long years ago."

"Now there's a thought. A train robber and kidnapper who talks like an anarchist."

"I'm no anarchist. I believe in the law if it's upheld fairly against all."

The chief's deep-set eyes shined behind his gold spectacles. His dumb Irish mug swollen red and pocked from years of abusing the bottle. He sniffed the putrid air. Wiggled his nose like a rabbit. I was still covered in stink. A month had passed since my last bath. The chief covered his nose with a handkerchief embroidered with yarn flowers, to block the lingering odor.

He clucked his tongue in pity. "Let me tell you something, Patrick. We currently have a population of more than four hundred inmates in our Douglas County jail. That makes us the largest jail in the state. But I'm going to give you my undivided attention. After you're so beaten and starved that you can barely lift a glass of water to take a drink, I'll have you killed by a couple of big niggers right out in our jail yard just for giving them a steak for lunch. Now, what do you say to that?"

"You're the chief, and I'm your prisoner."

"You won't tell me the truth, eh?"

"The truth about what?"

"Do you think I'm a fool?"

"You're an Irishman, ain't you?"

"Just like yourself."

"Just like myself."

Donahue nodded at my manacles. "How do you fancy your new jewelry?"

"They're just aces," I said and shook my chains like bracelets.

"I heard you were a funny man."

"Just another bloke trying to get by without too much trouble."

"And yet here you are, turned in of your own accord."

"That's right. Of my own accord. Like I said, I'm not looking for trouble."

"And yet trouble's all you made. I could make more for you if you want. A lot more than you could handle. Or I could make your time here as easy as a milk bath with Lotta Crabtree."

"She's the one with the big moons, right?" I asked.

"You are a funny man."

"I don't mean to be."

Donahue hitched up his trousers without moving from his seat on the bench on the opposite side of the wagon. His shoes gleamed, buffed to an opalescent sheen. The finest cordovan leather. Blue smoke came out of his nostrils. "I predicted, didn't I? You read the papers. I predicted that one day I'd bring you to justice."

I squinted. "That's not true. If I recollect right, I recollect that you said one day you'd make me uncomfortable."

"Well, are you?"

"Not in the slightest. Hell, I don't mind county court. I got me a few pals there I've been meaning to say hello to anyway."

"You're not going to county, Paddy boy. You're headed to the federal building. Have you any friends there?"

The police wagon, built with little more structural integrity than a tin can, rattled onward through the swelling snow. The undercarriage bounced us around worse than a dinghy on a choppy sea. The grumbling engine as loud as a congested giant.

"One or two," I said.

Donahue whirled more smoke. He'd whittled his cigar to a stub. "You're going to need more than that."

III

I LAY WITH my skin burning on the ticking of my jailhouse cot, the cheers of the crowd at the train station lingering in my ears. I'd been washed like a flea-bitten horse: doused in unslaked lime from an oaken bucket while I stood in the buff cupping my genitals, sprayed off with a cloth hose in a stall with a floor drain, and deloused in disinfectant powder. The jail barber, a Negro totally lacking in tonsorial talent, sheared my beard and hacked off my hair with a pair of buttonhole scissors.

A day and night passed in solitude. Then a whole week.

Time drudged at a sluggish pace. They gave me a hunk of gray bread and a jar of water for my first jail supper. It'd been so long since I had anything to eat that the bread tasted like cake. I drank a bit of the water, stale as rain. The rest of my meals consisted of boiled ham and cans of imitation oysters and maggoty puddings on a tin tray with a clay cup of chicory coffee so foul it smelled like it had been brewed with old bath water.

Some six or seven lawyers had stopped by my cell to offer their services free of charge just for the chance, as one of them called it, to represent the most notorious criminal the good state of Nebraska had ever known.

So it was when the eighth such attorney came to call that I paid him little heed, my attention focused on the pages of a cardboard Bible bloated from old water damage. The bumbling turnkey procured a chair for the lawyer, drug it into the cell with its legs scraping loudly against the cold floor.

"Thank you kindly," the attorney said.

He wore a startling purple suit pitted with eggs of sweat under the arms, and bifocals as thick as driving goggles. A tincture of silver in his parted hair. After sweeping off the chair bottom, he crossed his legs and dug around in a leather briefcase that was scarred as if it had been used as a shield in a knife fight.

"You're wasting your time with the sales pitch, counselor," I said without taking my eyes off my Bible. I turned the page and lost three more to the ground as they fell out of the book's damaged spine. Half of Deuteronomy was already scattered at the foot of my cot. "I'm going to defend myself."

"You have a lot of experience with the law, do you?"

"I've a lot of experience breaking it."

The lawyer scoffed. "You're in a heap of trouble."

"You don't say?"

"My name is A. S. Ritchie. That's Alexander Samuel Ritchie, formerly of the Thomas & Harp firm. Top of my class at West Virginia Law. I was assistant district attorney for—"

I slammed my Bible shut and sat up against the wall. "Just another big shot come to get his name in lights. I've already had six other fellas visit me today. One of them even told me he'd pay me just so he could say he was my lawyer."

"My fee is two hundred dollars a week."

I curled my lips and tucked the curls of my eyeglasses behind my ears. "Well, you're a crack-up in a purple suit, ain't you? I just told you six other blokes offered me representation free of charge, and I sent them all packing."

"There's five or six more still waiting, too," Ritchie said and took out a tortoiseshell snuffbox from a velvet pouch. He pinched a tobacco clot and inhaled it through his left nostril, sniffling three times as he snapped the box shut. I watched his deliberate movements. A very deliberate man. Ritchie crossed his left leg over his right knee, revealing three inches of lavender sock as he flicked loose tobacco off his thumb and wiped his nose with a frilly handkerchief. He wore white canvas sneakers as scuffed up as old gym shoes.

"I brought you a little something. A gift," he said, sniffled twice more, and searched his briefcase. He pulled out a bottle of Albanian brandy with a hand-painted label. "Aged twelve years in oak with a hint of peach. Sure to burn your blood on a cold night."

I straightened up at the sight of the bottle.

"I hear you fancy the purple."

"You might've heard right."

Ritchie cradled the bottle like a tuxedoed waiter presenting wine tableside. "All I'm asking for is ten minutes of your undivided attention, and this is yours. If you don't like what I have to say, I'll be on my way and you'll be analgesic in under an hour."

"I'm agreeable," I replied and uncorked the brandy with my teeth. I pressed the bottleneck to my nose and inhaled deeply. Oak and peach. It couldn't have smelled better if it was perfume. "Goddamn," I said and put my lips to the bottle.

"Hold your horses. You need a glass for something that good. As a practitioner of the law, there are a lot of crimes I can abide in this world or I'd be out of business. But drinking a ninety-dollar brandy out of the bottle isn't one of them," Ritchie said and handed me a crystal tumbler he unwrapped from protective paper.

This lawyer was a very curious fellow.

Very odd indeed.

"What else have you got in that valise?" I asked.

Ritchie smiled and produced another item: a folded newspaper. He tossed a week-old copy of the *Omaha Evening Bee* on my cot.

The headline read in bold stamp: BEEF TRUST TRIAL TO THE SUPREME COURT.

I considered the paper and poured a whisker of brandy into the gifted glass and swallowed the first grateful swig after rinsing it around in my mouth. It burned smooth fire down my throat. I poured another helping and swirled it in the glass.

"Well, counselor," I said. "Let's have the spiel."

"All in good time. First I want to know, did you do it?"

"Do what?"

"Steal that Cudahy boy for ransom."

I shook my head. "Most defense attorneys don't care if their clients are guilty or not."

"I'm not a defense attorney, Mr. Crowe, I'm a county prosecutor."

"Well, thanks for the brandy anyway, fella."

Ritchie sat back and recrossed his legs. "I'm to represent you in court, if you'll have me. But you don't need a defense. This case? You need to be on the offensive. Now, let me guess, every other attorney that's come calling has promised you a nice plea bargain. Maybe some soft time in Lincoln. Plead guilty, avoid court, sentenced to a couple, three years, out in eighteen months, something like that?"

"Something like that."

"Fairy dust and tall tales and promises of El Dorado are the favorite fictions of every criminal lawyer who sets their own fee. And you? You're a shining penny. They see a lot of billable hours when they look at you, and they won't even have to set foot in a courtroom beyond the five minutes it'll take to enter your plea and collect their check."

"Haven't you been listening or are you just deaf? They all told me they'd work for free. Every single one of them."

Ritchie laughed. "Have you ever been lied to before or was that your first time?"

I took down more of the brandy.

"Make a deal, Pat Crowe. That's all you'll hear from every two-bit attorney that walks in here. Take the easy road. But I aim to get you into court, not sidestep it. This case needs to be heard. You won't be on trial for stealing some rich man's son. The rich man'll be on trial for stealing money from every person who ever took a bite of his steak or paid three times more than they had to for a pound of his meat. You see that paper there?"

I looked at the print.

Ritchie snorted more snuff off his thumb. "You ever heard of the Beef Trust?"

I shook my head.

"Did you ever wonder why your old pal Ed Cudahy was so adamant about shutting down your little shop? If you didn't think that was odd, then you haven't been thinking at all."

"Tom Dennison had more to do with it than Cudahy ever did."

Ritchie laughed boldly. "Tom Dennison? You must be joking. The man's a political pawn. He's an intimidating sort, no doubt. But he doesn't break eggs unless he's given the say-so."

"You must not know him as well as I do."

Ritchie was still cackling. "It's you who don't know him. Tom Dennison. What a hoot. I've sent six of his men to the federal penitentiary in my time. The man's done everything to go after me short of poisoning my soup and shooting up my house. Oh, I know him, alright. But he's got about as much to do with what happened to your butcher shop as a flea does giving a dog a bad day."

"He's the one who bankrolled me."

"Think, Pat. With whose money? It wasn't his, I guarantee it."

"He kidnapped me once."

"And he left daggers on my desk as threats whenever one of his bozos got pinched for offing a whore or rigging election boxes. That's his shtick. He's an errand boy who employs a few toughs to get done what the men with real power want him to get done."

"Still doesn't change the fact."

"Well, if you're so sure of that, why didn't you abduct one of his kids?"

"Because he hasn't got any."

"He's got two, in fact. A boy and a girl. Christopher's six and Annabelle's two. But not many know that. Not many know what I know, and I'm trying to pull back the curtain for you."

"Is that right? What else do you know?" I asked accusingly.

"I know your piddly little butcher shop wasn't open more than six months before Cudahy ran you and your friend out of there even though you were selling less than a fifth of a single percent in a whole week than the Cudahy company sold in half a day. So let me illuminate something for you that you might've guessed at before but never could put a finger on. The Cudahy Packing Company isn't just the Cudahy Packing Company. Not by itself. It's also the Armour and Swift Company, Wilson, Morris, six of such giant meatpackers all total. The Big Six, they call them. For years they've engaged in a conspiracy to fix prices and divide the livestock market so they can triple and quadruple the cost of meat across the board. They blacklist competitors, even little nowhere outfits like yours. They take rebates from railroads, set the price of ice."

"It's a monopoly. I know that. Everyone knows that."

"Technically speaking, it's not a monopoly. It's six separate companies acting as one without sharing anything but secret hand-shakes in backrooms. But President Roosevelt? He doesn't care what's technical and what isn't. He's got a big stick and he's smash-ing windows and knocking heads. So is the attorney general. Him and me? We were roommates at West Virginia. Philander Knox is his name. He's a tornado in a hundred-dollar suit getting set to level some big buildings."

I gulped another brandy. "What does any of this have to do with me?"

"That case is going to the Supreme Court next month."

"And I'm going on trial for kidnapping a kid."

"No you're not. That's what I've been trying to tell you. Edward Cudahy is going on two trials. While his empire gets battered around in Chicago, he's also going to be getting what-fer here in Omaha. The timing couldn't be more perfect. I don't know why you decided to come out from whatever hole you were hiding in after five years, but I'm sure glad you did. This goes all the way up to the top, Pat. When you kidnapped Cudahy's son and got away with some of his money, you did something that every poor sonofabitch in the country wished they'd done themselves but didn't have the gall. Think about that reception you got at the train station. You're a goddamn hero and you don't even know it."

"I know what I am," I said dourly.

"Don't play it small, and stop talking stupid. Let me help you."

"Help you do what? Get a new tax levied on him or something? No, thank you. I could see the noose if this goes wrong. I'm nobody's lamb."

"You won't see a day in prison if I have a say in it."

I laughed. "You said you worked for the district attorney's office?"

"That's right."

"Another government man with his own agenda."

"My office doesn't know I'm here."

"Going rogue then, are you?"

"I wouldn't use that word myself. There are much bigger things at play here. This baby's federal. You remember how I said I used to be roommates with the attorney general? Who do you think put me up to this? I didn't come down here on a Saturday when it's three miserable degrees outside to tempt you with a good bottle of brandy because I'm hurting for case work."

I considered the angles. Another wobble of brandy down the

chute and a mighty belch to follow it. This attorney was too crooked to be anything else but true. Still, I felt like I was being played fiddle easy while being in on the fix all at the same time.

I said, "Even so, best case scenario, you might make a small dent. What happens to me in the process is an afterthought. I know how this works."

"If all we wanted to do was make a dent, then sure, that's all we would do. And if I wanted to see you in a noose, I'd get a good seat in the balcony and watch you knot the rope yourself. But neither of those things would do us any good. We're going after all of it. But to take down a giant, you don't stand toe to toe with him and swing at his head. You go after the ankles. The rest will come tumbling down. But to do that I have to know, did you do it?"

"Would you like it in writing?"

"It's not like that. You've already had four nice swallows from that bottle, and anything you tell me now would be inadmissible anyway. But you and me? We have to trust each other and I have to know."

I stood from my cot and stretched, bottle still in hand. "Truth to tell, we did it just like they say we did. We snatched that kid in front of his own house and got a load of gold for it."

"Speaking of we, what about your old partner, Billy Cavanaugh? Where's he about? How's he still running around while you're sitting in here?"

"I thought you knew everything?"

Ritchie reared back in his chair. "Now's not the time to be coy."

I paced my cell, three steps between the bars to the back wall. "I haven't seen Billy in near on four years."

"So you don't know where he is?"

"Sure I know where he is. He's in Arizona. A little shithole called Nogales."

"How can you be sure of that if you haven't seen him in four years?"

My face seized up. I sat back down on my cot and hung my head. The brandy roasted my belly. Split my memory wide open. Billy wasn't in Nogales. The river had taken him elsewhere.

I closed my eyes and saw again where it all had ended.

The bullet holes in the orange walls of the crumbling cantina.

The waspy rattle of a howitzer.

The giant sicario in the dirty white hat, his eyes glowing like a deer's in the pitch black.

Even after all that time, my heart flounced at the image. A moment passed, and I opened my eyes. I considered the curious attorney in his purple suit and scuffed white shoes and was about to tell him what I'd never said out loud before but then realized I didn't need to. Ritchie already knew just by the look of me.

IV

TOWARD AUGUST IN the summer of nineteen-aught-one, some eight months passed since our kidnapping of the Cudahy boy, Billy and I made residence in the deep bottom of Arizona five miles from the Mexican border. A little hamlet called Nogales. Twenty or so mud homes, a few of adobe and tin, sitting in a passageway of black walnut trees, a village more populated by roosters than men.

That far south everything was upside down. Rats lived in the trees like squirrels. Desert bats burrowed in mesquite like rabbits. The painted *mujeres* taller than the mustachioed hombres. Milk stools taller than most of the men. The nearby Santa Cruz River, a bright chemical orange from a flooded iron mine, flowed north against the compass.

Together we had evaded tracking parties of Pinkerton detectives as far west as Pueblo and as far north as the bald mountains of Utah. A posse of five hired mercenaries led by a Winnebago chief who could track a beetle over a rock while blindfolded nearly gunned us down in the soak lands around Salt Lake, where a man couldn't make a footprint without creating fossil. A three-story hotel not three months erected burned in our wake when the posse tried to smoke us out by lighting the lobby curtains on fire. The new lumber burned faster than matchboard, sent up green flames. A manhunt of proportions the country had never seen. The *New York Post* famously dubbed the chase "The Thrill of the Nation."

Every homemaker in horn-rimmed spectacles and every Jim Dandy in a wrinkled suit paid the nickel when a headline promised a new tale of our escape.

Sightings were reported the globe over. Our pictures were sent broadcast daily, worming in code through telegraph wires from one outpost to the next, placarded on street poles and diner windows and train station bulletins. One day I was spotted in Cape Girardeau,

Missouri, and the very next day seen in Florida on Buzzard Island. Other reports had Billy on a steamship headed for Honduras and, six hours later, claimed his likeness to be holed up at Turtle Mountain Indian Reservation in North Dakota.

That entire summer, we rode south through intense heat wearing wide-brimmed hats to block out the sun and kept dry in yellow slickers during heavy downpours. For six straight months, we committed more bank and train robberies than the Jesse James and Cole Younger gangs combined. Flash floods stranded us on high chunks of rocks twice in three weeks and nearly broke the leg of my blue roan during a close escape. Coursing through southern Colorado and northern New Mexico, the temperature would drop fifty or sixty degrees at nighttime. We'd shiver ourselves to sleep outside desert mining towns that, come midday, would be glimpsed from afar through sheets of heat haze as if we were looking at a mirage.

We slept on horse blankets in stinking pup tents. We slept under desert willows that dropped newly hatched tree spiders on our snoozing faces. When we could find them, we slept in caves notched into the base of sky islands that rose up from the Chihuahua desert floor so high the peaks were covered with snow.

When it rained, we dug square moats in the ground around our camp to keep our bedrolls dry. At certain intervals we stopped to rest and water our horses in the shade. I considered my compass and gauged the land and sky in every direction, as if all the world and the universe above was something containable inside my head.

Every new moment was so temporary, so ethereal, like the existence of a mayfly.

Now it was Nogales.

For three weeks we lived in the belfry of an abandoned adobe church, hotter than the furnace of a dying star, guano baking on the roof tiles. Middle August and the mercury eased past triple digits sometimes before breakfast and stayed perched until the sun was rising somewhere over Greece. We scrubbed our clothes on a washboard in the river with a cake of lye and stole roosters at night to stew them in a crock of scald. Soon the whole bell tower floor was covered with enough chicken feathers to start a mattress factory.

We'd converted some of the Cudahy gold to greenbacks as we traveled south through Utah and kept the bills stuffed in the bottom of our horse grain sacks for safe keeping.

We found little pleasure and didn't assume to find much more of it for some time yet.

Nogales gave us hope.

Three weeks without incident, and we began to relax for the first time in over half a year. How many horses had we been through? Four? Five? At every friendly juncture, we sold and bought new ponies to change our look: Appaloosas as heavily spotted as dalmatians, sorrels without markings, even once a pair of mustangs that were nearly as big as moose. I adopted a new costume in Santa Fe: a flat straw hat and a spade beard on my chin like that of a goat, thirty pounds heavier in the gut. Billy stained his hair with boot polish, learned a touch of Spanish, wore a velvet cape and gloves, and started calling himself Jimendo the Magician.

So came the last Thursday of the month.

We felt safe enough to eat in public, no more boiled rooster in the abandoned church, and found a little cantina with faded orange walls and clay floors. We pushed open the batwing doors and surveyed the establishment with the apprehension of ghosts suddenly made visible by knocking over the flour jar. Ten tiny tables, only three of which were occupied, were lit by individual candle lamps. Moths the size of small birds thumped against the shades.

I nodded. As good a place as any.

We took up a table by the back wall, spied the pair of old caballeros playing dominoes along the windowsill, and noted the gigantic revolvers in the beaded holsters at their hips.

A lumpy waitress brought us a gourd of pulque with two cups. We toasted our glasses and drank fast, the pulque as thick as treacle and white as milk, with the flavor of spoiled milk that had been yellowing on a hot porch stoop. Next came plates of tortillas with wooden bowls of rice and pork and poblanos.

We ate and drank until we were plump drunk. Outside a hard blue sky past dusk, the last ten minutes of deep blue before full nightfall. The cantina was as quiet and hot as our hideout in the church belfry but much more pleasant. I sweated through the seat of my pants so fully the bottom of my wicker chair sagged with wetness. The shoe polish in Billy's hair ran down his cheekbone in rivulets.

"I feel pretty good," I said.

Billy agreed. "This isn't such a bad place to wind up."

I held up my glass of pulque. "This stuff ain't much of a substitute for brandy."

"We can't live in that church for much longer."

"What do you propose?"

"We got more money than we've ever had, and we haven't spent hardly a dime of it. Would it be so bad to get a hotel for a while?"

"Lot of risk in that. Hell, we shouldn't even be in here. You see them old beaners over there with the dominoes?"

Billy spied the pair of hombres with the big pistols as he poured more pulque.

"Those are thirty-eights they're carrying," I said.

"So what?"

"Not exactly dude ranch pistols. Those fellas are hired guns."

"Old Mexican army more likely. Hell, they're both north of sixty."

"We ought to slip out the back, quietly," I said.

"You're paranoid. We've been here a good hour and those old boys would've moved on us by now if they were going to move on us at all."

"Not if they're professionals. They seen us drinking. Wouldn't it be easier for them if we were both drunk? The bigger one there in the white hat? He's a *sicario* for sure."

Billy finished off the last of his pulque in a giant swallow, spilled some down the side of his mouth, and wiped it from his chin with his sleeve. "You're going to spook yourself silly if you keep thinking that way. I'm telling you, I won't sleep one more night in that church or eat any more goddamn rooster. Not one more."

"We ought to skedaddle. Get us some tequila bagged up," I said.

"You can go if you want, but I'm staying here."

"We need to leave now."

"No sir, no way. I'll be sleeping in a real bed tonight, and I'll be having a nice *puta* in there with me. I ain't using my hand again so long as I can afford not to. It's shameful. Facing the wall while you're snoring and with the goddamn owls watching all the time. Tell you what, if some fat old caballero wants to try at my bounty, he can get a bellyful of buckshot doing it," Billy said with a belch. He patted his scattergun that he'd leaned against the table like a cane and went up to the bar counter for another gourd of pulque.

I groaned and kept my eyes trained on the two Mexican gunmen.

The big one in the white ten-gallon hat had a walrus mustache and deep-set eyes that seemed to hold attention on the entire room like the stare of an enigmatic portrait: everywhere you went no matter the angle, they followed you. I didn't know just how large he was until he stood to use the outhouse. Nearly six and a half feet tall in a pair of hobnail boots. Every footfall a stomp. His pearl-handled revolvers were custom engraved.

If he was old Mexican army, he'd given up war long ago.

Billy returned to the table while the big man was outside relieving himself. I said it was time to go, no arguments. Midnight drew near and with it came the howling of lobos out on the grasslands. The cantina, nearly empty just ten minutes ago, was now at full capacity. We gathered our shotgun and rifle and exited the back of the cantina in an alleyway overgrown with grapevine between the hovels of rabbit warrens. We paused at the end of the egress where it opened into a stone courtyard strung with paper lanterns.

I studied the empty gravel *avenida* in both directions, cast in pale pitch from a gorged moon. An ash can burned waste next to an old hunk of furniture scorched past recognition. Perhaps once a couch or a bedstead that smoldered like an animal carcass rotting under a pounding sun. There wasn't a sound to be heard except for faint barroom music.

Billy lurked behind me with his coach gun lazy in his hands. A ragpicker appeared in shadow across the street as he crossed a tavern window and disappeared again. A handcart of muskmelon abandoned in front of a mud house. I nodded, and we set forth down the side of the street, nearly hugging the building fronts.

We weren't more than a few paces down the sidewalk when the giant Mexican in the white hat appeared in the middle of the street like an apparition rendered visible out of thin air. I braced Billy with my free hand, the other hovering over the revolver at my hip. The *sicario* stood there calmly as if he'd been waiting for us the whole while and knew we'd show at this very juncture. His face was darkness. His eyes reflected light. Billy and I waited, unable to move. The big man made a soft sound like a grunt and walked off the street behind a building.

I gasped relief.

We watched the man until he was gone, and behind us there was a loud flap like that of the wing of some prehistoric creature taking flight. I turned. Across the *avenida* a dusty tarp flung off a mobile Gatling gun on a two-wheeled frame and three men behind it, one wrestling the tarp into a ball, the other two squatting behind the cannon. In the last hiccup of silence before its six-barreled cylinder began to spin, I grabbed Billy by his shirtsleeve but could not move his legs.

"Oh, my God," I said.

A fusillade of grapeshot broke open the silent street in a whirl as I hustled Billy behind a parapet in the courtyard, hunkering down over him like a mother would a child while a cyclone chewed up their house. The barrage of bullets streamed scattershot, bursting stone flowerpots into smithereens and mowing down whole walls into rubble over our heads. Adobe brick exploded in chunks, and terra-cotta burst apart into pink dust from the shelling as the field cannon continued to spray the courtyard.

We crawled deeper into the courtyard, squirming like crabs until we reached a thick barrier and sat up against its hold. The Gatling whirred ceaselessly. I could hear nothing but the stunned humming of my own shot eardrums. Billy was shot through the chest as adobe dust settled all around us. His shirt filled with blood, and his eyelids drooped as he floated in and out of consciousness. I slapped his face like trying to wake a deep sleeper. His stomach gushed and his chest heaved and there was nothing to be done for him.

"Jesus Christ! You're full of holes!" I screamed and my scream was barely audible.

Billy heaved up blood like slow vomit.

I wiped my friend's forehead.

"It's—it's just—a knick," Billy managed.

"Goddamn, Bill, you're dying."

"I got five minutes left. Help me outta here."

I held him and knew that he didn't have the better half of a minute left let alone five, and I stroked him as his blood covered my clothes. There was nothing else said between us as the salvo screamed banshee over our heads crosswise. Brick dust turned our faces pale as silver miners. One more day in that old church, one less hour in that cantina, one more of anything in our favor, I thought. The Gatling rang so loud it was almost quiet, the noise a kind of silence of its own creation. Bullets oscillated across the building fronts without much care for aim but only for volume, and suddenly the sonorous flow of machine-gun fire whistled to a halt.

Only the cranking of the empty breech could be heard.

I waited for another barrage, but it never came. The Gatling was spent of ammunition. It sighed down slowly like a beast stricken with sleep, its empty cylinders spinning to a stop. I listened for screams but heard only silence. Cannon smoke dissipated. Cordite burned the air. Billy was dead in my arms and not a goodbye word shared between us.

All those years and nothing for a farewell but the cradling of his body.

A portion of adobe wall collapsed nearby. Bullet holes everywhere, the courtyard riddled and steaming still. I held Billy's head in my lap and pushed him gently to the ground so I could get at the pistols on his hip. I coughed powder. A chunk of daub on my hat brim. My clothes ghostly, scoured. Our scattergun and rifle had been dropped somewhere in the street when we ducked for cover.

I wiped the white dust from my eyes and listened hard. The entire world hushed as if abandoned all at once. Then the crunch of approaching footsteps. Two different beats, two different men. The big Mexican was coming from the left. I could tell the difference in his heavy footfalls. Maybe twenty yards away. Then fifteen. Cautious but not overly so. I cocked both of Billy's pistols as I hunkered down against the collapsing parapet.

A voice called, softly, "¿Puede ver algo?"

"No. Cállate," replied another.

A moment passed. The big Mexican's footsteps stopped. I breathed deep, knew deep down that the breath was likely my last, and snapped up from my sitting position against the wall firing both of my pistols in the direction I'd last heard the men talking—until my chambers clicked empty.

Two bodies collapsed, ten feet apart.

I couldn't believe my luck. I'd gunned down both men with blind fire. The big *sicario* in the white hat hadn't been more than three paces away from discovering my hiding place behind the parapet. His head was sprayed off from the eyebrows up. The other was wounded but still alive. He moaned prone on the ground.

I dropped the empty pistols and made for the dead sicario's pearl-handled revolvers. A streak of brain slashed the ground next to his big white hat. So much for him. I picked up the revolvers and fired three shots into the wounded man's back.

"So much for you, too, *compañero*."

There were still two others out there somewhere in the smoky street. I stepped into plain sight past the wreckage of the courtyard and called, "Any man who doesn't want to get killed better not show face or I'll gun you down and then I'll burn this whole fucking town to the ground."

"¿Cabrón?" A voice called after a moment.

I scanned my pistols about the street. "Who's there and where are you?"

The remaining pair of men who'd helped operate the Gatling stepped out from a pile of stacked stone with their hands raised.

"No estados armados," one of them said.

"You speak English?" I asked.

"No. No inglés."

"*Salir*," I said, only knowing a few words of broken Spanish. "*Salir* or I'll kill you. Salir or muerte, pendejos!"

The two men looked at each other and took off at a dead sprint down the street where it emptied toward the grasslands. I trained my new revolvers upon them and slapped off six shots, hitting both men in the back as they fled. A woman cried from a window somewhere in the distance. I looked about the street, flashing my revolvers in every direction. Oil lamps burned in the windows of the jacales lining the avenue. A group of terrified onlookers stood in a huddle outside the cantina, which was partially collapsed from stray cannon fire.

I yelled at them to scat.

"Vámonos," I demanded and waved my revolvers, but it did no good. I snuffled and coughed more powder as I walked over to the bodies of the men I just killed and searched their pockets. They had no guns. They'd told the truth. No *armados*. Probably poor chicken farmers hired out locally by the man in the white hat. Too bad, I thought and clicked my tongue pitifully. I plugged each man twice more to make sure he stayed dead.

I considered how I might get Billy's corpse out of town. No time to dig a grave. I stood thinking in the street where anyone might take a shot at gunning me down. A small lizard scampered over my boot. Poor goddamn Billy, full of grapeshot. His last laborious breaths pulling more tin into his lungs. Goddamn if that was quick but painful. Our horses were a mile away, hitched back at the abandoned church. Hardly another pony in that town. Nearly every hombre a chicken farmer and too poor to afford a mule.

There was only the orange river.

The shallow, wide Santa Cruz.

I picked Billy up under his armpits and drug him out of the rubble. Nearly the whole town had come outside to witness the aftermath. I screamed at them to move along. I cried and screamed and threatened their lives, and they didn't budge. A man and his son stepped forward with a wheelbarrow to offer their assistance.

"You take him to the river, no?" the man asked and nodded at his cart.

I nodded. "Yes. To the river."

Together we lifted Billy's body into the wheelbarrow, his arms and legs akimbo over the sides. The Santa Cruz ran parallel to the outskirts of Nogales where a mill sat abandoned after the ruptured iron mine polluted the water. When I got to the riverbank, I looked behind me and expected the townsfolk to be following, but no one was there. They'd let me be. Only the howl of distant wolves and the long grasses stirred by the nighttime desert winds and the fat moon as big as Jupiter, the silence astounding.

"Goddamn, Billy," I said. "Goddamn."

I lifted his body out of the wheelbarrow and pulled him into the water until I was chest deep. There were no words. Taking one last long look at his face, I let him go.

V

In the south courtroom on the top floor of the Douglas County Federal Building, I sat alone at the defense table, dressed in a loud tangerine suit. At ten minutes before nine, my attorney Samuel Ritchie entered in a fuss and dumped his leather suitcase and stack of books on the tabletop. "This is how you dress for your first day in court?"

I fanned out my lapels. "What's wrong with it? It's spiffy."

"It's cheerful, but this isn't Easter dinner. It's your trial."

"It was the only suit the county had that fit me."

Ritchie plopped down in his chair. "Fit you? Your cuffs are halfway up your arm."

I shied. The suit was two sizes too small for my frame. I put my hands below the desk to hide my sleeves. "What about you and your purple duds?"

Ritchie, perpetually clad in some shade of purple, straightened his jacket. "It's my trademark. And purple's a sight different than orange. Doesn't stop traffic when I cross the street. And speaking of stopping traffic, here comes the original stoplight himself," Ritchie said with a smiling gesture as District Attorney Louie Black, head of the prosecution, made his way down the aisle in a new gracklehead blue suit. His burnsides were matched in volume only by his mustache. His wild hair mussed up in stylish disarray. A pair of octagon spectacles pushed into his doughy face. A young but obese lawyer known for his shrewd logic and outright lack of subtlety, he was born and raised in Biloxi, Mississippi, and spoke with a southern drawl as heavy as peach farmer.

When asked in an interview with the *Omaha Evening Bee* the week before, he had called Ritchie a "whippersnapper" and a "blatherskite."

In response, Ritchie had weighed the comment with as much seriousness as a schoolyard taunt and stated, "If that's the harshest dish that my esteemed brother-of-the-bar can serve up, why, he'd better go back to law school to learn some new jabs."

Black offered his hand to Ritchie before settling in at his own table across the aisle.

"Well-hell, if it isn't Mr. Purple, attorney-at-law," he said.

Ritchie stood, and they shook furiously.

Black looked at me while he and Ritchie continued to pump hands. "How's our famous child abductor doing today? He sure must feel fancy in that nice orange suit, no doubt. Two peas in a pod you both must be. Say, you know who else wears purple and orange together? The inmates on death row at Sing Sing."

"You're a goddamn idiot, Louie," Ritchie said softly and finally released himself from the overlong handshake. "You know damn well your horse-raping cousin-in-law never wore any orange or purple, and he was on that row for eight years before they finally gave him the noose."

Black laughed like a man lost of mind and grabbed Ritchie firmly by the shoulder to pull him close. "You make fun of my wife's inbred but well-meaning family all you want, counselor, and I'll return serve by pissing my own drawers out of glee when Mr. Crowe here strangles to death from a broken neck."

I could smell the alcohol on this district attorney's breath. I asked, "Just how much gin have you had this morning, prosecutor?"

"Oh, only a pinch and a shard if you fancy a strict breakfast as do I, and you both are going down in a blaze of brimstone unbeknownst to man even in the darkest scripture of our vengeful Lord. So let me save you a lot of undue heartache and national embarrassment and make you one last substantial offer of which will disappear in the next two minutes before the honorable, elderly, alcoholic Judge Sutton, with whom I play pilotta every Sunday, arrives and the offer is this: plead guilty to both the kidnapping and robbery, and the state will only ask for twenty meager years of Mr. Crowe's dour life."

Ritchie jerked. "Twenty years, huh? Have you seen your jury? Not one of them has a full set of teeth that belongs to them from birth."

"Sympathy for the poor by the poor be damn, counselor. Your client will be hanging from the gallows if you don't take a plea bargain right now, and you know I've never been one to fib. As they say in Biloxi, last chance for romance."

Ritchie said, "By romance you wouldn't happen to mean pay-ing shoeshine boys five dollars for an alleyway tug after another lonely night of swilling pig vodka?"

Attorney Black chuckled at the insinuation. "You ought not go making light of a man on course to becoming an elder statesman come fall. Not a smart career move."

"Yeah, I heard you're taking a crack at the governor's mansion. I'm sure you'll have the vote of every monkeyshine in the city. But who am I to judge love?"

Black laughed again so fiercely his whole stomach shook. "Too bad you can't judge that or anything else. We'll leave that to my dear friend Josiah Sutton," he said and, as if on cue, Judge Sutton entered the courtroom from his chambers. He instructed the bailiff to bring in the jury and momentarily glanced at me.

I smiled wholeheartedly in my orange suit.

The entire room hushed as if the spectators knew they were about to witness a drama that would soon vanish into myth.

A coin dropped on the tile floor.

A woman captured a cough in her hanky.

The most publicized federal trial in the history of the state was about to begin.

The jury consisted of fourteen men with two on standby in case of emergency or illness: seven farmers, a carpenter, a rancher, a poul-try man, an oil station manager, and three insurance salesmen. Two of them wore their overall bibs with their ties because they didn't own a suit. The judge's bench was situated at the east end of the courtroom. To his left was the jury box and, to his right, desks for the court clerk and court reporter. The gallery was filled to capacity with newspaper reporters. Six bailiffs were on duty for the entire length of the trial, under the charge of Deputy United States Marshal Earl Little.

"It's a funny thing," Black said from his table across the aisle moments before court was called to order. He dipped a pen beak into an inkwell, scribbled something on a legal pad. "A real funny thing. Last week a scribe from the *Bee* wrote: 'Everyone knows who kid-napped Edward Cudahy Junior. But what we of Omaha and the rest of the western world want to know is who kidnapped Patrick Crowe.'"

Ritchie feigned a smile. He massaged his eyes under his spectacles. "What in heavens do you mean?"

"What in heavens do you mean?" Black mocked in a fake, gurgled tone without looking up from his notes. He continued to scribble furiously. "What I mean is that the timing of all of this is curious. Hell, I don't know. Curious is a generous word. Too generous. I'd say it's conspiratorial. All of a sudden this Beef Trust baloney from President Bolshevik comes down the pike, and the elusive Pat Crowe miraculously resurfaces on his own after five long years?"

My attorney scoffed. "It wasn't for lack of trying. The poor fellows of the distinguished Omaha police department. Don't kick them around too hard. After all, every once in a great while one of them catches the trots."

I laughed loudly.

"Something amusing to you, son?" Black asked me.

I said nothing.

Black stopped his scribbling. "An honest man would've come forth immediately. 'Why, sir, I've seen my likeness pasted on street poles and winders all over town, and I can't say why. Here I am.' Like Uriah from the Bible staring down his own death, an honest man would've said, 'Here I be. Here I am. I have done no wrong and yet you pursue me still.'"

The court came to order.

Black rose from his chair, as did the rest of the courtroom. He looked over at Ritchie and me while he drummed his pen on his open palm. Quietly he hummed with a smile: "Oh where oh where has Pat Crowe gone? Oh where oh where could he have been?"

VI

From San Francisco, I set sail for foreign ports on a Pacific Mail ocean liner, with nine thousand dollars of the Cudahy money tucked secretly in a pair of specially tailored treasure pockets in my coat lining, a spare change of clothes, and the pearl revolvers I lifted off the dead sicario in Nogales.

First to Yokohoma, Japan.

Forty days it took to cross the gelid Pacific, the sea all the wrong color: sometimes as pale as frothed gin, other times as pink as blood in milk, but never the clear blue I'd seen in picture books. In storm, the ocean splashed the steamer about like a bath toy. Rain shifted directions every five minutes. Swells sluiced over the gunwale, settled inches deep in the sleeping quarters. The sun a useless ornament behind a pellicle of sea cloud. Twice a dead child was wrapped in a tarp and, after a ceremony was held, tossed overboard. The wail of bawling mothers and men stomach sick. Vomit in wooden buckets and knife fights over crackers and all the known world long vanished with a small measure of soggy thankfulness.

There was no staying hidden forever. Not even in Japan. For two weeks I stole frozen shipments of eel right off the dock while it was being unloaded and resold it by the yard on a different wharf two or three piers away. When that forgery ran its course, I boarded another vessel headed to Natal, South Africa. I arrived in the city of Durban on the steamship *Ryndam* in the second week of January, nineteen hundred and two.

The first sight of foggy coast in a month.

It took eleven weeks and a journey of thirteen thousand miles to separate myself from the Pinkerton thugs that lurked in nearly every city and the reward posters of my face plastered on nearly every street pole.

Here, half a world away, I might find a haven. There was some money hidden away along my ribcage, a rumor of diamonds in the hills, and not a soul on the lookout for my likeness anywhere on the entire continent.

The future was hopeful and empty all at once.

Not a few steps off the gangplank and I saw the streets swathed with Canadian and British soldiers as the Second Boer War neared its end. The final mop up of the rebel armies was the reported line in most of the newspaper cable dispatches. Soon all South Africa would be under the rule of Great Britain, another colony in which to plant their flag. War held little interest for me. All I cared for after nearly two months at sea was a heavy meal and a few cups of grog and a bed in a room of its own that didn't sway in the belly of the ship. At a fancy wharf hotel, I ate a plate of salted cod with apricot jam, drank two bottles of banana wine, and hired a suite on the top floor.

I slept for a day and a half straight before setting out for supplies. A ragged village shop without a proper name advertised all sorts of wares: army surplus, canvas tents, gardening tools, hosiery, oils. Inside an elder English gentleman occupied the counter behind a single beer tap that was little more than an old sink pipe screwed into a barrel.

I approached with a handwritten list. "A little glass of whiskey, friend. I'm chilled."

"Chilled, mate? This is high summer."

"I'll have a whiskey all the same."

"None to be had. This isn't a saloon. I've beer and I've tea and a little bit of gin from my own stores at top cost."

"Gin, then," I said.

The proprietor poured me a gargle from a dark blue apothecary jug and made note of the pearl repeaters on my hip. "Long way from home for an American cowboy. You're not one of those mercenaries hired on by the rebels are you?"

"What if I was?" I said and brought the gin to my lips.

The storekeeper put his hand over the glass before I could drink. "Then I wouldn't serve you good London gin or anything else. This store is property of Her Majesty's army."

I shooed away the man's hand and drank. "I'm prospecting for diamonds."

"Diamonds?" the clerk said rudely. "God blind me. In the middle of war country? What a cock-up. You won't find any diamonds in Durban that aren't under store glass."

"Heading into the Drakensberg Mountains."

"The Dragons? That's a week's ride, and rides are hard to hire into the interior. Lot of coin that'll cost you. Friendly advice? You'll spend more getting there than you will ever dig up even if you got lady luck on your side. Those mountains are picked clean."

I ignored him and read the supplies from my list: a Winchester or another good name rifle along with three boxes of ammunition, a hammer, a handsaw, nails, a shovel, braided rope and pulleys for a windlass, lumber to build a headframe, two large buckets, a mining pick, and all the dynamite he had in stock. Vittles, too. Nothing snooty. Hardtack, beans, jerked meat, pickled eggs, anything that came in a can. A bedroll and pup tent. Matches, canteen, tinderbox. A map of the midlands, a compass. Fishing pole and tackle. A draft horse and a wagon to haul my goods.

"This isn't one of your fancy New York City department stores. Do you see ten stories with a lift? What I've got on the shelves is all I have," the clerk said.

I showed him a thick roll of Yankee greenbacks. "Not to mention I'll have every drop of gin you got, too. I'd prefer whiskey or brandy, but since you ain't got neither, I suppose a little of the queen's eyewater will suffice."

The clerk smartened up at the sight of the cash and helped me find what he had in stock. What he didn't have, well, he knew where to get it. Recommendations at a cost, of course. This was war country, after all. Everything for a price, even directions. By midday, after stops at three other village shops and a lumber mill, I had finished my errands and loaded the supplies into a flatbed wagon with a dependable pony. I finally tracked down three bottles of smuggled whiskey in an old apothecary, along with a handful of stinkweed cigars. I hired a guide to take me into the interior, a Canadian fellow who was setting out across the Orange Free State that afternoon.

"What a merry coincidence that is," the Canadian had said.

We sashayed off without delay, wagon to wagon, and rode until sundown over the rangeland of thorny acacia and tussock grass. Conversation was minimal. A few banal niceties and nothing more. For three straight days nothing but the endless flat of the veld. Land as empty as Nebraska prairie. Everywhere the stubble of low shrub and long aprons of scorched ash where wildfire had seared the veld down to stone. Here and there a sugar cane farm and a collection of grass huts. Once I spotted a pair of white rhinos, and the sight of the animals finally made the terrain feel extraterrestrial. Toward the end of the week, the landscape shifted to plateaus of hilly velvet. We came upon a thicket of alpine grassland along the Tugela River.

"This is where we part," my Canadian guide told me. "If you head up that pass to the north you'll find some good spots to dig in a day's ride or so. Don't stray too far east or your horse won't be able to manage the climb back down."

I stood in my wagon seat and shook his hand. "I appreciate you letting me tag along."

"Don't mention it, eh? Always been friendly with the yanks, I have."

"I don't see any mountains yet," I said and nodded at the horizon so cottoned with cloud there was no way to tell the sun's direction with a naked eye.

"Oh, they're there. They'll spring up on you once the weather clears out."

"Good enough," I said, touched my hat brim in farewell, and continued north until it was too dark to manage another mile. I made a fireless camp on a giant rock that night, and in the morning, sure as sunup, the Drakensberg Mountains were towering over me. Some of the peaks were as flat as tabletops, and others rose as singularly as cathedral spires. I had been in the foothills without knowing it. All the cloud cover wiped away as cleanly as a swept floor, the South African weather as mutable as it was in the Midwest. I rode on through an erosion gulley as narrow as a cart path to the northern cape where the basalt wall of the mountains rose steep as a wall hung by an expert carpenter.

Toward evening, the last hues of day coaxing purple, I settled on a spot that looked as good as any for shaft mining and had myself a little lonely celebration. Dinner cooked over a small twig fire: canned meat, rusk bread, red beans. Two days prior, I'd caught a fine mess of yellow fish with the Canuck, and I fried them up and ate them so scorching hot I could barely taste their flavor. The moon arrived on schedule and plenty of whiskey came along with it, whiskey that didn't taste much like any whiskey I ever had before but still did the good work of turning my head humid. I smoked two of my stinkweeds and put my bare feet up to the fire with my trousers unbuckled and thought to myself what a good old time I was having and boy wouldn't Billy just be in stitches if he were still alive to share the moment.

A sudden donsie washed over me, brought on by the whiskey and pull-grass cigars that set my head spinning.

Poor goddamn Billy.

I drank another whiskey and lit a new stinkweed. My ragged hat, pushed low, covered my eyes. How much sadness could fit into one happy night?

Come first light also came sickness. I puked cold on rock. My stomach shriveled up like gut punch. Old fire a pile of ash strewn with bottle and can. The horse I paid for in Durban whinnied pitifully like a mother ashamed. I staggered to my feet and told the horse to fuck off.

There was work to be done.

For three days I set about constructing the headframe with the windlass for pulling up buckets of waste rock, with the hopes I might find a little scrap of precious stone among the rubble. I blew dynamite with extended fuses and dug out what had collapsed into the hole, digging sometimes nine and ten hours in a day.

By week's end I'd created a shaft twenty feet deep and nailed some lumber into the hole to serve as a ladder. Fissure water leaked into the bottom of the shaft like a well and was as hot as if brewed. I hoisted the water and gangue rock and climbed back out of the shaft to breathe open air. Alone at night with a cup of whiskey and a wispy fire, I engaged in long talks with my horse. She neighed and hoofed rock and barely made a sound otherwise.

"Some conversationalist you are," I said to her and chuckled twice.

The horse stared blankly, and I laughed again.

Every new morning I pushed on.

In the evenings I filtered the rock through a shaking screen while the sun drooped. I studied promising shards and chunks through a quizzing glass. All that alluvium sifted through in the hope of finding one scintilla of diamond but finding none. Ten days in and I would've taken a cheap hunk of iron for my efforts. Every morning the shaft filled again with a foot of water even though it hadn't rained since my arrival. Day after day I came out of the hole gasping and soaked, my arms dead from swinging the pick. Three weeks passed. I was nearly out of alcohol and tobacco, and my spirit was failing.

On the first of February, I woke and hitched the wagon to my horse to head back down to Durban. An arrowhead of geese in the bathwater sky. I came out of the mountains a thousand dollars poorer than when I entered them, without a single rock worth study, just as the sour English storekeeper had warned. A day's ride back onto the veld and I came upon my first glimpse of humanity since parting with my Canadian guide: a ragged outfit of rebel Boer infantry in a camp of sagging tents.

I rode up headlong and declared myself a friend to their cause.

"Who's in charge around here?" I asked, still stationed on my wagon seat.

A tattered chief stepped forward. Five other men staggered behind him. He wore a giant pith helmet and a bandolier slung crosswise over his chest and a large shot pouch on his hip, giving him the appearance of a man hunting big game rather than one at war. "I'm the commander here. You got a lot of nerve riding up on us like that."

"Name's Herbert Malcolm." I doffed my hat. "And you?"

"I'm Fritz Bebout and this is my outfit."

I surveyed the camp. "Outfit? There ain't but six of you."

"Lost a lot of good men in the last few weeks. This is what's left of us."

"Lobsterbacks been giving you what-fer, have they?"

"Lobsterbacks?"

"Red coats," I clarified.

"You're American?" Fritz asked.

"That's right. You speak pretty good English for a Boer."

"I speak four tongues. English, French, Afrikaans, Dutch."

I stepped down from my wagon and rummaged through my saddlebag before finding my last bottle of stoppered whiskey. I took a slug and handed to it Fritz. "You men look like you could use a good drink. That's choice whiskey bought in Durban. Go on. Pass it around."

Fritz took a swallow and handed it to the men behind him. "What's your business here?"

"Looking for a good fight, so I am," I said and sparked a stinkweed. "You fellows are fighting for your home. I know what that's like."

"You were a solider?"

"No. But I've had just about everything that was ever worth anything taken away from me. Just like the Brits are trying to do to you."

"If you weren't a solider, then you know nothing about war."

"I suppose maybe not, but I've been in a few gunfights in my time. One ain't much different from the next."

"They're all different," Fritz argued, his hand on the pommel of a short sword on his hip sheath. "Only an American would be so stupid to think otherwise."

"Well, us Americans, we've kicked almighty hell out of old Mother England twice now, and that was with rocks and sticks we did that. So I figured I'd bounce on down here from them mountains to show face and help you kick the hell out of her again, if you'll have me."

Fritz and his squad of ragtags could barely believe their ears. They stood there stunned, staring at me. After a moment, Fritz said, "You just come riding in here on your sorrowful little wagon hoping to join the rebellion? That's hard news to purchase."

I opened my coat to show my pearl revolvers. "Not just my wagon, friend. I got me a fine brace of Betsies on my hip and a Winchester in my scabbard and I can hit just about anything in range of a hundred yards."

"That so? Well, if you want to enlist, I suppose we could use every man we can get."

The whiskey bottle made it back around the circle. I hobbled down another mighty swallow and slapped Fritz on the shoulder. "That's more like it, Fritzy. I hereby swear devotion to your banners. Now, what've you boys got boiling in that pot over there? I'm famished."

VII

THE FACTORY WHISTLES were honking and the streetcar bells chiming as the first day of witness testimony in the Cudahy kidnapping case was set to begin. A Monday morning glossy with February frost. The cottony winter light made the morning feel more like late afternoon. The courtroom filled to capacity. Up in the gallery, the newspaper boys stood in their somber felt hats, their tongues hanging out like bullfrogs.

Ritchie patted me on the back. He'd bought me a new suit with his own money, a handsome tailored cassimere with big lapels and blue threading.

Government counsel called Edward Cudahy Sr. to the stand at nine sharp. He bounded down the aisle, plump as I'd ever seen him. He stopped at the fourth row of seats to kiss his wife and hug his son, Eddie Junior, who was now twenty-one years old and a sturdy six feet tall with a premature receding hairline. I hardly recognized the young man. He'd married the year before while I was on the bum in Montana. The wedding was big society news. I got wind of the affair too late to make a surprise visit at the ceremony but did send along my own tardy congratulations via post:

No one could wish you greater happiness in the hands of your new kidnapper than I do. Here's hoping you will cherish no ill will over our former escapade, and enjoy this one more.

Signed, Your Old Kidnapper

I hope the kid got a kick out of that. I truly do. My sour humor was cheap theatre of the fifth rank and most probably not as hysterical to him as it was to me. Don't mistake me. The note was not composed out of malice. Nor was it pure jest. In hindsight I can see how it could have been misinterpreted as ridicule. Or, even worse, torment. Rather, I had hoped those few simple lines might lighten the heaviness of our stunted but sordid past. I've always said this and always will: Edward Junior was as fine a man as I've ever come across.

Among the other spectators in the courtroom were Tom Dennison and Billy Nesselhous, who stood in the back corner like men loitering under a streetlamp. There, too, was my sister Sallie, but no Hattie or Matilda. I looked for them everywhere and hoped I might get a glimpse of them only to have my hopes dashed.

The courtroom was overly humid. Six wooden ceiling fans scrolled at a fast clip but provided no ventilation. They only seemed to thicken the air as if whisking up a batter. The benches of the courtroom were as long as pig troughs, oiled to a reflective glaze, and could hold sixty spectators. The room filled with more than eighty persons. Members of the audience sat shoulder to shoulder, fanning themselves with pamphlets and cigar coupons. Judge Sutton commented on the uncomfortable conditions and asked that the court be cleared of any person who could not find a seat. Some twenty or thirty extra persons were standing at the rear of the room, and the overflow capacity was something he deemed to be adding to the mugginess.

As court came to order, Cudahy took his seat in the witness box and immediately asked for a glass of water. Government attorney Louie Black, dressed in a suit of houndstooth brown with a nauseously checkered tie and his hair slicked with rose oil, began his line of questioning.

"Good morning," he said to Mr. Cudahy.

"Good morning."

"Could you please state your name for the record?"

"Edward Cudahy."

"Edward Cudahy Senior, father to Edward Cudahy Junior?"

"Yes, sir."

"Mr. Cudahy, where were you on the night of December 18, 1900?"

Cudahy cleared his throat. His triple chins shook. "I was at a business dinner with some associates of mine until about ten o'clock when I returned home."

"Where do you live?"

"Here in Omaha. On South Dewey Avenue."

"3716 South Dewey, is that correct?"

"Yes, sir."

"And when you came home on the night of December 18, 1900, did you notice anything strange about your residence?"

"Strange? I should say so. My son was missing."

"Your son Edward Junior?"

"Yes, sir. My one and only."

"How old was your son at the time?"

"Sixteen."

"Sixteen years old, you say? Did he break curfew? Forget track of time? Get caught out on lovers' lane with one of the girls from his school?"

"No, sir. I didn't say he was late. I said he was missing. He was kidnapped."

The courtroom gasped communally even though everyone in the whole city and beyond knew the circumstances and details of the abduction. The newspapers had detailed every facet of my crime and reported every rumor for nearly six months. At various points, the horse I had rode up to the Cudahy mansion to deliver the ransom note had been seven different breeds and colors. Everyone in the city knew everything about the abduction, even the things that weren't true. And still they gasped at the knowledge, much like people will laugh again at a joke they've heard before.

Black circled around, hands clasped behind his back. "Kidnapped? How do you know he was kidnapped?"

Cudahy then read the ransom letter that had been left on his front lawn the morning after his son went missing. People whispered and groaned at the threatening details. As Cudahy recited the letter, his eyes filled much like an actor auditioning for a role of heartbreak. He emoted and paused, clenched his hand on the arm of his chair. His voice nearly broke apart when he read: "'If there is any attempt to capture us we will not try to get the money, but return your son to you after we have put acid in his eyes and blinded him. We will castrate him surgically with a pair of elastrator pliers so that he may never bear children. Being your only son, he will not be able to pass on your family name. The Cudahy line will end with him.'"

Attorney Black thanked him for his courage and gave him a moment to compose himself. Cudahy brushed his mustache with his kerchief a few times. The ransom letter was entered into evidence.

Black waddled about with a slipshod shuffle, coaxing his wild hair by rubbing a hand through its messiness, and asked, "Do you know who your son's captors were?"

"I only know of one for certain," Cudahy said, staring at me from the witness stand.

"And who was that? Is one of the kidnappers in this room today?"

"He is. He sits right there before me now." Cudahy pointed at me. "Patrick Crowe."

Ritchie was on his feet. "Objection, Your Honor. Hearsay. There is no way Mr. Cudahy could possibly know the identity of any supposed kidnapper without direct proof or eyewitness account."

"Your Honor," Black said. "We are about to find out why Mr. Cudahy is so sure of the identity of one of the kidnappers if you'd only permit me to follow that path."

"Overruled," the judge said without hesitation. "Let us see what can be gathered still from this line of inquiry."

Black licked his lips. "Thank you, Your Honor. Now, Mr. Cudahy, to ease the suspicious mind of defense counsel and the curiosity of our audience and the analytical reasoning of this jury, do tell us, how have you come to the conclusion that Patrick Crowe was one of the men who abducted your son, threatened his life, and stole away with a quarter of a thousand dollars of your money in the black of night?"

Cudahy slugged down some water from his glass. "There are several determining factors," he said with a rehearsed polish. "I've known Pat Crowe for a number of years. He used to work for me in my South Omaha stockyards. It was there he learned the trade of butchering and was able to make for himself his own butcher shop some short time later. I've talked with him in person a number of times, and I know his voice, his manner, his whole person, really. It would be impossible to mistake him. He's a character of whom it is hard for any man to forget."

"Ah, but knowing a man in general or even specifically is one thing," Black said. "How do you know it was him who stole your child?"

"Well," Cudahy said. "Like I said, I've talked to him many times before. And the last time I heard his voice was the dawn of the day after my son went missing. A man called my home in the very early hours to alert me of the ransom letter left on my front lawn. I heard his voice then telling me about the letter and to follow its instructions and that voice was no different than the one of the man whom I had conversed with many times before."

"Patrick Crowe called your house you say?"

"Yes, he did. About seven in the morning on December the nineteenth, not a few hours since my son went missing. He told me I would find a note attached to a stick in my yard and gave a brief description of that letter's contents. I knew it was him the moment he spoke."

"And how would you describe Mr. Crowe's voice?"

"Well, he has an Irish brogue. A strong voice. Not deep, I would say, but strong. Unmistakable."

"So, once again, to be as clear as we can in this chamber here today, is there any doubt in your mind as to who kidnapped your son?"

"There is no question in my mind. It was Pat Crowe."

"Thank you, Mr. Cudahy," Black said. "No more questions, Your Honor."

Ritchie rose to cross-examine. Today was a fine day for his best purple suit: a mauve three-piece, the most popular shade of the previous decade. He adjusted his mallow bow tie and studied a set of notes, his canvas shoes squeaking on the floor. He took his time in approaching the witness stand. Sleet snapped at the large windows. A pair of radiators hissed. The courtroom waited with bated breath.

Finally he asked, "Mr. Cudahy, you say you are certain without a doubt that it was Pat Crowe who abducted your son on the night in question, December 18, 1900?"

"Yes. I'm certain."

"How certain, sir? Could you perhaps apply a percentage to that certainty?"

"One hundred percent," Cudahy said.

"So there is no doubt, not even a sliver, the slightest chance, that someone else could have been the man to have taken your son?"

"No, sir. There is no doubt."

"And you know this because you are familiar with Pat Crowe's voice?"

"That's correct."

"I'm curious. For I, too, want to be as clear to this court as my esteemed colleague, Mr. Black. Was there any other information or clue you might be able to share with us today that makes you so certain that the captor was Pat Crowe?"

Cudahy stammered, worked his mouth like he was imagining an answer. "I'm not sure what you're asking me to divulge."

"Oh," Ritchie said with a short chuckle. "I mean did you have any other evidence besides a familiarity with Mr. Crowe's voice that led you to believe he was your son's abductor? Did you or anyone else see him snatch your child off the street? Did he announce himself during this alleged phone call to your house? Did he ring your residence and say, 'Pat Crowe calling for Mr. Edward Cudahy'? Did he sign this ransom letter with his signature? 'Sincerely and eternally yours, Patrick Joseph Crowe'? Maybe with a little curlicue flourish on the top of the capital C that would distinguish his handwriting?"

The audience shared a communal laugh.

"No, sir. None of those things. What kind of man would do such a thing?"

"So it would be safe to say your certainty as to the identity of the kidnapper is based on his voice and his voice alone?"

"Yes, it is."

"And you say his voice was discernable based on a couple qualities. Chiefly that he spoke with an Irish brogue?"

"That's right."

Ritchie massaged his chin with a smirk. "Well, now, that is rare. I can't say I've ever heard anyone else in this city who speaks with an Irish accent."

The court laughed again, laughed as hard as they might at a punch line in a vaudeville routine, and Judge Sutton was liberal in the use of his mallet to silence them.

"Mr. Cudahy, do you know how many citizens of this city are first or second generation Irish immigrants?"

"I cannot say. I'm sure there are many."

"Many is right. Let me illuminate for you just how many," Ritchie said and read from a small notepad. "According to the 1900 census, the twelfth census conducted in this country, one of the questions asked was the place of birth of each individual and the place of birth of the parents of each individual. The figures reported in the *Omaha Daily News* about that 1900 census listed the population of our city at 102,555. Now, of that number, some fifty-four thousand residents listed their place of birth or their parents' place of birth as Ireland. That's almost exactly half of our city's population that were first or second generation Irish Americans who, no doubt, would have spoken with what you called an Irish brogue."

"Objection," Black yelled. "This pantheon of pathetic statistics doesn't disprove that my client was familiar enough with the defendant's voice to have been able to recognize it no matter how many others may have shared his heritage. He's misleading the jury."

Ritchie replied, "Your Honor, it was only minutes ago you allowed Mr. Black to continue with his questioning of Mr. Cudahy to establish the identity of the kidnapper based on the familiarity he had with the defendant's voice when I argued otherwise. You allowed for him to gather what he could from that inquiry, and now I would ask you grant me that same freedom."

Judge Sutton weighed the proposition for a moment. "Overruled. But let me warn you, Mr. Ritchie, that your trajectory seems thin to me, sir. Very thin, indeed."

"Thank you, Your Honor. But I would say that sheer proven numbers as collected by our nation's government is not thin at all.

It proves something of serious weight in this case. The ability for Mr. Cudahy to be able to distinguish the voice of one man from nearly half a hundred thousand other citizens of this city who share his so-called Irish brogue would be quite a feat," Ritchie said and redirected his attention to Mr. Cudahy.

He asked, "Mr. Cudahy, what is your occupation?"

"I'm the founder and president of the Cudahy Packing Company."

"Very well. And what is your education, sir?"

"I have a bachelor's degree from Columbia University."

"And what was your field of study?"

"Economics and business administration."

"Economics and business administration? Very impressive. And during your time as a student, did you ever study linguistics or speech pathology?"

"I did not."

Black was out of his chair again. "Objection, Your Honor. Mr. Cudahy's education has no bearing on the fact his child was stolen for ransom. Defense counsel is leading this jury down the primrose path."

"It's exactly the opposite, Your Honor," Ritchie said. "Mr. Cudahy's ability to tell one person's voice apart from thousands and thousands of others just like it is of keen bearing in his testimony. His ability to say with what he called a 'one hundred percent certainty' that the voice on the other end of the line that called his home on the morning after his son's disappearance was Pat Crowe's and no other is the only quality with which he could make any kind of identification. And I ask you, are we to believe, is this jury to believe, that when a man's life is at stake we should take Mr. Cudahy's word for it when he has neither the experience or education to come to such a conclusion?"

Judge Sutton wrinkled his brow. He seemed exasperated already even though it was only the second hour of testimony. "Objection sustained. Mr. Cudahy swore under oath that he believed the voice he heard was that of the defendant, and I see no reason why that fact should be challenged at this point."

Ritchie, flabbergasted, turned to the audience, broke the fourth wall. "Why, if Pat Crowe were, say, a Hungarian with a certain and distinguishable vowel harmony or maybe spoke with a south Turkish accent, then we might say, 'Well, that's pretty unique in this town.' But his voice is not unique, is it? It's one of more than fifty thousand!" He turned to the judge. "And you say that's no reason for me to challenge the ability of Mr. Cudahy to discern between the accents of a number of citizens that make up half of this city's population?"

Judge Sutton slammed his gavel. "Mr. Ritchie, there will be no place for grandstanding in my court. One more outburst like that from you and I will find you in contempt."

"I apologize to the court, Your Honor. I will cut at this apple from the other side," Ritchie said and reasserted himself in front of the witness stand. "Mr. Cudahy, in the year 1899, how many people worked for you?"

"I can't say to an exact figure."

"Well, estimate. Put us in the ballpark, if you would."

Cudahy shifted in his chair. "Maybe three thousand. A little more."

"You're close. According to your employment records in the year 1899, some forty-six hundred people worked for you."

"That sounds right."

"It doesn't just sound right. It's an exact figure taken from your own documents. Now, of those nearly five thousand people who worked for you in that year, how many did you know by name?"

"In that year specifically? It's impossible to say. That was over five years ago. I make a concerted effort to get to know as many of my employees as I can."

"Well, according to your best guess just moments ago concerning how many folks worked for you in that year, you were off by sixteen hundred. So would it be safe to say you maybe knew a third of your employees by name? Perhaps less?"

"I was and still am the owner and operator of a large business," Cudahy said, his voice heightened. He was aggressively on the defensive now. "And like I already told you, it would be nearly impossible to know every person who worked for me on a first name basis. There simply isn't enough time in the day. I, sir, am one of the single largest employers in this city and have been for some time now. That's why we have a managerial structure in business."

"Yes, sir. That only makes sense. But let me ask you this. Earlier you said that Pat Crowe worked for you in the stockyards for some time. To be exact, he was an employee of the Cudahy Packing Company for seven months in the year 1899. In that time he worked mainly as a cargo loader. That is to say he worked largely in the capacity of hauling beef from the slaughterhouses into railroad cars for transport. Now, is that a high-ranking position in your company?"

"No, sir. It is not."

"And would you say that, as the owner and chief executive officer, you get to know many of the folks who work as cargo loaders in your stockyards?"

"Not as many as I would like."

"Then how, sir, can you say that you knew Pat Crowe well?"

"I never said I knew him well. I said I knew him."

"What you actually said not even thirty minutes ago was that you've known Pat Crowe for a number of long years. You said you talked with him in person a number of times and that you knew his whole person. His whole person. You, sir, talked about him like you worked with him in close capacity every day. I wrote it down here," Ritchie said and flipped over a page on his notepad. "You said that, and I quote, 'It would be impossible to mistake him. He's a character of whom it is hard for any man to forget.' And now you're telling us you didn't know him well? Well, sir, which is it?"

"I know him well enough."

"Well enough to remember him distinctly when he only worked for you for seven months when you can hardly even remember how many people worked for you in that entire fiscal year? In an area of your business you admitted to hardly ever having direct managerial contact with?"

"Yes. I've answered this question twice now. I knew the man well enough."

"Well enough to be able to distinguish his voice over the phone more than a year after his last day of employment, all because he had an Irish brogue?"

Black shot out of his chair so fast he nearly kicked it over. "Objection!"

"Don't bother, Your Honor," Ritchie said and headed back to his seat next to me at the defense table with a grin and a strut. "I withdraw the question."

VIII

DAYBREAK ON THE highveld. A tin sun and cold sunburst. Another morning gathered without color or warmth as my new Boer brethren and I rode horseback across the thirstland. For three days we'd traveled and nary a sign of man in all that time. The whole empty gray veld as lonely as a lunar valley. Here and there a baobab tree chattering with blue monkeys. Here and there a dusty cheetah as starved as a wolf in winter.

We rode near on thirty miles through the powdery afternoon. Along a rutted road, our bullock wagon rumbled and ached as if on the verge of collapse. Scalding wind blew dirt like sleet. Above, a scarred sky of high cirrus. I wiped the dirt from my face and drank from my water bugle. I raved for roast beef and honey biscuits. Nothing here to hearten a man but his own jollities. Fritz and I jibbed back and forth for a spell as we strode over the red grasses south of a sharp line of kopjes. Telegraph wires skirting an abandoned rail line had been cut and buried for miles at a stretch by a British reconnoitering party. Ahead, nothing but more cinder plain magnetizing in its longness.

We camped for water under the fragmented shade of an umbrella tree while the sun burned the hottest hour of the day, and then continued on through the cradle of the midlands. By and by we came upon the remains of a sugar cane farm ten miles west of Pongola. Dolerite cliffs bordered the ash land. The farm, sunken by fire, lay in a giant heap of blackened stick and rubble that was still smoldering even though Fritz calculated the fire happened days ago. Maybe even a whole week. Fires on the veld could simmer and smoke for a month before wafting out, he said.

He took off his pith helmet and wiped out the inside with a handkerchief and spat. I halted alongside, told my horse to shush. The six infantrymen behind us sullen and slumped of shoulder, the long war stamped upon their faces. A trio of springboks nosed through the scrap and ash. Bearded vultures, also in trio, watched our arrival from a felled tree trunk split down the middle like the abandoned makings of a canoe.

We dismounted our horses and searched the remains. Searching for what, we did not know. A body to bury. A machete for salvaging. A cask of good cape rum left unmolested by the fire and those who had started it. I wiped off the seat of my pants and looked over the scorched canebrake. So barren from fire, it didn't appear burnt, but frozen. A gray sun behind gray cloud over a gray landscape that looked nothing like countryside in the midst of war, but one long since deserted after war.

Fritz pitied the sight and took some wheat papers out of his shirt pocket. His tobacco baggie dangled from his teeth by the pull string. "Cane in these parts used to grow twenty, thirty foot high. Good carrizo cane. Now look at her, this country."

I pushed my hat back and mopped my brow. "Looks a lot like home to me."

"What's home to you?"

"Flatness in every direction," I said.

A cryptic howling echoed over the surrounding hills.

All the men looked east. Fritz finished rolling his cigarette.

"Wolves?" I asked.

Fritz shook his head. "You're on the wrong continent to hope for wolves, cowboy."

"Jackals, then?"

"Ridgebacks."

"Ridgebacks?"

"British scout dogs. They picked up our scent."

"Hell, that ain't hard. You all stink worse than skunk trappers."

"Stink or not, it's time to pull foot," Fritz said and mounted his horse after sparking his cigarette, the howls of the pack dogs growing closer over the dusking hills. We seven raced hard along the woodland edge of the Vaal River, the upland thick with groundcover of wild dagga and dogbane blossom. The hills rose taller the farther east we traveled, and soon enough, almost by accident, we found ourselves in a deep cut between the ridges. The road so narrow we were forced to pace our horses in a single line through the passage.

Sky echoed with voices that were not our own. The ridge above us crested with the faraway shapes of men. Fritz stopped his horse. His was the face of a man who saw his own death coming slowly from a short distance away.

I swung my horse around to flee in the direction we had come as the man behind me dropped from his saddle sideways and hit the ground with a thud. I loosed my pony and nearly landed face-down after getting my foot caught in the stirrup trying to dismount in such a hurry. I got on my haunches in the dirt and turned the man over.

He'd been hit square in the chest with a rifle ball. A clean shot through the heart and not a sound heard. No crack of gunshot, no rifle echo.

Only the hollow voices above.

I crouched behind my horse and drew my left hip pistol. Three of the Boer fighters at the back of our train retreated west through the cut. A volley of rifle fire like unexplainable rainfall from a cloudless sky picked them off in a matter of a few wild seconds, and their horses fell with them. I looked in every direction. Twenty yards away, Fritz returned blind fire from horseback and was clipped three or four times before he could even see long enough to aim. His horse took as many bullets. The salvo rang out from both sides of the kopjes, and still I couldn't see a single shooter.

All of the men dead except for me.

No time for calculating dumb luck.

Evening sky dark around the edges but nearly as light as full day looking straight up from the bottom of the ravine. I might as well have been a dot of red paint on white paper for whoever was on the other end of those rifles.

I crawled on my stomach through the dust with a pistol in each hand and hadn't made it more than a few feet when I felt the bullet hit me in my left shoulder. The shot close enough to my spine that it emptied me of breath. I rolled onto my back and sucked at the sky. Could not get any air into my lungs. I patted my chest above my heart and groped around inside my shirt along my collarbone, searching for an exit wound.

There was none. The ball stopped somewhere in my shoulder blade, deep in the muscle. Wondered maybe if it went into my lung. Probably must have as hard as it was to draw wind. I panted and continued crawling without being able to breathe beyond shallow hiccups. Rifle shots caromed off rock and dirt, inches from my head.

My vision blurred and I spat blood. Keep crawling, I told myself. They haven't killed you yet. I looked back. My horse shot thrice and kicking its legs on the ground. The ping of bullets nearly missing me as I pulled myself through the brush. Voices yelling overhead, words inaudible. Finally after squirming for nearly fifty feet along the base of the escarpment, I was able to screen myself in thorn shrub. I sat up against rock and strained for breath. Blood down my back, hot as sweat. The upper half of my left arm had numbed, and my fingers tingled as if I had fallen asleep on the limb. Lucky it wasn't my good shooting hand. If there was such a thing as luck in a bind such as this. Surely there was. Had the bullet hit an inch more to the left or the right, I would have died in considerable pain.

The rifle fire ceased momentarily. I looked around. A small pass as narrow as a staircase through the kopje some forty feet yonder. Steep but manageable.

I could make it if I tried.

On the other side, back the way we came before, was a stretch of shallow river, if I remembered right. I waddled up and out of the gulch with my dead arm dangling and the other clutching my revolver. Twice I collapsed to my knees. My throat swelled from thirst. If offered toilet water I'd have drank the bowl dry. Time lapsed languorously, and so unaware of its passing was I that when I ascended the ridge, night had fallen completely.

I fell to my stomach again and writhed through the olid undergrowth toward the direction in which I thought I might find water. I could hear the tracing of water, could smell river. Voices echoed in the distance still. The ridgebacks howling. Maybe a good two hundred yards away. From what I could tell, it sounded like they had climbed down into the gulch to look for me. Hadn't figured on me being able to climb out. Hell, I hadn't given the proposition much chance myself. On and on I crawled through the tall grasses, heedless of all else save for my thirst and the pulsing pain in my shoulder. At the edge of the wadi, I stumbled down a slope and nearly lost consciousness but pulled myself to the riverbank. If I never did anything else with the remainder of this life, I would drink water until my gut burst. I may die yet, but I won't die thirsty. When I got to the waterline I thrust my head into the stream and nearly drowned myself gulping. The water tasted like I imagined urine might taste, and more than likely it would make me sick enough to shit out my organs in a soup, and I did not care.

I drank and drank until my stomach cramped. I turned onto my back and gasped for sweet air and then drank some more. Finally full, I ripped off my shirt and buried my shoulder into the frigid mud. I pawed mud onto the gash for a salve to plug the bleeding and slow any infection, and then closed my eyes.

What followed for the next few hours I could not say.

When I woke again the night was still Cimmerian.

Wan light and utter quiet. Needle grass quaking in moonglow. I sat up and could no longer feel any pain in my shoulder, but my left leg stung worse than electrocution. The river trickled behind me. I went to roll up my pants but could not on account of my calf having swollen three times its normal size. I tried peeling off my boot in vain. My foot gorged too fat. Had to get the jackknife off my belt and saw at the leather. A great amount of pain, but I didn't scream. Pain worse than removing a bandage from a bad burn. I cut and cut until I finally made an incision all the way to my boot heel. I lay back and shook my leg until my boot wiggled off, and kicked it away, exhausted.

My foot was the size of a miracle fruit. A wonder it hadn't split my boot apart at the stitching while I slept. My stomach heaved and I vomited down my shirt like an infant unable to control his reflexes. I gurgled up bile and spit it clean of my mouth. There was blood in my vomit, and I figured death wasn't far along but it sure was taking its sweet time in arriving.

Hardly able to bend over again, I ripped my pant cuff all the way to the knee. Enough moonlight to see I'd been snakebit. I pawed at the piercings where fang had punctured skin. Two or three times I'd been bit just above the ankle. Hard to tell with all the bloating, but it was at least two times.

I stood on my good leg and hobbled about to find my revolver in the mud. The kind of snake and the severity of the venom were hard to gauge, but I didn't count on the dose to be anything shy of lethal. Maybe a mamba or a viper, the only two types I knew of by name in the area. I patted my pockets and found my cowhide flask. Sloshed it around to measure how much was left. Maybe an inch of whiskey. I tipped it back and stood for a moment but was unable to keep it down. More puke down my shirtfront. I gagged so hard I nearly asphyxiated on my own regurgitation. Impossible to walk in my condition. I crept into the river and, keeping to the slow running shallows, floated down it some distance.

Wading was all I could manage.

I drifted downstream for miles. The flickering fires of British encampments in the bluffs beyond, glowing orange flecks of campsites all over the distant dark hills. No telling where I was headed or how I might stumble upon remedy. The river turned at several bends but remained flat until morning broke over the range. I treaded water and never allowed myself deeper than where I could stand. There was no route to follow. For nearly half a day longer I sloshed my way down the watercourse, figuring it must lead out of the war land at some point. Finally, at long last, I saw a farmhouse set back against a stunted maize field. Purple maize as bright as coneflower. I'd never seen corn such a color except as ornaments in a cornucopia.

I paddled toward the shore.

The snake bite gave me more pain than the gunshot ever could. The swelling in my leg had risen halfway up my thigh by the time I dragged myself out of the river. A slow venom but nasty business all the same. My pants had come wholly apart on the left half and I tore them off all the way to my beltline. I reapplied a mud poultice to my shoulder to stopper the bleeding as best was possible. I didn't want to fathom how much blood I'd lost or how severe the infection.

My stomach was empty, but I continued to heave dryly. Everything inside me seized and rippled. Still, I was starved. I picked two ears of the violet corn from a stalk at the edge of the property and ate it raw. It was as hard as flint and nearly inedible, and still I chewed it down to the cob and saved the other ear in my remaining pant pocket as I hobbled toward the whitewashed farmhouse. A pair of jacaranda trees as brilliantly purple as the maize swayed over the roof even though I could feel no wind. Two children, a boy and girl both of fair complexion, were playing in the dirt at the bottom of the porch stoop. I waved from a safe distance. I hollered a greeting and the children stared for a moment before retreating inside. They cried shrilly. Inside the farmhouse a sound like a giant pot hitting the floor.

I stood waiting.

You fool, I told myself. You scared the damn kids and whoever their forbearers might be won't be too pleased at that. I listened closely. Footfalls from deep inside the house and then the screen door swung open. Behind a small-bore rifle came a giant old woman with a sprig of white hair that flowed like a beard in a breeze even though there was still no wind. With a bandolier slung over her cooking apron, she thrust the gun in my direction like a bayonet. A good thirty feet separated us.

She screamed at me in words unknowable.

Maybe Dutch, maybe Afrikaans.

I tried to speak but could manage no sound. I gestured at my wounds and begged for sympathy. What a sight I was: half of my pants completely torn away, my exposed leg swollen to elephantine mutation from the snake bites, my shirtfront torn and covered in old vomit, my entire left arm dead from numbing. I fell to my knees and looked skyward as if awaiting execution. A momentary rain came down nails, slowed to a dapple, then stopped altogether. A single passing cloud over a quivering sun.

Late summer lightning as faint as rumor past the flanked hills beyond.

The elderly woman screamed at me once more and continued to thrust her rifle.

"Kill me," I said hoarsely though I figured my words were lost on her.

She approached five steps, halving the distance between us. I bent my head low, and the last thing I saw when I collapsed sideways into the mud were the pair of swaying jacaranda trees over the pitched roof of the farmhouse and the downcast eyes of the woman screaming at me still as she pushed her rifle into my chest before all went blank.

IX

THE SECOND AND third day of the trial passed with little flair as a slew of what the Omaha papers called "small-time" witnesses took the stand. Mrs. Jesse Witten, neighbor of our Grover Street hideout, identified me as one of the two men living in that cottage. She testified she had seen me enter and exit the house often, usually with supplies, and that I had been the one to paste paper over the windows to darken the commotion within.

In rebuttal, Ritchie pressed her on key points of my appearance. She told the court I kept my blond hair long about my shoulders and wore a beard without glasses. However, I currently wore my hair short above the ear and was clean-shaven and nearly thirty pounds trimmer, with periscopic spectacles. How could she explain the distinct physical differences between the man she fingered as me five years ago and the man who now sat at the defense table?

The courthouse crowd mumbled at the discrepancy. The proletariat gallery sent up wild cheers when Ritchie challenged her on the remarkable disparity between those characteristics and on her failing eyesight. He called her an octogenarian who wore corrective prescription goggles of triple magnification. He claimed that she could just as easily mistake a raccoon for a dog as she could identify a man whom she claimed she saw come and go only at night from a distance of nearly fifty yards.

Next came a number of witnesses who all claimed to have seen me riding a horse around the Grover cottage and the Cudahy mansion. A young stable worker swore he saw me atop a palomino mare that could have very well been gray or white or even tan on the day after Edward Junior's disappearance. He admitted the early morning light could have made an impression on the horse's coat. Ritchie laughed off his testimony as that which came from a boy who couldn't tell the difference between sugar and flour if it was on his tongue.

A second witness agreed that the horse I rode was indeed cream in color, but he could not remember the breed or if the person atop the pony was tall or short, old or young. "Why," Ritchie had said, "if the horse was indeed white or ashen, perhaps it was the pale horse of the apocalypse and the rider upon him was Death with Hades following close behind!"

The audience again broke out in raucous laughter at his allusion to the book of Revelation. Ritchie swayed back and forth clutching his jacket lapels, often smiling at the audience as if he were a play actor and the courtroom his stage. A third witness swore the horse was not white at all, but a dark red mare. A fifth claimed the animal was a piebald pony and the rider was dark-skinned and dressed in a bathrobe.

Ritchie scratched his ear and declared to the jury, "Why, maybe the person who allegedly stole Cudahy's son wasn't riding a horse at all. Perhaps he was saddled upon a wooden Pegasus on a carousel while circus music played on a loop."

Even I had a chuckle at that one.

Judge Sutton rapped his gavel and warned Ritchie that making light of witness testimony in such a fashion was an affront to the integrity of his court.

"I disagree, Your Honor," Ritchie said in response, stroking his necktie. "The only thing that risks the integrity of this court is the botched testimony itself and the caliber of the witnesses presented to us by government counsel."

Judge Sutton was furious. "It's not in your place to judge testimony. You are skating treacherously close to being held in contempt. Do not try my patience once more."

"I wouldn't dare, Your Honor. And I thank you for your patience. But someone in this room, maybe many somebodies, have perjured themselves on the stand here today, and I think I'm within my bounds to call the jury's attention to these many discrepancies. For either we are listening to the tall tales of liars or we have come across something much grander: the very first chameleon horse known to science. And I, for one, stand very suspicious of both."

On the afternoon of the third day, a factory worker named Toby Glynn took the stand in his stained boiler suit and sooty face.

He told the story of how he heard me bragging in the Yarrow Saloon about the Cudahy abduction and all the gold I'd made from the ransom.

Let me say this: I hadn't been in an Omaha saloon since the kidnapping. I'd never even heard of the Yarrow before. The things people will say just to be heard. The fabrications we create just to remind the world we exist.

Glynn said he'd been drinking whiskey and didn't pay for a single pour as I bought rounds for the whole house with my twenty-dollar gold pieces all night long. When pressed, Glynn admitted he didn't know who I was until that night. He also admitted he had five or six whiskeys and, weighing only one hundred and thirty pounds, was surely intoxicated by such an amount. Could his memory be colored by drink?

Perhaps, he admitted, but doubtful.

Ritchie pressed harder about young Glynn's intentions. What prompted him to come forth and bear witness against a man he hardly knew, had never met before or after that supposed night in the Yarrow Saloon?

Glynn chewed his tongue as he thought on his reply.

"Well," he said after a very labored pause. "I came forth for Mr. Cudahy and his family."

Ritchie froze. "Oh? And do you know the Cudahy family well?"

Glynn stammered again. He was completely stymied. "I don't know them at all."

"And yet you came forth on their behalf?"

"Objection," Louie Black said. "The witness's intentions have nothing to do with what he saw or his testimony toward that fact."

Ritchie rebutted, "Your Honor, motivation is a powerful thing. How often is it necessary to prove a motive when establishing a reason behind a crime? How often in these hallowed chambers do we search for a man's motivation for committing crime? And so I ask the same of this witness, of any witness, because motivation can just as easily sway testimony as it can birth criminality. If I cannot challenge the veracity of this witness in such a manner—"

Judge Sutton stopped Ritchie with a wave of his hand. If the judge didn't interrupt him, Ritchie was liable to go on for an hour or more before taking time to breathe. The man had more gas in his lungs than a filibuster. Besides, Judge Sutton agreed. "Objection overruled. The witness will answer the question."

Glynn asked Ritchie to repeat the question. He studied on it longer with more chewing of his tongue and finally said, "I came forth because if I proved to be a friend to Mr. Cudahy, he might find it necessary to repay the favor."

"Repay the favor? Do you have business pending before the court yourself that Mr. Cudahy might serve witness to?"

"No, sir. I'm a law-abiding man."

"Well then, Mr. Glynn, I'm confused. How would Mr. Cudahy repay this favor? That's what you referred to in your testimony as, correct? A favor?"

Glynn licked his lips. "Why, with cash, of course."

The courtroom gasped.

"With cash? You mean to say you came forth hoping to be paid for your testimony?"

Glynn, in his soiled boiler coveralls and ashy face, responded firmly as if avowing his faith: "Isn't that all right? Heck, the jury gets paid. You get paid. The judge gets paid. Everyone in this court gets paid. What makes me so different?"

Ritchie smiled. He looked at Louie Black who was palming his red face. "Nothing at all makes you different. Everyone in this court would like to get a little of Mr. Cudahy's money if they could. You're no different at all."

To close out the last day of court before the weekend recess, Louie Black called Edward Cudahy Junior to the stand. The young man now stood nearly as tall as myself and just as strong of shoulder. He'd filled out about the chest and was handsome of jaw. He wore a tartan suit and pomaded hair in early recession along his temples. He was three weeks away from his twenty-first birthday, but looked closer to thirty and nowhere near the slender, peach-cheeked teenager I remembered snatching in front of his house five years earlier.

Louie Black wasted little time in cutting to the paste.

Yes, Eddie said, I was kidnapped by two men on my very own

street. They knocked me bonkers over the head and threw a blanket about me and hauled me away in a wagon. There were two men. Yes, one of them is here today in this court. There he sits. Pat Crowe. I know the man from top to bottom. They blindfolded me and kept me tied to a chair in an empty house for two days, but it seemed longer than two weeks.

Black asked him about that house. "Is it true you assisted the Omaha police in finding that hideout cottage on Grover Street?"

"Yes, sir. As soon as I stepped inside I knew it was the place. I saw all the cigarette butts on the floor that I had smoked while tied to a chair."

"But you say you were blindfolded the whole time?"

"That's right. They blinded me with a shirt, but they should've put plugs in my ears, too. I knew from the echo of the floorboards that it was an empty house. I could hear the tooting of our packing plant whistles and our locomotives. I couldn't have been more than a mile away."

Black ran his thumbs down the inside of his suspender straps. "Tell us more about this experience. How did your abductors treat you?"

"Treat me? Well, I never did much but sit there in that chair. They fed me coffee, crackers, cigarettes. A little whiskey and ham. They treated me pretty well."

Black wobbled as if shocked. "Treated you pretty well?"

"As well as someone who's kidnapped you could treat you, I suppose."

"Well, then, it was a high time at the old Grover Street cottage, was it?"

"No, sir. I did not mean to imply that at all. I was scared to death. Scared for my life. I urinated on myself. I wasn't allowed use of a toilet. The men, they drank a lot, and I feared they might harm me after they got drunk. I didn't know if I'd survive the next five minutes or if I'd ever see my family again."

Black asked, "Would you know these men again?"

"There were two of them. And one of them is Pat Crowe, like I said before. I could never forget him. I'd know him among all creation."

"And how can you be so sure of that? Defense counsel has

raised many points of contention here in this court about the ability of multiple witnesses to identify your captor, despite the fact that they all have identified the same one. So, tell us, how are you certain that one of your kidnappers was the defendant?"

Eddie nodded at me. I shrank in my chair.

He said, "Because I met him just four days earlier. He came to our house to converse with my dad one morning before I left for school."

"Pat Crowe came to your house on Dewey Avenue? The same street on which he nabbed you off the sidewalk under the cover of dusk?"

"That's right."

"Interesting indeed. Very curious. Can you tell us about that meeting?"

"Well, he was in a desperate state to look at him."

"Pat Crowe, you mean?"

"Yes. He was shaking from the cold and looked sickly in the face and had a pretty nasty cough. It'd been snowing out and he didn't even have a coat about him. My dad knew him from when he was one of his employees at the packinghouse. He'd fallen on hard times. I think he was inebriated and begging. My dad offered him a good job in California. It seems he never took that offer. Looking back on it, he wasn't there for any other reason than to get a good look at me. To size me up. Four nights later, him and his pal approached me on our street. They'd dressed up like police detectives and told me I was under arrest for robbing my aunt. Of course, that was just their ruse. Next thing I knew, I was pelted over the head, and everything went dark. I was knocked out for a good while. I don't remember anything else after that until we arrived at their hideout. They forced me inside and bound me to a chair."

"Did they talk to you in that house while you were tied up?"

"Yes. One of them was almost always in the room with me. Usually both were. The other man, Pat's partner, was a drunk. He slurred his words and stunk of whiskey."

"And what kind of things did they say to you?"

"Some of it I don't remember too clearly anymore. I've tried to clear my head of it."

"That's only natural, I'd say. No one likes to recall traumatic episodes from their past. But is there anything at all you can tell the court in this regard?"

Eddie worked his hands together like a worried mother. "There is one something I'll never forget no matter how hard I try. Pat Crowe, he said to me, he said that I better hope my father loves me more than his money. He said if my dad didn't come forth with the gold that he, well"—Eddie sputtered, his voice strained—"that he'd slit my throat and dig a grave in the basement of that house. He said, 'If your dad fails to deliver the money, you're going into that grave and these barrels of quicklime will be your only coffin lining. It will be poured all around you after I have killed you. You will simply disappear, and no one on this earth will ever know what has become of you.'"

X

I woke from dream to the sound of trumpeting rain on a thatch roof. Laying on my back, staring at a ceiling unfamiliar, I blinked as rapidly as an animal come out of hibernation to unbearable sunshine. I choked on my phlegm and sat up spitting on my chin. My nostrils flared. The aromatic smell of acacia wood breaking apart in a mud stove. Dangling lines of eggplant and yellow carrots as long as femurs were strung about the walls like jute. A pair of grease lamps illuminated a farmhouse kitchen in threads. My vision a cluster of white spangles.

I sat up fully and wiped my mouth.

I was shirtless with bandaging over my left shoulder and suddenly, in a flush, I remembered the bullet I took and the ambush in the deep red gully and wading downriver across the treeless flats of the unsunned veld. Thought I might vomit but did not. My recovering leg was encased in a puttee. A heavy nerve of rain strummed the roofing. I strained for a look out the window above my straw bed. Outside, a thundery sky and gristly downpour thrashed the field of purple corn. Adjacent to the maize line was a pink stone corral for a few heads of starving cattle who ran about in circles, soaked and terrified.

"You're a considerable man to have survived," a voice said from the back corner of the damp kitchen.

I turned. The giant old woman with the sprig of white hair sat on an upturned pail, husking corn into another pail between her knees. She wore pantaloons, cloth shoes, and a man's shirtsleeves.

"Where am I?" I asked and massaged my aching eyelids.

The woman tossed some old husks into the cookstove. The fire belched upon receiving the weak tinder and then flared down again. "The Hotel Baroque."

"You speak English."

"I know English. Most trekboers do. Rather'd not speak it."

"Language of your enemy and so on and so forth?"

The old woman rose and shuffled over to a cutting table where she mealed together a concoction of spider weed, goat milk, eucalyptus leaves, and some kind of jam that looked like black honey into a wooden bowl. I watched her intently. Three long wizardly hairs on her chin. Her flabby arms shook from the effort of muddling the ingredients. "I removed the bullet from your shoulder and cleaned the wound, but you'll need to keep it in bandages or it will get infected," she said and brought me the bowl and told me to drink the batter. "You've a mild dose of fever. This will make you feel right pert."

I sipped the medicine. A greasy, dark milk. "Where are your children?"

"Laid to rest in a church plot back in Ladysmith."

"Jesus. How long have I been out?"

"Two and one-half days."

My face blanked. "And your children? Gone and buried in that time?"

The woman returned to husking corn. She dropped a fresh ear into a cauldron of boiling water on top of her mud stove. Her voice was impassive but kind. "My children died long ago."

"I saw them. Two little fair-haired ones. On your stoop. A boy and a girl."

"You were hallucinating."

I sat down my bowl.

"Are you hungry?"

"I could eat like all wrath."

She dropped two more ears into the scald. "Making corn soup."

"I wouldn't mind getting corned, myself."

The woman scoffed. "I don't have any trim for quaffing."

"I'm not particular miss . . . ?"

"Rutts. My family name is Rutts."

I struggled on a smile. "I'm Fritz Bebout."

"If you say so. I've a little antifogmatic in the cupboard," Rutts said and, with great aching effort, rose again to pour me a dop of white alcohol from an oviform bottle stoppered with a cob. I accepted the clay mug with two hands and thanked her mightily. The liquor was as strong as moonshine with the lethal taste of sorghum and sourwood.

"Have you a smoke?" I asked.

"I haven't."

"A chaw of turbaccur, maybe?"

Rutts nodded and procured a pouch of goldflake from somewhere deep in her apron. I scooted over to the edge of the bed, and together we sat dipping the leaves and spitting juice onto the fragrant roasting logs in her stove.

I put my wrapped leg up on one of the corn pails. "Probably a mamba, right?"

"You'd been dead if it were a mamba. A boomslang it was most probably."

"You saved my life," I said.

"I'll queue you up a bath for your leg. It needs soaking," Rutts replied and made business scooting herself into a backroom to heat the bath before dinner. The tub was a giant copper vessel large enough to hold three men, and the water was heated underneath by a cairn of hot rocks. I tested the temperature. Hot enough to cook my skin right off the bone. I managed my ankle and calf into the boil in order to soak my wound but couldn't tolerate the heat for more than a few seconds.

Come nightfall we ate supper sitting before the mud stove. I slopped up corn soup and cowpeas from a biscuit tin with a bent spoon. I ate three bowls and tore into some rocky bread for dipping and indulged in another chaw of goldflake afterward and sipped more fog while the rain swooped music against the thatch roof. Old woman Rutts broke the silence by asking, "What's your real name? You surely aren't any Fritz Bebout."

I was in no state to draw up memory, and I said as much.

"You owe me at least your name."

"I owe you more than that. My name's Pat Crowe."

"An Irish lad, then?"

"American," I said. My head swarmed from the mug of fog. "I suppose you could say I haven't any home, though, really."

"Everyone has a home. Even those who've abandoned it," Rutts said and rose from her cane chair for her bedroom without saying another word.

In the morning she drew another bath for me, this one much cooler. I soaked my whole body and got the crust off my skin with a currycomb. A cross breeze blew in through a pair of open windows. While drying myself with a ratty towel, two separate voices and the faint clatter of hooves echoed outside. I scanned the landscape through a window, my feet still in the bath. Two British soldiers on horseback approached through a wide aisle in the purple corn. They donned green tunics and khaki helmets and rode their horses at a walk. A pair of Waler ponies by the look of them. Hearty creatures shipped in from Australia. Horses bred for war that could trek nearly as much ground without water as camels. The English never cultivated anything on their own merit. Not even their goddamn horses. Everything was seized, claimed, or imported. I peeked my head out of the bathroom door.

"Got a pair of scouts out there in your corn," I said in an urgent whisper.

Rutts sat unalarmed by the stove. "I know. They're early."

"Early? You're expecting them?"

"They've come for reparations."

"How's that?"

"I give them food and drink and a place to bunk for the night and whatever else they want. In turn, they don't burn down my barn or my crops."

"Whatever else they want?"

"Sometimes if they get drunk enough it comes to that."

"That's some arrangement."

"Reason how my farm is one of the few still left standing."

I came out of the washroom holding my towel around my waist. "Fetch me my clothes and revolver."

"Best not. Best to stay hidden if I were you."

I grabbed my pearl-handled pistol and bandolier belt off a knob by the front door and hurried about for my clothes.

"Your laundry is on the boil," Rutts said and nodded at the pot of water cooking my tattered shirt and pants. I stammered and fussed and checked the cylinder of my revolver to make sure it was loaded. Hoof beats circled outside the farmhouse. There was no time to react as the riders came calling. I climbed naked out of the washroom window with my revolver in hand and scampered into the tall purple corn. I crawled through the stalks to the other side of the house in order to get a vantage point. Knelt down in the dirt and waited. I could see the backs of the soldiers up on their horses still. They sat on their ponies a few feet in front of the farmhouse discussing payment with the old woman.

I strained to hear.

"Hellu, Maggie," one of the riders said in greeting. "We've come for our due and proper."

"You're a week early," Rutts replied from the doorway.

"Are we now? Say, I suppose we might be."

"Suppose you'll have to indulge us anyhow," the other rider said.

"I haven't much for giving. A little milk. Some corn. I'm plumb out of liquor and bread and potatoes."

"Oh, come now, old girl. Surely you can do better than that. Unless maybe you'd like to take a ride with us back to Pinewood."

The second rider added, "And this is such a nice farm. Shame to have to torch her."

I swelled with raw ire. A deep guttural hatred so awkward and unknowable that it was nearly ancestral in my bones and my throat. I felt it neither in my head nor my heart. Rather it was inside my follicles, in my pores. An emotion so ancient, so somatic, I could not help myself. I bolted out of the corn as naked as I'd entered it. I held my pearl pistol behind my back, clasped against my buttocks with both hands.

I smiled like a lunatic and called out to the pair of soldiers from a safe distance of about thirty yards. "Either one of you nancies be able to spare me a change of clothes?"

The soldiers turned in their saddles. The fatter of the two, a piggish man with a lampshade mustache, was chewing on his helmet string like a toddler. The second man tugged on his lead rope to turn his horse around fully and set his rifle across his lap. Neither man could quite believe his eyes.

"Criminy, George," the second man said to the first. His cigar nearly fell out of his mouth. "He's butt naked."

I stepped forward. "Nothing gets past you, friend."

"Sir, you do know your John Thomas is dangling in the free wind?"

I considered my own genitals and cocked the pistol hammer behind my back. "You got a keen eye. Attention to the obvious. I like that in a man."

The soldiers sat staring. Saddle leather squeaked under their weight. They could not stop staring, and I could not stop smiling.

"You boys fancy a little uphill gardening?" I asked. Judging by the blank expressions on their faces, my homosexual allusion had escaped them. A moment passed, and I stepped closer again. Twenty yards between us now. "Gets lonely out here on the veld, don't it?"

"Maybe he's one of those escaped from Barberton last month," the first man said.

"Barberton?" I asked and paused as if drawing up a thought. "Oh yes. I heard of that place. That's the prison camp where you keep all the fellas naked, right? A little slap and tickle at Her Majesty's pleasure? I heard it told the queen's army has been going a little against clocks up in those parts, if you know what I mean."

The second soldier steadied his rifle but was still too confused to aim the barrel. He looked at his partner like he'd been struck over the head. "This bloke's off his onion."

"What the devil are you doing out here without any clothes on?" the other asked.

"Looking for a good time," I said. "Looks like I found one."

"He's crazier'n hell."

The man with the rifle finally put it to sights. "Off with you, you crazy bastard."

I took little heart in the threat. "I'll give you a half crown for your coat and drawers."

"And where would you be keeping such a coin? Two inches deep in your own arse?"

Both of the soldiers laughed at that.

I said, "Now that's not very nice. Not very nice at all. Seems basic manners were little taught to you boys."

"You hardly need manners when you're the one holding the gun," the second man with the rifle said and put a boot heel into his horse's flank to approach.

"Well, I can't argue with that logic," I said, whipped out my pistol from behind my back, and shot the encroaching soldier clean through his neck. His artery ruptured, and he clasped both hands over his throat as it jetted blood. I'd never seen that much blood come out of a man that quickly. Before he even had time to fall off his horse, I fired two more shots squarely into the other soldier's chest and watched him drop from his saddle in a bundle. His horse took off at a full gallop like a shot out of a gate stall and drug his body around in the mud, his foot still caught in the stirrup.

It was a hell of a time corralling the two war horses into Miss Rutts's paddock and even sillier than it was difficult on account I was still naked as I tried to coax the horses with nothing more than a switch. Rutts watched me dance around in circles trying to calm and steer the ponies. I looked back at her now and then. She was smiling widely. Watching me hop around naked as a jaybird fooling with those damn horses must've brought her more amusement than she'd had doing anything else in many years. Maybe ever.

The foolishness went on for the better part of an hour before I could manage both horses past the gate and lock them up. Next came the task of lugging the two bodies nearly a hundred yards to the other side of the farmhouse. I stripped each man of his clothing before I pulled them one at a time by their legs over the stone well. I stood panting and heaving for a long while and drank from the well bucket before finally dressing myself in the uniform of the slimmer soldier. I donned his pants, boots, green tunic, and even his khaki helmet. Everything except the man's skivvies and socks. The pants didn't fit at all. They sagged off my hips like I'd cinched on a potato sack. When I finally came back to the house it was well into the morning.

"Believe I'll need me another bath before the day's out," I said to Rutts when I stomped into the small kitchen. She smiled and smiled from her chair at the table.

"Did you enjoy that show?" I asked.

Rutts blushed and studied her feet.

"That real fat one I pegged in the throat? God. He must've been one surprised sonofabitch to have gotten shot by a fella in the buff."

"He must've been, yes," Rutts said.

I took off my new helmet. "Well, that sorry pair won't be harassing you anymore."

"If not them, it'll be someone else. On and on it'll go."

I tossed the cloth purse I'd lifted off one of the dead soldiers on the table. It was full of shillings and British gold. "You might be able to get some relief with that coin there. I'd maybe find a nice place to stash it under your floorboards."

"I'd rather go hungry for torture than make use of that currency."

"One kind of coin buys milk the same as any other."

"It'd put my soul at hazard."

I seized up a chair. Kicked my bare feet on the lip of the mud stove after taking off my new riding boots. I'd found a clay pipe in the belongings of one of the soldiers and set about to having a smoke. "I sure do get a kick out of you, missus. A real kick. And, well, just between you and me and the gatepost, you go ahead and do what you want with that coin. But don't say I never left you anything."

Rutts noted my improved disposition. "You're in a fine fettle."

"Turned out to be a pretty good day after all."

"So you'll be leaving off, then?"

I wheezed on my new pipe like an asthmatic. "Come first light tomorrow. Got to get those bodies and horses off your property. If some other troops come snooping around, well, you know what that means better than I do."

"And after that?"

"After that?" I chewed on the thought. The pipe made me dizzy and reflective. "Well, after that I'm going to make port dressed up as a wounded British soldier in my new duds. Bullet wound in my back will come in handy for that. I'll sail up to London and then back to New York. Next I'll have me a drink of good old-fashioned American brandy, eat two or three platters of oysters on ice, hire up a whore that suits me as good as did my first horse. Maybe one with strawberry curls and some chunk to her. But, first things first. I got two new rifles, fifty pounds of ammunition, a horse to sell and one to ride. There'll be couple of graves to dig when I get enough distance between me and your homestead. That and one helluva long boat ride. But I tell you what, I can taste that brandy and them oysters already. I can smell the lavender in that whore's hair. Strong as pollen, I can smell it now."

XI

WHAT THE DAY had melted, night froze again. Come the bluing of dawn, icicles as long as stalactites hung from the courthouse eaves. I rolled over on my jailhouse cot. It took me a moment to realize someone was standing at my cell door. A man dressed in a plaid suit and sheepskin coat held a long garment bag hooked over his shoulder by a single finger. The man kicked the bars of my cell after considering his timepiece. He dropped it back into his vest pocket with a labored sigh. I blinked myself awake, sat up in a torpor state. My hair as wild as cockscomb. I rubbed my tongue all over my mouth. My teeth felt like they were growing fur.

With clear eyes I looked again at the man standing before my cell bars.

Tom Dennison.

A pall of smoke around his head. Hazy as a nebula. He smoked a gold cigarette in an ivory holder. Wore fine doeskin gloves.

"Good morning, kitten," he said and tossed me a beautiful golden banana between the bars. "I brought you breakfast."

I nearly fumbled the fruit. Looked at it in my open palms like an artifact. "Didn't you read the sign?"

Dennison balked. "And justice for all?"

"Don't feed the animals," I said, stripped the banana, and masticated half of it in two huge bites like I was being clocked by a timer.

"This cold is ungodly. I do hope you're keeping warm in here."

I scarfed the rest of the banana, smacked my lips like chewing library paste. I gestured at the privy in the corner of my cell. "My toilet water froze overnight. Can you believe that?"

"I can believe almost anything when it comes to you, Patrick."

"Froze like pond ice. Goddamnest thing," I said and pitched the peel into the toilet where, sure enough, it landed on ice without sinking. "You got another nanner on you?"

"I've something better," Dennison said and unzipped the garment bag. "A cheviot suit. Hand-tailored to your measurements. Tan with pink stripes. Ain't it something?"

"That's swell of you. Just what every jailbird needs," I said, my cheeks still bulging with banana, and pinched my own black and white prison stripes. "A good striped suit."

"You're not a jailbird anymore. I'm springing you."

"You tell the guards that on your way up?"

Dennison closed the garment bag. "I posted your bail. We've something to discuss."

"My bail? That's seven thousand dollars."

"What're friends for?"

I lay back down. "Well, they shore ain't for floating seven large. That's what banks and loan sharks are for. And you. Whatever you are."

"You're in no spot to be refusing charity," a new voice called out from the down the hall.

I stood and went to my bars and rested my hands between the slats. My attorney hobbled over with a limp, clutching his briefcase against his chest with both arms as if it were a source of heat, chattering and cursing the cold.

"What're you doing here?" I asked.

Ritchie said, "There's not much time to discuss. I invited Tom here. He's here to help. We have an ace in the hole, and it's time to play the card."

I took out a smuggled cheroot from my prison waistband and set fire to the clipped cigar with my last match. I rasped the bars with my knuckles. "I'm not going anywhere with this clown," I said and gestured at Dennison. "Being in his debt is like being in the grave."

Dennison smiled. "I'd be in your debt, actually, as it is."

I didn't take the bait. "I see, said the blind man to the deaf dog."

"You need to trust me," Ritchie said.

My eyelids were still heavy with sleep. My words sluggish, like talking in a dream. "Trust you? Trusting you this far is what's going to get me a life sentence in Joliet. Goddamn you. I thought you was a sorcerer, not a lawyer. That's what they call you, isn't it? The sorcerer in the purple suit?"

"And what about what they call you?"

"Hell, what about all that big talk you gave me when you came courting with that fancy bottle of brandy? Where's that guy with all the big friends in Washington? I'd like him to show face. That guy would get me outta this trap."

"He's right, Sammy," Dennison agreed. "You know, the next time you want a good spanking, take it down at one of my clubs and not in that goddamn courtroom."

Ritchie brayed. "I'm awful glad you're so worried about it, Tom."

"Yeah, you and that Louie Blue, you two are putting on quite the show," Dennison said. "Yes, sir. That audience is getting to experience all sorts of thrills without paying a cent."

"Louie Black. Not Louie Blue," Ritchie corrected him.

Dennison clucked. "Well, gee woops, Sam. Like I give a sweet one what color his name is. Man's a one-term district attorney who fell into the gig backwards two years out of the public defender's office, and you're piddling around in that courtroom like he's the god of all thunder."

"It's you who ought to be paying more attention. Louie's been the D.A. for two terms now with a strong push to be this state's next governor," Ritchie said.

Dennison laughed.

"What's so goddamn funny?" I asked.

"The state's next governor is exactly what he's going to be," Dennison said. "I've always found you can get yourself full by satisfying the appetites of other men."

I paced my cell like a puma in a zoo cage. I sucked on my cheroot with a hungry compulsion, blowing smoke all over. "You know something? Most everything you say wouldn't make sense to a crazy man."

"Governor Black," Dennison said. "Kind of has a ring to it, wouldn't you say?"

I finally registered the plan. Louie Black wanted the governor's mansion. Tom Dennison wanted to pick up the scraps of the stockyard empire after it crumbled apart following the Beef Trust trial. Cudahy was the linchpin. See him lose in Omaha, and the Big Six monopoly would get taken to task in Chicago. All Louie Black needed to do was step out of the way, and he'd find himself anointed the most powerful man in the state by the kingmaker who used the political system like a checkbook.

"Oh, that's keen," I said to Dennison. "That's really something. You're like a rat got into the wheat cellar. You know that? Nibbling and gnawing at everyone else's stores."

"It's the best remedy," Ritchie said and called for the turnkey who came over with a giant ring of keys and unlocked my cell gate.

Dennison stepped inside and handed me the garment bag. "It's the only remedy."

I stood there stymied. "What about good lawyering? Why not try that instead?"

Ritchie said, "This is lawyering, son."

Dennison clapped me on the back. "Come now, Paddy boy. How about you get dressed and the three of us go make a new friend?"

XII

I fled Africa as a stowaway on a hospital ship due for London, and paid a surgeon a considerable sum to properly mend the bullet wound in my back. From England I took the first Cunard liner to New York and did largely what I told old Mrs. Rutts I would do: booked the Randolph suite at the Astoria Hotel, ate an epicurean supper of bluepoint oysters and lobster thermidor, hired a hot medicinal bath, drank my fill of Benedictine, and dollied around with a strawberry-haired whore with a forty-inch bust and a rump like a horse.

The Boer republics, I learned from an extra edition of the *Post*, had fallen. The news struck me as gravely as if the headline reported the death of my sister. The rebellion was quite dead, but I was still somehow alive and not sure how thankful I was for that mercy. All told, I'd been away overseas for eight months.

I thought on good old Mrs. Rutts. On the morning I left, I didn't wake her to say goodbye. I stopped in her doorway, watched her sleep, and was nearly overcome with the emotion to kiss her on her forehead. Instead I parted the same way I'd arrived: dizzy and swollen of heart, my leg and arm in little better condition, unable to find the right words. I left her nearly every dollar I still had secretly sown into my jacket. I took only what I needed to see myself through to the States with a little to spare for frivolity once I got there. She might burn it in her mud stove for kindling or bury it in her cornfield. But that was up to her, stubborn old gal that she was. At the very least, she would understand my gratefulness. Or so I hoped. I could not measure my gratitude by any other gauge besides maybe writing her a few lines of verse, but oftentimes even words full of poetry have no heart, for the heart has no tongue.

The rest of the money from the Cudahy ransom was still buried in a nectarine orchard in Nogales where Billy had died. I thought then I might never go back to retrieve it. Some things must simply be left buried.

From New York, I rode to Chicago and then on to Nebraska in the wheat car of a freight train and nearly froze in transit. The chilly springtime wind, gusting sometimes over forty miles an hour, hardened my clothes to bark. I switched trains at a division point, sleeping again in wild hay while enduring fierce wind, and gained Omaha for the first time in over two years since the kidnapping. I'd been harried across the globe, had not been seen or heard from in all that time. Still, when I stepped off the platform, there was my likeness pasted on circulars everywhere: PAT CROWE WANTED.

The fifty-thousand-dollar reward offered by Cudahy for my capture, dead or alive, was still in force. There was no point at which the man would give up the search. The Pinkerton thugs demanded a wage of a thousand dollars a week for their efforts and had found nothing, and still Cudahy paid them their salary. Burlington detectives still skimmed the hills and rode the trains and frequently stalked my old stomping grounds in hopes of apprehending me.

I was cautious, but not overly so. My appearance had changed dramatically since I was last in the city. I'd trimmed my beard to a Vandyke style, cut my hair above the ear and stained it with bootblack, carried thirty extra pounds in my gut. I donned simple clothing that gave me the look of a banker or a merchant. Still, I dared not dally on the streets and hired a suite in a pink hotel. A young bellhop brought me a supper of liver and onions and black coffee as strong as a doorjamb. Wheat was scattered all about the room from my time riding in the open freight car. It was in my hair, in my socks. I introduced myself as Jonathan Loveless. I told the bellhop I was in the wheat business and had been inspecting grain silos all day.

"Reason why I'm covered in all this pasturage," I said and tipped the lad handsomely.

The boy smiled. He knew right off who I really was. My changed appearance might fool a man at a glance, but up close I was still unmistakable. I asked the bellhop to bring me two glasses of forty-rod and again gave him a nice gratuity.

"They've been snooping around here a lot, looking for you," the bellhop said when he returned with the whiskey.

I peeled off a sock and shook it loose of wheat strands. "Who do you think I am?"

"Everyone knows who you are. And the police sure are set on nabbing you."

"Do you favor them?"

"I favor the fifty thousand dollars they're offering for your head."

"And you really think they'll fork it over if you squeal?"

The bellhop thought on that. "No. They probably might not."

I unfolded another bill from my roll. "They probably might not is right. They'll say you never said boo. But me? I pay cash up front to my friends."

The bellhop snatched the money.

"Now, you wouldn't be telling anybody about my residence here, would you?"

"No, sir. Not when you pay me twenty dollars for a fifty-cent whiskey."

I laughed and shook out my other sock. "And there's more where that came from. I'm not asking you to do anything illegal, but if you see any John Law snooping around, you come and knock on this door twice. Is that something you can manage?"

The bellhop smiled again. "Certainly so, Mr. Loveless."

I relaxed some after that. Swallowed two thunderbolt pills for my splitting headache and slept like a dead man all day and far into the next night. About eight o'clock the following morning, the young bellhop came pounding on my door.

I jumped out of bed and into my trousers.

"They're coming for you, old boy," the bellhop said through the door and then fled down the hallway. I went to the window. Three posses were rallying on the hotel from every avenue. Some of the men were plainclothes detectives, some uniformed officers, and others were dressed like farmers.

I was hemmed in on all sides. I cinched on my gun belt and stomped on my boots and made for the roof of the hotel via a back staircase. From there I scaled down the lone fire escape and jumped to the lower roof of a nearby building. Once on the street, I bought a newspaper from a magazine stand and immersed myself in the pages as I walked among pedestrians starting out their day. Clear of the city sidewalks, I fled at a sprint toward the Missouri River.

Another score of men crept along the north edge of the river: local farmers with their double-barreled quail guns and a few piebald hunting dogs howling and some of the men mounted on sorry old cow horses that weren't fit to pull a toy wagon. I guessed them to be thirty or forty strong. I bellied down in the brittle river cane and crawled for the bank. The river was sheeny with skim ice around the shallows and as blue as the deep ocean in others. I scrabbled through the slough while the posse from the north rode overland. A light drilling of spring snow started. Mud as trapping as quicksand. I heaved for breath and scanned the shore in every direction.

Past a low tailrace I spotted a huddle of fishing skiffs moored to a small dock. Wind whorled the new spring snow, but the sky was largely clear save for the leavings of a few battered clouds. The sun was well out and felt warm on my skin. My whole front half caked with cold mud. Yet another posse was on my trail from the opposite direction. They advanced in formation like trained infantry, and I could do naught else besides make a dash for the dock. There were three boats there. Flat-bottom punts used for fishing gizzard shad and walleye. I set two adrift and climbed into the third and rowed for my life.

The posse climbed down the bluff toward the riverbank on their stomachs and opened fire. I kept my sculls to the water. I rowed through the lacey ice with great effort until my skiff broke clear of the shallows and was out toward midstream. A few of the men shook off their coats and ditched their guns and swam for the boats I set loose. I quit my oar long enough to fire a few shots at the swimmers and hit one of them in the arm just as he was about to dive into water barely knee deep. I could have killed him with ease. I aimed my pistol and was about to make the man's wife a widow and his children forever fatherless, but refrained.

Two of the other swimmers turned back to assist the man. I lost three hunters from my pursuit instead of just one by the simple abstinence of my pistol. I rowed faster. Precipitous gunfire echoed from a grove of cottonwoods so close to the shoreline that their roots grew into the river. More shooters crested a hummock over-looking the water and fired down upon me in brittle bursts but never came within twenty feet of my boat, as if I was under the protection of aegis. I nearly bent the oar with my effort and soon found myself with the advantage of the down current.

The ambuscade perched on the northern edge shouted and fired their pitiful flintlocks blindly. Buckshot scattered the water. The boom of double-aught-like musketry. A blessed thing they only had farmhands on the other end of those shotguns. If there had been one trained rifle among that mob, I would've been sunk. I rowed and the two posses sprinted along the banks to keep pace with my skiff. I returned fire in the hiccups of silence, volleying shots back and forth between hard bursts of frantic rowing.

Water began to fill the bottom of my skiff. Some lucky shot had put a hole in the side of the boat. I cursed and rowed harder. I paddled for the far shore as a keelboat approached from the south. Both posses were losing ground on foot. For a moment I thought I might be able to outdistance them all the way to Kansas, but then my skiff breached a sandbar. The Missouri was at dearth before thaw, shallow as the Platte in spots.

I could not pry the vessel loose. Bullets plowed all around me. I jumped into the freezing water and pulled at the bow and dug at the sand with my oar, using it like a crowbar to jack the boat free of the sand. It was no use. The punt was stuck but good. The water was so shallow in that part of the river that I could stand with it up to my chest. I was twenty yards from the Iowa shore, and I swam with my last energy for life and liberty.

I sprinted through a camass meadow and floundered my way through a thin line of blackjack trees, soaked and muddy still and every breath as tortuous in my throat and lungs as if I'd been keen-ing all day. A flood of sunlight split the sky. I came upon a soybean field still to be planted and overrun with pigweed, and I slowed my pace to a walk. I could not run one more step. I was too spent to lace my shoes, which had nearly come off my feet from the weight of gathered mud.

Downriver, some members of the second posse had seized boats and were rowing across the Missouri. They were dogged in their pursuit. The promise of fifty thousand dollars will spur many a man to endure extremes and go to lengths he could not possibly brave otherwise. These men rode under the oriflamme of mammon and for nothing else. I jogged toward a secluded barn. It was a fatigued mile from the river, and I nearly collapsed upon reaching it. I chucked myself into the doors, barreling them open with a heave of my shoulder, and fell into more hay. If I never again lay in straw or paced another river with death upon my tail, I would live a happy remainder of my days.

There was only one pony in the stalls. A paint horse with pinto spotting. I saddled the animal with a pillion and crusty blanket and led it from the stables. Throwing myself upon it took my last ounce of energy. I was completely sapped and begged the creature for good speed. Just as I was riding out of the barn, a woman's voice wailed from the farmhouse porch.

"Cletus! Cletus! Some sommabitch is stealing our nag!"

"Off to see the wizard, lady," I screamed with shortened breath. "Back in a jiffy."

I larruped the horse with my boot heels and rode the poor beast as hard as she would allow for near on fifteen miles until she was just as taxed as me. The horizon behind me an empty line. Even the men who had horses surely didn't drive them over the river. I paced my stolen nag for the rest of the day, trotting over swards of exposed hardpan where the plain was as dusty as the desert and fields of early globe mallow had shriveled in the unexpected chill.

I walked the horse until night dropped. The moon rose in a sickle, and a brisk wind came with it. I could smell myself through my clothes. The odor as strong as ripening cheese. I neared Neola, Iowa, and turned south toward the Rock Island Railroad junction. I stopped outside the depot, which was vacant for the evening, hid the saddle in a ditch, and turned my stolen horse loose.

The pony loped after me, nickering somber tones in her nostrils that I'd never imagined possible from a horse. I embraced her. "You're one true hussy, old cousin. I don't want any goodbyes, either. I surely don't. It's a rotten charge, us parting. But that woman will be missing you, and those boys on my tail would know you from a mile away."

I led the animal into a rancher's paddock on the other side of the train station, closed the gate with a cinch, and ran for the rail yards, sprinting over the circuitous tracks. I'd missed the last passenger train for the night and would have to wait until morning before I could catch a ride out of the city.

XIII

Tom Dennison's touring car was the most beautiful machine I had ever seen: green as pulverized lime, with brass fittings, deep leather seats that could seat five more comfortably than most people's drawing rooms, and eighteen actual horsepower. Dennison's driver, a young mulatto with a pencil-thin mustache, wore white leather gloves and a chauffer's cap. We coasted over the icy avenues with the sluggish, confident pace of a canal barge. Slush splattered out from under the fenders like a continual sneeze. Snow as fat as soap curds fell from a bone pale sky. A gloriously crystalline morning. We tobogganed around a slick curve. Dennison chewed an extinguished cigar stump and studied a daily racing form. He liked a filly by the name of Kiss and Tell in the noon handicap at Tijuana.

Finally we came to the Jewish section of town. A little four-block stretch where the city, according to Dennison, kept its best delis and its stupidest lawyers. Enchantingly enough, Louie Black's apartment was above a kosher delicatessen dubbed Zimmerman's.

I exited the car after Ritchie and Dennison, into the talcum snowfall. We paused momentarily in front of the deli, and the sight of the shop brought back memories of my own butchery. I stood there staring through the shop windows like a dunce trying to make sense of an equation on a chalkboard. Stood there moon-eyed and full of heartsickness, grinning like an idiot. Lamb shanks as big as cavemen's clubs hung on a rack in a neat row. Cheese wheels the size of wagon tires. Glittering bottles of sacramental wine. Barrels of gefilte fish. Knuckled pickles in jars of brine.

"Hey, wistful one," Dennison called to me. "Time and tide tarry for no man."

I shrugged snow off my shoulders. I followed Dennison and my attorney to the third floor, clomping up the staircase. Dennison stopped before Louie Black's door. He cinched up his tie and pounded on the door like he was police. We waited for nearly half a minute before the door creaked open. The district attorney heaved behind the gap. He'd left the chain lock in place. I could see his left eye through the crack in the door. His blue iris orbited wildly.

"Counselor Black? It's Tom Dennison come by."

"I'm not decent."

"When have you ever been good?"

"I'm in my skivvies," Black clarified.

"Forget your pants," Dennison told him. "This is urgent."

The door opened fully. Black waved us in and bellied up to his table without pants. His shirttails covered his underwear and his tartan socks were held halfway up his calves with elastic supporters, no shoes. His apartment stank of old water and unwashed feet. Dennison took off his hat and sat down next to Black at his small card table.

Ritchie and I huddled in the kitchenette over a sink full of dress socks soaking in discolored water.

"Do you always eat breakfast without any pants on?" Dennison asked.

"It's my home," Black said.

Dennison raised a palm. "Whatever makes you comfortable."

I pinched a putrid soaking sock out of the mess.

"Laundry in the kitchen?" I asked and dropped the sock back in the suds.

"I'm frugal," Black said and resumed his breakfast of frankfurters and runny eggs. He worked his knife and fork like gearshift levers.

I watched him eat with a rueful smile. The table was cluttered with heavily fingerprinted jars of jellies and mustards. Spoon handles jutted out of condiment containers. The first creak of daylight shot through the windows. Black doused his eggs and wieners in mustard, his mustaches twitching, and asked, "Which one of you idiots sprung baby doll here?"

"Never you mind that," Dennison said, holding his hat in his lap. "Nothing's been done but legal."

"Some fancy new threads you got there, too, laddie," Black said to me.

I considered my new pinstripe suit. "One thing the prison

system in this country always got right was fashion. An hour ago I was wearing stripes cost me nothing. Now here I am with fifty dollars' worth of yarn on my shoulders and I'm wearing them still."

"We haven't much time, Lou," Dennison said.

Black slurped a poached egg. "And mine's paid with nickels?"

"A little bird came tweeting in my ear that you're dreaming of waking up in the governor's mansion next January. Place has a lot of pillars. Big old Corinthian columns. Twelve bathrooms. Four fireplaces. And the chandeliers? Very hoity-toity."

"What do you really want, Tom?"

"Well, I came by to see if it's really true. I came by to see if you really got a hankering for big boy politics."

"I don't see how that's any of your affair."

I looked around the apartment. The walls peeled. A humming icebox leaked water into a drip pan on the floor like casket ice. A ramshackle piano in the corner of the main room was in no better condition than cordwood.

"Have you a map somewhere in this dump?" Dennison asked Black.

"A map?"

"Yes. A state map of Nebraska. In one of your desk drawers maybe?"

"I thought you wanted to get serious?"

Dennison snapped open his cigarette case like a clamshell. "I'm serious as can be. Now, I haven't looked at a map myself in a long while, but last time I did, Omaha was the biggest city in the state by a furlong and an oxgang."

"What's your point?"

"Votes are the point," Dennison said and popped a match. He set fire to a yellow cigarette. "More than a third of the whole state lives in this city. My city. And I'd bet my last tenpenny you wouldn't mind having that kind of number on your half come November. Well, sir, I can deliver it to you in the bottom of a hat."

Black shook his head. "Gee whiz, would you really now?"

"Lawyers, even district attorneys, don't want to stay lawyers forever."

"It might be maybe that I've got certain gubernatorial aspirations."

Dennison faked a theatrical gasp and wagged his eyebrows madly. "So it is true!"

I giggled like a child who broke wind in a church.

Black folded a triangle of toast in his mouth. "What's your problem?" he asked me.

Dennison answered before I could. "He's a little disturbed. Under a lot of undue stress, as you can imagine."

"As he should be," Black said. "He's the most vile criminal this state's ever known. By the time I'm done with him, he'll be working in a button factory at Madison prison."

Dennison grimaced like he'd stubbed a toe. "Oh hell, Lou. You talk like you're one of the sainted sons of Zebedee. Besides, if there weren't any crime in the world, what would we do for detective novels?"

"Or lawyers?" I added. Ritchie stuck his tongue out at me.

"Or governors," Dennison said.

Black wiped his mouth with the napkin tucked into his shirt. "Don't be a heel. It's no damn secret. The whole state knows I plan on running for the job."

"Running for the job? For governor? That's a hell of a funny thing for you to say," Dennison said. "Goddamn, Louie. Nobody runs for governor."

"Well, they sure as hell don't walk for it," Black said.

"That's right. They don't do anything except pay for it. Same as any other job. Don't matter if you're a piano player in a dime-a-dance or a busboy at a lunch counter. If you want a gig, you pay to get it. Then you keep on paying to keep it."

"I've paid my dues," Black said.

Dennison smarted. "Your dues? Jesus Christ. Your dues? To whom? Do you even know what the fuck you're talking about? How is it that someone who wants to be governor is so ignorant that he doesn't even know how a body gets picked for the job?"

"By the good people of the state," Black said. "By democracy. That's how."

"Well, that's real cute. Cutesy. The good people of this state have about as much to do with this state's elections as I have with the weather in Russia. Democracy is an ideology. But ideologies don't win elections. Votes do."

"You're talking about voter fraud?"

Dennison sucked his cigarette like it was his last request. He exhaled smoke through his nostrils as a bull expels steam before charging a matador's cape. Ritchie and I stood silently by the sink, waiting for an eruption that never came. Both of us had seen Dennison split heads over sillier things. But Tom calmed himself and sucked his cigarette down to the cotton.

Black sweated over his plate of eggs and frankfurters.

"Let me fill you in on a little secret," Dennison said and poked the district attorney in his gut. "You don't lose weight by cutting the crusts off your egg salad sandwiches, and you don't win the governorship because of what happens at the polls in November. You win it as you sit here in your underwear or not at all."

Black stared at Dennison blankly.

"What? You think we run a neat and tidy little pickup service with all the cab companies and streetcar firms to get a bunch of hicks and nigras from one polling place to another like we did for the mayor? Idiot that he was," Dennison said. "Then come the next morning you wake up in the capital taking your oath to protect the Constitution and all that jazz? Tell me, Lou, what exactly do you and all your carpetbagger chums down at the Fontenelle actually know about anything?"

Black blushed and spit a mouthful of egg into his napkin. "Well, if you're going to sit there and belittle me in my own home, the hell with you."

"Really, Tom, how many people on God's green earth know anything about the intricacies of electoral politics?" Ritchie asked as he cleared his throat.

"Well, I do, for one. And what am I? Some bagman gambler who made a few dollars from whores and craps tables. So I'd like to think that someone who wants to be that very thing and holds his hands out asking for it would trouble himself with the knowing of how he is supposed to get it in the first place."

"I'm not asking for anything," Black said. "You're the one came here proselytizing like some goddamn Bible salesman and interrupted me during my breakfast."

"Looky here, Lou, I didn't mean to offend your fragile sensibilities. If you want an apology, you have it. What you need, though, is something different."

After a moment of silence, as if waiting for Dennison to finish his thought, Black finally said, "Well, get on and tell me then."

Dennison chuckled at Black's eagerness. He had the man by the tail, dangling him right over the scalding pot. He gestured at me, standing by the sink. "Reason I brought Patrick here with us this morning is so you might get to know him a smidge. See for yourself he's not such a bad fellow. He doesn't deserve to be sent to the penitentiary any more than you deserve to be sent to the governor's mansion. But I'm telling you, if one happens, the other won't."

Black shoved his plate to the middle of the table. "You want me to throw the case?"

"I want you to stop trying so hard to win it," Dennison said.

Ritchie came over to the table. "In particular one detail of vast importance. The boy's father is due to return to the stand this week after he gets back from Chicago. Well, I've heard it told that old Mr. Cudahy and his driver had a confrontation with a pair of men out on the highway that night they supposedly left all that gold out there. I'd make certain neither of them get around to mentioning that fact while they're on the stand."

"Well, counselor, I appreciate that recommendation. That's very clandestine of you."

"It would make it almost impossible to convict on robbery charges if that little detail was left in omission," Ritchie said.

I looked at my attorney as if he was as pretty as Venus riding her seashell. He was a goddamn work of art. The entire scene had unfolded before me like it had been rehearsed a hundred times. I shook my head in a little bit of awe. The scam was so well orchestrated for both sides it was impossible not to admire the geminated architecture.

Black nodded. He understood. "Is that all?"

"That and a little less zeal from you in front of that jury box," Dennison added.

Black pointed his fork at Dennison. "What's in it for you? Honest, now."

"Honest? It means a helluva lot of money to me."

Black chuckled. "Plan on squeezing the stockyards after they all get knocked back on their keisters? Ho, ho. Isn't there enough graft to be had in this city with the gambling and the hoors? Now you're cutting in on the meat business, too?"

"I'm a businessman with an eye for expansion, you could say," Dennison admitted.

"You're a pariah," Black said.

"Well, I'm glad to know someone else in this room is aware that I don't run the world."

Black was soused by the idea. "This is some favor you're asking."

"And what would you call being handed the keys to a certain Georgian Colonial on a shaded avenue in our state capital? Passing the salt shaker?"

"I'd call it a bribe of a state's attorney."

"Are you soft, man? Or just stupid? Your wool hasn't been white for a long time. No lambs among us here. Just us old goats yammering on and on. And a man like you ought to know what you really are."

"A man like me?" Black asked. "What do you know about what kind of man I am or what kind of man I'm not?"

"Well, I ain't peeping on you through your bedroom curtains. But let's just say that some of the—" Dennison paused. "How should I put this delicately? That some of the wild goings-on in your bedchamber could really put a damper on your campaign if word got out."

"That sounds threatening," Black said. "But seeing as how you think you know something about me, let me say this about you. Say I do wrangle the big gig. Say I end up governor. You and I will be at each other's throats the whole way down the flowered lane. How friendly will you be when I push for counties deciding their own stances on prohibition? You want to stall unionization. I want it on the fast tracks. You also got some of the same railroad boys in your pocket that I'd like to hang up on a clothesline and—"

Dennison interrupted. "Who gives a damn about politics? Not politicians, I guarantee you. You know something, Lou? You're boring the ever-living hell outta me."

"And you're stressing me to bloat."

"I'm glad to see that hasn't dulled your appetite at least," Dennison said.

Black raised an eyebrow.

Dennison pointed at Black's shirtfront. "You got catsup on your good shirt."

"Damn frankfurter," Black said after glancing at the stain.

"Frankfurters for breakfast," Dennison murmured and shook his head. "Listen here, Lou, there's something you need to get educated about if you're ever going to be a state man."

"I'm all ears."

"Some folks are good, some folks are bad, and laws won't ever change that. Not if there was only one of them left in the whole Constitution. Saints will always follow it and bad'ns, they'll always break it. Besides, laws that people don't believe in can't be enforced if whole armies tried it. Hell, anymore these days, there are so many laws that people are either lawbreakers or hypocrites," Dennison said and stood from his chair.

Ritchie and I followed him to the door.

Before leaving, Dennison added a cryptic farewell for Louie to chew over with the remainder of his breakfast. He said, "Lou? For my part? I hate a damn hypocrite."

XIV

I RODE THROUGH five states and countless towns after my escape over the Missouri River, continuing to wander without a plan or destination in mind. I was near broke already, having spent most of the money on food and whiskey. Then I was arrested for drunkenness in Columbia, Missouri, and spent the night sleeping it off in a polly cage. When I sobered up the next morning and was released by the county deputy, my pockets were a thousand dollars lighter than they had been when I entered the jailhouse.

"That there's a finder's fee," the deputy had told me when he turned me loose. "State of Nebraska's got a re-ward out for you for five hundred dollars, Pat Crowe. Colorado and New Mexico, too. Oh yes, I've seen your likeness on just about every telegraph pole in this city and others. So I figure five hundred to turn you in, plus another five hundred for not turning you in. Trick is you're a free man and I double what those Nebraska marshals would've paid for your hide. That seem alright by you?"

I searched my pockets. "Awful steep price for overindulging in this town."

"Well, if it don't suit you none, I can just give it all back and lock you up again," the deputy drawled and twirled his ring of long keys. "Tell you what, we got us a coin box in the telegraph office next door that makes long-distance phone calls. Maybe I drop a line or two to a couple friends of mine in Omaha, and we just wait and see who might show up to collect."

"No," I said with some lingering dizziness as I struggled to get my arms through my coat sleeves. "You go on and keep that swag. You earned it."

The deputy swung his boots back up onto his desk, his big spurs jangling against the wood. He spit a clot of tobacco into a brass cuspidor that sounded like a nail hitting the bottom of a tin can. "A famous man like you is always welcome back now, you hear?"

All that was left to my name was six hundred dollars and my weixel wood pipe, which I kept in its own velvet-lined case. I decided Chicago might be as good a place as any to build up my bankroll again. I bought an old Colt six-shooter and a bottle of corn whiskey and hired a room on the third floor of a flophouse on the corner of Wabash.

The room had a good view of the street below. I could see every building all the way to the end of the block.

I took several drinks from the bottle as I continually spied out the window. The hour was drawing near nine. Down the hall, a woman started in with shrill screaming. I jumped from my chair, grabbed my revolver off the table. Standing with my ear to the door, I listened for approaching footsteps. Three minutes passed before I sat down again and pulled the string on the dangling light bulb, darkening the room save for the light crawling in around the edges of the closed curtain.

For the fifth time in two minutes I looked down at the street. An hour passed, and I finished off half of the bottle. Warmed by the liquor, I finally relaxed enough to lie down and close my eyes, hoping to sleep off the rest of the day.

A booming series of knocks woke me from my slumber. I jolted out of bed and threw on my crumpled suit. The Chicago police called out from the hallway as they continued to pound on the door, announcing their presence. I stashed my money in my left boot and stamped them both on my feet and hid my revolver in my pant pocket.

The officers knocked again. "Chicago Police. Open up."

"Use the knob," I said groggily. "It works."

The door opened slowly and standing in the hallway were two Chicago policemen. Both were thin and clean-shaven and no older than me.

"Howdy, officers," I said.

"Is this the man?" one of the officers asked the other.

"Yeah, this is the feller," the other replied.

"Who do you think I am?" I asked. I was sitting on the edge of my iron bed with my head in my hands.

The two officers stepped into the room. "You're Pat Crowe. The man who kidnapped the Cudahy boy. The whole country is in a fit looking for you."

I shrugged. "You sure you got the right fella? My name's Jonathan Loveless. I don't know anything about any Cudahy boy."

The first patrolman aimed his pistol at my chest. "Come on down to the police box with us and we'll see what's what."

"Be cool, fella. If your finger slips, that Betsey might go off and put a slug in me."

"And no happiness lost at that. You're a goddamn child abductor."

"Merci beaucoup," I said and saluted with my liquor bottle. "I see you're a harbinger."

"A what now?" the officer asked.

"Oh, you know, a fortune-teller. A soothsayer. You and your crystal ball. You've never seen me before in your life."

"You're the bird I've seen on every wanted poster this side of the Missouri."

"I already told you I don't know anything about that business."

The officers looked at each other. I sat there the whole time, unafraid of arrest or gunshot. My calmness unnerved them.

"You're coming with us to sort it out any which way," the second officer said after a moment of hesitation.

"Alright. But you boys are making a mistake," I said and left willingly with the officers. We went down the stairs and came out onto the plank sidewalk past a pharmacy and a general store. They hadn't handcuffed me, only walked alongside me with one officer gripping my wrist like I was a lost child. I turned to the bull holding my wrist and whispered, "Hey, bud, I got near on half a grand in my hip pocket here. I'll give you both the lot of it if you'll close your eyes for a moment and let me have a gallop back down the street."

The officer wavered and looked around, as if being watched. His grip on my wrist loosened and I reached down into my pocket as if to fetch the money. But the cash was tucked away in my boot, and I gripped the butt of my revolver. The officer seized my hand again and pulled it out of my pocket by the sleeve. I yanked my arm away and lifted my shooter, aiming right between the policeman's eyes. The second officer fumbled for his own weapon, and I fired a bullet into his shoulder. He fell to his knees, and I fired a second shot at the other officer whose grip I'd shaken off. The bullet would've found the officer's heart at point-blank range, but he grabbed my other hand and jerked it in front of my gun barrel just as I squeezed the trigger.

The gunshot went straight through my wrist, shattering bone before lodging itself somewhere deep in my palm. I yanked myself away. My hand gushed blood in runnels. There was no time for contrition. I fired a third time, hitting the officer in the side of his face, blowing off a whole hunk of his jaw. The first officer squirmed on the flagstone next to him. When he got up to his knees, I let loose another shot clean in the left side of his belly, just below his heart. He fell onto his stomach and hunkered over his wound.

I hobbled down the sidewalk as a crowd rushed over.

I was halfway down Clark Street when two detectives in three-piece suits wandered out of a café eating fried doughnuts wrapped in paper napkins. I nearly ran straight into them. Cries of murder were hollered out by the shocked bystanders. The detectives saw my bloodied wrist and grabbed me around my bicep to halt my progress.

I pointed back to the crowd that had gathered by the wounded officers. "Somebody tried to rob me and killed two policemen!"

The detectives let go of me and dropped their doughnuts, heading toward the crowd as the cries of "Murder!" and "Stop that man!" grew louder.

I hadn't gotten ten yards away when the detectives turned back around and caught up to me, knocking my legs out with a solid whack of a baton on the back of my knees. I fell to the sidewalk and scraped my forehead. A huge gleaming gash bled down the side of my face, and I was back on my feet in a fit, sprinting into a nearby alley. My wrist poured blood the whole way. A bullet flew past my head and turned a chunk of brick building side into dust as I came onto the street again.

More bullets skimmed across the avenue and dinged off store signs.

A mob of twenty or more townsfolk had joined the detectives in their pursuit, shouting that they were after a cop killer. I turned and fired three shots without aiming as I sprinted toward the back of a building under construction. Not looking where I was going, I fell headfirst into a trough of plaster, sticky as birdlime. I was covered in the gunk from head to foot. The paste ran down into my eyes and partially blinded me. I was shaking off the mortar and blinking out the sting and wiping my eyes with my hand as I broke into the building, which was nothing more than four floors of skeletal wood and clapboard.

There were no doors or windows hung.

The cover was scarce at best.

I climbed the half-finished stairs to the second level and collapsed behind a pile of sawn lumber. After dropping down, I tore off a piece of my right shirtsleeve and used the ripped cloth like a bandage. I wrapped it around my wounded wrist and tied it off into a makeshift tourniquet. The material soaked through with blood. More pistol shots rang out from the floor below. I crawled over to the makings of a window frame and looked down onto the street. The mob had doubled in size.

They carried numerous objects: bricks, rocks, glass bottles. Gunshots echoed, many of them fired into the air by the police as warning shots. A group of men with biceps as big as bread loaves urged the crowd into storming the building to pull the cop killer out of hiding and string him up. One man wearing a slouch hat and saddled on a quarter horse rode to the front swell of the horde. He carried a braided towrope at least twenty feet in length. Four women in cotton print dresses handed out stones from water pails, and folks were slinging them through the open windows.

The mob surrounded the building on all sides like a moat of wool hats and box caps. As the assault party converged, the police ascended the staircase. Some of them were accidentally struck by the rocks and bricks thrown by the crowd. I stuck my head out the window frame and fired off four more shots just as a lucky chunk of lobbed pavement hit me in the forehead. I took to the stairs again, mopping at the wound with a green neckerchief as I came out onto the tarred roof and lay flat on my stomach to avoid gunfire from the street below.

A group of men stole two construction lamps from the dig site and used the kerosene to soak the first floor of the building. Once the fire was started, it engulfed the wood in a giant burst like a backdraft. Ten minutes passed, and I couldn't do anything but lie there gushing blood and envisioning my own demise.

Two fire pumpers arrived on the scene, pushing through the crowd until they were surrounded and unable to advance. The firemen managed to attach a pair of canvas hoses to a hydrant, but were cut by the mob as some screamed to let me burn. One wagon was rocked back and forth by ten men until it tipped over. The ladders were stolen and leaned against the front of the building. The most daring members of the raid climbed the rungs to get to the third floor windows. Spindrifts of smoke whirled as the hour approached noon. At least ten men had managed their way onto the second and third floors of the building. To slow their progression, police discharged warning shots down what was to become an elevator shaft.

I gathered my strength and crawled over the edge of the roof. The tar covering had melted down into a jam from the intense heat one story below. I pulled my coat over my head and stumbled my way back down the only staircase not in flames.

Though I was surrounded by the mob on the street, nobody recognized me as the one they were after. I joined their ranks, lobbing rocks at the burning building and shouting for the cop killer to burn. Easily as that, I became one of them. I was in the mob, and not a single policeman or angry citizen noticed my bleeding wrist or the pair of gashes on my head.

Slowly I backed away from the masses and wandered off into an alley with my jacket still smoking and my head faint from blood loss. I tossed my bloodied shirtsleeve into a trash bin and washed my wound in a chilly horse trough. Three blocks away I came upon a livery stable connected to a feed and grain store. There were four geldings in twelve ramshackle stables. The barn was constructed of logs plastered together with straw and pink paste. Creeping into the stable, I selected a chestnut mare from one of the paddocks. I bridled the animal and fastened it with a square-skirted saddle. Without being seen, I rode the horse out of town, heading back in the same direction from which I arrived two days before.

For five miles I thrashed the horse east along the flood basin outside of the city until the streets gave way to open prairie. I stopped every ten minutes to scan the terrain ahead. The bullet was still lodged in my wrist, but I'd at least managed to slow the bleeding to a trickle by knotting my belt around my forearm. My horse panted and neighed. It hadn't carried the weight of a rider for some time, more than likely. By and by, I came upon a creek as pale as shallow seawater, and I followed its elbow bend south until nightfall.

I continued to ride south for nearly a week, stopping only to sleep for an hour at a time and to water and feed my stolen nag. Rode south all the way out of Will County before I turned east. Sopping cornfields tilled lower than a sock line. Cold prairie like flat pale lilac. A long forest of red maple and plane trees running along the bed of the Kankakee River.

A man could get lost forever in those woods.

I followed the watershed through four separate Illinois counties. Given enough luck and a swirling wind, I could come out clean a hundred miles away and be ordering peach cobbler in a café with oilcloths on the tabletops before the week was half over and contemplating how close to the ocean I could get if I kept heading east with six hundred dollars in my boot and the afternoon sun always on my back, the voices of the pursuant echoing across the plains like the chants of ghosts.

XV

COURT RESUMED ON a Monday morning filthy with snow clouds. The forecast called for a high of two degrees, and spectators filled the courtroom shivering like mice in a huddle with their coats reeking of lamp smoke and coal. They stomped the slush off their gum boots and galoshes as they took their seats. Tom Dennison and Billy Nesselhous arrived early for the day to ensure seats three rows behind the prosecution table. They spoke with each other cheek by jowl in hushed tones, their arms crossed. Dennison had come to see just how seriously Louie Black had taken their early morning conversation two days ago.

I sat for long periods of time with my eyes closed. Though I may have looked to be asleep, I was alert and listening closely to every word as Louie Black recalled Edward Cudahy Senior to the stand. He'd been away in Chicago as a defendant in the Beef Trust trial, and the wear on his person was evident in his walk and his face. His complexion was as pale as pastry, and it was not a stretch to guess he was drained of all heart from his legal battles. His eyes bulged as if he'd forgone two nights' sleep. He labored into the witness chair.

"Mr. Cudahy," Black began. "As weary as you are, I thank you again for your return to the stand in order that we may bring some things to light that we did not get a chance to visit upon during your testimony last week. Mr. Cudahy, you are a Catholic, are you not?"

"I am," Cudahy said.

"And are you a practicing Catholic in good standing with the church?"

"Yes, sir. My family and I take in the Sunday service at Saint Stephen's every week come rain or shine. It's an important part of our lives."

"Who is the pastor at that parish?"

"Father Dan Murphy."

"And how long have you known Father Murphy?"

"Well, for as long as he's been at Saint Stephen's. Maybe eight or nine years now."

"Is Pat Crowe also a communicant of that same church?"

"I'm not able to say."

"But would you be able to say that Pat Crowe has been in communication with Father Murphy at some point in the last calendar year?"

Cudahy squeezed both of his armrests. "Yes. I would say so with assuredness."

Black smiled and paused. He stepped away from his lectern and looked out into the courtroom where Tom Dennison was sitting next to Billy Nesselhous. He paused to wipe his spectacles with a handkerchief. Without replacing them on his face, he wagged them about as he posed a new question to his witness:

"And how do you know that Pat Crowe was in contact with Father Murphy?"

Cudahy produced an envelope from his suit coat. "Well, by documentation. I have here a confession letter to the crime written and signed by Pat Crowe himself that he gave to Father Murphy just this past spring."

Black took the letter and said, "Your Honor, the state proposes to enter this letter into evidence as Exhibit Four-B."

Ritchie jumped from his chair. We'd been waiting, fearing, the arrival of this letter to the court. We thought Dennison's meeting with Louie Black that past weekend might have been enough motivation for the district attorney to keep the letter out of evidence.

But there was simply no way of avoiding its existence.

There was quite a fight ahead of us now.

Ritchie said, "Objection. Your Honor, if such a communication is even indeed legitimate and not a forgery, then said communication is sacred to the confessional. As stated, this supposed letter sprung upon the court is a communication between priest and parishioner no different than the sacrament of confession itself. It's clearly in the class of privileged communications as though still in the hands of the priest to whom it was originally confided."

"I should say not, sir, and say not with overwhelming vigor,"

Black said and approached Judge Sutton's bench. He spoke loudly enough that the entire court could still hear his argument. "Your Honor, the state contends that this letter now in possession of Mr. Cudahy was not given in the nature of a confession as a sacrament of the Catholic Church. Its purpose was not the seeking of spiritual comfort or intercession with omnipotence. It was sent to the recipient Father Daniel Murphy to get him to act as an intermediary with Mr. Cudahy so that he might consent to a dismissal of the prosecution. That much will be abundantly clear if Your Honor would allow the contents of the letter to be read to the court."

Ritchie hustled to the judge's bench. "Your Honor, ecclesiastical law is to become of some importance in this case, and in the matter of this letter, we cannot separate or ignore such law from this chamber."

Black retorted, "The letter itself also directs it should be turned over to another priest, and the state contends that this in itself shows it was not a confession to remain forever locked within the chamber of one person."

Judge Sutton, shrunken in his great swaying robe and already exhausted by this early argument, opened his mouth to address the matter, but Ritchie was quicker with his tongue.

"Yes," Ritchie said, "even if that is true, that very fact seems to establish its own sacredness as a confession, confirming it to spiritual advisers and that it was not to be made public no matter if it did find its way into the hands of a third party as Mr. Cudahy sits there clutching it now and grinning like a cat that just swallowed the family canary."

Judge Sutton raised a flat hand. "You're both feeling very talkative today. I might be for an evening session to let you both continue to groan on and on about the importance of canon law and religious mandate until you're each blue in the face, but I simply don't think our jurors could stand it, nor could I. As to the letter, I side with the state. We will hear the content of the letter in its entirety. If it comes to pass that its contents deem it to be under the protection of privileged communications, we will address that matter then, but not before."

"At what price, Your Honor?" Ritchie demanded. "The damage will already be done by then to prejudice this jury."

"No, sir, it will not. The jury is fully aware of their responsibilities and the charges at hand. Your objection is noted but overruled."

As Ritchie returned to his seat, Black stationed himself in front of the witness box and urged Cudahy to read the letter to the court slowly and clearly. "Unless you feel unable, sir, in which case I would be glad to recite it for the court."

"No," Cudahy said. "I can manage."

"Please," Black replied. "Is there a date or heading on the letter? An address, perhaps?"

Cudahy examined the letter. "No, sir. It simply begins, 'Dear Father—'"

"Loud and clear, now," Black instructed him.

"'Dear Father Dan, I wrote you a letter from Chicago a few months ago and your answer was very encouraging to me as I have for several years thought of reforming and starting life anew. In your letter you said that you did not believe half of what was written about me and the assaults on my character. Well, that is the truth. I have been accused of hundreds of crimes which I never committed.

"'For the past four years my suffering has been intense. My daughter doesn't know me any better than a stranger and my estranged wife, whom I have tried to reconcile with numerous times in the past, has made a new life with a new man. I am an outcast, a disgrace to the mother that gave me birth. And to add to my suffering I have wronged a man that has been a friend to me. I am guilty of the Cudahy affair. I am to blame for the whole crime. After it was over I regretted my act and offered to return eleven thousand dollars to Mr. Cudahy, but he refused to take it. I was hunted from every corner of the country and so I went to Japan and then on to South Africa where I joined the Boer rebel army and was badly wounded, being shot in the shoulder.

"'I returned to America and repeatedly tried to make peace with the man I wronged. Now I am going to give myself up and take whatever comes. If Mr. Cudahy would show me mercy I would come out all right and start life anew. Cudahy is a remarkably good man. I have known him many years and must say he is generous and forgiving. It would be hard to find a better man. But he feels he owes it as his duty to the public to prosecute me. Now I could stand trial and beat the case, but that would not relieve me of the burden that is crushing out the last ray of happiness in my waste of a life.

"'Now I wish that you would write to Mr. and Mrs. Cudahy and pray for mercy, for as they do so will those who come after them. Tell them of my character and my desire to repent. I feel sure that Mr. Cudahy knows it is an old and well-established fact having long since been proven so by scientific research that if the parents are honest, their offspring, though it may wander away into sin, will eventually abandon evil and return to the good. Remember this and Mr. Cudahy knows as does hundreds of others in this city that I showed mercy to his son when he was in my power. If I cared to surround myself with stolen gold I could have ten million inside of thirty days. But I have found no happiness in evil and am going to return to the teaching of my childhood. If I must suffer, I will not repine.

"'Please forward this letter to the Reverend Father Lillihan in Colorado from whom I received my first communion and who buried my poor mother and just recently my elderly father. I wish to prepare myself for the day that is sure to come when I must return to them. Write to Mr. and Mrs. Cudahy and ask them to show me some mercy.

"'This is all and I will say goodbye. Please tend to this as soon as possible. The Cudahys are good Catholics and letters that you or Father Lillihan write to them will never be known by the public. Your Brother in Faith, Patrick Joseph Crowe.'"

Attorney Black thanked Mr. Cudahy for his sturdy and unemotional recitation of the letter to the court and turned over his witness to the defense.

Ritchie, sweating through his shirt at both the neck and under his arms, loosed his tie and rolled his sleeves. "Mr. Cudahy, how exactly did you come into possession of this letter?"

"Through Father Murphy."

"Yes. But how? Did he slip it into your coat pocket while doling out the Eucharist or maybe folded it into your wife's purse after he asked you to help him with the spelling?"

Black said, "Objection. Implying facts not evidence. Furthermore, the inference that Father Murphy had anything to do with the authorship of this letter is hearsay."

"Sustained. Mr. Ritchie, the court would be delighted if you kept the commentary to yourself and asked your questions without insinuation," Judge Sutton ruled.

Ritchie turned. "Mr. Cudahy, in what manner did Father Murphy give you the letter?"

"He handed it to me one day after a Sunday service. Oftentimes after Mass we gather for coffee and doughnuts. A community hour, we call it. That's when he approached me. He told me he'd been in communication with Pat Crowe and that he'd received a letter from the man and he thought I should be made aware of its message."

"I see. And when did this occur?"

"A few weeks ago."

"Can you be more specific?"

"Four Sundays ago. The second week of January, I believe."

"And yet this letter was written last spring, you said?"

"That's correct. There's no date on the correspondence, but Father Murphy told me he received it last spring."

"And did Father Murphy tell you why he waited so long to deliver this letter to you?"

"He did not."

Ritchie smiled and paced toward the jury box. "Was the delay in his giving you this letter maybe due to the fact that he felt some hesitation about whether or not he should break his sacred vow by divulging the secrets of one of his parishioners?"

"Objection, Your Honor," Black said. "Mr. Cudahy cannot possibly assume the motivations of another. Nor does the state condone his constant implications that Father Murphy has violated the seal of confession when the letter has already been admitted and read to the court."

"Sustained," Sutton replied.

"I will change course, Your Honor. Mr. Cudahy, when did you learn that Pat Crowe would stand trial and that you would be called upon as a witness in this trial?"

"I cannot remember exactly. Maybe two months ago."

"You're close. The start date of this trial was set almost exactly six weeks ago."

"That sounds right."

"And you said you received this letter about four weeks ago?"

"Yes, sir."

"Well, a boon synchronism that is. Do you suppose, sir, that the appearance of this letter and Father Murphy's giving it to you might have been inspired by this impending trial?"

Black was on his feet again. "Objection, Your Honor. If defense counsel wishes to ask questions about Father Murphy's intent, then let him save those questions for the man himself and not Mr. Cudahy."

"That would be something!" Ritchie said and flapped his hands wildly. "How I would love to get Father Murphy on this stand. Strangely, I see the good old priest is not currently on your list of witnesses set to appear. I wonder why."

Judge Sutton sagged in his chair. He looked ready to tear off his robe and pitch it in the trash and wander off naked down the court aisle if that's what it took to escape the grinding irritations of the day's proceedings. "Objection sustained. Mr. Ritchie, you're trying the patience of this court. If you keep this up we'll be here until Christmas. We're nearly at the end of things and I ask you one final time to refrain from making such implications."

"I apologize," Ritchie said. "Mr. Cudahy, have you ever taken part in the sacrament of confession with Father Murphy as a communicant of Saint Stephen's parish?"

"Yes, I have. Many times."

"And would you like to share with the court the sins you confessed to?"

"I would not."

"And would you like Father Murphy to come here and voice those sins you told him in faith so that the whole world might come to know them?"

"Of course I would not," Cudahy said firmly.

Ritchie smiled. "Of course not. No one would."

"Objection. Immaterial."

"Sustained," Judge Sutton said and addressed the jury. "The court will strike the last two questions and Mr. Cudahy's response to those questions from the record and the jury will purge them from their minds."

Ritchie struck a new pose. "Mr. Cudahy, do you trust Father Murphy?"

"Yes, I do. He's a fine priest."

"Do you trust him to hold the secrets that you've confessed to him no matter how much those secrets might be of service or help to someone else?"

"Yes, I do."

"Well, sir, how can you be so certain of your trust in this regard when Father Murphy has already broken that trust with another?"

Black stood again. "I object, Your Honor. As the letter states, Pat Crowe sought Father Murphy to help him deliver this message to Cudahy. That much was made explicit by the letter itself. It was the wish of the writer, Pat Crowe, in his own words, that his confession was never meant to be kept secret."

"Sustained," Judge Sutton said wearily.

Ritchie continued, "And yet, Mr. Cudahy, Father Murphy delayed over half a year in relaying this message to you. Why did he wait so long to pass it along?"

"I cannot say."

"You cannot say, and yet you trust him still?"

"Objection, Your Honor. The witness has already answered the question, and he stated that he trusts Father Murphy."

"Sustained. Mr. Ritchie, I urge you to get off this point. It's trodden ground."

Ritchie smacked his lips. "Mr. Cudahy, did you write this letter?"

"No, sir."

"Did Father Murphy write this letter?"

"Objection."

"Sustained."

"Your Honor," Ritchie said, "I'm simply trying to ascertain the authenticity of this letter and probe the possibility that it's a forgery. Why, any man could pen a fake letter of confession, sign the author of that letter as Pat Crowe, and send it off to any one of the clergymen at the Cudahy's parish. The existence of this letter and how it came into Edward Cudahy's possession is a preposterous story. No priest in Christendom would turn over to an outsider such a confidential communication as charged by the state."

Judge Sutton pawed his forehead. "I don't argue with your intent, Mr. Ritchie. But I ask you to please reserve your speech-making for your closing statement, not witness testimony."

Ritchie turned back to Cudahy. "Mr. Cudahy, you have offered a fifty-thousand-dollar reward for the capture of Pat Crowe, have you not?"

"I have."

"And how long has that reward been in effect?"

"I put it in effect the day my son returned home safely, and it stayed in effect until Pat Crowe finally turned himself in."

"And how much information did you receive from people, from complete strangers far and wide, concerning the possible where-abouts of Pat Crowe in response to that reward?"

"Heaps and heaps," Cudahy said.

"And how much of these 'heaps and heaps' actually led you to capturing Pat Crowe?"

"None of it."

"None of it," Ritchie repeated. "So it would be fair to say that all of the responses you received to your reward offering fifty thou-sand dollars for the capture of Pat Crowe were speculative and unhelpful?"

"I suppose you could say that."

"Would you also suppose that some of the information you received in response to your reward was imagined entirely by peo-ple hoping to capture some of that reward?"

"I cannot say. I would think not. I cannot see how someone making up false information would lead to any monetary gain, especially from me."

"But is it possible?"

"It's possible, but doubtful."

"And would you say that this letter of confession supposedly written by Pat Crowe could have been written in forgery by a per-son hoping to cash in on a portion of your reward?"

"No, I don't think so. I haven't paid a cent of that reward to any person."

"Yes, but that withstanding, is it possible, sir? Is it possible that the letter is a forgery written by someone with the hope of gaining reward much like all the other unhelpful and speculative information you received over the years about Pat Crowe?"

Cudahy sat forward, finally provoked into aggression. He coughed into his hanky and pointed a finger at Ritchie with the hanky balled up in his fist. His voice rattled with a deep tenor. His entire face shook with effort. "No it would not, like I said before. I don't know how much clearer I can say it. Your logic is flawed, sir. False information, people making things up out of thin air, as you say, would not help us find Pat Crowe and therefore would get them no closer to any kind of reward."

Ritchie volleyed back a strong outburst of his own: "But it sure is helpful to you now, isn't it? I mean, if this letter is indeed fake and yet still somehow manages its way into this case as evidence, then it is helpful to you. It might seal the fate of my client no matter its veracity or lack thereof and you profit from it either way. Now, isn't that true?"

"Object—" Black began but was interrupted.

"I believe the letter to be true," Cudahy said with a stony assuredness.

Ritchie pounced. "Yes. But I didn't ask if you believed it to be true. You can believe all you want and swear under oath about your belief until the breath of life passes from your lips, but that belief doesn't make it so. Hell, for centuries people believed the earth was flat and that the sun revolved around the earth and we all know now how wrong those poor idiots were. But, what I asked you, sir, is if it was possible this letter was not written by Pat Crowe. If it was possible that it was not true."

"Objection," Black said, knocking over his chair. "How many times will the court allow defense counsel to ask the witness the same question over and over again?"

"Sustained. Mr. Ritchie, the witness has already sworn under oath that he believes the letter to be true. There's nothing else he can add to this matter. I advise you to move along, sir."

"Fine," Ritchie said. "I only have a couple more questions for you, Mr. Cudahy. When you were on the stand for the first time last week, I asked you how you knew for a certainty that Pat Crowe was one of the men who kidnapped your son and stole away with twenty-five thousand dollars of your money. Do you remember that conversation?"

"I do," Cudahy said.

"And what was the sole reason you gave for being able to identify Pat Crowe?"

"I said I knew him by his voice."

"That's right. By his voice and his voice alone, you said. Do you remember that?"

"I do."

Ritchie snatched the confession letter from the evidence table and waved it about the room. He asked, "And yet you were in possession of this confession letter last week when you gave that testimony?"

Cudahy paused.

"Mr. Cudahy?"

"Could you repeat the question?"

Ritchie flung the letter back on the table. "Were you in possession of this letter last week when you admitted the only way you were able to identify Pat Crowe was by his voice?"

"Yes, I was."

"Well, then, I'm quite confused, sir, as I'm sure is the rest of this court. How could you have stated the only reason you could identify Pat Crowe was by his voice during a telephone call made to your house when, in fact, you had in your grasp a confession letter to the crime?"

Cudahy again didn't respond.

Ritchie pressed harder. "Was it because, perhaps, this letter actually didn't even exist last week? Was it because, out of the clear blue sky, this letter actually came into existence after that day in court and not before?"

"Objection, Your Honor!" Black yelled. "Calls for assumption."

"Overruled. The witness will answer."

Cudahy stammered. "No, sir. The letter was in my possession the whole time."

"Then why did you not mention it? Don't you think that would have been something worth telling when you were asked about your ability to identify Pat Crowe? Why, you had the entire crime admitted to in print and signed, supposedly, by the defendant. That's a pretty damning piece of evidence, wouldn't you say? And yet you still swore the only way you knew him was by the sound of his voice?"

"I was nervous and under a lot of stress. My whole family has been under an undue amount of stress to have to go back and revisit the abduction of my son."

"And I can appreciate that. But, stress and nervousness aside, were you under oath then? Were you under oath when you admitted to only being able to identify Pat Crowe by his voice when you actually could identify him by this letter?"

"I was."

"Could you speak up, sir, so the whole court can hear you?"

"Yes, I was under oath," Cudahy said with more volume, but not much more.

"And are you under oath now?"

Cudahy sank in his chair. "I am," he said meekly.

Ritchie smirked. Sweat ran down his cheeks in rills. He took a dramatic pause to wipe his face with a pocket linen and to allow the gravity of Cudahy's admission sink in for the court. Finally, he asked, "Why did you lie under oath, Mr. Cudahy? Why perjure yourself on the stand when all you had to do was reveal the existence of this letter when I asked you about the identity of Pat Crowe the first time?"

Black was on his feet again. "Objection, Your Honor! Mr. Cudahy is not on trial here. The accusation that he perjured himself on the stand is not only badgering and misquoting the witness, but slanderous nonsense. He and his split serpent's tongue. How foul! He's manipulated and confused this witness—"

"Overruled," Judge Sutton said. "The court is very much interested to hear Mr. Cudahy's response on this matter. And may I warn you, Mr. Cudahy, to consider your answers carefully, sir. Very carefully, indeed."

Ritchie rested a hand on the witness rail. "Answer the question, please."

It took Cudahy a moment to gather himself. He looked to Attorney Black with trepidation and then to Judge Sutton. His stomach shook with each breath. "I was advised to hold onto that information."

"Advised by whom? Attorney Black?"

"Yes. I wanted to tell about the letter right away. But I was advised not to."

"Why? Why hold onto the best card you had to play until now?"

"I cannot say."

"Cannot or will not?"

Cudahy sat silent.

"Was it because Mr. Black and his team thought that the letter was possibly a forgery and wanted to ensure that it was genuine?"

Black jumped out of his chair. "Objection. Calls for speculation. Furthermore, the authenticity of this confession letter has been tried and tried again when it's already been accepted as evidence."

"And it's acceptance as evidence is exactly the issue at hand," Ritchie said before Judge Sutton could rule on the objection. "And I also wonder at the delay by you, Mr. Black. I surely hope for your sake and the sake of this court that the state is not withholding evidence."

"How dare you!" Black said.

"Mr. Ritchie—" Judge Sutton began, but was interrupted.

"What's next, I wonder? Why, if this trial were to drag into next week we might be privileged to photographic evidence. If we should find ourselves still at battle in these chambers come the first of March, maybe Mr. Cudahy would be recalled to the stand for a third or fourth time armed with a daguerreotype of Pat Crowe posing for the camera with Cudahy's son tied to a chair or him rolling around in all of that ghostly gold left out on the highway!"

The courtroom audience burst into applause and shouts of dismay.

Judge Sutton pounded his gavel. "That's enough! That's quite enough. I will clear this courtroom not only today but for the remainder of this trial if I hear one more shout or cackle or even a sneeze or any other interruption of any kind."

The courtroom fell silent as if turned off by a switch.

Ritchie attempted to lighten the mood. He pulled out his handkerchief. "I feel a slight cough coming on, Your Honor. Will you pardon me?"

"That's quite enough from you too, Mr. Ritchie," the judge said.

Ritchie slammed the defense table. "Oh, it's not enough yet. Not by a long measure. Your Honor, this entire charade orchestrated by the prosecution is an atrocity. Louie Black and his bunch have withheld evidence for the purpose of timing. This is a federal trial, not a theatrical performance. Why, if given the chance, Mr. Black would like to turn this courtroom into a stage, divulging points of the plot when he saw fit to stir and manipulate this jury. I've never heard of such a tactic in my twenty-plus years as a lawyer. It flirts with perjury and witness tampering. Why, it's a wonder that the jury does not rise in their box in protest and render their verdict right here!"

Another smattering of applause, this one much more subdued after Judge Sutton's threat to clear the room, quickly rose then died.

Ritchie smiled. He could not help himself but to fan the flames. "Well, it seems at least a few good bystanders of Omaha here today don't appreciate a man lying under oath any more than they do being robbed every time they put a piece of his meat in their mouths."

The courtroom cheered again, and some of the audience members were standing and hollering with their hands cupped over their mouths to amplify their voices. There was no stopping the pandemonium. The wick had been lit, and there was no smothering the spark. Judge Sutton rose in his giant robe and pounded his mallet like he was trying to bolt down a coffin lid. Over and over he whacked his gavel while the shouting continued. A few of the spectators in the gallery were throwing down coins from their pockets in the direction of the witness stand, aiming their pennies and nickels at Cudahy.

"That thief wants all of our money!" somebody yelled from the balcony. "Well, boys, let him have it! Let him have it all!"

More coins flew through the air. They rained down from the gallery and from across the room. The crowd was at a fever pitch, ready to break into riot. I turned in my chair to look back at the erupting audience. I sat stunned but could not stop grinning. I'd been separated from the world for so long. And yet I had never been alone. I had company all along. I was among the many, and stood for the many. Someone cheered my name.

"Hooray for Pat Crowe!" one man hollered.

"Let him steal that boy again for double the price!" screamed another.

Then a chorus broke out: "Hooray for Pat Crowe! Hooray!"

Judge Sutton rapped his gavel ceaselessly. "Order! Order, I say! I want this entire room cleared now! Bailiffs, remove the witness and the jury. Clear this room! I will have order! Bailiff, get Mr. Cudahy out of here now, I say. The rest of you, get that jury out of here!"

Ritchie dodged coins like hail with his arms raised over his head and sat next to me at the defense table with a contemptuous smile. With coins still raining down and even a couple of shoes thrown in the air and people waving their hats and screaming madly, the hysteria pitched all around us both, we two sat together quietly.

Ritchie touched me on my knee.

He said, "Come tomorrow it's you who will run for governor."

XVI

SIX WEEKS AFTER nearly burning to death in Chicago, I was almost reduced to ashes again in Oklahoma. Without a map and having to stay off the roads both night and day, I soon found myself much farther south than I'd originally planned. I was hoping for the cosmopolitan swag of the eastern seaboard. Instead my route, trimmed on all sides by a country frenzied at the possibility of my capture, led me into Indian Territory.

The country of southwest Oklahoma was very little under plow, and I rode lazily over a tall grass prairie for two weeks before I found a settlement of five sod blockhouses on the edge of the Wichita Mountains. Distant rain like piping along the horizon. Fields of dead blue corn and huckleberry brush and jointed sand grass. Creeks as skinny as lodgepoles. Ancient ponds untouched by man, as perfect as if painted on canvas. The entire damn territory the color of a cemetery in winter even though spring days were well at hand.

I was near starving and my horse was worse off yet. I'd retreated so far from the eye of the world that I felt I might never see another sign of man for the rest of my days, until I came across a collection of crooked huts at the base of the Wichita range. I set up camp a half mile away from a snug little farm covered with pear and apricot trees. I took my utensils and bedroll off my mare, and let it drink from a spring to its heart's content. The sky was gold, and the sun still well in the sky when I set out to stealing some of the unripe fruit, using my shirt like a basket to collect as much as I could manage.

That night I slept on the ground without a fire and rose early to see if any of the folks in that sad conglomeration had anything worth bartering. At the last house on the edge of a wide arroyo, I was greeted by a man who called himself a traveling preacher. He was side-whiskered with a shaved lip and wore a big wooden crucifix around his neck like an albatross.

"Come on inside, son, and bask in the light of the Lord," the man said.

I thanked him with a silent nod. Before I was five paces into the cramped house, I learned the man had been as far south as Georgia and as far west as Oregon and ran his church out of his traveling bag.

"Ain't so many like me no more," the preacher said. "Folks that live near steeples have got God easy. It's the ones out here in the rough that need faith more urgently than all the rest and so is why I've committed myself to making sure that neither hell nor high water nor drought nor blight of any devil-kind keeps folks from being able to worship the Lord appropriately."

I was so rot from my travels I could smell my own horrible odor through my flannel suit. I took off my hat in the scullery and sat down at the table.

"Can you speak English, son?" the preacher man asked.

I tossed a gold piece on the table. "By the dollar full."

The preacher perked up. "That's a handsome coin."

"I trust you have a hot breakfast on the boil."

The preacher put his lower lip over his upper. "This ain't no restaurant."

I tossed another coin on the table.

"Well, I was done full myself already. I got coffee and chicken tumale and the works, yessiree," the preacher said. As soon as he scooped up my two coins, he transformed from a man of the pulpit to a man of the apron and served me a plate of everything he had on the stove: fried taters, a mess of beans, flour tortillas, and chicken tamale. He poured me a cup of undercooked coffee from a granite pot, and gave me a glass of goat milk. I devoured the food and asked if the man had any eggs.

"Ain't seen a chicken in these parts for some time," the man said.

"I'm eating chicken."

"That's canned. Been eating it since I passed through Kentucky."

"Mmm," I said with a full mouth. "You're a daisy, Mr. Preacher Man. I've been living off cattleman's gumbo for a month."

"Cattleman's gumbo?"

"That's grass and flowers boiled in creek water. One more tea-spoon of that and I was sure my gut was going to burst."

"You're a bundle of nerves, son. You need the Lord in your life."

I twirled my fork in the air. My mouth too full to force in another bite. "I need ham in my belly. A sacred something can only fill the soul if the stomach ain't empty."

"That's desperation talking."

I shook my head. "That's biology talking back."

"What's your life's ambition, son?"

"My life's ambition?" I chewed and chewed and thought on the question. "To live so long I don't have no regrets for living."

"That's the talk of a man with a sinful past. After you eat, you should repent."

"I was entertaining the idea of a nap."

"Have you accepted the Lord Jesus Christ as your savior?"

"I'd accept the King of Squeedunk as the one true creator and name my horse after your firstborn if you had another plateful to part with."

The preacher took my plate and refilled it from his giant cook pan over a woodstove that was hot enough to smelt pig iron.

I had the fork in my mouth again. "Thank you, waiter."

"I'm a servant of God," the preacher snapped.

"Well, I must be God then because you're serving me right fine. Now how's about another cup of that brown water you're passing off as coffee?"

The preacher snatched the plate away from me and tossed the food back into his pan, scraping it clean.

I rose from my chair like a man ready for a brawl. "I gave you two double eagles for that grub. That's more than I'd pay for a T-bone in a New York restaurant. Now you fill that plate back up you sonofa-bitch, or I'll fill it myself and take back my gold and maybe even give you a good backhand for upsetting me."

"I will not have blasphemy spoken in my home."

"You'll have that and more if you want coin to pay for your Bible leather."

The preacher stood firm. "I won't have threats, either. Kindly leave, sir, and take whatever devil's gotten inside you right along with you."

I strutted right up to the preacher as if ready to strike him but only patted him lightly on the cheek and let out a belly laugh. I yanked my plate back and began piling up beans and tamale with a wooden spoon. "I like your stuff, Mr. Preacher Man. Glad to meet a man of faith that ain't a wimp like most the rest of your kind."

"I asked you to leave."

"And I decided to stay," I said and went back to the crooked little table with a full plate in hand. "Say, bub, have you got a wash bucket around here? Could use me a good soak. I smell worse than a paper mill on a hot day."

The preacher frowned but could do nothing to get rid of me. He joined me at the table and, as if studying a wild animal, watched me inhale his food. I paid him for a tub of hot water and a cake of soap and had myself a bath and took a nap on the preacher's cot. I'd been sleeping out of doors since fleeing Chicago and even that little bit of sackcloth pulled taut on some old laundry poles felt as comfortable as goose down.

I woke late in the evening and listened to the preacher's sermon for the townsfolk in the center of their makeshift neighborhood. Afterward, I lured a few of the older men into a card game behind one of their huts. One of them kept a little frontier whiskey in a carboy wrapped in rope. We had a grand old time sipping the gunk and worrying our aces and deuces over a pot of nothing more than a few bent pennies as the stars filled the sky. When the rest of the players turned in for the night, I went out into the long grass and sat listening to a quiet so stark I could hear my own pulse.

Come daybreak I said goodbye to the preacher and bought a few cans of his chicken tamale and red beans and dry soda biscuits for the days ahead. I saddled my pony after feeding it some grain and headed north over a piece of high prairie. It was still young in the summer, and soon the air filled with the throbbing sound of grasshoppers. By noontime on my third day of traveling after leaving the preacher's house, they were so thick that they darkened the sun like a penumbra. In those wild places they arrived by the thousands like a plague of locusts, carried by the zephyrs in the same fashion fish go along an ocean current, thick as rain shadows.

They descended in droves and destroyed whole acres of land in giant disintegrating feasts and floated off again aboard another tide of wind. I'd heard stories about grasshopper clouds so dense they crashed through windows in dizzy clots, had to be shoveled off rooftops and railroad tracks. When in full force, grasshoppers were more destructive than anything else on the prairie. Blizzards and cyclones and grass fires could not contend with their horrible circumstance. I was glad as I'd ever been to be clear of their path come the time I crossed an oxbow lake at the top of Comanche country.

Another week had gone by when I thought myself to be somewhere in middle Oklahoma. I swigged water from my canteen and glassed the region to the north with an old spyglass. Nothing in sight for another day's worth of riding but more chop hills and soapweed clumps. Scattered among the tall grasses were a few decrepit oaks, sword-shaped yucca, and pink wild onion blooms.

Before riding again, I looked at the horizon behind me to see a line of smoke spilling out in coils a mile away. This was not another cloud of grasshoppers. I could tell from its shape and color that this was the smoke of a prairie fire. The wind was blowing at my back and soon the flames would be upon me even if I were saddled on a thoroughbred race horse. The heavy growth of dry grass under the burning sun was quicker kindling than gun powder. Given the height of the smoke, I knew the fire was spreading at a speed faster than any animal or machine in creation.

Still there was nothing to do but spur my half-hearted pony into the fit of its life, hollering and kicking her into a fury like I was coming down the last furlong of the Epsom Derby. I leaned low, keeping my head nearly upon the nape of my horse's neck with one hand gripping the pommel of my saddle as we flew through the grassland that had no end in sight.

The flames were gaining and grew taller than a city skyline. Once more than a mile off, the fire was now less than a quarter mile behind us, and I felt the heat at my back. Birds screamed through the air. Some sailed too low and had all their feathers burned from their bodies and dropped down like stones into the fire to perish.

Just when the flames were so close that I considered shooting my horse and then myself, I saw two Indians ahead of me. A squaw and what looked to be her daughter were running on foot, their tribe nowhere in sight. The afternoon sky as dark as if filled with storm clouds. When I was upon them, I slowed my horse to scoop them both up. The squaw climbed on behind me and squeezed her daughter between us. It was a fool's errand to take on the extra weight, but I couldn't have ridden past them knowing that all I was doing was extending my own life a mere few minutes more than their own.

My horse panted severely and was on the verge of collapse when we came upon the oddest and grandest sight: an oasis of short grass bordered on the backside by a rocky cliff. I spurred my pony's flanks until I broke skin, begging her for one last sprint toward the lowland. We didn't reach that rough and low chunk of grass with more than seconds to spare. A half a minute later and we would have burned alive. My horse fell over sideways when I finally let up on the reins and dismounted. The ends of her tail were singed and her skin was so warm that some of her fur had turned colors. The two Indian women I'd saved embraced each other and chanted and cried in deep bellows.

I knelt down, resting my butt on the back of my boots. The fire engulfed everything around us but was unable to spread against that stunted oasis. I was as drained as a spent athlete. Like my poor horse's hide, my back was so warm it was a wonder my clothes hadn't combusted. The smoke was smothering, and I put my shirt over my mouth, using the fabric as a filter. I couldn't see more than a few feet around me. The entire prairie as fumy as the afterglow of cannon warfare on a battlefield.

Nausea dizzied my head, and I vomited from all the smoke I'd inhaled. I could not quit puking, and my eyes burned to near blindness. Once my stomach stopped seizing, I crawled over to my pony and rubbed her neck and kissed her as deeply as one might give a goodbye smooch to a dying lover. She was breathing so hard I thought her lungs might never fill. Over and over I whispered into her ear, "Thank you for saving my life," until I collapsed next to her on the ground from a fatigue so strong it felt like falling backwards into death.

The next morning my horse was dead. The wildfire had finally extinguished itself, leaving behind a wasteland of scorched earth. The oasis of stunted grass, which had saved my life and the lives of the two Indian women, served as a firebreak, the flashover spreading around us in a giant circle. In every other direction, the charred landscape had turned the earth into rock and dust. The prairie was still smoking slightly in some places, giving off wisps from the blackened ground as if the entire range had been doused all at once. Isolated fire bands still flickered in spots. The tall grass was burnt down to the roots so completely it revealed a new shape to the land: pocked and cratered as the surface of the moon and nearly the same color.

I spooned my dead horse, rubbing her along her ribcage.

The two squaws came over and plopped down next to me, their skin and long buckskin breechcloths covered in soot. The older of the two wore her hair short and parted down the middle, exposing a line in the center of her scalp that was painted with yellow clay. Her daughter, or at least what I guessed to be her daughter, wore a single feather and an array of beads in her long braids. Beneath the ash on their faces, their cheeks were covered in orange circles of grease paint.

They spoke to me in clipped phrases, repeating the words *kuuna* and *puuku* and *paa* over and over while they pointed north. From their gesturing and grunts, I was finally able to figure they were Comanche women and meant to show me to their tribe. How far away their camp was and how long we would have to walk I could not ascertain.

I grabbed up my grub bag, which still contained a few cans of chicken tamale, and took my shotgun out of my saddle scabbard and strapped it over my back and left everything else behind, including my horse.

Without means to bury her, I left her in the same position she had fallen to die. I felt as sorry for the loss as I had about anything else I'd ever experienced and set to crying so hard it left streaks down my ashen cheeks. Once on foot, the mother squaw offered me the buffalo pouch she used as a water bag. A few dribbles were left and I shook them into my mouth, barely enough to wet my tongue.

Together we walked across the smoldering fields. I allowed them to lead the way, trailing by a few yards. Twelve noon and it was still as dark as twilight. A fire cloud seemingly large enough to cover the entire state remained in the phosphorescent sky, as widespread as volcanic ash. I marveled at its size, voluminous enough to produce its own weather.

We trudged over the ash grove at the pace of a funeral march. Wherever prairie dog holes had been smoked out, the dead carcasses of rattlesnakes and owls who had invaded those underground homes overnight were not far away. By and by we came across a brook bordered by trees that had been burnt as thin and limbless as street poles. We washed our faces and drank from our cupped hands, even though the water was full of ash, and kept moving north.

I guessed we'd traveled five or six miles when we ascended a low bluff and finally glimpsed a sunken valley that hadn't been touched by fire.

Wild sage and rye grass as green and glittery as Christmas tinsel. A green so vivid to my senses it was as if I were experiencing the color for the first time. I patted my clothes again to knock off more dust. I could have kept patting at my shirt for a week straight and still it would've let off a cloud with each whack, like an old rug.

The mother squaw pointed and yapped like a pup.

The young one leapt and clapped her hands and took off at a dash.

I squinted against all the color. Even the sky was clear and my eyes adjusted to the brightness like coming inside a dark room after being out in the sun all day.

At the bottom of the tableland was a migratory collection of skin tipis arranged in a circle. Maybe ten or so. Before setting off down the hillside, I checked the chamber of my revolver and dropped two shells into my short tom gun. The Comanche reputation preceded them. I was not about to wander into their campsite without being able to take out at least seven of them if I could still aim well enough despite the dizziness in my head from all the smoke I'd inhaled.

Past the camp was a narrow band of the Cimarron River, its water reddened with clay deposits. I must've been close enough to

Ingalls or Stillwater to make it there in a day's travel, even by foot. But that valley was the unassigned land of all things wild. If I wanted to survive through the night, I'd have to trust that these Comanche would do me no harm and even welcome me as a guest for my deed on the plains, which saved two of their tribeswomen.

I walked through the center of the tipi grounds, timid and wide-eyed and my fingers ready to draw pistol at the first sign of aggression. I'd lost sight of the two women I saved from the fire. A different pair of squaws were scraping a buffalo hide clean, using antlers like flensing knives. They stared at me as if I were a ghost from the moon. Dirty chickens wandered about without a pen, free as feral cats. Hung strips of meat and a whole armadillo smoked over a fire of dung chips. The fire pit was dug deep in the ground and lined with a buffalo stomach that held boiling water like a cloth pot.

At least twenty good horses were tied up to a long rail, many of them a mix of breeds and colors. They'd most likely been acquired by accident or theft.

By the look of the misshapen tipis, these were a nomadic people. They put as much care into the sloppy erection of their huts as a magpie would into a nest. Four travois fashioned from cottonwood poles were unloaded at the edge of the camp, ready to be packed up again at a moment's notice and to haul their belongings like sunken wagons. If they'd been there three days, they'd be gone in three more, moving along the rivers in a caravan to chase buffalo around as ardently as street urchins might follow a penny-dainty man selling ice-cream scrolls from a pushcart.

As I came into the hub of their settlement, one of the squaws started hooting. Soon I was surrounded by twenty-some Comanche. They did not appear ready for violence but were simply curious. Most of the men were shirtless and covered in paint as vibrant as berry juice. I raised my hand in a friendly greeting, hoping to be taken in as a guest. The circle of redskins pushed closer, as if inspecting a new type of animal they'd never seen before and were wary that it might be dangerous.

A man wearing a long headdress approached. A large piece of chain mail was draped over his shoulders. He'd likely bartered it from fur trappers. He said something that I couldn't understand, not even in context, but knew enough to gather that he was the chief. The two squaws I saved from the fire were standing behind him and croaking out words that sounded like they might be identifying me as the man they'd invited to follow them after their brush with death.

The chief came forward and opened his arms. He directed me toward the edge of camp. I followed him over to where their horses were hitched. The chief used a series of gestures to suggest that I should pick one for myself. I selected a black gelding with a spirited disposition. The chief hollered out a command and one of the tribesmen brought over a buffalo hide saddle and fastened it on my new horse, cinching the girth snug under the belly. I thanked the chief by bowing repeatedly. We shook hands and came to understand we would always be friendly.

That night I smoked the feathered stone pipe of peace with the old chief and six of his tribesmen. Together we shared in a feast of buffalo tongue, roasted armadillo meat, corn cake, and plenty of firewater. I'd never tasted anything that strong and was soon beaming drunk. I was given my own tipi for the night and, just as I was closing my eyes to have my best sleep in a month, the elder squaw I'd saved from the fire flipped open the flap and stood before me. She held a buffalo robe in her arms.

These Comanche were the most hospitable people I had ever come across. Every rumor I'd heard about them now seemed as gross a slander as had ever been spoken.

I thanked her and invited her to sit down. Instead she disrobed and crawled on top of me. I was hesitant at first. Surely this woman was past marrying age and belonged to one of the men, but I was unable to fight off her aggressive advances in my drunken state. Her lady parts had a gamey smell, and her torso was covered in old cracking paint, and her mouth tasted like decomposing animal matter or worse.

Still, I didn't care.

I hadn't had a woman without paying for it since Hattie.

Being with the squaw was like the very first time all over again. Afterward, she curled up next to me, and we fell asleep together naked on the buffalo robe.

When I woke in the morning the squaw was gone, along with the rest of the tribe. I staggered out of the tipi to see the entire camp had packed up and moved along, stolen away under moonlight with no indication as to which direction they fled out. The valley was as empty of signs of life as if undiscovered by man. There were no traces of the fire pits they'd dug in the ground or even footprints left behind. All that remained was my tipi and my new black horse tied up to a wooden stake in the ground.

I dressed in my old suit of clothes, which were soiled with my stink. My gelding was covered in handprints of bright paint and stripes of clay down to its fetlocks. I lifted her left front leg. No shoes on her hooves. Most likely it was a wild breed stolen during a night raid. The Comanche also left me a parfleche pouch filled with mesquite beans, saskatoon berries, pemmican in an old meal bag, and a rawhide drinking gizzard the size of a cow udder. I collapsed the tipi and scrolled up the hide, along with my buffalo robe, into a pair of bedrolls and tied them off onto the back of my new saddle.

Sunlight feathered out behind thin clouds.

The sky lined with sunbeams like quillwork.

I mounted my horse and had some trouble settling it down before it stopped bucking and spinning in circles. I orientated myself northward and started off at a brisk lope through the tall grasses. My head was still swimming from the firewater I drank the night before. After two days of riding I found a dogtrot trading post with a yellow tin roof and papered windows that kept the sunlight from fading the boxed products on the shelves. I bought a needlework shirt and a new ninety-cent hat and ordered a lemon phosphate at the counter.

Where to go? Certainly not back to Omaha.

There was nothing left for me there.

I looked at a wrinkled map and thought: Montana. Give me a pair of reliable pistols and a calico with some getaway getup in her gallop and a sheet town with a bank way the hell out in the middle of nowhere and I'll be a vibrant man yet, one who isn't tuckered out on life.

I sipped my phosphate and considered the map again.

Montana.

That's where the Big Nose George Gang had hailed from, the

same gang that visited my family farm in the days of my youth. I'll never forget what Big Nose told me the morning he and his riders lit out for new terrain.

"The simple, honest life? That game ain't worth the candle, son," he had said. "I'll tell you one something I wished had been told me when I was a sprout.

"Being miserable ain't the same as being good."

XVII

WEDNESDAY MORNING. THE day after Saint Valentine's, nineteen-aught-five. The clock hands marked the time as ten minutes before nine. Both counsels were prepared to make their closing arguments. The courtroom was hushed as if in silent prayer. More hats and dresses waited down in the lobby and spilled out into the streets. Wagons and buggies were parked on both sides of the street for three solid blocks in every direction.

Leaving his purple suit coat draped over his chair at the defense table, attorney Ritchie rose to address the court. His white canvas shoes squeaked across the waxed floor. He ran his thumbs along the inside of his suspenders and cleared phlegm from his throat and patted one hand against his stomach. He began:

"May it please the court and gentlemen of the jury: I must congratulate you and congratulate counsel on the other side upon the fact that we are closing out this beast and that we may soon go to our homes and sleep the sleep of the righteous. I also wish to congratulate this defendant upon the fairness and kindness with which the public press of this city has treated him during the progress of this trial so that no prejudice might be created against him."

Black rose to his feet. "If the court please, I would request that no references be made to anything outside of this case."

"Mr. Ritchie," Judge Sutton said, "the newspaper reports have not reached the jury, and the jury has no knowledge of what the press may have said about this case."

Ritchie tapped a pencil against his hand. "I hope I shall not again be interrupted by government counsel during my final statement to this court. I was only giving thanks to the press for their fair treatment of this trial and did not intend nor will I make any specific comments about the details of their reporting."

He continued, "If I may begin again, I would say that the kidnapping of children is not something that has occurred often. And it hasn't occurred to Edward Cudahy Junior. Not by our state law, it hasn't. In order to be considered a kidnapping in Nebraska, the captured person must be ten years of age or younger and must be transported across state lines. Neither applies to the young Mr. Cudahy. As you know well by now, he was sixteen at the time of his very brief disappearance and was never more than three miles away from his own home. By law, no kidnapping ever occurred. So I began to wonder what crime, if any, had been committed.

"I have heard of the old crime of robbery. This is the crime that the state insists my client committed. Yet, I did not so readily distinguish that this was robbery and thought possible that it might not be. A charge of robbery as it applies in this case cannot be sustained under state law, either. For robbery, it's necessary to show that the person robbed is in personal fear of violence and that the person robbed must also be close enough to the robber to be within his presence when the crime is committed. A man in Omaha cannot commit robbery of a man in Asia through written threats. Even if the person thus influenced sends the money through the mail or by messenger, it does not come within the robbery statute.

"So this case is not one of robbery. And it's not a case of kidnapping. The law of Nebraska, very clearly defined, wouldn't allow for either. So I racked my brain all throughout this trial as to what crime I was defending my client from. I'm still not sure what the state prosecution, crack them that they are, wants you to convict Pat Crowe of. I was sure it was not arson. I was sure it was not murder. I was sure that it wasn't any one of a number of crimes that I have heard of. So I am left to wonder, often gape-mouthed, what kind of offense you of the jury might be able to find Pat Crowe guilty.

"And yet, over the past two weeks, when I heard the witnesses relate the story of gold being placed on Center Street, I was reminded of what my father told me about the rainbow in the days of my youth. He said if you go away over to where the rainbow touches the earth and hunt around you will find some pots of gold. Well, after I had my collegiate education I took the few little traps I had and tied them in a handkerchief, and I came out west, and I am still going west trying to find those pots of gold. It occurs to me now, at the ripe old age of forty-seven, that these are the same pots that Cudahy left out on Center Street, and they are the same pots that Pat Crowe was supposed to have found out on Center Street."

The audience erupted with laughter. It was not sustained for very long at the banging of Judge Sutton's mallet. Ritchie smiled and wiped the glaze from his forehead with a pocket linen and wadded it back into his trousers. He said, "I get the idea from the district attorney that it is your duty to punish somebody because Cudahy's child was stolen. He warns you that Cudahy is a rich man, and he asks if you will treat him just the same as you would a poor man. You say certainly you will. And I will treat him just the same as I would a poor man in my argument. Just exactly the same.

"But these other people that live out there in the neighborhood of that cottage, these policemen and people like the Glynns and Chief Donahue and people of that kind, they won't treat this case the same. They would not treat your child the same as they would treat Mr. Cudahy's child.

"Suppose on the nineteenth day of December 1900, a poor colored lady had gone to the police station in Omaha and said to the desk sergeant, 'My poor littah Rastus has run away. He has gone somewheres, and I can't find him. Please, surr, please, would you help me get back my poor little boy?' Do you know what that policeman would say? He'd say, 'We haven't got any time, we are looking for the millionaire's child.' He would say, 'If we find the stray, we will pick him up.' Just as though it were a horse or a dog. But when Mr. Cudahy's child is lost, everybody gets out and hustles to find him.

"Mr. Cudahy came here on the witness stand and shed a few crocodile tears expecting to get the sympathy of this jury. Had the jury been comprised of millionaires, honorable Judge Sutton might have the pleasure of assigning Pat Crowe to a prison cell for a term of fourteen years or longer. But you are not millionaires. And, not being millionaires, you know that much more entitled to sympathy is the poor child who has no wealthy father. The poor child that must be fed on chuck steak and scraps and cannot eat real genuine meat and grow like young Cudahy Junior has into the sturdy, wealthy cattle buyer he is today. All the sympathy must be given to Mr. Cudahy, the millionaire.

"Yet, not a hair on the boy's head had been touched. He was uninjured. At first he was frightened a little and, according to his version of things, it was all over in little more than a day's time. When it became known that Mr. Cudahy's boy had been stolen and that he was the millionaire packer of South Omaha, people began to gather to tell what they knew or find out what they could say that would be favorable to the conviction of someone. They didn't care much who.

"Don't you see that is just as natural as that water should run down a hill? Flies always gather on the sugar barrel. They never go near the vinegar. It turns out so in this case. Young Mr. Glynn rang the key note to this whole trial when he said, 'Why, I am in this for the cash that there is in it, for the money that there is in it.' They are all in it for the money that there is in it. Their testimony is colored by it. It's natural that this should be so. We cannot blame these poor people very much for trying to get a little of Cudahy's money. He has been trying all his life to get all they had!" Ritchie said with a thunderous assuredness, and his words were met with immediate applause that nearly broke out into a standing ovation while Judge Sutton slammed his gavel for silence.

Ritchie turned to look at the courtroom audience for the first time since starting his final argument. He'd been so focused on the jury, he'd failed to see just how packed the room had become. Extra chairs had been brought in and filled the space inside the bar. Thirty or forty additional seats flanked the bench on both sides and occupied every inch of the room within the bailiff's rail.

He looked at me soddenly. My eyes filled, my hands placed neatly on my lap. Ritchie stared at me and the pause was noticeable to every person in the court.

Everyone was now looking at me sit silently and alone.

"One day you might come to sit where Pat Crowe now sits," Ritchie finally said. "Any one of us might find ourselves in his chair someday. It's not an impossibility. The law says that if any man is brought in here and charged with a crime, that we shall not raise presumption against him. The law is that he shall be considered innocent until the state proves him to be guilty beyond a reasonable doubt. The law has said further that no man shall be compelled to give evidence against himself. That he shall have a right to sit in court and hear the witnesses against him. These are the great principles which are thrown around you and around us all.

"Are those great principles to be set aside and to be taken off like the plumes that the silly girl wears on her hat? Are they to be cast aside and put on at pleasure? Or are they real? Are they substantial? Are they the things that apply to the real issues of life? When men are tried for life and liberty, that life and liberty cannot be taken without due process of law.

"We were not all right when we started. We had one little thing in our Constitution that was not right and is still not right. It was said that everybody was equal to everybody else. It was supposed that this earth was a place where every man was every other man's brother and that God was the father of us all. But I warn you that the time is coming on apace where we realize that not every man is every other man's brother.

"Not every man is equal to everyone else. Here is a lie of the blackest and foulest disgrace to ever blot the pages of our history. How can we say everyone is equal to everyone else when, on one street in our city, children walk about in rags hoping for a stray apple to tumble off a produce wagon so that they might fight over it and almost tear the clothes off each other trying to get at it and, on another street not more than a few blocks away, children of the very same age dressed in fine department store clothing ride in painted carriages to elite schools where they sharpen their minds so that one day when they are fully educated and grown they might never worry themselves about anything more than which restaurant they will dine in and which they will not. They will never have to claw for an apple rolling toward a gutter, and they will never be brothers and sisters with those who do. Yet we still operate under the principle that all men are equal as if it's an inherent truth when we all know it is the greatest lie ever penned in the history of our country.

"Pat Crowe is not equal to Mr. Edward Cudahy. Nor am I or Judge Sutton. I'd wager no one else in this courtroom is equal to Mr. Cudahy. Very few in this country can equal his station. But here in this chamber you twelve men have the opportunity to live up to that forever fraying and fleeting virtue. You have the opportunity to judge Pat Crowe as an equal to a man who, in every other realm of the world, has so few. This is the power of the law. To finally see the scales of justice on an equal balance."

Ritchie paused to wipe the fog off his eyeglasses with his pocket hanky and, before placing his newly cleaned spectacles back on his face, took a survey of the audience. He looked again at me and paced the front of the courtroom.

He said, "Now we are upon it. Here as I stand, this is the last opportunity—whether I am doing my duty well or poorly—that Pat Crowe will have to be heard. He will be heard for better or for worse now. And so we come to this consideration: whether the money was lost by Cudahy and whether it was lost through the criminal agency of another and whether these facts are proven beyond a reasonable doubt. And why did Mr. Cudahy, as he claimed on the witness stand, put a sum of twenty-five thousand dollars out in the middle of a desolate street seven miles west of town? Because a letter found on his front lawn instructed him to do it.

"You are all familiar with this letter. It was analyzed and read and reread in this court many times over. But who put the letter there? I don't know who put it there. The state says you must guess, you must dream that Pat Crowe put it there because there has been a great crime committed and we need a hostage and somebody must be convicted. It must be Pat Crowe. We have got to convict him or everybody's child in Omaha will be carried off.

"What was the first thing that Mr. Cudahy did with that letter? He read it to his wife, in the presence of his groom and his stable hand and his housemaid. He read it to the Chief of Police Bill Donahue. The contents of that letter were known to everybody that was there. No secret at all made of it. Every policeman in Omaha knew the contents of that letter. Hired Pinkerton agents numbering more than thirty men knew what the letter said. A man named Sears who remained in Cudahy's employ just ten days after this transaction and went to Sioux City, he knew the contents of that letter. He carried that information in his brain when he went down to his boardinghouse that night. Fifty or sixty other men from the packinghouse came up there and knew the contents of that letter.

"Now if the money was placed out there on Center Street, let us see who got it. Everybody told everybody else in town, and everyone knew that Mr. Cudahy was going out with a rig with a lantern tied on the dash. A red lantern. Everybody in town knew that there was going to be a lantern on the highway where the fellows were going to get the money that he was going to take out there. But, of course, no one else could've gotten that money except for Patrick Crowe and William Cavanaugh. They were the only ones who could possibly set up the lantern on the highway to catch the cash when it came along.

"I wish I had been in on that. I wish I had known the contents of that letter, and I might have taken a chance at it myself," Ritchie said, garnering more laughter from the audience. "I wish I hadn't been one of the few poor idiots in town who didn't know that a millionaire packer was going out on a dark road in the middle of the night to leave twenty-five thousand dollars in gold on the side of the road. Go on out there with a lantern and find yourself a rainbow's pot of gold."

The courtroom erupted again, much to Judge Sutton's dismay. After silencing the room with his gavel, he warned that the next outburst would force him to clear the courtroom. He said the next person to make a display in his court would be ushered out onto the street with force, and again the spectators were as silent as a church congregation.

Ritchie continued, "Why, it was all too easy. There was too much silk in that for anything. Anyone could get a lantern and tie black and white ribbons on it and go upon that highway and stick it out. Oh, tell me, pray, how do you know that anybody ever got that money who was in the plot to take the boy?

"We do not find twenty-five thousand dollars on the highway every Wednesday evening, and we are all looking out for twenty-five thousand dollars on the highway. If we learn from someone that it is going to be put there, we will go out there and take chances on getting it. Ah, but they will say, the Father Murphy letter, this supposed confession to the crime, proves the corpus delicti and that Pat Crowe, over his own signature, tells Mr. Cudahy that he offered him back eleven thousand dollars.

"Why didn't Mr. Cudahy swear to that on the stand? I never saw, I never knew of a greater omission. Mr. Cudahy was offered back eleven thousand dollars, and he was on the stand two hours two separate times, and he never said anything about it besides the reciting of it in that supposed letter of confession. Never said another word about it. Not a word.

"Another circumstance that is of great value in this case: some hoboes got into that Grover Street cottage after Eddie Cudahy returned home. They had a gasoline lamp with two burners and a red tank there. They had some old jute hung on the walls, and they were in that house a couple days and moved out. Ah! There is a weighty circumstance in this case. A circumstance that proves something. I could take you to all the empty houses there are in Omaha and South Omaha, and I can show you that nearly the same thing has occurred in any one of them. Those were possibly some poor devils who did not have money enough to buy a week's board or to buy a bed. So they go into that house and sleep for a few nights and then went on further to be buffeted to and from by the cold winds of adversity. Every vacant house on the edge of the city is subject to such use.

"But the state would like to make you believe that because there were cigarette stubs on the floor and because there was a gasoline stove and an old oaken bucket in the front room that these things were left there by Pat Crowe. They would like to make you believe that Pat Crowe is guilty simply by calling attention to these things. I expect that if we had all the literature that Mr. Cudahy received in answer to his advertisement that he would give fifty thousand dollars for the capture of Pat Crowe, we would have answers that could fill this courtroom from the floor to the ceiling.

"Witnesses who come that way are witnesses who come with the purpose of gain. Their testimony must therefore be scrutinized very carefully, very carefully indeed. Just the same as the evidence of the policemen who are pursuing one path and no other all the time. Archimedes of old who invented the fulcrum and the lever, he claimed that if he could get a place to stand on he could lift the world. If you will give me a million dollars and make me vice president of the Cudahy Packing Company, I can pretty near move the social world in the city of Omaha.

"And as much as I admire my friend, the district attorney here, who shows so much enthusiasm and warmth for Mr. Cudahy and for the state, so mingled that you cannot distinguish them, I wonder how much of that warmth and enthusiasm you will attribute to Mr. Cudahy's gold. Ah! Ah! How they sidestep for him when he comes in here. Everybody gives him the center of the path as he walks up to take the witness stand. How they bow in obeisance.

"Gentlemen of the jury, the people of the United States are homely, poor people. The middle class and the laborers, they are the bulwark of American liberty and the strength of American society. They are not to be hoodwinked by the shedding of a few crocodile tears of the wealthy and the powerful. There are people right here in this courtroom now who expect to get something in some way out of this. We would all like to get hold of some of Mr. Cudahy's money if we could. But I don't see how we are going to do it unless we run him for mayor on the Republican ticket," Ritchie said and earned his fourth round of hearty laughter from the spectators. Even I had a chuckle at that one. I could not help it. Ritchie continued, "Then he will open up his barrel, and those people will all gather around his standard again.

"But what has been presented to you by the prosecution? Evidence or want of evidence? There is nothing in this case that shows one single thing that Pat Crowe ever had was found anywhere near the Cudahy house or the Grover Street cottage or anywhere else. No proof that he ever made a mark anywhere pertaining to this case. Not a single thing. If you could get a piece of board that was broken off from that hideaway cottage and another piece of board that fitted right into it that came from Pat Crowe, then you would be getting near something tangible. But you cannot draw inferences from things like buckets and cigarette stubs.

"Then we have the testimony of Edward Cudahy Senior. His anxiety to bear witness against Pat Crowe was exhibited the second time he was on the stand. The counsel for the state asked, 'Did you ever see Pat Crowe again after he worked for you in your market in South Omaha?' He answered yes. He had forgotten that the first time he was on the stand. He was asked it, but for some reason he did not answer it. But the second time he said, 'Yes, Pat Crowe was at my house.' He then went on to detail what Pat Crowe had told him. He said Pat Crowe came to his house in an ailing state and that he wanted nothing more than for Cudahy to see the poor condition he was in. Mr. Cudahy said that Pat Crowe asked him for a drink at seven in the morning and that he appeared to be a drunkard on the bum.

"Now, if any living human being can tell me what that has to do with this case I would like to know. What was the point of Mr. Cudahy revealing these details to the court? Was he trying to railroad this man by blackening his character with admissions that were unrelated to the alleged crime and Crowe's relation to it? I cannot see any other reason for such details other than that purpose. Oh, and Mr. Cudahy also revealed the he gave Pat Crowe one of his old secondhand coats he was not using. Talk about the heart of the millionaire! There is one thing in this world that is perhaps the coldest and chilliest thing in it, and it is a million dollars. There is only one thing that is colder and chillier and more heartless, and that is two million."

Applause rang out in the courtroom and, again, Judge Sutton's gavel brought it to a halt with some seven or eight whacks of his judicial hammer.

Ritchie pressed forward. Pacing with his hands in his pockets, he said, "Now, in closing, let us talk a little while about this so-called confession letter written to Father Murphy, the letter that was introduced in evidence by Mr. Cudahy. Attorney Black is going to claim that Father Murphy is a good man and that when he gave that letter up to Mr. Cudahy, he gave it up to the public to help the state. He gave it to him for the purpose of convicting Pat Crowe and punishing a great criminal.

"Is there any evidence of that in this case? Why didn't Father Murphy go on the stand and swear to it if that kind of a confession was made to him? I will tell you why not. It is the same reason two and two don't make five and the same reason elephants don't give birth to baby birds. Because it is impossible. I tell you, gentlemen of the jury, it is a moral impossibility that Father Murphy gave that letter to Mr. Cudahy or that it is a genuine letter. A moral impossibility. For Mr. Black to claim otherwise is a blasphemous slander upon that old and ancient faith and upon the priests and ministers of that faith.

"I am not a Catholic. Sometimes I wish I were when I see what good they do in this world. When I see on every hill in Omaha a Catholic charity. When I see down here on the east side of the city a hospital to which white and black, rich and poor, saint or devil, can go free of charge to be cured. My hat goes off to Catholicism. It is, without a doubt, one of the very few institutions in this world dedicated to unconditional goodness. We cannot but believe that they will keep the secrets that are entrusted to them by their communicants. That is a jurisdiction which no one hitherto has touched and which the mightiest of earth have always respected.

"For more than twelve centuries this honored church, in one way and another, has gone forth succoring the sick, caring for the helpless. And Mr. Black would have you believe that a priest of that faith gave to Mr. Cudahy a letter which was to be used as evidence against Pat Crowe. Believe everything and anything else in this case, but do not believe that this good old priest would have been guilty of such perfidy as that. You will not cast such slander upon the men who devote their whole lives to the caring for the weak, the sick, the sinful, and those who look up to them for aid and consolation.

"This relation of priest and communicant is a sacred jurisdiction. It is a relation which no vandal shall enter and devastate. It is morally impossible that could have been done. It is a malicious, cowardly, and perjured falsehood. The most despicable falsehood ever dropped from the lips of a perjured man. If anyone here has the effrontery to even intimate that Father Murphy betrayed the secrets of his holy church, I say that the man who says that lies and I have never met Father Murphy in my life.

"I also never met Pat Crowe before I met him a few months ago when hired as his lawyer. Many people condemn me for having taken this case. My wife didn't want me to take this case. I myself wasn't sure I should take it. But against all better judgment, even my own judgment, here I am in its deepest throes.

"Here we all are. It's like every other case where everybody knows all about it and nobody knows anything about it. Here is what is irrefutable, the only thing that is known for sure: young

Edward Cudahy went missing one night on December 18, 1900, and when he came home less than two days later, he came home to his mother and father and never a hair injured or a single scratch upon him. And these men are crying out madly for the blood of Pat Crowe.

"I am glad that I stayed by him in his adversity. I am glad that he can go forth from this courtroom knowing that there was someone in this world who would stand between him and the bloodhounds that are pursuing him.

"When William H. Seward, the Secretary of State for Abraham Lincoln, was practicing law in Auburn, New York, a poor colored man was defended by him for murder. The colored man had killed his neighbor's whole family. His whole family. Seward took the case. Everybody said, 'Why, Seward, you must lose the case. The murder was cold-blooded.' Seward told the court and he told the jury that the colored man was crazy. He told them the colored man was crazy and you ought not to convict him. Seward stayed by him. He was convicted. Seward took the case to the Supreme Court and the case was reversed. It came back and that poor black man died in prison. After he was dead they held a postmortem and found a diseased brain. A diseased brain. And there is not a page in the history of Secretary Seward that will shine brighter than that page which reads of his defense of that poor colored man.

"Take Pat Crowe if you will and hurry his bones across the stones on the theory that he is a beggar. Shoot him down and put him in his coffin rather than send him to the penitentiary to rot and die. Try him on identity. Try him on circumstantial evidence if you will, but make no mistake. Judge not lest you be also judged.

"I ask you to let him go. I do not ask you to let him go on the theory that he must be given another chance to try and live as you would like to. I ask that you let him go because the state has not proven him guilty. I ask you to let him go because the identification and the circumstances here are so weak and uncertain that it would be monstrous to base a conviction upon them. Go home to your children when you go out of this courtroom and let them say of you in the coming years when you are gone that you had the courage to stand up and be counted in favor of giving a man his liberty who was accused of a crime when the evidence against him was weak and unsatisfactory.

"We are doing the best that we can here in this life. We must all of us be gathered sooner or later to our fathers. Rich and poor, white and black, all of us are bound to go one day to that bed on which we shall lie for the last time. As the breath of life passes from you and kind and loving hands come to wipe away the death damp from your brows and you must pass in swift and solemn judgment on every act of your lives, do not let a verdict of guilty against Pat Crowe come up in that final hour to vex your peaceful departure from the scenes of earth.

"Say 'Not guilty,' the only just and true verdict in this case. Say 'Not guilty,' and He who said that it is easier for a camel to go through the eye of a needle than for a rich man to enter the kingdom of heaven, He who stills the tempest and who notes the sparrow's fall, He who looks over us day and night at our best and at our worst, will bless you all."

XVIII

THE MILLARD HOTEL was a five-story chunk of pale brick on the South Sixteenth Street Mall. Holed up on the top floor, the jury deliberated all night and early into the morning before finally coming to a decision.

Court came to order for the final time at nine sharp. Judge Sutton swayed in from his chambers. His demeanor was that of a man beaten. The county clerk called in the jury.

Ritchie and I rose to our feet.

My head spun like the cosmos.

I stood behind the defense table with my hands clasped before my groin and smiling thinly as the jury took their seats on the platform. My thick morass of stained hair was pushed back but not combed. I wore a checkered suit with a paisley tie in a loose knot. Ritchie clapped me on the back like I'd just won the heavyweight championship. Judge Sutton called on jury foreman Casey Young, an oil station manager from Fremont. He asked him if the jury had reached a verdict.

"We have, Your Honor," Young said flatly.

Sutton, who late the night before became ill with grip, fumbled his fingers on his forehead. Finally, it was over. At long last.

At the defense table, I closed my eyes and smiled.

Young cleared his throat. "We do find the defendant not guilty."

Like the boom of a mortar shell came the roaring cheers of the densely packed courtroom. Men shouted and pumped their fists in the air. Women covered their faces with gloved hands. Applause turned into a standing ovation. Judge Sutton took great effort to stop the demonstration. He pounded his gavel until the room quieted.

He said, "It's incredibly upsetting that the acquittal of a blatant criminal in this courtroom should be celebrated with cheering."

A bystander in the gallery hollered: "You go to hell, Judge!"
Another yelled: "And take Cudahy with you!"

Sutton stamped his gavel again and again. The room fell to whispers. I stood smiling and shaking hands with my attorney. Sutton individually asked each juror if they felt the same way. He asked: "Was this, and is it still, your verdict?"

One by one, each juror responded without wavering: "It is."

Juror number seven, a feeble old man who wore the same red tie over his coveralls for the whole trial and trembled with every effort like a man stricken with fear, added to his response: "And let me say something else. Pat Crowe is no criminal. He's a hero."

The courtroom cheered again.

"That's quite enough," Sutton said.

The trial was over. I was a free man. I stood and began to shake hands with the jury when Sutton forbade I do so.

I turned to the judge and spoke my first and only words of the whole trial: "You can rot, Judge. The case is over and these men are no longer jurors. They're my friends, and I can shake hands with friends, and you can't stop me from doing it."

Sutton ordered the room to be cleared. Before the court calmed and before the jury filed out of their box, I exited the room as fast as I could through the crowd. I heaved my way down the center aisle as people in the audience reached out, some of them patting me on the shoulder, some of them grabbing at my suit sleeves. Many people were standing, some remained seated.

Most cheered, a few booed.

Standing at the back of the courtroom was Tom Dennison attired like a rajah in his flawless diamonds and onyx and a brilliant silk suit. His arms crossed in a pensive pose while he chewed his gum like a piece of fat. His cold penetrating eyes never changed expression. He clasped his mouth tightly.

I stopped before him. Dennison offered his hand. We shook.

He guffawed. "That verdict was a real gas, kid."

I agreed. "Not bad for a butcher from Colorado, is it?"

"You come out alright, Paddy boy. I sure am glad. I got a car waiting for you outside with a case of my best barleycorn. You just tell my man where you want to go."

I stammered. Old Dennison had turned out alright in the end.

"You got any notions in mind?" Dennison asked.

"I was thinking Philadelphia," I said after a moment. The court-room continued to throb and shriek as people exited their seats. The throng pushed in a bottleneck toward the doors, and the word of the verdict was now echoing and chanting in the streets.

"What's in Philly?"

I thought on Billy's sister, Mabel. It wouldn't hurt to see. Just in case. "A woman and a little more trouble."

Dennison smiled. "I guess I won't be seeing you, then, kid."

"I guess not," I said and thanked him again as I exited the courtroom.

In the hallway I headed for the elevators. Thirty reporters barked off questions. Down in the first floor lobby, a new mob swelled around me as I was led outside, bulbs flashing. Tom Dennison's touring car idled on the curb, his young mulatto driver at the wheel, waiting to ferry me out of town.

A grip of halcyon weather lightened the city. The rattle of fire-fly motors and autocars filled the streets. Breakfast sausages sold from sidewalk carts. Gumball machines stocked by men in paper hats outside confectioneries. Store glass flashed like giant helio-graphs. Trolleys began their morning routes. The whole city alive and welcoming the thaw. A high of forty-two degrees expected by midday. Gutter buckets gurgled like mud pots.

The reporters continued to fire off their questions. I answered those that could be heard through the clangor with a few flippant responses.

"Whaddaya say, Pat? How are you feeling this morning?" was the first audible question that arose from the chorus.

I was all smiles. "As fine as frog's hair, boys. Nothing like the first hint of spring."

"What do you think of the verdict?"

"It's the bunk," I said.

"Do you believe the jurors were convinced that you had noth-ing to do with the kidnapping?"

I stopped to give a full response. A hive circled around me. Ritchie stayed close at my side, beaming like a proud parent.

I said, "I don't know what they thought any more than you do. I'm satisfied of one thing. There are a good many people in this world who like to eat meat once or twice a day, and they don't like being picked poor to put a little food on their family's table. We all of us in this country ought to be able to eat a decent meal without fear of poverty."

The reporters fired off another salvo of questions. I pushed down the steps. I reached the sidewalk and stood before Dennison's touring car with the door opened. I shook hands with Ritchie and bid him farewell. Told him we were friends for life and took one final look out at the courthouse. Its steps flooded like a wedding congregation filing out of a church to send off the bride and groom.

"What do you think of the prosecution?" one reporter asked.

"Yes, what make you of Louie Black?" asked another.

"Well," I said with contemplation. "I hope that bird has an easier time as governor than he did as a lawyer."

"Now that the trial's over, tell us, Pat, did you kidnap Cudahy's son?"

I shook my head, stepped into the car and held the door open to give one last response before darting away. "What's worse? To steal one child or starve many?"

"What influence did Tom Dennison have on the outcome here today?" a newsman asked.

"I don't know anything about him."

"What did Dennison say to you as he left the court?"

I slammed the door shut and stuck my head out the window. "He wished me good luck and God bless."

"Are you and Dennison pals?"

"I don't know anything about the man."

"Is this verdict a victory for the people of Omaha or another black mark upon her? Was this trial influenced by the men who run the city's vice elements?"

I smiled. "I sure am sorry to let you down, but I haven't anything to say on the subject."

"That's pretty boring," one of the reporters added.

The touring car bounced forward in the slush. As camera flash-pans continued to snap and explode, the lime green monstrosity hiccupped with a jolt. A spray of snow water kicked up by aching tires. I leaned my head out of the window once more.

"I'm a boring man," I said into the wind. "And you can print that, for what it's worth."

All Things Made New

LET ME TELL you something about love: it's no one else's goddamn business. Out of all the sayings about love that are meant to whittle it down or size it up, there is only one thing about that abortive emotion that has always been and will forever remain true: it belongs only to you. You cannot give it to another. Sure, it can be showcased. But so can an automobile or a feathered coat or well-arranged produce. That's nothing special. Anything can be put behind a pretty display window for others to moon over.

I never stopped loving Hattie.

Whether she felt the same way or not was a moot point.

Love isn't a transaction.

So, here I am an old man with shaking hands and a face lined in sadness, and I saddle up my courage and set off to find her. I comb my thinning hair and put on my best pair of duck trousers and a shirt with pearl buttons. Hattie was working as a housemaid for a wealthy rancher ten miles west of town. The Dunbar Family Ranch. Five hundred head of cattle, three barns and two stables, horse pasture, carriage house, bunkhouse, springhouse, a good stream with a water mill. I come upon the homestead early in the evening. The sun going down crepuscular behind willow trees. I wait on the edge of the property until night falls in full. Sunflowers as tall as teenagers along the roadbed. A thundershower looms in the distance. The sky is leaden, the color of guncotton. Lightning partitions the horizon. I imagine the bolt cracking the earth wide open. Trees drip, clouds drip, rooftops drip. All the world in a sob.

I don't know what I expect.

I don't go in for fanciful notions of atonement or miracle.

What little I do know is this: you never know anything.

I spot her just as the lights in the windows of the bunkhouse are dimmed. She walks down a gravel lane carrying a heaping basket of laundry toward a catchall shed that serves as her sleeping quarters. I approach the porch and stand with one hand against each side of the screen door, looking in at her as she goes about sorting the laundry she'd carried over in the basket. It takes her some time to turn around from her work to see me standing there. She spooks for a moment, but only a moment.

A smile forms at the corners of her mouth.

Hattie.

I open the screen door and strut into the room as if I were there on king's business. Neither of us says a word to each other. I push my straw hat back on my head just enough to reveal my ebbing hairline and grin like a fool. Hattie watches me move about her small room with her hands on her hips.

She says, "Well, just let yourself in why don't you?"

"Thanks," I say. "Believe I will."

I examine her living conditions. There was new wallpaper hung, a floral pattern of pale rose. Real electric lighting. A brass bed with creased sheets. I test the mattress with my hand. It feels bouncy. Free of ticking. She has a cast iron cookstove for heat. A calico cat jumps off a short bookcase and rubs itself against my left boot.

I kneel down and pet the creature. "Say, here's three somethings I thought I'd never see all in one go. You lodging in spinsterhood with a pet pussycat and washing other people's unmentionables."

Hattie doesn't respond. Her yellow hair streaked through with gray. I evaluate the room once more. "This place ain't so bad," I tell her. "You got print flowers on your wall and a neat little bed and some bound books. Place is fixed up nice and spritely. Good and warm in here, too."

Hattie just stands there with her hands on her hips, exhausted and frayed.

I mosey to her bookshelf and pick up a handsome leather tome. "Well, what do we got here? Tennyson's *Idylls of the King*," I say, pronouncing *idylls* as *idea-lees* like some kind of goddamn moron. I mumble something about the full-page engravings and then say more clearly: "Brilliant rays of fairy romance from the lights of genius."

I scan more of the titles. "Hmm," I say. "Longfellow's early poetry. Emerson. Hmm. You used to hate poetry. At least the stuff I used to write you."

"Those aren't mine," Hattie says. "They were left here by the last resident."

"Good taste, that gal," I say and pick up a ball of knitting. "Ah, what's this now? Florence crochet silk. You sew now, too? My. And they say people don't change."

I find a couple bottles of perfume and recite their labels. Quadruple extract of violet. Lily of the valley. "It's important to smell good when you're scrubbing rich folk's dirty drawers. That's for certain. Yes, ma'am. And what's this? A turkey duster?"

Hattie snatches the duster from my hand. "Why did you come here?"

I shrug and shake my tobacco pouch. "I don't know, now that you ask it. I thought maybe you might like to go sparking in private. For old time's sake."

Hattie grimaces.

"Or maybe we could play us a card game. Maybe a little Roger Cuddle?"

"I don't have any cards."

"Well, let's skip the Roger part altogether and just cuddle. That's how the sparking usually starts, anyway."

Hattie lights a cigarette and sits down on her bed. "You got ants in your pants."

I smile. "Yeah. Them buggers ain't the only thing I got in there."

"Boy, aren't you just romantic as hell?"

"I tried romance the first time with you and it didn't go over so hot. This time I thought I'd give old-fashioned immorality a go."

Hattie blows smoke dispassionately.

I come around the room full circle. "Tell you what, I got me an old army blanket out there on my saddle roll. How about we go spread it over your master's flower bed and have ourselves a little reacquainting tryst?"

"That sounds very Presbyterian," she says.

"Well, if it'd make you feel better, we can get eloped first. There's a chapel down the road a piece. Have us a couple prime rib dinners at Pelinko's afterward to celebrate? I'd even consider a bridal tour in Kansas City if you're feeling rambunctious. Then maybe you and I spend the second half of our lives pretending like the first halves never happened."

Hattie squashes out her cigarette. "The second half?"

I blush. "Well, at least the next half year. Who knows how much time we've left? I'm old, and you're not too far off. I don't know about you, but I still feel as spritely as the devil."

If Hattie is anything else besides bored and unimpressed, she's a good enough actress to cloak it. She asks, "Aren't there other women in the world for you to harass?"

I sit down on the other end of her bed. "I've harassed plenty," I say. "But nobody else gave me the mitten like you. You used to be quite the little noisemaker. I just thought I'd come by one last time and see if you can still howl like you used to."

"Well, ain't that just keen."

"Why did you run off on hubby number two? Little George Cudahy, right? Or was it Tom? I can't remember. He deny you a pearl necklace or something?"

"He left me, if you must know. After he found out you had a hand in all that kidnapping business with his nephew, well, he figured I must've motivated that some. For you."

I cluck my tongue. My heart sags. "That whole family's rotten to the core," I tell her.

"And what're you?"

"I'm the handsome sonofabitch that spent all day prettying up for you is what I am."

Hattie squashes her cigarette into the soil of a potted plant.

I spot a bottle of brandy on top of her bookshelf. "Hey now, I say. How about we have us a cap of that purple?"

"Never did give up the drink, did you?"

"I've got the dipsomania."

"You're a lousy drunk is all you are."

"If you want to get into one of our old rows about what we're both lousy at, we can have that discussion. I was hoping to be past all that by now."

Hattie softens. "Why did you come here? Really?"

I pour myself an inch of brandy into a coffee mug and take it down. I say, "Well, darling, I've harassed other women like you say. All kinds. Thirty years is a long time for a man to be on his lonesome. There were big old buffalo gals and dainty little deacons' daughters and even a squaw once and all other kinds in between. I'm a sight wiser for it now and still stupid enough to come back here and see about you. I thought you at least ought to know I still love you. I thought that might be something worth telling. So, here I am, telling you. I love you as much as I did the day we moved into that little pink house on Orchard Avenue. You remember our first night together in that place? We hadn't a stick of furniture yet, and we slept on a couple old blankets right on the floor? God, I'll never forget that in all my born days."

"Oh, Pat," Hattie says without much emotion. "We were both too young and naïve about the world to have had that last."

"And now I'm near on sixty."

"You're well past sixty."

"I might be yet. I might be seventy. God knows."

"We were carried by storm to the altar."

"And by storm I was driven from my home."

"There's no use in thinking we can replicate those days now."

"I know it," I say and dig a folded sheet of paper out of my pocket. I hand the square to Hattie, but she doesn't reach for it.

"More poetry?" she asks.

"No. Not poetry."

"Unless it's a treasure map, I don't want it."

I smile and wag the paper. "A funny notion that is," I say.

Hattie takes the sheet and studies the contents with a furrowed brow.

Lo and behold: a map.

I tell her: "I got some eight or nine thousand dollars buried in a little nectarine orchard down in Arizona by the Mexican border. Nogales is the name of the town. You'll have to dig about three feet under the exact tree marked there, but it's all yours if you're game enough to go find it."

"And where would we go after that?"

"Wherever you wanted. Nine thousand isn't a fortune, but it's enough to start a new life without having to be some rancher's laun-dress and sleeping in a shed. You could buy a cozy house, some fur-niture, maybe use the excess to start a millinery store or whatever it is you fancy doing in the daytime."

"The money you got from that kidnapping?" Hattie scoffs. "I won't have it."

I help myself to another spot of brandy. I say, "That was thirty years ago and more."

"I won't have it," she says again.

"Then it'll just sit there in the ground."

"You won't go for it, yourself?"

"No. I reckon not. Unless you wanted me to accompany you." Hattie tosses the map.

"We could be happy again for what short while we have left," I say. "It's not such an extravagant idea."

"It's all extravagance and nothing else."

"Yeah, I suppose that's all it's ever been," I say, step forward, and plant a deep kiss on Hattie's lips. She doesn't fight me off but doesn't return the affection either. I linger only for a couple sec-onds. I refit my hat to a jaunty tilt and go to her door again, ready to leave. We stare at one another. I rub my lips with two fingers. We stare at each other longer before I step out. A farewell smooch for old times' sake.

Here's another thing I will cherish in sadness.

It's hard to believe I've survived this long.

I always behaved like I'd be dead before I was forty. Yet, here I am still. It's kind of cruel to think about. Washing my underwear in my wall sink with blue starch. Heating my pottage over a cook-stove that barely gets hot enough to bring water to boil. My skiv-vies are worn to threading, and from my pottage, I tongue a strand of hair and pull it out of my mouth to see it's as long as a spaghetti noodle.

But. I'm not dead. There's a twinkle left yet.

Some things must be dug up.

I book passage on a train to Arizona to get what's left of the Cudahy gold. A long trip, yes. I have no other program. The rail-road goes only so far. I must walk the remaining six miles from the depot to Nogales. Desert heat thrashes the earth. After an hour of walking my socks are as soaked as if I had bathed in them. I might not make it far. The mercury is nearly in the triple digits, and the pounding sun could roast a man half my age.

I stop to relieve myself. My urine is dark. The odor as strong as brine. My canteen is dry, and I dig for groundwater under a clump of cactus flower, finding enough to wet my swollen tongue and push onward.

Come nightfall I set up camp along a tiny sliver of forded brook. I manage a small fire with the flint and char cloth from my tinder-box. Dry my wool socks by draping them on the end of a stick and holding them above the fire like bait on a fishing line. For supper I munch on wafers wrapped in wax paper and a can of chicken paste. Drink a little barleycorn and lots of creek water and sleep on a bed of slough grass.

The brook gurgles behind me. I wash my hands from my canteen and light the end of a green cigar. After finishing it down to the nub, I douse the small fire and sleep the rest of the night next to the smoldering embers with nothing but the stars for covering.

By the next midday, I reach Nogales. I'm hot and tired, my clothes stick to my skin and my neck is burnt from the sun. According to my wrinkled section of map, the nectarine orchard isn't more than a mile away. I hurry over to a stone well and drink from a ladle in the bucket until my belly is as full as if I'd eaten two suppers. The water is barely potable. I can taste the iron on my lips.

At a local apothecary, I purchase a small tin of willow extract pills for headaches, a box of ammunition for my revolver, and two bottles of cream soda. After an hour of sitting in refrigerated air, I'm rejuvenated enough to hoof it toward the orchard where the remaining share of the Cudahy gold is still buried.

Or so I hope. Who knows what may have happened to it by now. It takes me a while to find the orange river. The Santa Cruz. The water as bright as cinnamon. I follow its moccasin bend to the spot marked on my map. Clouds tear apart and knit back together. Airglow in the gaps of sky. Rakings of desert light, pale as moon-beams, shoot through cloudbreak.

The ground is as hard as frozen rock and as hot to the touch as cooking stones. I dig and dig until my arms quake. After two hours of working my shovel, I've barely made a deep enough hole to bury a cat in a shoebox. It takes my every last energy and every last sliver of daylight before my shovel bangs on iron.

I fall to my knees and paw away at the dirt. There she is. Our old carriage trunk. I pop open the lid with my jackknife, and the smell hits me first. My heart skips two beats. The hidden gold is right where Billy and I had buried it more than thirty years ago.

I gasp. Open my mouth to the sky.

The first time I plunk down one of those gold coins to pay for a glass of brandy in a saloon or a cup of coffee at a lunch counter, the clerk in his funny wedge hat will raise an eyebrow and look me over suspiciously.

He'll say: "That's some curious coin, mister."

I will smile. Give him pause.

Ask him for directions to Sunburst or Shinbone. I'm heading east. Or west. Whatever notion comes to me in the moment. Take a good long look, friend. Telephone my description and destination to the authorities.

"An old man in a linsey-woolsey shirt riding a blue roan," he'll say over the wire.

"Yes, that's right, officer. An old man on a blue horse. A linsey-woolsey shirt. You know. One of them old-timey threads with yarn flowers stitched all over it.

"He said he was headed up Nebraska way.

"Yes, sir. Very suspicious this coin. Come on down to the store and take a look-see for yourself. Yes, sir. A damn old coin. A liberty gold coin. Issued 1900. He gave it over for a glass of brandy and asked for no change.

"Yes, sir. He's probably one of them goddamn highwaymen."

Then the clerk will ring off.

I will be pursued again.

The bandits of today use petrol automobiles for fast getaways, and the criminals of tomorrow will use celestial flying machines beyond our current imaginations. But for now, for the sake of the past, for that last bit of faraway sun going down behind the ancient hills, they still might give hunt to an old man on a hobbled nag.

There's still some promise left in a life lived under moonlight. South has always been a fine direction for a man on the downslope. Florida has a promise particular. State shaped like a gun could use a good gunman. I will cut as many capers as luck will allow by day, and by night, I'll rumba in Cuban-themed ballrooms in ghostly creole hotels. There'll be plates of fried plantains and black beans and plenty of sugarcane rum. I'll slap my guns at bank managers wearing their sleeve garters and hullo to all the dark ladies in the perfumed whorehouses and ride under scudding clouds tracing transparent over the sun. I will hear the summertime coyotes yip loneliness, and I will howl back in my own song and be not remorseful of my time above ground when some lawman from Gainesville or Clearwater in snakeskin boots finally guns me down in a bog.

There are wonders I've yet to see or have only seen in part.

I will gig my horse and set off to find them.

And, for one final time, if fate be the same inescapable doxy I've always known her to be, this world will be chasing me down yet.

AUTHOR'S NOTE

PAT CROWE'S STORY is a true story. However, his story as it's told in *World, Chase Me Down* is a work of fiction. In retelling this story, I have tried to stay true to the historical accuracy of the main events as best I could. That said, many elements were changed for the sake of creating a strong plot and characters. I built this story from a foundation of fact, then molded the story and its details to create the fiction. Many names have been changed. Names that were not changed are not representative of their actual, real-life persons, but of my own imagination.

In creating fiction from history, I relied on many texts centering around, not only the story of Pat Crowe, but also the backdrop of Omaha during the turn of the twentieth century. That list includes *Spreading Evil: Pat Crowe's Autobiography* by Pat Crowe; *Pat Crowe: His Story, Confession, and Reformation* by Pat Crowe; *The Last Outlaw: The Life of Pat Crowe* by John Koblas; *A Dirty, Wicked Town* by David L. Bristow; and *Political Bossism in Mid-America* by Orville D. Menard. I also relied on the historical collections of the *Omaha World-Herald* and the *Omaha Bee* provided by the Omaha Public Library.

I'd also like to note: Large parts of Edward Cudahy Jr.'s ransom letter and Pat Crowe's confession letter are taken directly from Pat Crowe's autobiography, *Spreading Evil*. Likewise, large parts of the closing argument by Pat's attorney Albert S. Ritchie were taken from his actual final address to the jury in the book *Pat Crowe: His Story, Confession, and Reformation* by Pat Crowe. All three historical documents were altered for the purposes of this fictional retelling.

ACKNOWLEDGMENTS

My DEEPEST THANKS to everyone at Penguin Books and to my editor, John Siciliano, for his support and faith in this book. I owe a great debt to my agent, Christopher Rhodes, who plucked this novel out of obscurity and took a giant leap of faith on my behalf. His guidance and tireless effort is something I can never repay.

For all of my writing teachers at both Creighton University and the University of Northern Michigan that have helped me along the way, especially Susan Aizenberg, Katie Hansen, Jennifer Howard, Brent Spencer, and Mary Helen Stefaniak. Without their tutelage and the generous sharing of their knowledge over the years, this book would never have been possible. Also, every city deserves a library as devoted to the preservation of its local history as the good folks at the Omaha Public Library do every day—thank you.

There are also many others who gave me support through the years: Justin Daugherty, Colin Clancy, Ted Wheeler, Timothy Schaffert, Elizabeth Rosner, Ross Browne, Jane Ryder, Ian Pelnar, Leslie and Jared Birchard, Taylor Brown, Rebecca Johns, Laura Soldner, J. D. Rummel, Russell Prather, Brian James Beerman, Amanda and Kyle Gilbertson, and Michael Burke.

Finally, to all of my family and friends, I owe you everything. For all your love and support, thank you to my parents, Dan and Nancy. For his friendship and exceptional technical wizardry, my brother Thomas. And, last but certainly not least, for my wife April and my daughter, Cecelia. I love you both more than you will ever know.